S0-BRZ-106

ALIEN MEETINGS ...

A wavering image formed on the tube. "I outrage! I do not endure! You are gave one minutes, Eastern Standard Time, for total abandon of vicinity!"

"Gentlemen, don't get carried away," Magnan called out over the hiss of static. "I'm sure this can all be worked out equitably—"

"Such indignant my language lack! My goodness! Drat! Other obscenity as required!"

"It will not avail you to rant," Slith whispered. "My guns stand ready to answer your slurs."

"My frustrate!" Okkyokk yelled and brandished a pair of limbs tipped with shredding devices. "Gosh, such wish to know sensation of plait all five eyes into single superocular, followed by pluck like obscene daisy—"

"To wait in patience until the happy moment when I officiate at your burial, in the ceremonial sand-box," Slith countered.

... AND TERRAN DIPLOMACY

"Well, at least they're still speaking to each other," Magnan said as the exchange raged on. "That's something."

It's a good thing Retief was there!

RETIEF
AT
LARGE
KEITH
LAUMER

ACE SCIENCE FICTION BOOKS
NEW YORK

"Cultural Exchange," copyright © 1962 by Digest Productions Corp.

"Saline Solution," copyright © 1963 by Digest Productions Corp.

"The Castle of Light," copyright © 1964 by Galaxy Publishing Corp.

"Wicker Wonderland," copyright © 1964 by Galaxy Publishing Corp.: first published in *If* under the title "The City that Grew in the Sea."

"The Brass God," copyright © 1964 by Galaxy Publishing Corp.: first published in *If* under the title "Retief, God-Speaker."

"Mechanical Advantage," copyright © 1966 by Galaxy Publishing Corp.: first published in *If* under the title "Retief, the Long-Awaited Master."

"Dam Nuisance," copyright © 1966 by Galaxy Publishing Corp.

"Grime and Punishment," copyright © 1967 by Galaxy Publishing Corp.: first published in *If* under the title "Clear as Mud."

"The Forbidden City," copyright © 1967 by Galaxy Publishing Corp.: first published in *If* under the title "Retief, War Criminal."

"The Piecemakers," copyright © 1970 by Universal Publishing and Distributing Corp.

"Ballot and Bandits," copyright © 1970 by Universal Publishing and Distributing Corp.

"Pime Doesn't Cray," copyright © 1971 by Universal Publishing and Distributing Corp.

RETIEF AT LARGE

An Ace Science Fiction Book / published by arrangement with the author

PRINTING HISTORY
First Ace Printing / August 1978
Sixth printing / May 1985

All rights reserved.
Copyright © 1978 by Keith Laumer
Cover art by Bob Adragna
This book may not be reproduced in whole or in part,
by mimeograph or any other means, without permission.
For information address: The Berkley Publishing Group,
200 Madison Avenue, New York, New York 10016.

ISBN: 0-441-71507-9

Ace Science Fiction Books are published by
The Berkley Publishing Group,
200 Madison Avenue, New York, New York 10016.
PRINTED IN THE UNITED STATES OF AMERICA

TABLE OF CONTENTS

CULTURAL EXCHANGE

I

SECOND SECRETARY MAGNAN took his green-lined cape and orange-feathered beret from the clothes tree. "I'm off now, Retief," he said. "I hope you'll manage the administrative routine during my absence without any unfortunate incidents."

"That seems a modest enough hope," Retief said. "I'll try to live up to it."

"I don't appreciate frivolity with reference to this Division," Magnan said testily. "When I first came here, the Manpower Utilization Directorate, Division of Libraries and Education was a shambles. I fancy I've made MUDDLE what it is today. Frankly, I question the wisdom of placing you in charge of such a sensitive desk, even for two weeks. But remember. Yours is purely a rubber-stamp function."

"In that case, let's leave it to Miss Furkle. I'll take a couple of weeks off myself. With her poundage, she could bring plenty of pressure to bear."

"I assume you jest, Retief," Magnan said sadly. "I should expect even you to appreciate that Bogan participation in the Exchange Program may be the first step toward sublimation of their aggressions into more cultivated channels."

"I see they're sending two thousand students to d'Land," Retief said, glancing at the Memo for Record. "That's a sizable sublimation."

Magnan nodded. "The Bogans have launched no less than four military campaigns in the last two decades. They're known as the Hoodlums of the Nicodemean Cluster. Now, perhaps, we shall see them breaking that precedent and entering into the cultural life of the Galaxy."

"Breaking and entering," Retief said. "You may have something there. But I'm wondering what they'll study on d'Land. That's an industrial world of the poor but honest variety."

"Academic details are the affair of the students and their professors," Magnan said. "Our function is merely to bring them together. See that you don't antagonize the Bogan representative. This will be an excellent opportunity for you to practice your diplomatic restraint—not your strong point, I'm sure you'll agree."

A buzzer sounded. Retief punched a button. "What is it, Miss Furkle?"

"That—bucolic person from Lovenbroy is here again." On the small desk screen, Miss Furkle's meaty features were compressed in disapproval.

"This fellow's a confounded pest. I'll leave him to you, Retief," Magnan said. "Tell him something. Get rid of him. And remember: here at Corps HQ, all eyes are upon you."

"If I'd thought of that, I'd have worn my other suit," Retief said.

Magnan snorted and passed from view. Retief punched Miss Furkle's button.

"Send the bucolic person in."

A tall broad man with bronze skin and gray hair, wearing tight trousers of heavy cloth, a loose shirt open at the neck and a short jacket, stepped into the room. He had a bundle under his arm. He paused at sight of Retief, looked him over momentarily, then advanced and held out his hand. Retief took it. For a moment the two big men stood, face to face. The newcomer's jaw muscles knotted. Then he winced.

Retief dropped his hand and motioned to a chair.

"That's nice knuckle work, mister," the stranger said, massaging his hand. "First time anybody ever did that to me. My fault though. I started it, I guess." He grinned and sat down.

"What can I do for you?" Retief said.

"You work for this Culture bunch, do you? Funny. I thought they were all ribbon-counter boys. Never mind. I'm Hank Arapoulous. I'm a farmer. What I wanted to see you about was—" He shifted in his chair. "Well, out on Lovenbroy we've got a serious problem. The wine crop is just about ready. We start picking in another two, three months. Now I don't know if you're familiar with the Bacchus vines we grow . . . ?"

"No," Retief said. "Have a cigar?" He pushed a box across the desk. Arapoulous took one. "Bacchus vines are an unusual crop," he said, puffing the cigar

3

alight. "Only mature every twelve years. In between, the vines don't need a lot of attention, so our time's mostly our own. We like to farm, though. Spend a lot of time developing new forms. Apples the size of a melon—and sweet—"

"Sounds very pleasant," Retief said. "Where does the Libraries and Education Division come in?"

Arapoulous leaned forward. "We go in pretty heavy for the arts. Folks can't spend all their time hybridizing plants. We've turned all the land area we've got into parks and farms. Course, we left some sizable forest areas for hunting and such. Lovenbroy's a nice place, Mr. Retief."

"It sounds like it, Mr. Arapoulous. Just what—"

"Call me Hank. We've got long seasons back home. Five of 'em. Our year's about eighteen Terry months. Cold as hell in winter; eccentric orbit, you know. Blue-black sky, stars visible all day. We do mostly painting and sculpture in the winter. Then Spring; still plenty cold. Lots of skiing, bob-sledding, ice skating; and it's the season for woodworkers. Our furniture—"

"I've seen some of your furniture," Retief said. "Beautiful work."

Arapoulous nodded. "All local timbers too. Lots of metals in our soil and those sulphates give the woods some color, I'll tell you. Then comes the Monsoon. Rain—it comes down in sheets. But the sun's getting closer. Shines all the time. Ever seen it pouring rain in the sunshine? That's the music-writing season. Then summer. Summer's hot. We stay inside in the daytime and have beach parties all night. Lots of beach on Lovenbroy; we're mostly islands. That's the drama and symphony time. The theatres are set up on the sand, or anchored offshore. You have the music and the surf and the bonfires and stars—we're close to the center of a globular cluster, you know . . .''

"You say it's time now for the wine crop?"

"That's right. Autumn's our harvest season. Most years we have just the ordinary crops. Fruit, grain, that kind of thing; getting it in doesn't take long. We spend most of the time on architecture, getting new places ready for the winter or remodeling the older ones. We spend a lot of time in our houses. We like to have them comfortable. But this year's different. This is Wine Year."

Arapoulous puffed on his cigar, looked worriedly at Retief. "Our wine crop is our big money crop," he said. "We make enough to keep us going. But this year . . ."

"The crop isn't panning out?"

"Oh, the crop's fine. One of the best I can remember. Course, I'm only twenty-eight; I can't remember but two other harvests. The problem's not the crop."

"Have you lost your markets? That sounds like a matter for the Commercial—"

"Lost our markets? Mister, nobody that ever tasted our wines ever settled for anything else!"

"It sounds like I've been missing something," said Retief. "I'll have to try them some time."

Arapoulous put his bundle on the desk, pulled off the wrappings. "No time like the present," he said.

Retief looked at the two squat bottles, one green, one amber, both dusty, with faded labels, and blackened corks secured by wire.

"Drinking on duty is frowned on in the Corps, Mr. Arapoulous," he said.

"This isn't *drinking*. It's just wine." Arapoulous pulled the wire retainer loose, thumbed the cork. It rose slowly, then popped in the air. Arapoulous caught it. Aromatic fumes wafted from the bottle. "Besides, my feelings would be hurt if you didn't join me." He winked.

Retief took two thin-walled glasses from a table beside the desk. "Come to think of it, we also have to be careful about violating quaint native customs."

Arapoulous filled the glasses. Retief picked one up, sniffed the deep rust-colored fluid, tasted it, then took a healthy swallow. He looked at Arapoulous thoughtfully.

"Hmmm. It tastes like salted pecans, with an undercurrent of crusted port."

"Don't try to describe it, Mr. Retief," Arapoulous said. He took a mouthful of wine, swished it around his teeth, swallowed. "It's Bacchus wine, that's all. Nothing like it in the Galaxy." He pushed the second bottle toward Retief. "The custom back home is to alternate red wine and black."

Retief put aside his cigar, pulled the wires loose, nudged the cork, caught it as it popped up.

"Bad luck if you miss the cork," Arapoulous said, nodding. "You probably never heard about the trouble we had on Lovenbroy a few years back?"

"Can't say that I did, Hank." Retief poured the black wine into two fresh glasses. "Here's to the harvest."

"We've got plenty of minerals on Lovenbroy," Arapoulous said, swallowing wine. "But we don't plan to wreck the landscape mining 'em. We like to farm. About ten years back some neighbors of ours landed a force. They figured they knew better what to do with our minerals than we did. Wanted to strip-mine, smelt ore. We convinced 'em otherwise. But it took a year, and we lost a lot of men."

"That's too bad," Retief said. "I'd say this one tastes more like roast beef and popcorn over a Riesling base."

"It put us in a bad spot," Arapoulous went on. "We had to borrow money from a world called Croanie. Mortgaged our crops. Had to start exporting art work too. Plenty of buyers, but it's not the same when you're doing it for strangers."

"Say, this business of alternating drinks is the real McCoy," Retief said. "What's the problem? Croanie about to foreclose?"

"Well, the loan's due. The wine crop would put us in the clear. But we need harvest hands. Picking Bacchus grapes isn't a job you can turn over to machinery—and anyway we wouldn't if we could. Vintage season is the high point of living on Lovenbroy. Everybody joins in. First, there's the picking in the fields. Miles and miles of vineyards covering the mountain sides, and crowding the river banks, with gardens here and there. Big vines, eight feet high, loaded with fruit, and deep grass growing between. The wine-carriers keep on the run, bringing wine to the pickers. There's prizes for the biggest day's output, bets on who can fill the most baskets in an hour . . . The sun's high and bright, and it's just cool enough to give you plenty of energy. Come nightfall, the tables are set up in the garden plots, and the feast is laid on: roast turkeys, beef, hams, all kinds of fowl. Big salads. Plenty of fruit. Fresh-baked bread . . . and wine, plenty of wine. The cooking's done by a different crew each night in each garden, and there's prizes for the best crews.

"Then the wine-making. We still tramp out the vintage. That's mostly for the young folks but anybody's welcome. That's when things start to get loosened up. Matter of fact, pretty near half our young-uns are born after a vintage. All bets are off then. It keeps a fellow on his toes though. Ever tried to hold onto a gal wearing nothing but a layer of grape juice?"

"Never did," Retief said. "You say most of the children are born after a vintage. That would make them only twelve years old by the time—"

"Oh, that's Lovenbroy years; they'd be eighteen, Terry reckoning."

"I was thinking you looked a little mature for twenty-eight," Retief said.

"Forty-two, Terry years," Arapoulous said. "But this year it looks bad. We've got a bumper crop—and we're short-handed. If we don't get a big vintage, Croanie steps in. Lord knows what they'll do to the land. Then next vintage time, with them holding half our grape acreage—"

"You hocked the vineyards?"

"Yep. Pretty dumb, huh? But we figured twelve years was a long time."

"On the whole," Retief said, "I think I prefer the black. But the red is hard to beat . . ."

"What we figured was, maybe you Culture boys could help us out. A loan to see us through the vintage, enough to hire extra hands. Then we'd repay it in sculpture, painting, furniture—"

"Sorry, Hank. All we do here is work out itineraries for traveling side-shows, that kind of thing. Now, if you needed a troop of Groaci noseflute players—"

"Can they pick grapes?"

"Nope. Anyway, they can't stand the daylight. Have you talked this over with the Labor Office?"

"Sure did. They said they'd fix us up with all the electronics specialists and computer programmers we wanted—but no field hands. Said it was what they classified as menial drudgery: you'd have thought I was trying to buy slaves."

The buzzer sounded. Miss Furkle's features appeared on the desk screen.

"You're due at the Intergroup Council in five minutes," she said. "Then afterwards, there are the Bogan students to meet."

"Thanks." Retief finished his glass, stood. "I have to run, Hank," he said. "Let me think this over. Maybe I can come up with something. Check with me day after tomorrow. And you'd better leave the bottles here. Cultural exhibits, you know."

II

As the council meeting broke up, Retief caught the eye of a colleague across the table.

"Mr. Whaffle, you mentioned a shipment going to a place called Croanie. What are they getting?"

Whaffle blinked. "You're the fellow who's filling in for Magnan, over at MUDDLE," he said. "Properly speaking, equipment grants are the sole concern of the Motorized Equipment Depot, Division of Loans and

Exchanges." He pursed his lips. "However, I suppose there's no harm in telling you. They'll be receiving heavy mining equipment."

"Drill rigs, that sort of thing?"

"Strip mining gear." Whaffle took a slip of paper from a breast pocket, blinked at it. "Bolo Model WV/1 tractors, to be specific. Why is MUDDLE interested in MEDDLE's activities?"

"Forgive my curiosity, Mr. Whaffle. It's just that Croanie cropped up earlier today. It seems she holds a mortgage on some vineyards over on—"

"That's not MEDDLE's affair, sir," Whaffle cut in. "I have sufficient problems as Chief of MEDDLE without probing into MUDDLE's business."

"Speaking of tractors," another man put in, "we over at the Special Committee for Rehabilitation and Overhaul of Under-developed Nations' General Economies have been trying for months to get a request for mining equipment for d'Land through MEDDLE—"

"SCROUNGE was late on the scene," Whaffle said. "First come, first served. That's our policy at MEDDLE. Good day, gentlemen." He strode off, briefcase under his arm.

"That's the trouble with peaceful worlds," the SCROUNGE committeeman said. "Boge is a trouble-maker, so every agency in the Corps is out to pacify her. While my chance to make a record—that is, assist peace-loving d'Land—comes to naught." He shook his head.

"What kind of university do they have on d'Land?" asked Retief. "We're sending them two thousand exchange students. It must be quite an institution."

"University? D'Land has one under-endowed technical college."

"Will all the exchange students be studying at the Technical College?"

"Two thousand students? Hah! Two *hundred* students would overtax the facilities of the college."

"I wonder if the Bogans know that?"

"The Bogans? Why, most of d'Land's difficulties are due to the unwise trade agreement she entered into with Boge. Two thousand students indeed!" He snorted and walked away.

Retief stopped by the office to pick up a short cape, then rode the elevator to the roof of the 230-story Corps HQ building and hailed a cab to the port. The Bogan students had arrived early. Retief saw them lined up on the ramp waiting to go through customs. It would be half an hour before they were cleared through. He turned into the bar and ordered a beer.

A tall young fellow on the next stool raised his glass.

"Happy days," he said.

"And nights to match."

"You said it." He gulped half his beer. "My name's Karsh. Mr. Karsh. Yep, Mr. Karsh. Boy, this is a drag, sitting around this place waiting . . ."

"You meeting somebody?"

"Yeah. Bunch of babies. Kids. How they expect—Never mind. Have one on me."

"Thanks. You a Scoutmaster?"

"I'll tell you what I am. I'm a cradle-robber. You know—" he turned to Retief— "not one of those kids is over eighteen." He hiccupped. "Students, you know. Never saw a student with a beard, did you?"

"Lots of times. You're meeting the students, are

you?''

The young fellow blinked at Retief. "Oh, you know about it, huh?"

"I represent MUDDLE."

Karsh finished his beer, ordered another. "I came on ahead. Sort of an advance guard for the kids. I trained 'em myself. Treated it like a game, but they can handle a CSU. Don't know how they'll act under pressure. If I had my old platoon—"

He looked at his beer glass, pushed it back. "Had enough," he said. "So long, friend. Or are you coming along?"

Retief nodded. "Might as well."

At the exit to the Customs enclosure, Retief watched as the first of the Bogan students came through, caught sight of Karsh and snapped to attention, his chest out.

"Drop that, mister," Karsh snapped. "Is that any way for a student to act?"

The youth, a round-faced lad with broad shoulders, grinned.

"Heck, no," he said. "Say, uh, Mr. Karsh, are we gonna get to go to town? We fellas were thinking—"

"You were, hah? You act like a bunch of school kids! I mean . . . no! Now line up!"

"We have quarters ready for the students," Retief said. "If you'd like to bring them around to the west side. I have a couple of copters laid on."

"Thanks," said Karsh. "They'll stay here until take-off time. Can't have the little dears wandering around loose. Might get ideas about going over the hill." He hiccupped. "I mean they might play hookey."

"We've scheduled your reembarkation for noon tomorrow. That's a long wait. MUDDLE's arranged theater tickets and a dinner.''

"Sorry," Karsh said. "As soon as the baggage gets here, we're off." He hiccupped again. "Can't travel without our baggage, y'know."

"Suit yourself," Retief said. "Where's the baggage now?"

"Coming in aboard a Croanie lighter."

"Maybe you'd like to arrange for a meal for the students here."

"Sure," Karsh said. "That's a good idea. Why don't you join us?" Karsh winked. "And bring a few beers."

"Not this time," Retief said. He watched the students, still emerging from Customs. "They seem to be all boys," he commented. "No female students?"

"Maybe later," Karsh said. "You know, after we see how the first bunch is received."

Back at the MUDDLE office, Retief buzzed Miss Furkle.

"Do you know the name of the institution these Bogan students are bound for?"

"Why, the University at d'Land, of course."

"Would that be the Technical College?"

Miss Furkle's mouth puckered. "I'm sure I've never pried into these details."

"Where does doing your job stop and prying begin, Miss Furkle?" Retief said. "Personally, I'm curious as to just what it is these students are travelling so far to study—at Corps expense."

"Mr. Magnan never—"

"For the present, Miss Furkle, Mr. Magnan is vacationing. That leaves me with the question of two thousand young male students headed for a world with no classrooms for them . . . a world in need of tractors. But the tractors are on their way to Croanie, a world under obligation to Boge. And Croanie holds a mortgage on the best grape acreage on Lovenbroy.''

''Well!'' Miss Furkle snapped, small eyes glaring under unplucked brows. ''I hope you're not questioning Mr. Magnan's wisdom!''

''About Mr. Magnan's wisdom there can be no question,'' Retief said. ''But never mind. I'd like you to look up an item for me. How many tractors will Croanie be getting under the MEDDLE program?''

''Why, that's entirely MEDDLE business,'' Miss Furkle said. ''Mr. Magnan always—''

''I'm sure he did. Let me know about the tractors as soon as you can.''

Miss Furkle sniffed and disappeared from the screen. Retief left the office, descended forty-one stories, followed a corridor to the Corps Library. In the stacks he thumbed through catalogues, pored over indices.

''Can I help you?'' someone chirped. A tiny librarian stood at his elbow.

''Thank you, ma'am,'' Retief said. ''I'm looking for information on a mining rig. A Bolo model WV tractor.''

''You won't find it in the industrial section,'' the librarian said. ''Come along.'' Retief followed her along the stacks to a well-lit section lettered ARMAMENTS. She took a tape from the shelf, plugged it into the viewer, flipped through and stopped at a squat armored vehicle.

''That's the model WV,'' she said. ''It's what is

14

known as a continental siege unit. It carries four men, with a half-megaton/second firepower.''

"There must be an error somewhere," Retief said. "The Bolo model I want is a tractor, Model WV M-1—"

"Oh, the modification was the addition of a bulldozer blade for demolition work. That must be what confused you."

"Probably—among other things. Thank you."

Miss Furkle was waiting at the office. "I have the information you wanted," she said. "I've had it for over ten minutes. I was under the impression you needed it urgently, and I went to great lengths—"

"Sure," Retief said. "Shoot. How many tractors?"

"Five hundred."

"Are you sure?"

Miss Furkle's chins quivered. "Well! If you feel I'm incompetent—"

"Just questioning the possibility of a mistake, Miss Furkle. Five hundred tractors is a lot of equipment."

"Was there anything further?" Miss Furkle inquired frigidly.

"I sincerely hope not," Retief said.

III

Leaning back in Magnan's padded chair with power swivel and hip-u-matic contour, Retief leafed through a folder labelled "CERP 7-602-Ba; CROANIE (general).'' He paused at a page headed "Industry."

Still reading, he opened the desk drawer, took out the two bottles of Bacchus wine and two glasses. He poured an inch of wine into each and sipped the black wine meditatively.

It would be a pity, he reflected, if anything should interfere with the production of such vintages . . .

Half an hour later he laid the folder aside, keyed the phone and put through a call to the Croanie Legation. He asked for the Commercial Attache.

"Retief here, Corps HQ," he said airily. "About the MEDDLE shipment, the tractors. I'm wondering if there's been a slip up. My records show we're shipping five hundred units . . ."

"That's correct. Five hundred."

Retief waited.

"Ah . . . are you there, Retief?"

"I'm still here. And I'm still wondering about the five hundred tractors."

"It's perfectly in order. I thought it was all settled. Mr. Whaffle—"

"One unit would require a good-sized plant to handle its output," Retief said. "Now Croanie subsists on her fisheries. She has perhaps half a dozen pint-sized processing plants. Maybe, in a bind, they could handle the ore ten WV's could scrape up . . . if Croanie had any ore. It doesn't. By the way, isn't a WV a poor choice as a mining outfit? I should think—"

"See here, Retief! Why all this interest in a few surplus tractors? And in any event, what business is it of yours how we plan to use the equipment? That's an internal affair of my government. Mr. Whaffle—"

"I'm not Mr. Whaffle. What are you going to do with the other four hundred and ninety tractors?"

"I understood the grant was to be with no strings attached!"

"I know it's bad manners to ask questions. It's an old diplomatic tradition that any time you can get anybody to accept anything as a gift, you've scored points in the game. But if Croanie has some scheme cooking—"

"Nothing like that, Retief. It's a mere business transaction."

"What kind of business do you do with a Bolo WV? With or without a blade attached, it's what's known as a continental siege unit."

"Great Heavens, Retief! Don't jump to conclusions! Would you have us branded as warmongers? Frankly—is this a closed line?"

"Certainly. You may speak freely."

"The tractors are for transshipment. We've gotten ourselves into a difficult situation, balance-of-payments-wise. This is an accommodation to a group with which we have rather strong business ties."

"I understand you hold a mortgage on the best land on Lovenbroy," Retief said. "Any connection?"

"Why . . . ah . . . no. Of course not, ha ha."

"Who gets the tractors eventually?"

"Retief, this is unwarranted interference!"

"Who gets them?"

"They happen to be going to Lovenbroy. But I scarcely see—"

"And who's the friend you're helping out with an unauthorized transshipment of grant material?"

"Why . . . ah . . . I've been working with a Mr. Gulver, a Bogan representative."

"And when will they be shipped?"

"Why, they went out a week ago. They'll be half way there by now. But look here, Retief, this isn't what you're thinking!"

"How do you know what I'm thinking? I don't know myself." Retief rang off, buzzed the secretary.

"Miss Furkle, I'd like to be notified immediately of any new applications that might come in from the Bogan Consulate for placement of students."

"Well, it happens, by coincidence, that I have an application here now. Mr. Gulver of the Consulate brought it in."

"Is Mr. Gulver in the office? I'd like to see him."

"I'll ask him if he has time."

"Great. Thanks." It was half a minute before a thick-necked red-faced man in a tight hat walked in. He wore an old-fashioned suit, a drab shirt, shiny shoes with round toes and an ill-tempered expression.

"What is it you wish?" he barked. "I understood in my discussions with the other . . . ah . . . civilian there'd be no further need for these irritating conferences."

"I've just learned you're placing more students abroad, Mr. Gulver. How many this time?"

"Two thousand."

"And where will they be going?"

"Croanie. It's all in the application form I've handed in. Your job is to provide transportation."

"Will there by any other students embarking this season?"

"Why . . . perhaps. That's Boge's business." Gulver looked at Retief with pursed lips. "As a matter of fact, we had in mind dispatching another two thousand to Featherweight."

"Another under-populated world—and in the same cluster, I believe," Retief said. "Your people must be unusually interested in that region of space."

"If that's all you wanted to know, I'll be on my way. I have matters of importance to see to."

After Gulver left, Retief called Miss Furkle in. "I'd like to have a break-out of all the student movements that have been planned under the present program," he said. "And see if you can get a summary of what MEDDLE has been shipping lately."

Miss Furkle compressed her lips. "If Mr. Magnan were here, I'm sure he wouldn't dream of interfering in the work of other departments. I . . . overheard your conversation with the gentleman from the Croanie Legation—"

"The lists, Miss Furkle."

"I'm not accustomed," Miss Furkle said, "to intruding in matters outside our interest cluster."

"That's worse than listening in on phone conversations, eh? But never mind. I need the information, Miss Furkle."

"Loyalty to my Chief—"

"Loyalty to your pay-check should send you scuttling for the material I've asked for," Retief said. "I'm taking full responsibility. Now scat."

The buzzer sounded. Retief flipped a key. "MUD-DLE, Retief speaking . . ."

Arapoulous's brown face appeared on the desk screen. "How-do, Retief. Okay if I come up?"

"Sure, Hank. I want to talk to you."

In the office, Arapoulous took a chair. "Sorry if I'm rushing you, Retief," he said. "But have you got anything for me?"

Retief waved at the wine bottles. "What do you know about Croanie?"

"Croanie? Not much of a place. Mostly ocean. All

right if you like fish, I guess. We import our seafood from there. Nice prawns in monsoon time. Over a foot long."

"You on good terms with them?"

"Sure, I guess so. Course, they're pretty thick with Boge."

"So?"

"Didn't I tell you? Boge was the bunch that tried to take us over here a dozen years back. They'd've made it too, if they hadn't had a lot of bad luck. Their armor went in the drink, and without armor they're easy game."

Miss Furkle buzzed. "I have your lists," she said shortly.

"Bring them in, please."

The secretary placed the papers on the desk. Arapoulous caught her eye and grinned. She sniffed and marched from the room.

"What that gal needs is a slippery time in the grape mash," Arapoulous observed. Retief thumbed through the papers, pausing to read from time to time. He finished and looked at Arapoulous.

"How many men do you need for the harvest, Hank?" Retief inquired.

Arapoulous sniffed his wine glass and looked thoughtful.

"A hundred would help," he said. "A thousand would be better. Cheers."

"What would you say to two thousand?"

"Two thousand? Retief, you're not fooling?"

"I hope not." He picked up the phone, called the Port Authority, asked for the dispatch clerk.

"Hello, Jim. Say, I have a favor to ask of you. You

20

know that contingent of Bogan students. They're traveling aboard the two CDT transports. I'm interested in the baggage that goes with the students. Has it arrived yet? Okay, I'll wait.''

Jim came back to the phone. ''Yeah, Retief, it's here. Just arrived. But there's a funny thing. It's not consigned to d'Land. It's ticketed clear through to Lovenbroy.''

''Listen, Jim,'' Retief said. ''I want you to go over to the warehouse and take a look at that baggage for me.''

Retief waited while the dispatch clerk carried out the errand. The level in the two bottles had gone down an inch when Jim returned to the phone.

''Hey, I took a look at that luggage, Retief. Something funny going on. Guns. 2mm needlers, Mark XII hand blasters, power pistols—''

''It's okay, Jim. Nothing to worry about. Just a mix-up. Now, Jim, I'm going to ask you to do something more for me. I'm covering for a friend. It seems he slipped up. I wouldn't want word to get out, you understand. I'll send along a written change order in the morning that will cover you officially. Meanwhile, here's what I want you to do . . .''

Retief gave instructions, then rang off and turned to Arapoulous.

''As soon as I get off a couple of TWX's, I think we'd better get down to the port, Hank. I think I'd like to see the students off personally.''

IV

Karsh met Retief as he entered the Departures enclosure at the port.

"What's going on here?" he demanded. "There's some funny business with my baggage consignment. They won't let me see it! I've got a feeling it's not being loaded."

"You'd better hurry, Mr. Karsh," Retief said. "You're scheduled to blast off in less than an hour. Are the students all loaded?"

"Yes, blast you! What about my baggage? Those vessels aren't moving without it!"

"No need to get so upset about a few toothbrushes, is there, Mr. Karsh?" Retief said blandly. "Still, if you're worried—" He turned to Arapoulous.

"Hank, why don't you walk Mr. Karsh over to the warehouse and . . . ah . . . take care of him?"

"I know just how to handle it," Arapoulous said.

The dispatch clerk came up to Retief. "I caught the tractor equipment," he said. "Funny kind of mistake, but it's okay now. They're being off-loaded at d'Land. I talked to the traffic controller there. He said they weren't looking for any students."

"The labels got switched, Jim. The students go where the baggage was consigned. Too bad about the mistake, but the Armaments Office will have a man along in a little while to dispose of the guns. Keep an eye out for the luggage. No telling where it's gotten to."

"Here!" a hoarse voice yelled. Retief turned. A

disheveled figure in a tight hat was crossing the enclosure, arms waving.

"Hi there, Mr. Gulver," Retief called. "How's Boge's business coming along?"

"Piracy!" Gulver blurted as he came up to Retief, puffing hard. "You've got a hand in this, I don't doubt! Where's that Magnan fellow?"

"What seems to be the problem?" Retief said.

"Hold those transports! I've just been notified that the baggage shipment has been impounded. I'll remind you, that shipment enjoys diplomatic free entry!"

"Who told you it was impounded?"

"Never mind! I have my sources!"

Two tall men buttoned into gray tunics came up. "Are you Mr. Retief of CDT?" one said.

"That's right."

"What about my baggage!" Gulver cut in. "And I'm warning you, if those ships lift without—"

"These gentlemen are from the Armaments Control Commission," Retief said. "Would you like to come along and claim your baggage, Mr. Gulver?"

"From where? I—" Gulver turned two shades redder about the ears. "Armaments?"

"The only shipment I've held up seems to be somebody's arsenal," Retief said. "Now if you claim this is your baggage . . ."

"Why, impossible," Gulver said in a strained voice. "Armaments? Ridiculous. There's been an error . . ."

At the baggage warehouse Gulver looked glumly at the opened cases of guns. "No, of course not," he said, dully. "Not my baggage. Not my baggage at all."

Arapoulous appeared, supporting the stumbling figure of Mr. Karsh.

"What—what's this?" Gulver spluttered. "Karsh? What's happened?"

"He had a little fall. He'll be okay," Arapoulous said.

"You'd better help him to the ship," Retief said. "It's ready to lift. We wouldn't want him to miss it."

"Leave him to me!" Gulver snapped, his eyes slashing at Karsh. "I'll see he's dealt with."

"I couldn't think of it," Retief said. "He's a guest of the Corps, you know. We'll see him safely aboard."

Gulver turned, signaled frantically. Three heavy-set men in identical drab suits detached themselves from the wall, crossed to the group.

"Take this man," Gulver snapped, indicating Karsh, who looked at him dazedly, reached up to rub his head.

"We take our hospitality seriously," Retief said. "We'll see him aboard the vessel."

Gulver opened his mouth.

"I know you feel bad about finding guns instead of school books in your luggage," Retief said, looking Gulver in the eye. "You'll be busy straightening out the details of the mix-up. You'll want to avoid further complications."

"Ah. Ulp. Yes," Gulver said. He appeared unhappy.

Arapoulous went on to the passenger conveyor, turned to wave.

"Your man—he's going too?" Gulver blurted.

"He's not our man, properly speaking," Retief said. "He lives on Lovenbroy."

"Lovenbroy?" Gulver choked. "But . . . the . . . I . . ."

"I know you said the students were bound for d'Land," Retief said. "But I guess that was just another aspect of the general confusion. The course plugged into the navigators was to Lovenbroy. You'll be glad to know they're still headed there—even without the baggage."

"Perhaps," Gulver said grimly, "perhaps they'll manage without it."

"By the way," Retief said. "There was another funny mix-up. There were some tractors—for industrial use, you'll recall. I believe you cooperated with Croanie in arranging the grant through MEDDLE. They were erroneously consigned to Lovenbroy, a purely agricultural world. I saved you some embarrassment, I trust, Mr. Gulver, by arranging to have them offloaded at d'Land."

"D'Land! You've put the CSU's in the hands of Boge's bitterest enemies!"

"But they're only tractors, Mr. Gulver. Peaceful devices. Isn't that correct?"

"That's . . . correct." Gulver sagged. Then he snapped erect. "Hold the ships!" he yelled. "I'm canceling the student exchange—"

His voice was drowned by the rumble as the first of the monster transports rose from the launch pit, followed a moment later by the second. Retief watched them out of sight, then turned to Gulver.

"They're off," he said. "Let's hope they get a liberal education."

V

Retief lay on his back in deep grass by a stream, eating grapes. A tall figure appeared on the knoll above him and waved.

"Retief!" Hank Arapoulous bounded down the slope and embraced Retief, slapping him on the back. "I heard you were here—and I've got news for you. You won the final day's picking competition. Over two hundred bushels! That's a record!"

"Let's get on over to the garden. Sounds like the celebration's about to start."

In the flower-crowded park among the stripped vines, Retief and Arapoulous made their way to a laden table under the lanterns. A tall girl dressed in loose white, and with long golden hair, came up to Arapoulous.

"Delinda, this is Retief—today's winner. And he's also the fellow that got those workers for us."

Delinda smiled at Retief. "I've heard about you, Mr. Retief. We weren't sure about the boys at first. Two thousand Bogans, and all confused about their baggage that went astray. But they seemed to like the picking." She smiled again.

"That's not all. Our gals liked the boys," Hank said. "Even Bogans aren't so bad, minus their irons. A lot of 'em will be staying on. But how come you didn't tell me you were coming, Retief? I'd have laid on some kind of big welcome."

"I liked the welcome I got. And I didn't have much

26

notice. Mr. Magnan was a little upset when he got back. It seemes I exceeded my authority."

Arapoulous laughed. "I had a feeling you were wheeling pretty free, Retief. I hope you didn't get into any trouble over it."

"No trouble," Retief said. "A few people were a little unhappy with me. It seemes I'm not ready for important assignments at Departmental level. I was shipped off here to the boondocks to get a little more experience."

"Delinda, look after Retief," said Arapoulous. "I'll see you later. I've got to see to the wine judging." He disappeared in the crowd.

"Congratulations on winning the day," said Delinda. "I noticed you at work. You were wonderful. I'm glad you're going to have the prize."

"Thanks. I noticed you too, flitting around in that white nightie of yours. But why weren't you picking grapes with the rest of us?"

"I had a special assignment."

"Too bad. You should have had a chance at the prize."

Delinda took Retief's hand. "I wouldn't have anyway," she said. "I'm the prize."

SALINE SOLUTION

I

CONSUL-GENERAL MAGNAN gingerly fingered the heavily rubberbanded sheaf of dog-eared documents. "I haven't rushed into precipitate action on this claim. Retief," he said. "The Consulate has grave responsibilities here in the Belt. One must weigh all aspects of the situation, consider the ramifications. What consequences would arise from a grant of minerals rights on the planetoid to this claimant?"

"The claim looked all right to me," Retief said. "Seventeen copies with attachments. Why not process it? You've had it on your desk for a week."

Magnan's eyebrows went up. "You've a personal interest in this claim, Retief?"

"Every day you wait is costing them money. That hulk they use for an ore-carrier is in a parking orbit piling up demurrage."

"I see you've become emotionally involved in the affairs of a group of obscure miners. You haven't yet learned the true diplomat's happy faculty of non-identification with specifics—or should I say identification with non-specifics?''

"They're not a wealthy outfit, you know. In fact, I understand this claim is their sole asset—unless you want to count the ore-carrier.''

"The Consulate is not concerned with the internal financial problems of the Sam's Last Chance Number Nine Mining Company.''

"Careful,'' Retief said. "You almost identified yourself with a specific that time.''

"Hardly, my dear Retief,'' Magnan said blandly. "The implication is mightier than the affidavit. You should study the records of the giants of galactic diplomacy: Crodfoller, Passwyn, Spradley, Nitworth, Sternwheeler, Rumpwhistle. The roll-call of those names rings like the majestic tread of . . . of . . .''

"Dinosaurs?'' Retief suggested.

"An apt simile,'' Magnan nodded. "Those mighty figures, those armored hides—''

"Those tiny brains—''

Magnan smiled sadly. "I see you're indulging your penchant for distorted facetiae. Perhaps one day you'll learn their true worth.''

"I already have my suspicions.''

The intercom chimed. Miss Gumble's features appeared on the desk screen.

"Mr. Leatherwell to see you, Mr. Magnan. He has no appointment—''

Magnan's eyebrows went up. "Send Mr. Leatherwell right in.'' He looked at Retief. "I had no idea Leatherwell was planning a call. I wonder what he's after?'' Magnan looked anxious. "He's an important figure in Belt minerals circles. It's important to avoid arousing antagonism, while maintaining non-commitment. You may as well stay. You might pick up some valuable pointers technique-wise."

The door swung wide. Leatherwell strode into the room, his massive paunch buckled into fashionable vests of turquoise velvet and hung with the latest in fluorescent watch charms. He extended a large palm and pumped Magnan's flaccid arm vigorously.

"Ah, there, Mr. Consul-General. Good of you to receive me." He wiped his hand absently on his thigh, eyeing Retief questioningly.

"Mr. Retief, my Vice-Consul and Minerals Officer," Magnan said. "Do take a chair, Mr. Leatherwell. In what capacity can I serve today?"

"I am here, gentlemen," Leatherwell said, putting an immense yellow briefcase on Magnan's desk and settling himself in a power rocker, "on behalf of my company, General Minerals. General Minerals has long been aware, gentlemen, of the austere conditions obtaining here in the Belt, to which public servants like yourselves are subjected." Leatherwell bobbed with the pitch of the rocker, smiling complacently at Magnan. "General Minerals is more than a great industrial combine. It is an organization with a heart." Leatherwell reached for his breast pocket, missed, tried again. "How do you turn this damned thing off?" he growled.

Magnan half-rose, peering over Leatherwell's briefcase. "The switch just there—on the arm."

The executive fumbled. There was a *click,* and the chair subsided with a sigh of compressed air.

"That's better." Leatherwell drew out a long slip of blue paper.

"To alleviate the boredom and brighten the lives of

that hardy group of Terrestrials laboring here on Ceres to bring free enterprise to the Belt, General Minerals is presenting to the Consulate—on their behalf—one hundred thousand credits for the construction of a Joy Center, to be quipped with the latest and finest in recreational equipment, including a Gourmet Model C banquet synthesizer, a forty-foot sublimation chamber, a five thousand tape library—with a number of choice items unobtainable in Boston—a twenty-foot Tri-D tank and other amenities too numerous to mention." Leatherwell leaned back, beaming expectantly.

"Why, Mr. Leatherwell. We're overwhelmed, of course." Magnan smiled dazedly past the briefcase. "But I wonder if it's quite proper . . ."

"The gift is to the people, Mr. Consul. You merely accept on their behalf."

"I wonder if General Minerals realizes that the hardy Terrestrials laboring on Ceres are limited to the Consular staff?" Retief said. "And the staff consists of Mr. Magnan, Miss Gumble and myself."

"Mr. Leatherwell is hardly interested in these details, Retief," Magnan cut in. "A public-spirited offer indeed, sir. As Terrestrial Consul—and on behalf of all Terrestrials here in the Belt—I accept with a humble awareness of—"

"Now, there was one other little matter." Leatherwell leaned forward to open the briefcase, glancing over Magnan's littered desktop. He extracted a bundle of papers, dropped them on the desk, then drew out a heavy document and passed it across to Magnan.

"Just a routine claim. I'd like to see it rushed through, as we have in mind some loading operations in the vicinity next week."

"Certainly Mr. Leatherwell."

Magnan glanced at the papers, paused to read. He looked up. "Ah—"

"Something the matter, Mr. Consul?" Leatherwell demanded.

"It's just that—ah—I seem to recall—as a matter of fact . . ." Magnan looked at Retief. Retief took the papers, looked over the top sheet.

"95739-A. Sorry, Mr. Leatherwell. General Minerals has been anticipated. We're processing a prior claim."

"Prior claim?" Leatherwell barked. "You've issued the grant?"

"Oh, no indeed, Mr. Leatherwell," Magnan replied quickly. "The claim hasn't yet been processed."

"Then there's no difficulty," Leatherwell boomed. He glanced at his finger watch. "If you don't mind, I'll wait and take the grant along with me. I assume it will only take a minute or two to sign it and affix seals and so on?"

"The other claim was filed a full week ago—" Retief started.

"Bah!" Leatherwell waved a hand impatiently. "These details can be arranged." He fixed an eye on Magnan. "I'm sure all of us here understand that it's in the public interest that minerals properties go to responsible firms, with adequate capital for proper development."

"Why, ah," Magnan said.

"The Sam's Last Chance Number Nine Mining Company is a duly chartered firm. Their claim is valid."

"I know that hole-in-corner concern," Leatherwell snapped. "Mere irresponsible opportunists. General

Minerals has spent millions—millions, I say—of the stockholders' funds in minerals explorations. Are they to be balked in realizing a fair return on their investment because these . . . these . . . adventurers have stumbled on a deposit? Not that the property is of any real value, of course," he added. "Quite an ordinary bit of rock. But General Minerals would find it convenient to consolidate its holdings."

"There are plenty of other rocks floating around in the Belt. Why not—"

"One moment, Retief," Magnan cut in. He looked across the desk at his junior with a severe expression. "As Consul-General, I'm quite capable of determining the relative merits of claims. As Mr. Leatherwell has pointed out, it's in the public interest to consider the question in depth."

Leatherwell cleared his throat. "I might state at this time that General Minerals is prepared to be generous in dealing with these interlopers. I believe we would be prepared to go so far as to offer them free title to certain GM holdings in exchange for their release of any alleged rights to the property in question—merely to simplify matters, of course."

"That seems more than fair to me," Magnan glowed.

"The Sam's people have a clear priority," Retief said. "I logged the claim in last Friday."

"They have far from a clear title." Leatherwell snapped. "And I can assure you GM will contest their claim, if need be, to the Supreme Court!"

"Just what holdings did you have in mind offering them, Mr. Leatherwell?" Magnan asked nervously.

Leatherwell reached into his briefcase and drew out a paper.

"2645-P," he read. "A quite massive body. Crustal material, I imagine. It should satisfy these squatters' desire to own real estate in the Belt."

"I'll make a note of that," Magnan said, reaching for a pad.

"That's a Bona Fide offer, Mr. Leatherwell?" Retief asked.

"Certainly!"

"I'll record it as such," Magnan said, scribbling.

"And who knows?" Leatherwell said. "It may turn out to contain some surprisingly rich finds."

"And if they won't accept it?" Retief asked.

"Then I daresay General Minerals will find a remedy in the courts, sir!"

"Oh, I hardly think that will be necessary," Magnan said.

"Then there's another routine matter," Leatherwell said. He passed a second document across to Magnan. "GM is requesting an injunction to restrain these same parties from aggravated trespass. I'd appreciate it if you'd push it through at once. There's a matter of a load of illegally obtained ore involved, as well."

"Certainly Mr. Leatherwell. I'll see to it myself."

"No need for that. The papers are all drawn up. Our legal department will vouch for their correctness. Just sign here." Leatherwell spread out the paper and handed Magnan a pen.

"Wouldn't it be a good idea to read that over first?" Retief said.

Leatherwell frowned impatiently. "You'll have adequate time to familiarize yourself with the details later, Retief," Magnan snapped, taking the pen. "No need to waste Mr. Leatherwell's valuable time." He scratched a signature on the paper.

Leatherwell rose, gathered up his papers from Magnan's desk, dumped them into the briefcase. "Riff-raff, of course. Their kind has no business in the Belt."

Retief rose, crossed to the desk, and held out a hand. "I believe you gathered in an official document along with your own, Mr. Leatherwell. By error, of course."

"What's that?" Leatherwell bridled. Retief smiled, waiting. Magnan opened his mouth.

"It was under your papers, Mr. Leatherwell," Retief said. "It's the thick one, with the rubber bands."

Leatherwell dug in his briefcase, produced the document. "Well, fancy finding this here," he growled. He shoved the papers into Retief's hand.

"You're a very observant young fellow." He closed the briefcase with a snap. "I trust you'll have a bright future with the CDT."

"Really, Retief," Magnan said reprovingly. "There was no need to trouble Mr. Leatherwell."

Leatherwell directed a sharp look at Retief and a bland one at Magnan. "I trust you'll communicate the proposal to the interested parties. Inasmuch as time is of the essence to the GM position, our offer can only be held open until 0900 Greenwich, tomorrow. I'll call again at that time to finalize matters. I trust there'll be no impediment to a satisfactory settlement at that time. I should dislike to embark on lengthy litigation."

Magnan hurried around his desk to open the door. He turned back to fix Retief with an exasperated frown.

"A crass display of boorishness, Retief," he snapped. "You've embarrassed a most influential member of the business community—and for nothing more than a few miserable forms."

"Those forms represent somebody's stake in what might be a valuable property."

"They're mere paper until they've been processed!"

"Still—"

"My responsibility is to the Public interest—not to a fly-by-night group of prospectors."

"They found it first."

"Bah! A worthless rock. After Mr. Leatherwell's munificent gesture—"

"Better rush his check through before he thinks it over and changes his mind."

"Good heavens!" Magnan clutched the check, buzzed for Miss Gumble. She swept in, took Magnan's instructions and left. Retief waited while Magnan glanced over the injunction, then nodded.

"Quite in order. A person called Sam Mancziewicz appears to be the principal. The address given is the Jolly Barge Hotel; that would be that converted derelict ship in orbit 6942, I assume?"

Retief nodded. "That's what they call it."

"As for the ore-carrier, I'd best impound it, pending the settlement of the matter." Magnan drew a form from a drawer, filled in blanks, shoved the paper across the desk. He turned and consulted a wall chart. "The hotel is nearby at the moment, as it happens. Take the Consulate dinghy. If you get out there right away, you'll catch them before the evening binge has developed fully."

"I take it that's your diplomatic way of telling me

that I'm now a process server.'' Retief took the papers and tucked them into an inside pocket.

"One of the many functions a diplomat is called on to perform in a small consular post. Excellent experience. I needn't warn you to be circumspect. These miners are an unruly lot—especially when receiving bad news.''

"Aren't we all.'' Retief rose. "I don't suppose there's any prospect of your signing off that claim so that I can take a little good news along, too?''

"None whatever,'' Magnan snapped. "They've been made a most generous offer. If that fails to satisfy them, they have recourse through the courts.''

"Fighting a suit like that costs money. The Sam's Last Chance Mining Company hasn't got any.''

"Need I remind you—''

"I know. That's none of our concern.''

"On your way out,'' Magnan said as Retief turned to the door, "ask Miss Gumble to bring in the Gourmet catalog from the Commercial Library. I want to check on the specifications of the Model C banquet synthesizer.''

An hour later, nine hundred miles from Ceres and fast approaching the Jolly Barge Hotel, Retief keyed the skiff's transmitter.

"CDT 347-89 calling Navy FP-VO-6.''

"Navy VO-6 here, CDT,'' a prompt voice came back. A flickering image appeared on the small screen. "Oh, hi there, Mr. Retief. What brings you out in the cold night air?''

"Hello, Henry. I'm estimating the Jolly Barge in ten minutes. It looks like a busy night ahead. I may be moving around a little. How about keeping an eye on me? I'll be carrying a personnel beacon. Monitor it, and if I switch it into high, come in fast. I can't afford to be held up. I've got a big meeting in the morning.''

"Sure thing, Mr. Retief. We'll keep an eye open.''

Retief dropped a ten-credit note on the bar, accepted a glass and a squat bottle of black Marsberry brandy and turned to survey the low-ceilinged room, a former hydroponics deck now known as the Jungle Bar. Under the low ceiling, unpruned *Ipomoea batatas* and *Lathyrus odoratus* vines sprawled in a tangle that filtered the light of the S-spectrum glare panels to a muted green. A six-foot trideo screen, salvaged from the wreck of a Concordiat transport, blared taped music in the style of two centuries past. At the tables, heavy-shouldered men in bright-dyed suit liners played cards, clanked bottles and shouted.

Carrying the bottle and glass, Retief moved across to an empty chair at one of the tables.

"You gentlemen mind if I join you?''

Five unshaven faces turned to study Retief's six foot three, his close cut black hair, his non-commital gray coverall, the scars on his knuckles. A redhead with a broken nose nodded. ''Pull up a chair, stranger.''

"You workin' a claim, pardner?''

"Just looking around.''

"Try a shot of this rock juice.''

"Don't do it, Mister. He makes it himself.''

"Best rock juice this side of Luna.''

"Say, feller—''

"The name's Retief.''

"Retief, you every play Drift?''

"Can't say that I did."

"Don't gamble with Sam, pardner. He's the local champ."

"How do you play it?"

The black-browed miner who had suggested the game rolled back his sleeve to reveal sinewy forearm, put his elbow on the table.

"You hook forefingers, and put a glass right up on top. The man that takes a swallow wins. If the drink spills, it's drinks for the house."

"A man don't often win outright," the redhead said cheerfully. "But it makes for plenty of drinkin'."

Retief put his elbow on the table. "I'll give it a try."

The two men hooked forefingers. The redhead poured a tumbler half full of rock juice, place it atop the two fists. "Okay, boys. Go!"

The man named Sam gritted his teeth; his biceps tensed, knuckles grew white. The glass trembled. Then it moved—toward Retief. Sam hunched his shoulders, straining.

"That's the stuff, Mister!"

"What's the matter, Sam? You tired?"

The glass moved steadily closer to Retief's face.

"A hundred the new man makes it!"

"Watch Sam! Any minute now . . ."

The glass slowed, paused. Retief's wrist twitched and the glass crashed to the table top. A shout went up. Sam leaned back with a sigh, massaging his hand.

"That's some arm you got, Mister," he said. "If you hadn't jumped just then . . ."

"I guess the drinks are on me," Retief said.

Two hours later Retief's Marsberry bottle stood empty on the table beside half a dozen others.

"We were lucky," Sam Mancziewicz was saying. "You figure the original volume of the planet; say 245,000,000,000 cubic miles. The deBerry theory calls for a collapsed-crystal core no more than a mile in diameter. There's your odds."

"And you believe you've found a fragment of this core?"

"Damn right we have. Couple of million tons if it's an ounce. And at three credits a ton delivered at Port Syrtis, we're set for life. About time, too. Twenty years I've been in the Belt. Got two kids I haven't seen for five years. Things are going to be different now."

"Hey, Sam; tone it down. You don't have to broadcast to every claim jumper in the Belt."

"Our claim's on file at the Consulate," Sam said. "As soon as we get the grant—"

"When's that gonna be? We been waitin' a week now."

"I've never seen any collapsed-crystal metal," Retief said. "I'd like to take a look at it."

"Sure. Come on, I'll run you over. It's about an hour's run. We'll take our skiff. You want to go along, Willy?"

"I got a bottle to go," Willy said. "See you in the morning."

The two men descended in the lift to the boat bay, suited up and strapped into the cramped boat. A bored attendant cycled the launch doors, levered the release that propelled the skiff out and clear of the Jolly Barge Hotel. Retief caught a glimpse of a tower of lights spinning majestically against the black of space as the drive hurled the tiny boat away.

II

Retief's feet sank ankle deep into the powdery surface that glinted like snow in the glare of the distant sun.

"It's funny stuff," Sam's voice sounded in his ear. "Under a gee of gravity, you'd sink out of sight. The stuff cuts diamond like butter—but temperature changes break it down into a powder. A lot of it's used just like this, as an industrial abrasive. Easy to load, too. Just drop a suction line, put on ambient pressure and start pumping."

"And this whole rock is made of the same material?"

"Sure is. We ran plenty of test bores and a full schedule of soundings. I've got the reports back aboard *Gertie*—that's our lighter."

"And you've already loaded a cargo here?"

"Yep. We're running out of capital fast. I need to get that cargo to port in a hurry—before the outfit goes into involuntary bankruptcy. With this, that'd be a crime."

"What do you know about General Minerals, Sam?"

"You thinking of hiring on with them? Better read the fine print in your contract before you sign. Sneakiest bunch this side of a burglar's convention."

"They own a chunk of rock known as 2645-P. Do you suppose we could find it?"

"Oh, you're buying it, hey? Sure, we can find it.

You damn sure want to look it over good if General Minerals is selling.''

Back aboard the skiff, Mancziewicz flipped the pages of the chart book, consulted a table. ''Yep, she's not too far off. Let's go see what GM's trying to unload.''

The skiff hovered two miles from the giant boulder known as 2645-P. Retief and Mancziewicz looked it over at high magnification. ''It don't look like much, Retief,'' Sam said. ''Let's go down and take a closer look.''

The boat dropped rapidly toward the scarred surface of the tiny world, a floating mountain, glaring black and white in the spotlight of the sun. Sam frowned at his instrument panel.

''That's funny. My ion counter is revving up. Looks like a drive trail, not more than an hour or two old. Somebody's been here.''

The boat grounded. Retief and Sam got out. The stony surface was littered with rock fragments varying in size from pebbles to great slabs twenty feet long, tumbled in a loose bed of dust and sand. Retief pushed off gently, drifted up to a vantage point atop an upended wedge of rock. Sam joined him.

''This is all igneous stuff,'' he said. ''Not likely we'll find much here that would pay the freight to Syrtis—unless maybe you lucked onto some Bodean artifacts. They bring plenty.''

He flipped a binocular in place as he talked, scanned the riven landscape. ''Hey!'' he said. ''Over there!''

Retief followed Sam's pointing glove. He studied the dark patch against a smooth expanse of eroded rock.

42

"A friend of mine came across a chunk of the old planetary surface two years ago," Sam said thoughtfully. "Had a tunnel in it that'd been used as a storage depot by the Bodeans. Took out over two ton of hardware. Course, nobody's discovered how the stuff works yet, but it brings top prices."

"Looks like water erosion," Retief said.

"Yep. This could be another piece of surface, all right. Could be a cave over there. The Bodeans liked caves, too. Must have been some war—but then, if it hadn't been, they wouldn't have tucked so much stuff away underground where it could weather the planetary breakup."

They descended, crossed the jumbled rocks with light, thirty-foot leaps.

"It's a cave, all right," Sam said, stooping to peer into the five-foot bore. Retief followed him inside.

"Let's get some light in here." Mancziewicz flipped on a beam. It glinted back from dull polished surfaces of Bodean synthetic. Sam's low whistle sounded in Retief's headset.

"That's funny," Retief said.

"Funny, hell! It's hilarious. General Minerals trying to sell off a worthless rock to a tenderfoot—and it's loaded with Bodean artifacts. No telling how much is here: the tunnel seems to go quite a ways back."

"That's not what I mean. Do you notice your suit warming up?"

"Huh? Yeah, now that you mention it."

Retief rapped with a gauntleted hand on the satiny black curve of the nearest Bodean artifact. It clunked dully through the suit. "That's not metal," he said. "It's plastic."

"There's something fishy here," Sam said. "This erosion; it looks more like a heat beam."

"Sam," Retief said, turning, "it appears to me somebody has gone to a great deal of trouble to give a false impression here."

Sam snorted. "I told you they were a crafty bunch." He started out of the cave, then paused, went to one knee to study the floor. "But maybe they outsmarted themselves. Look here!"

Retief looked. Sam's beam reflected from a fused surface of milky white, shot through with dirty yellow. He snapped a pointed instrument in place on his gauntlet, dug at one of the yellow streaks. It furrowed under the gouge, a particle adhering to the instrument. With his left hand, Mancziewicz opened a pouch clipped to his belt, carefully deposited the sample in a small orifice on the device in the pouch. He flipped a key, squinted at a dial.

"Atomic weight 197.2," he said. Retief turned down the audio volume on his headset as Sam's laughter rang in his helmet.

"Those clowns were out to stick you, Retief," he gasped, still chuckling. "They salted the rock with a cave full of Bodean artifacts—"

"Fake Bodean artifacts," Retief put in.

"They planed off the rock so it would look like an old beach, and then cut this cave with beamers. And they were boring through practically solid gold!"

"As good as that?"

Mancziewicz flashed the light around. "This stuff will assay out at a thousand credits a ton, easy. If the vein doesn't run to five thousand tons, the beers are on me." He snapped off the light. "Let's get moving,

Retief. You want to sew this deal up before they get around to taking another look at it."

Back in the boat, Retief and Mancziewicz opened their helmets. "This calls for a drink," Sam said, extracting a pressure flask from the map case. "This rock's worth as much as mine, maybe more. You hit it lucky, Retief. Congratulations." He thrust out a hand.

"I'm afraid you've jumped to a couple of conclusions, Sam," Retief said. "I'm not out here to buy mining properties."

"You're not—then why—but man! Even if you didn't figure on buying . . ." He trailed off as Retief shook his head, unzipped his suit to reach to an inside pocket, take out a packet of folded papers.

"In my capacity as Terrestrial Vice-Consul, I'm serving you with an injunction restraining you from further exploitation of the body known as 95739-A." He handed a paper across to Sam. "I also have here an Order impounding the vessel *Gravel Gertie II*."

Sam took the papers silently, sat looking at them. He looked up at Retief. "Funny. When you beat me at Drift and then threw the game so you wouldn't show me up in front of the boys, I figured you for a right guy. I've been spilling my heart out to you like you were my old grandma. An old-timer in the game like me." He dropped a hand, brought it up with a Browning 2mm pointed at Retief's chest.

"I could shoot you and dump you here with a slab over you, toss these papers in the john and hightail it with the load . . ."

"That wouldn't do you much good in the long run, Sam. Besides you're not a criminal or an idiot."

Sam chewed his lip. "My claim is on file in the

45

Consulate, legal and proper. Maybe by now the grant's gone through.''

"Other people have their eye on your rock, Sam. Ever meet a fellow called Leatherwell?''

"General Minerals, huh? They haven't got a leg to stand on.''

"The last time I saw your claim, it was still lying in the pending file. Just a bundle of paper until it's validated by the Consul. If Leatherwell contests it . . . well, his lawyers are on annual retainer. How long could you keep the suit going, Sam?''

Mancziewicz closed his helmet with a decisive snap, motioned to Retief to do the same. He opened the hatch, sat with the gun on Retief.

"Get out, paper-pusher.'' His voice sounded thin in the headphones. "You'll get lonesome, maybe, but your suit will keep you alive a few days. I'll tip somebody off before you lose too much weight. I'm going back and see if I can't stir up a little action at the Consulate.''

Retief climbed out, walked off fifty yards. He watched as the skiff kicked off in a quickly dispersed cloud of dust, dwindled rapidly away to a bright speck that was lost against the stars. Then he extracted the locator beacon from the pocket of his suit and thumbed the control.

Twenty minutes later, aboard Navy FP-VO-6, Retief pulled off his helmet. "Fast work, Henry. I've got a couple of calls to make. Put me through to your HQ, will you? I want a word with Commander Hayle.''

The young naval officer raised the HQ, handed the mike to Retief.

"Vice-Consul F   ere, Commander. I'd like you
to intercept a skiff, bound from my present position
toward Ceres. There's a Mr. Mancziewicz aboard.
He's armed, but not dangerous. Collect him and see
that he's delivered to the Consulate at 0900 Greenwich
tomorrow.

"Next item: The Consulate has impounded an ore-
carrier, *Gravel Gertie II*. It's in a parking orbit ten
miles off Ceres. I want it taken in tow." Retief gave
detailed instruction. Then he asked for a connection
through the Navy switchboard to the Consulate. Magnan's voice answered.

"Retief speaking, Mr. Consul. I have some news
that I think will interest you—"

"Where are you, Retief? What's wrong with the
screen? Have you served the injunction?"

"I'm aboard the Navy patrol vessel. I've been out
looking over the situation, and I've made a surprising
discovery. I don't think we're going to have any trouble
with the Sam's people; they've looked over the
body—2645-P—and it seems General Minerals has
slipped up. There appears to be a highly valuable deposit there."

"Oh? What sort of deposit?"

"Mr. Mancziewicz mentioned collapsed crystal
metal," Retief said.

"Well, most interesting." Magnan's voice sounded
thoughtful.

"Just thought you'd like to know. This should
simplify the meeting in the morning."

"Yes," Magnan said. "Yes, indeed. I think this
makes everything very simple . . ."

At 0845 Greenwich, Retief stepped into the outer office of the Consular suite.

" . . . fantastic configuration," Leatherwell's bass voice rumbled, "covering literally acres. My xeno-geologists are somewhat confused by the formations. They had only a few hours to examine the site; but it's clear from the extent of the surface indications that we have a very rich find here. Very rich indeed. Beside it, 95739-A dwindles into insignificance. Very fast thinking on your part, Mr. Consul, to bring the matter to my attention."

"Not at all, Mr. Leatherwell. After all—"

"Our tentative theory is that the basic crystal frag-ment encountered the core material at some time, and gathered it in. Since we had been working on—that is, had landed to take samples on the other side of the body, this anomalous deposit escaped our attention completely."

Retief stepped into the room.

"Good morning, gentlemen. Has Mr. Mancziewicz arrived?"

"Mr. Mancziewicz is under restraint by the Navy. I've had a call that he'd be escorted here."

"Arrested, eh?" Leatherwell nodded. "I told you these people were an irresponsible group. In a way it seems a pity to waste a piece of property like 95739-A on them."

"I understood General Minerals was claiming that rock," Retief said, looking surprised.

Leatherwell and Magnan exchanged glances. "Ah, GM has decided to drop all claim to the body," Leath-erwell said. "As always, we wish to encourage enter-prise on the part of the small operators. Let them keep the property. After all GM has other deposits well worth exploiting." He smiled complacently.

"What about 2645-P? You've offered it to the Sam's group."

"That offer is naturally withdrawn!" Leatherwell snapped.

"I don't see how you can withdraw the offer," Retief said. "It's been officially recorded. It's a Bona Fide contract, binding on General Minerals, subject to—"

"Out of the goodness of our corporate heart," Leatherwell roared, "we've offered to relinquish our legitimate, rightful claim to asteroid 2645-P. And you have the infernal gall to spout legal technicalities! I have half a mind to withdraw my offer to withdraw!"

"Actually," Magnan put in, eyeing a corner of the room, "I'm not at all sure I could turn up the record of the offer of 2645-P. I noted it down on a bit of scratch paper—"

"That's all right," Retief said, "I had my pocket recorder going. I sealed the record and deposited it in the Consular archives."

There was a clatter of feet outside. Miss Gumble appeared on the desk screen. "There are a number of persons here—" she began.

The door banged open. Sam Mancziewicz stepped into the room, a sailor tugging at each arm. He shook them loose, stared around the room. His eyes lighted on Retief. "How did you get here . . . ?"

"Look here, Monkeywits or whatever your name is," Leatherwell began, popping out of his chair.

Mancziewicz whirled, seized the stout executive by the shirt front and lifted him onto his tiptoes. "You

double-barrelled copper-bottomed oak-lined son-of-
a—"

"Don't spoil him, Sam," Retief said casually.
"He's here to sign off all rights—if any—to 95739-A.
It's all yours—if you want it."

Sam glared into Leatherwell's eyes. "That right?"
he grated. Leatherwell bobbed his head, his chins compressed into bulging folds.

"However," Retief went on, "I wasn't at all sure
you'd still be agreeable, since he's made your company
a binding offer of 2645-P in return for clear title to
95739-A."

Mancziewicz looked across at Retief with narrowed
eyes. He released Leatherwell, who slumped into his
chair. Magnan darted around his desk to minister to the
magnate. Behind them, Retief closed one eye in a broad
wink at Mancziewicz.

" . . . still, if Mr. Leatherwell will agree, in addition to guaranteeing your title to 95739-A, to purchase
your output at four credits a ton, FOB his collection
station—"

Mancziewicz looked at Leatherwell. Leatherwell
hesitated, then nodded. "Agreed," he croaked.

" . . . and to open his commissary and postal
facilities to all prospectors operating in the belt . . ."

Leatherwell swallowed, eyes bulging, glanced at
Mancziewicz's face. He nodded. "Agreed."

" . . . then I think I'd sign an agreement releasing
him from his offer."

Mancziewicz looked at Magnan.

"You're the Terrestrial Consul-General." he said.
"Is that the straight goods?"

Magnan nodded. "If Mr. Leatherwell agrees—"

"He's already agreed," Retief said. "My pocket recorder, you know."

"Put it in writing," Mancziewicz said.

Magnan called in Miss Grumble. The others waited silently while Magnan dictated. He signed the paper with a flourish, passed it across to Mancziewicz. He read it, re-read it, then picked up the pen and signed. Magnan impressed the Consular seal on the paper.

"Now the grant," Retief said. Magnan signed the claim, added a seal. Mancziewicz tucked the papers away in an inner pocket. He rose.

"Well, gents, I guess maybe I had you figured wrong," he said. He looked at Retief. "Uh . . . got time for a drink?"

"I shouldn't drink during office hours," Retief said. He rose. "So I'll take the rest of the day off."

"I don't get it," Sam said signalling for refills. "What was the routine with the injunction—and impounding *Gertie?* You could have got hurt."

"I don't think so," Retief said. "If you'd meant business with that Browning, you'd have flipped the safety off. As for the injunction—orders are orders."

"I've been thinking," Sam said. "That gold deposit. It was a plant, too, wasn't it?"

"I'm just a bureaucrat, Sam. What would I know about gold?"

"A double-salting job," Sam said. "I was supposed to spot the phoney hardware—and then fall for the gold plant. When Leatherwell put his proposition to me, I'd grab it. The gold was worth plenty, I'd figure, and I couldn't afford a legal tangle with General Minerals. The lousy skunk! And you must have spotted it and put it up to him."

The bar-tender leaned across to Retief. "Wanted on the phone."

In the booth, Magnan's agitated face stared a Retief.

"Retief, Mr. Leatherwell's in a towering rage! The deposit on 2645-P; it was merely a surface film, barely a few inches thick! The entire deposit wouldn't fill an ore-boat." A horrified expression dawned on Magnan's face. "Retief," he gasped, "what did you do with the impounded ore-carrier?"

"Well, let me see," Retief said. "According to the Space Navigation Code, a body in orbit within twenty miles of any inhabited airless body constitutes a navigational hazard. Accordingly, I had it towed away."

"And the cargo?"

"Well, accelerating all that mass was an expensive business, so to save the taxpayer's credits, I had it dumped."

"Where?" Magnan croaked.

"On some unimportant asteroid—as specified by Regulations." He smiled blandly at Magnan. Magnan looked back numbly.

"But you said—"

"All I said was that there was what looked like a valuable deposit on 2645-P. It turned out to be a bogus gold mine that somebody had rigged up in a hurry. Curious, eh?"

"But you told me—"

"And you told Mr. Leatherwell. Indiscreet of you, Mr. Consul. That was a privileged communication; classified information, official use only."

"You led me to believe there was collapsed crystal!"

"I said Sam had mentioned it. He told me his asteroid was made of the stuff."

Magnan swallowed hard, twice. "By the way," he said dully. "You were right about the check. Half an hour ago Mr. Leatherwell tried to stop payment. He was too late."

"All in all, it's been a big day for Leatherwell," Retief said. "Anything else?"

"I hope not," Magnan said. "I sincerely hope not." He leaned close to the screen. "You'll consider the entire affair as . . . confidential? There's no point in unduly complicating relationships."

"Have no fear, Mr. Consul," Retief said cheerfully. "You won't find me identifying with anything as specific as triple-salting an asteroid."

Back at the table, Sam called for another bottle of rock juice.

"That Drift's a pretty good game," Retief said. "But let me show you one I learned out on Yill . . ."

THE CASTLE OF LIGHT

I

RETIEF SCALED his pale burgundy afternoon informal beret across the office, narrowly missing the clothes tree, and dumped the heavy carton he was carrying on his desk. A shapely brunette with a turned-up nose appeared at the connecting door to the next office.

"Miss Braswell," he said before she could speak. "I have here two handsome half-liter wine glasses which I'm about to field-test. Will you join me?"

She made a shushing motion, rolling her eyes toward the inner office. A narrow, agitated face appeared over her shoulder.

"Retief!" Consul-General Magnan burst out. "I've been at wit's end! How does it happen that every time catastrophe strikes you're out of the office?"

"It's merely a matter of timing," Retief said soothingly, stripping paper from the package. He pulled out a tulip-shaped goblet which seemed to be made of coils of jewel-colored glass welded together in an intricate pattern. He held it up to the light.

"Pretty, eh? And barely cool from the glass-blower."

"While you idled about the bazaar," Magnan snapped, his face an angry pink above a wide, stiff collar of yellow plastiweave, "I've been coping single-handed with disaster! I suggest you put aside your baubles; I'm calling a formal Emergency Staff Meeting in two minutes!"

"That means you, me and Miss Braswell, I take it, since the rest of the staff is off crater-viewing—"

"Just you and I." Magnan mopped at his face with a vast floral-patterned tissue. "This is a highly classified emergency."

"Oh, goody. I'll take the rest of the afternoon off and watch the festivities." Miss Braswell winked at Retief, extended the tip of her tongue in salute to the Consul-General's back, and was gone.

Retief plucked a bottle from his desk drawer and followed Magnan into the inner office. The senior officer yanked at his stiff collar, now wilting with perspiration.

"Why this couldn't have waited until Minister Barnshingle's return, I don't know," he said. "He's already a day overdue. I've tried to contact him, to no avail. This primitive line-of-sight local telescreen system—" He broke off. "Retief, kindly defer your tippling until after the crisis!"

"Oh, this isn't tippling, Mr. Magnan. I'm doing a commodity analysis for my next report. You fobbed the detail of Commercial Attache off on me, if you recall."

"As Charge d'affaires in the absence of the Minister, I forbid drinking on duty!" Magnan roared.

"Surely you jest, Mr. Magnan! It would mean the end of diplomacy as we know it."

"Well, not until after lunch, at least. And I hereby authorize you to postpone market research until further notice; we're facing a possible holocaust in a matter of hours!"

"What's it all about?"

Magnan plucked a sheet of yellow paper from his desk and handed it to Retief. "This came in over the autotyper forty minutes ago."

UNIDENTIFIED CONVOY COMPRISING FIFTY UHLAN CLASS VESSELS SIGHTED ON COURSE FOR YALC III ETA 1500 GST 33 OCT GSC. SIGNED POMFROY, ENSIGN PATROL NAVY 786-G.

"Uhlans," Retief said. "Those are thousand-man transports. And oh-nine-hundred on the thirty-third is just about two hours from now."

"This could be an invasion, Retief! A major breach of the peace! Can you imagine how it would look in my record if the planet were invaded under my very nose!"

"Tough on the natives, too," Retief commented. "What action have you taken so far?"

"Action? Why, I've canceled this afternoon's social engagements, checked out-going passenger schedules . . . and sharpened a number of pencils."

"Have you tried contacting this Ensign Pomfroy for a little more detail?"

"There's no one on duty in the Message Center but a

local Code Clerk. He's trying to raise him now.'' Magnan depressed a button on his desk. ''Oo-Gilitit, have you met with any success?''

''Pomfroy-Tic all same have organ cluster up ventral orifice—''

''Gilitit, I've warned you to watch your language!'' Magnan roared. ''It's no habit for a communications man to get into!'' He clicked off. ''Confounded locals! It's hopeless, of course. Our equipment was never designed for pinpointing moving patrol boats at four A-U's.''

''How do the Yalcan's feel about the situation?'' asked Retief, playing with the goblet still in his hand.

Magnan blinked. ''Why, as to that, I—ah—was just going to call Oo-Rilikuk.'' Magnan punched keys, tuned in a bland yellow and blue face with eyes like gold pinheads, and vertically-hinged jaws busy with an oily drumstick.

''Ah, there, Magnan,'' a voice like an unoiled wheel said. ''Just finished up my lunch. Roast haunch of giant locust. Delicious.'' A tongue like a length of green silken rope flicked a tidbit from a corner of the lipless mouth.

''Oo-Rilikuk, do you know anything of a large convoy due here today?''

Rilikuk dabbed at his chin with a gossamer napkin. ''I seem to recall issuing a number of visas to Groaci nationals in recent weeks.''

''Groaci? Fifty shiploads of them?''

''Something like that,'' the Yalcan said carelessly. ''By the way, if you haven't already made arrangements, perhaps you'd care to join my Bachelor's Group for the upcoming festivities—''

"You're not concerned? Perhaps you're not aware of the insidious reputation the Groaci enjoy!"

"I don't mind saying I've exercised a trifle of influence to procure a choice mud pocket. The rich, oleaginous kind, you know. And there'll be no shortage of nubile females along—though you're not organized to appreciate the latter, it's true—"

"May I ask the state of the planetary defenses, Rilikuk? I'm warning you, Groaci can't be trusted!"

"Planetary defenses?" Rilikuk issued a chirrup of amusement. "As confirmed pacifists, we've never felt the need for such an extravagance. Now, I'll be leaving the office in a few minutes. Suppose I drop by for you. We'll go on to my place for dinner, then off to the bog—"

"You're leaving the Foreign Office at a moment like this?" Magnan yelped. "They'll be landing in a matter of minutes!"

"I fear I'll have no time to devote to tourism this week, Magnan," Rilikuk said. "They'll just have to manage alone. After all, Voom Festival comes but once in ninety-four standard years."

Magnan rang off with a snort. "We'll receive scant help from that quarter." He swiveled to gaze out the unglazed window across the gay tiles of the plaza, lined with squat, one-story shops of embossed and colored ceramic brick, to the glittering minarets of the mile-distant temple complex.

"If these idlers invested less energy in shard-sorting and more in foreign affairs, I wouldn't be faced with this contretemps."

"If the CDT would talk Groac into selling them a

few thousand tons of sand, they wouldn't have to sort shards.''

"There are better uses for CDT bottoms than hauling sand, Retief . . . though I notice the local scrap pile is about depleted. Possibly now they'll turn to more profitable pursuits then lavishing the artistry of generations on tenantless shrines." He indicated the cluster of glass towers sparkling in the sun. "They might even consent to export a reasonable volume of glassware in place of the present token amounts.''

"Rarity keeps the price up; and they say they can't afford to let much glass off-world. It all goes back in the scrap piles when it's broken, for reuse."

Magnan stared across the plain, where the white plumes of small geysers puffed into brief life, while the pale smoke rising from the fumaroles rose straight up in the still air. Far above, a point of blue light twinkled.

"Odd," Magnan said, frowning. "I've never seen one of the moons in broad daylight before."

Retief came to the window.

"You still haven't. Apparently our Groaci friends are ahead of schedule. That's an ion drive, and it's not over twenty miles out."

II

Magnan bounded to his feet. "Get your hat, Retief! We'll confront these interlopers the moment they set foot on Yalcan soil! The Corps isn't letting this sort of thing pass without comment!"

"The Corps is always a fast group with a comment."
Retief said. "I'll give it that."

Outside, the plaza was a-bustle with shopkeepers
glittering in holiday glass jewelry, busily closing up
their stalls, erecting intricate decorations resembling
inverted chandeliers before the shuttered shops, and
exchanging shouted greetings. A long-bodied pink-
and-red-faced Yalcan in a white apron leaning in the
open door of a shop waved a jointed forearm.

"Retief-Tic! Do me honor of to drop in for last
Voom cup before I lock up. Your friend, too!"

"Sorry, Oo-Plif; duty calls."

"I see you've established your usual contacts among
the undesirable element," Magnan muttered, signaling a boat-shaped taxi edging through the press on fat
pneumatic wheels. "Look at these lackwits! Completely engrossed in their frivolity, while disaster de-
scends scarcely a mile away."

Retief eyed the descending ship as it settled in behind
the glittering spires of the temple-city.

"I wonder why they're landing there, instead of at
the port," Retief wondered.

"They've probably mistaken the shrine for the
town," Magnan snapped. "One must admit that it
makes a far more impressive display than this collection of mud huts!"

"Not the Groaci. They do their homework carefully
before they start anything."

The cab pulled up and Magnan barked directions at
the driver, who waved his forearms in the Yalcan
equivalent of a shrug.

"Speak to this fellow, Retief!" Magnan snapped.
"Obscure dialects are a hobby of yours, I believe."

Retief gave the driver instructions in the local patois and leaned back against the floppy cushions. Magnan perched on the edge of the seat and nipped at a hangnail. The car cleared the square, racketed down a side street streaming with locals headed for the bog, gunned out across the hard-baked mud-flat, swerving violently around the bubbling devil's cauldrons of hot mud that dotted the way. A small geyser erupted with a *whoosh!* and spattered the open vehicle with hot droplets. A whiff of rotten-egg smoke blew past. Off to the left, the sunlight glinted from the wide surface of the swamp, thickly scattered with exotic lily-like flowers. Here and there, tree-ferns grew in graceful clumps from the shallow water. Along the shore, bright-colored tents had been erected, and local celebrants clustered in groups among them, weaving to and fro and waving their multiple arms.

"It's disgraceful," Magnan sniffed. "They're already staggering and their infernal festival's hardly begun!"

"It's a native dance," Retief said. "Very cultural."

"What's the occasion for this idiotic celebration? It seems to have completely paralyzed whatever elementary sense of responsibility these flibertigibbets possess."

"It's related in some way to the conjunction of the four moons," Retief said. "But there's more to it than that. It seems to have an important religious significance. The dances are symbolic of death and rebirth, or something of the sort."

"Hmmph! I see the dancers are now falling flat on their faces! Religious ecstasy, no doubt!"

As they swept past the reeling locals, the driver made

cabalistic signs in the air and grabbed the steering bar just in time to swerve past a steam-jet that snored from a cleft boulder. Ahead, a cloud of dust was rolling out from the landing spot where the Groaci ship had settled in, a scant hundred yards from an outlying shrine, a sparkling fifty-foot tower of red, yellow and green glass.

"They're coming perilously close to violating the native holy place," Magnan observed as the taxi pulled up beside the ship. "There may be mob violence at any moment."

A pair of locals, emerging from one of the many fanciful glass arches adorning the entrances to the shrine complex, cast no more than a casual glance at the vessel as a port opened in its side and a spindle-legged Groaci in golfing knickers and loud socks appeared.

Magnan climbed hurriedly from the cab. "I want you to note my handling of this, Retief," he said behind his hand. "A firm word now may avert an incident."

"I'd better say a firm word to the driver, or we'll be walking back."

"Look, Mac-Tic, I got a reserved slot in a hot pocket of mud waiting for me," the driver called as he wheeled the car around. "Five minutes, okay?"

Retief handed the cabbie a ten credit token and followed Magnan across the scorched ground to the landing ladder. The Groaci descended, all five eye-stalks canted in different directions—One on Magnan.

"Minister Barnshingle," he said in his faint Groac voice before Magnan could speak. "I am Fiss, Tour Director for Groac Planetary Tours, Incorporated. I assume you've come to assist in clearing my little flock through the Customs and Immigration formalities. Now—''

"Tour Director, did you say, Mr. Fiss?" Magnan cut in. "Fifty shiploads of tourists?"

"Quite correct. I can assure you that passports and visas are all in order, and immunization records are up-to-date. Since we Groaci have no diplomatic mission to Yalc, it is most kind of the CDT to extend its good office."

"Just a minute, Mr. Fiss! How long are your tourists planning to stay on Yalc? Just during the Voom Festival, I assume?"

"I believe our visas read . . . ah . . . indefinite, Mr. Minister."

"I'm Magnan, Charge in the absence of the Minister," Magnan said.

Fiss waved his eyes. "The Minister is not here?"

"No, he's off mountain climbing. Very keen on sports. Now, ah, may I ask where your other forty-nine vessels might be?"

"Just where is the Minister to be found?" Fiss enquired.

"I really can't say," Magnan sniffed. "We've had no word for two days. Now, about your other ships." Magnan persisted.

"There are, I believe, forty-nine cities here on this charming little world," Fiss said smoothly. "One transport is calling at each."

"Curious way to conduct a tour." Magnan broke off as a cargo port rumbled open and a heavy six-wheeled vehicle churned out. Rows of multi-eyed Groaci heads peered over open sides, on which the words GROAC

PLANETARY TOURS, INC. had been hastily lettered. A second vehicle followed the first, and a third and fourth. Magnan gaped as the emerging carriers took up positions in an orderly double file.

"Here, what's this, Fiss?" he blurted. "These are tourists?"

"Of course? What else? Please note the presence of ladies and also a number of lovable Groaci grubs. Yes, innocent, fun-loving tourists all."

"Why are they in armored cars?" Magnan watched as the vehicles moved off in the direction of the towering glass temples. "Here, where are they going?"

"Since the entire populace is fully occupied with Voom festival activities," Fiss hissed blandly, "Groac Tours has thoughtfully arranged to occupy available unused housing."

"Why, that's the local Holy of Holies," Magnan expostulated. "You can't go in there!"

"The structures are not in use," Fiss whispered. "And I see no objection on the part of the aborigines." He indicated the cab driver who was watching indifferently as the first tractor moved under a graceful crystalline arch into the sparkling glass-bricked avenue.

"Hey, Mac-Tic," the driver called to Retief in Yalc. "Time's up. I wanna get there before the mud cools!"

"Are you out of your mind, Mr. Fiss?" Magnan demanded. "You're deliberately precipitating an incident! I'm warning you, I'll refer this to Sector HQ and call for a squadron of Peace Enforcers!"

"What need for Peace Enforcers, my dear fellow?" Fiss murmured. "Peace reigns! We are unarmed. No act of violence is contemplated."

"We'll see about this!" Magnan fumed. He turned and stamped toward the waiting taxi.

"So thoughtful of you to welcome us," Fiss's faint voice followed him. "I shall be calling at the Legation later to arrange a number of formalities. All quite legal, I assure you."

"It's worse than I thought," Magnan groaned to Retief as he climbed into the cab. "When a Groaci starts citing statutes, you can be sure there's mischief afoot!"

III

"This is incredible!" Magnan barked at the screen where Oo-Rilikuk's multi-colored visage nodded blandly against a background of sinuously moving Yal-can dancing-wenches. "You calmly admit that these foreigners are occupying every pagoda on the planet, strewing dope-stick butts and—"

"This is Voom season, Mr. Magnan," Rilikuk said reasonably. "What could be more fitting?"

"Your concept of propriety confounds me. There are fifty thousand of these fellows—and I have the distinct impression they're planning an extended stay!"

"Very likely," Rilikuk agreed, twitching in time to the music in the background. "And now, if you'll excuse me . . ." The screen blanked.

Magnan threw up his hands. "I don't like it, Retief. There's an aspect of this we're missing."

A chime sounded. The door opened and the Groaci

Fiss bustled in, breathing noisily under the weight of a heavy briefcase.

"Ah, Mr. Magnan! So good of you to await me. I have the papers here." He hoisted the case onto the desk and undid stout straps. "I'm sure you'll find all in order: Territorial claims, governmental charter, application for League membership—"

"What's this?" Magnan scanned the heavy documents. "What are you saying sir? That Yalc—that the Groaci—that you—"

"Quite right," Fiss nodded. "This world is now Groaci property."

There was a loud crash from the direction of the now deserted street. Magnan swiveled, stared out at a band of businesslike Groaci, hard at work on a shuttered shop with pry-bars.

"What are they doing?" he yelped. "Mr. Fiss, order those vandals away at once! The situation is getting out of hand!"

"Not at all. Those chaps are merely following my instructions. And now if you have any belongings you wish to take along—"

"Eh? Belongings? I'm not going anywhere."

"Permit me to contradict you," Fiss hissed softly, prodding a paper with a damp-looking finger. "This is the eviction order. I find that this humble structure will adequately fulfill my requirement for a field-office here in the village."

"F-field office?"

"I expect we shall be busy here for a few days," Fiss said. "Transferring useful items to our quarters," He waved airily toward the sparkling towers beyond the swamp.

"You're violating the Legation?" Magnan's eyes bulged.

"There has been a change of status quo since my arrival," Fiss pointed out. "No formal relations exist between my government and the CDT. Therefore this is merely an office, and you are unregistered aliens."

"This is an outrage!" Magnan sputtered. "I'm not leaving!"

"So?" Fiss murmured. He stepped to the door, opened it, waved in a quartet of bigger-than-average Groaci.

"To intimidate the soft ones," he hissed in Groaci. "To make threatening gestures."

Two of the newcomers stepped to Retief. He took them casually by their thin necks, escorted them to the window and tumbled them out. The second pair jumped at him in time to meet a stiff-arm which slammed both of them onto their backs. Fiss emitted a weak but impassioned bleat.

"Unhand them, brute! These are lawfully appointed bailiffs!"

Retief helped the stunned Groaci after their fellows and took a step toward Fiss. The Tour Director squeaked and darted through the door.

"Retief!" Magnan yelped. "Stop! After all, these papers—"

Retief gathered in the parchments, tossed them after the intruders. The outraged face of Tour Director Fiss appeared at the opening.

"Ruffians! Bandits! Our legal and just claim—"

"—isn't worth the plastic it's printed on," Retief stated. "And if any more tourists wander into the Legation I won't be so polite with them."

Fiss turned and made frantic gestures to the foraging crew. "To enter and evict the madmen!" he hissed. "To cast them forth bodily!"

The several dozen Groaci who had gathered moved in a body toward the Legation door.

"I'm disappointed in you, Fiss," Retief said, shaking his head sadly. "I thought you were going to pretend that this was all perfectly legal, and here you are about to violate a diplomatic mission in broad daylight."

Fiss hesitated, then hissed an order to his men. They halted.

"Very well, Soft One," he whispered. "What need of force? Unlike the higher races, you require water at frequent intervals, I believe. Since, alas, I cannot authorize further deliveries through the village mains, you will soon emerge to seek it. We will be waiting."

Magnan tottered to Retief's side. "Mr. Fiss," he croaked. "This is madness! You can't possibly hope to justify this outrageous seizure."

"On the contrary, Mr. Magnan," Fiss waved a fistful of paper. "If you will re-read your Colonial Code, Title Three, Section XI, paragraph 9b, you will find that, and I quote, 'any planetary body lacking an indigenous culture may be considered as available for homesteading by any Power covenant to these articles.' "

"Surely, Fiss, you don't imply that Yalc is uninhabited! Great Heavens, the world is known throughout the Sector for the beauty of its glass and ceramic work."

"I refer further to paragraph 12d, *ibidem*," Fiss bored on, "which provides the following criteria for determination of cultural level within the meaning of the Code (a) an active, organized government competent to represent native interests; (b) a degree of social organization characterized by cities of at least one thousand inhabitants; and (c) individual or group I.Q., (as applicable) averaging .8 "standard" as evidenced by GST Test scores."

"Have you lost your wits?" Magnan cut in. "You're standing in the midst of a Yalcan City! I deal daily with representatives of the Yalcan government! As for intelligence—"

"*Inhabited* city, Mr. Magnan, permit me to remind you. Minimum population, one thousand individuals." Fiss waved a hand at the empty street. "I see no individuals here."

"But they're all away participating in a festival!"

"As for government," Fiss continued blandly, "I have been totally unsuccessful in discovering any *active* organization. I confess I have been unable to secure a specimen of the local fauna for I.Q. Testing, but I feel sure any such effort would be unrewarding."

"You deliberately timed this coup to take advantage of local customs!" Magnan said in a shocked tone. "The code will be amended, Fiss!"

The Groaci vibrated his throat sac, a contemptuous gesture. "*Ex post facto* legal manipulations can hardly be expected to affect the present situation retroactively, my dear Magnan."

Magnan clutched at the edge of the window. "Retief," he gasped weakly. "This is insane, but I have a sudden, awful conviction that he's legally on firm ground."

"Of course," Fiss went on, "article 68 of the Code expressly prohibits occupation by force of any world, cultured or otherwise. However, since our arrival was carried out in complete tranquility, this is hardly germane."

"The festival will be over tomorrow," Magnan burst out. "What then?"

"Now that we have established legal possession of this planet," Fiss whispered, "it will, of course, be necessary to enforce the just laws which are even now being enacted. To this end, certain arms are of course necessary." He spat rapid Groacian at a trio of newcomers in black hipcloaks, who silently produced heavy particle-guns from sequinned holsters strapped to their thighs.

"You aren't planning—violence?" Magnan gasped. "Not against *us!*"

"As to that," Fiss whispered, "I was about to point out that naturally, a formal request for diplomatic status addressed to the present regime would, of course, receive consideration."

"Tour Director Fiss—" Magnan gulped.

"Planetary Coordinator Pro-Tem Fiss, if you please," the Groaci hissed. "It is unfortunate that the large Soft One acted in such haste, but I am prepared to overlook the incident."

"Why, ah, very good of you, I'm sure, Pla—"

"You're out of luck, Fiss," Retief cut in. "You'll have to conduct your piracy without CDT sanction."

Magnan tugged at Retief's sleeve. "Here, Retief! This is hardly a time for truculence!"

"It's as good a time as any, Mr. Magnan. And Minister Barnshingle might be irritated if he came back and discovered that these squatters had been recognized as a legal government."

Magnan groaned. "I . . . I suppose you're right."

"So? But, no matter, Soft One," Fiss whispered. "Why treat with underlings, eh? My scouts report a party of terrestrials in difficulty on an awkward slope some leagues from here. Doubtless the person Barnshingle of whom you speak will be grateful for relief. A timely rescue by selfless Groaci homesteaders will establish a correct mood for initiation of formal relations."

"The Minister's in trouble?" Magnan squeaked.

"He is at present dangling over a crevasse of awesome depth by a single strand of rope. Diplomat muscles appear unequal to the task of drawing him up."

There was a rending crunch from a shop across the plaza as a barred door collapsed under the impact of a power ram. Swarms of Groaci were systematically looting the stalls already opened, loading foodstuffs, glassware and other merchandise into wheeled vehicles.

"This is wholesale hijackery!" Magnan yelped. "Open pillage! Highway robbery! You can't do this without a license!"

"Curb your tongue, sir!" Fiss hissed. "I shall for a while indulge your arrogant preemption of Groaci property out of sentimental respect for the niceties of diplomatic usage, but I shall tolerate no insults!"

"Threats, Mr. Fiss?" Magnan choked.

"Call it what you will, Soft One," Fiss said. "When you are ready to acquiesce, send your word to me. Meantime, leave this building at your peril!"

IV

Dusk had fallen. The sounds of shattering locks and maneuvering vehicles continued in the streets outside.

Beyond the window, booted Groaci peace-keepers paced monotonously, heavy blast guns at the ready. Now and then, in a momentary lull, the sound of Yalcan voices raised in song could be heard from the bog, where torches flared, reflecting from the mirror-dark waters. The two lesser moons were high in the sky in their slow orbits; the third had risen above the horizon and cast purple shadows across the floor of the silent Legation office.

"It's nearly dark," Magnan muttered. "Retief, perhaps I'd better accompany you. Fiss may change his mind and batter the door down."

"He could come in through the window any time he decided to," Retief said. "He's nicely bluffed for the present, Mr. Magnan. And someone has to stay here to maintain occupancy of the Legation."

"On second thought, I'm changing my instructions," Magnan said decisively. "You'd better not go. After all, if Minister Barnshingle wishes to recognize the coup, I see no reason—"

"I don't think the Minister will be reasoning at his most lucid level while dangling over a precipice. And there's also Miss Braswell to consider. She's out there somewhere."

"Retief, you can't hope to find her without being apprehended! The city is swarming with armed Groaci!"

"I think I know the back streets better than they do. I'll stay out of sight. If I can reach Barnshingle before he signs anything, it may save a lot of embarrassment all around."

"Retief, as Charge—"

"Don't give me any instructions I can't follow, Mr. Magnan," Retief took a hand-light from a desk drawer, clipped it to his belt. "Just lie low and ignore whatever Fiss says to you. I'll be back in a few hours."

Retief stepped from a doorless opening into the shadows of a narrow alley running behind the Legation. He waited until a knobkneed Groaci in an elaborate helmet had strolled past the lighted intersection fifty feet distant, then jumped, pulled himself up onto the low, tiled roof of the adjacent building. In the light of the rising fourth moon, he moved quietly to the far side, lay flat looking down on a side street littered with items discarded by the looters.

One or two windows showed lights. A single armed Groaci stood under a corner street-lamp. Silently Retief worked his way along the roofs, jumping gaps between buildings, until he reached a narrow space leading back into darkness a few yards from the corner. He groped, found a chip of broken tile, tossed it down into the alley.

The Groaci cocked his eyes alertly, swung his gun around and came over to investigate, Retief tossed down another pebble; as the sentry entered the dark way, Retief dropped behind him, yanked him backward off his feet and caught the falling gun. He put the muzzle against the Groaci's pulsating throat sac.

"Tell me where the Terry female is being held," he

growled, "and maybe I won't tie knots in your eye-stalks."

"Iiiikkk!" the Groaci said. "To unhand me, de-monic one!"

"Of course, you may not know," Retief said. "In that case I'd have to regretfully kill you and strike up a new acquaintance, which would be a nuisance for both of us."

"The impropriety of assaulting an innocent tourist! To lodge a complaint with the Travellers Aid Society!"

"No, that was this morning," Retief corrected his prisoner. "This afternoon you're a peaceful home-steader. You can think of me as an unpacified aborigine, if it will help any." He jabbed with the gun. "Make up your mind. I'm on a tight schedule."

"The ghastliness of your fate," the Groaci hissed.

"Well, I have to hurry along," Retief said. "Pardon my thumbs; shooting is such a messy business, and noisy, too."

"To restrain yourself, prowler in the night! To show you the way to the Soft She—and to savor the moment when you writhe on the hooks!"

"That's right," Retief said agreeably. "Think about something cheerful." He prodded the captive guard to his feet. "In the meantime—" he switched to Groaci—"to play your cards right and maybe to live to see the dawn."

In a shadowy arcade running beside a rare two-story structure, Retief studied the dark windows in the wall opposite. Faint light gleamed behind two of the glass-less openings.

"I'll have to leave you here, I'm afraid, Tish," Retief said softly. "I'll just pop you into one of these

74

convenient garbage storage units. They have nicely fitted airtight doors, but you'll be all right for an hour or so. If your information is accurate, with luck I'll be back in plenty of time to let you out before you suffocate. Of course, if anything happens to delay me—well, that's just the little risk we have to run, eh?"

"To . . . to try the rear window first," Tish whispered.

"Whatever you say." Retief opened the door to the refuse bin and urged the Groaci inside. The alien clinched his olfactory sphincters tight and perched disconsolately on a heap of fruit rinds, locust carapaces and pottery shards, his head ducked under the low ceiling.

"To remember this trusting one," he said shakily. "To carefully avoid being killed before returning to release me."

"With a motivation like that, I'm sure to survive." Retief clamped the door shut, looked both ways, and darted across the street.

The wall tiles were deeply incised with decorative floral motifs. He found finger and toeholds, climbed quickly to the level of the windows, eased through into a dark room. He paused to listen; there were faint Groaci voices somewhere. In the dim-lit hall, they were more distinct. He moved silently along to the nearest room. The door opened at a touch.

Miss Braswell jumped up from a long, low Yalcan couch, her mouth open for a scream, cut off as she recognized Retief in the gloom.

"Why—Mr. Retief!"

"Shhh." He crossed to her. A length of rope was tied firmly to her ankle and looped around a massive clay sculpture. She was barefooted, and her brown hair was in a state of mild disarray; there was a streak of dirt along one cheek.

"What in the world is it all about?" she whispered. "I was just about to buy the darlingest hand-decorated chamber pot when all of a sudden a whole bunch of these nasty little creatures popped out of nowhere waving their eyes at me."

"How many are in the building now?" Retief attacked the heavy knots in the rope.

"Heavens, I have no idea. It's been pretty quiet for the last hour." She giggled. "That tickles. I tried to untie it, but I only broke a fingernail."

The knot yielded and Retief tossed the rope aside.

"Do you feel equal to a short climb?"

Miss Braswell came close to Retief. "Whatever you say, Mr. Retief," she murmured.

"Where are your shoes?"

"I kept kicking them when they were tying me up, so they took them. Ugh! Those creepy, damp hands!"

"If we should get separated, head for the Legation. Mr. Magnan is holding the fort."

"You mean—these awful little Groaci are there, too?"

"Haven't you heard? They're colonizing the place."

"Why, the nerve!"

There was a sudden hiss of nearby voices. Retief flattened himself against the wall just inside the door. Miss Braswell whirled and sat on the chaise-lounge. There was the soft clap of Groaci feet. A small figure stepped into the room.

"Ah, young woman," a soft Groaci voice hissed. "Time to be going along."

"Where?" the girl demanded loudly.

"To more comfortable quarters in more attractive surroundings."

"If it wasn't so ridiculous, I'd think you were on the make, you sticky little monster. Keep away from me!"

"You mammals are all alike," the Groaci whispered. "But it's pointless to flaunt those ugly objects at me, my girl." Two more Groaci had followed the first, who signalled. "To make fast its arms," he snapped. "To mind its talons—"

Miss Braswell jumped up and swung an open-handed slap that sent the flimsy alien reeling back; Retief stepped quickly behind the other two, cracked their heads together sharply, thrust them aside and chopped a hand across the leader's neck.

"Time to go," he breathed. At the window, he glanced out, then swung a leg over the sill. "It's easy; just hang on with your toes."

Miss Braswell giggled again. "It's so sort of sexy, being barefooted, isn't it?"

"That depends on what's attached to the feet," Retief said. "Hurry up, now. We're in enemy territory."

"Mr. Retief," she said from above, "Do you think I flaunt my ah . . ."

"Certainly not, Miss Braswell. They flaunt themselves."

There was a sudden drumming from the shadows of the arcade across the way.

"It just occurred to my friend Tish to use a little initiative," Retief called softly. He dropped to the street a few feet below. "Jump—I'll catch you."

The thumping continued. Miss Braswell squealed and let go, slammed against Retief's chest. He set her on her feet. "The Groaci have good ears. Come on!" They dashed for the nearest dark alley as a squad of armed Groaci Peace-keepers rounded a corner. There was a weak shout, a clatter of accoutrements as the four aliens broke into a run. Gripping Miss Braswell's hand, Retief dashed along the narrow way. Ahead, a wall loomed, blocking the passage. They skidded to a halt, turned to face the oncoming pursuers.

"Get to the roof," Retief snapped. "I'll slow them down!"

Between Retief and the Groaci, a six foot long grating set in the pavement suddenly dropped open with a clank of metal. The leading Groaci, coming on at a smart clip, plunged over the edge, followed an instant later by the second. Retief brought his light up, shone it in the eyes of the other two as the third runner reached the pitfall, dropped from sight. As the last of the four faltered, sensing something amiss, the long, sinuous form of a Yalcan native glided from a door set in the wall, gave the Groaci a hearty push, dusted both sets of hands, and inclined its head in a gracious nod.

"Ah, Retief-Tic—and Braswell-Ticcim! What jolly surprise! Please do honor to enter humble abode for refreshing snort before continuing!"

"Nice timing, Oo-Plif," Retief said. "I thought you'd be off to the festival by now."

The Yalcan reached inside the door, fumbled. The grating swung back in place. "I was busy with brisk trade when Five-eyes arrive," he explained. "Decide stick around to keep eye on store. Plenty time make scene at bog yet."

Miss Braswell shuddered as she crossed the grate. "What's down there?"

"Only good honest sewage, nice change for Five-eyes. After brisk swim, fetch up in bog, join in merry-making."

"I thought you Yalcans were pacifists," Retief commented, stepping inside a roughly finished passage running parallel with the outer wall of the building.

"All Yalcan love peace. More peaceful now noisy Five-eyes enjoying swim. Besides, only open drain cover; visitors dive in of own free will."

"I had the impression you helped that last fellow along."

"Always try to be helpful when possible. Listen, you want to talk, or want snort?"

They followed Oo-Plif along interior passages to emerge behind the bar of the darkened dram-shop, took seats at a low bench and accepted elaborate glasses of aromatic liquor.

"Oo-Plif, I'd appreciate it if you'd see Miss Braswell back to the Legation," Retief said. "I have to leave town on an urgent errand."

"Better stay close, Retief-Tic. Come along to bog in time for high point of Voom festival. Only couple hours now."

"I have an errand to run first, Oo-Plif. I've been delegated to find Minister Barnshingle and notify him that the Legation's under siege and that he shouldn't sign anything without reading the fine print."

"Barnshingle-Tic-Tic? Skinny Terran with receding lower mandible and abdomen like queen ripe with eggs?"

"Graphically put, Oo-Plif. He's supposed to be hanging around a mountain somewhere, if the Groaci haven't yet swooped down to the rescue."

Oo-Plif was wobbling his head, now enameled in orange and green holiday colors, in the Yalcan gesture of affirmation.

"Barnshingle-Tic-Tic here in city at present moment. Arrive half-hour ago amid heavy escort of Five-eyes."

"Hmmm. That simplifies matters, perhaps. I was expecting to have to steal a Groaci heli and hunt him down in the wilds. Did he seem to be a prisoner, Oo-Plif?"

"Hard to say, not get too good look. Busy helping Five-eyes find way to bog."

"Via the sewer, I take it?"

"Sure; plenty gratings round town. Must be fifty Five-eyes in swim now; plenty company."

"Are you sure they can swim?"

"Details, details," Oo-Plif said soothingly. "You want to go now, pay visit to Barnshingle-Tic-Tic?"

"As soon as Miss Braswell's taken care of."

"I'm going with you," the girl said quickly. "I wouldn't dream of missing the excitement."

V

"This system of hidden passages is certainly handy," Retief said. "How much farther?"

"Close now. Not really hidden passages; just space in double walls. Yalcan like build plenty strong."

They emerged into another of the innumerable alleys that characterized the town, crossed it, entered another door. Oo-Plif cautioned silence. "Place swarm with

Five-eyes. We sneak up and get lie of land, find way of rescue Barnshingle-Tic-Tic from rescuers.''

Five minutes later, crowded into a narrow, dusty passage in the heart of the sprawling building, Retief heard the booming tones of Barnshingle's voice nearby, and the breathy reply of a Groaci.

"Opening in back of closet just ahead," Oo-Plif whispered. "Get earful of proceedings there.''

Retief edged forward. Through the half-open closet door he caught a glimpse of Minister Barnshingle seated awkwardly in a low Yalcan easy chair, dressed in dusty hiking clothes. Half a dozen Groaci in vari-colored mufti surrounded him.

"—an exceedingly hairy experience, to be sure," Barnshingle was saying. "Most gratifying to see your heli appear, Drone-master Fiss. But I don't quite grasp the import of the present situation. Not that I'm suggesting that I'm being held against my will, you understand, but I really must hurry back to my office.''

"No need for haste, Mr. Minister," Fiss reassured him. "Everything has been conducted with scrupulous regard for legality, I assure you.''

"But there seemed to be hundreds of your . . . ah . . . esteemed compatriots about in the streets," Barnshingle pressed on. "And I had the distinct impression that there were a number of highly irregular activities in progress.''

"You refer perhaps to the efforts of some of our people to remove certain obstacles?''

"Breaking down doors, to be precise," Barnshingle said a trifle snappishly. "As well as hauling away wagon-loads of merchandise from shops the owners of which appeared to be absent.''

"Ah, yes, impulse buying. Hardly consonant with domestic thrift. But enough of this delightful gossip, Mr. Minister. The matter I wished to discuss with you . . ." Fiss gave the Minister a glowing account of his peaceful takeover, citing chapter and verse each time the astounded diplomat attempted to rumble a protest.

"And, of course," he finished, "I wished to acquaint your Excellency with the facts before permitting you to be subjected to ill-advised counsel by hotheads."

"B-but, great heavens, Drone-master—"

"Planetary Coordinator *Pro Tem*," Fiss interjected smoothly. "Now, I shall, of course, be happy to inspect your credentials at once in order to regularize relations between the Corps and my government."

"My credentials? But I've presented my credentials to Mr. Rillikuk of the Foreign Office!"

"This is hardly the time to reminisce over vanished regimes, Mr. Minister. Now—" Fiss leaned forward confidentially—"you and I are, if I may employ the term, men of the world. Not for us the fruitless expense of emotional energy over the *fait accompli*, eh? As for myself, I am most eager to show you around my offices in the finest of the towers of my capital."

"Towers? Capital?"

"The attractive edifices just beyond the swampy area where the local wildlife are now disporting themselves," Fiss explained. "I have assigned—"

"You've violated the native Sanctum Sanctorum?" Barnshingle gasped.

"An unfortunate choice of words," Fiss hissed.

"Would you have me establish my ministries here in this warren of huts?"

"The Yalcans—" Barnshingle said weakly.

"The name of the planet is now Grudlu," Fiss stated. "In honor of Grud, the patron Muse of practicality."

"Look here, Fiss! Are you asking me to turn my back on the Yalcans and recognize you as the *de jure* government here? Simply on the basis of this absurd legalistic rationalization of yours?"

"With the exception of a number of slanted adjectives, very succinctly put," Fiss whispered.

"Why in the world would I do a dastardly thing like that?" Barnshingle demanded.

"Why, good for him," Miss Braswell breathed behind Retief.

"Ah, yes, terms," Fiss said comfortably. "First, your mission would, of course, be raised at once to Embassy level, at Grudlun insistence, with yourself requested by name as Ambassador, naturally. Secondly, I have in mind certain local commercial properties which might make a valuable addition to your portfolio. I can let you in at investor's prices. The entire transaction to be conducted with the utmost discretion, of course, so as not to arouse comment among the coarse-minded. Then, of course, you'll wish to select a handsome penthouse for yourself in one of my more exclusive towers . . ."

"Penthouse? Ambassador? Portfolio?" Barnshingle babbled.

"I marvel at the patience your Excellency has displayed in tolerating the thinly veiled insult implied in

your assignment to grubby quarters in this kennel,"
Fiss commented. "Why a person could disappear in
this maze of old crockery and never be heard from
again."

"Disappear?" Barnshingle croaked. "And wha—
what if I refuse?"

"Refuse? Please, Mr. Minister—or more properly,
Mr. Ambassador—why release the fowl of fancy to
flutter among such morbid trees of speculation?"

"What about my staff? Will—"

"Suitable bribes will be offered," Fiss whispered
crisply. "Pray don't give it another thought. All surviv-
ing members of the Mission will present a united
front—with the exception of the two criminals now
sulking in the former Legation, of course," he added.

"Magnan? Why, he's one of my most reliable
men!"

"Perhaps something could be managed in the case of
Mr. Magnan, since you express an interest. As for the
other—he will return to Groac to stand trial for assorted
crimes against the peace and dignity of the Groacian
state."

"I really must protest—" Barnshingle said weakly.

"Your Excellency's loyalty is most touching. And
now, if you'd just care to sign here." An underling
handed Fiss a document which he passed to
Barnshingle.

"Why, the old phoney!" Miss Braswell gasped.
"He's going to do it!"

"It's time to break this up," Retief whispered to
Oo-Plif. "I'll take care of Fiss; you hit the others."

"On contrary, Retief-Tic," the Yalcan replied.

"Most improper to interfere with natural course of events."

"Maybe you don't understand; Barnshingle's about to sign away your rights to Yalc. By the time you drag it through the courts and recover, you may all be dead. The Groaci are zealous in the field of wildlife control."

"No matter. We Yalcans pacifistic folk. Not like butt in," Oo-Plif said quietly.

"In that case, I'll have to do it alone. You'll take care of Miss Braswell—"

"No, not even alone, dear Retief-Tic. Not in spirit of Yalcan Pacifism." Something hard prodded Retief's chest; he looked down at the power gun in Oo-Plif's lower right hand.

"Why, you old stinker," Miss Braswell said. "And I thought you were sweet!"

"Hope soon to recoup good opinion, Braswell-Ticcim," Oo-Plif said. "Now silence, please."

In the room, Barnshingle and Fiss were making congratulatory noises at each other.

"Matter of fact," Barnshingle said, "I never felt these Yalcans were ready for self-government. I'm sure your wardship will be just what they need."

"Please—no meddling in internal affairs," Fiss said. "And now let us away to more appropriate surroundings. Just wait until you see the view from your new suite, Mr. Ambassador . . ." They departed, chattering.

"Well, you've had your way, Oo-Plif," Retief said. "Your pacifism has a curiously spotty quality. Just why do you object to preventing our unfortunate Minister from making an idiot of himself?"

"Forgive use of weapon, Retief-Tic. Foolishness of Barnshingle Tic-Tic-Tic not important."

"He's a three-tic man now?"

"Promotion just received at hands of Five-eyes. Now away to bog, all buddies together, eh?"

"Where's the rest of Barnshingle's staff? They were together on the crater-viewing expedition?"

"All tucked away in house few alleys from here. Better get wiggle on now. Climax of festival arrive soon."

"Good night, does your silly old carnival mean more to you than your own planet?" Miss Braswell demanded.

"Voom festival of great national importance," Oo-Plif stated, opening and closing his bony mandibles like the two halves of a clam—a mannerism indicating polite amusement.

Following the Yalcan's instructions, Retief squeezed through narrow passages, found his way out into the inevitable dark alley, Miss Braswell's hand holding tightly to his. The sounds of looters and their vehicles had diminished to near-silence now. A turbine growled along a nearby street, going away. They came out into a side street, surveyed the deserted pavement, the scattered discards of the Groaci homesteaders. Above the low roof-lines, the mile-distant towers of the shrine were a blaze of gorgeous light.

"It looks so pretty, all lit up," Miss Braswell said. "I'm just amazed that you'd let those nasty little Groaci walk in and take it all away from you."

Oo-Plif laughed, a sound like sand in a bearing. "Towers tributes to deities. Fate of towers in deities' hands now."

"Hmmmph. They could have used a little help from you," Miss Braswell sniffed.

"Looks like the new owners have cleared out for now," Retief said. "All over at the towers, throwing a party in honor of Independence Day."

"Time go to dandy hot bog," Oo-Plif said. "Big event soon now."

Moving briskly along the empty street under the light of the fourth moon, now high in the sky, they reached the corner. Down the wider cross-avenue, the flaring torches of the revelers at the bog sparkled cheerfully. The faint sound of Yalcan voices raised in song were audible in the stillness.

"Just what is this big event we're hurrying to make?" Retief enquired.

Oo-Plif indicated the large satellite overhead. "When number four moon reach position ten degrees west of zenith—Voom!"

"Oh, astrological symbolism."

"Not know big word. Only one time every ninety-four years standard all four moon line up. When this happen—Voom!"

"Voom," Retief said. "Just what does the word signify?"

"Fine old Yalcan word," Oo-Pliff said. "Terry equivalent . . . ummm . . ."

"Probably untranslatable."

Oo-Plif snapped the fingers of his upper left hand.

"I remember," he said. "Mean 'earthquake!' "

Retief stopped dead.

"You did say—'earthquake?' "

"Correct, Retief-Tic."

Retief's left fist slammed out in a jack-hammer

punch to the Yalcan's midriff plates. The tall creature
ooffed, coiled into a ball, all four legs scrabbling, the
four arms groping wildly.

"Sorry, pal," Retief muttered, catching up the
power gun. "No time to argue." He grabbed Miss
Braswell's hand and started off at a dead run down the
deserted street toward the towering castle of light.

VI

They skidded to a halt at a gleam from an opening
door ahead. A pipe stem-legged Groaci hurried from a
building, a bulging sack over one knobby shoulder. A
second helmeted looter trotted behind, lugging a handsome ten-gallon spittoon.

"They've got a heli," Retief said softly. "We need
it. Wait here."

Miss Braswell clutched his hand even tighter. "I'm
scared!"

The two scavengers were clambering into their dark
machine now. Running lights sprang into diamond
brilliance. Turbos whirred. Retief disengaged his hand,
ran across the thirty feet of open pavement and jumped,
just as the heli lifted. There were faint, confused cries
from the startled Groaci. One fumbled out a power rifle
in time for Retief to jerk it from his grasp, toss it over
the side. The heli canted wildly, narrowly missing a
decorated cornice. Retief got a grip on a bony neck,
propelled the owner over the side, heard a faint yelp as
he hit. An instant later, the second followed. Retief
caught the controls, brought the heli around in a tight
turn, dropped it in beside Miss Braswell.

"Oh! I was afraid it was you that fell overboard, Mr. Retief!" She scrambled up beside him, lent a hand to tumble the gaboon out to smash thunderously on the tiles. On a nearby roof, the two dispossessed Groaci keened softly, like lost kittens. The heli jumped off, lifted swiftly past them and headed for the glass towers.

The city of glass spread over forty acres, a crystalline fantasy of towers, minarets, fragile balconies suspended over space, diaphanous fretwork, airy walkways spun like spiderwebs between slim spires ablaze with jewel-colored light. Retief brought the heli in high, settled in a stomach-lifting swoop toward the tallest of the towers.

"Miss Braswell, you can operate this thing, can't you?"

"Sure, I'm a good driver, but—"

Retief threw the drive into autohover three feet above a tiny terrace clinging to the spire. "Wait here. I'll be back as soon as I can. If anybody else shows up, get out of here fast and head for the bog!"

"The . . . the bog?"

"It's the safest place around when the quake hits!" He was over the side, across the five-foot wide shelf of water-clear glass, and through an opening arched with intertwined glass vines hung with sparkling scarlet and purple berries. A narrow stair wound down, debouching into a round chamber walled with transparent murals depicting gardens in the sun. Through the glass, lighted windows in the next tower were visible, and beyond, the silhouettes of half a dozen Groaci and a tall, paunchy Terrestrial.

Retief found more stairs, leaped down them, whirled through an archway of trellised glass flowers. A narrow crystal ribbon arched across the void to the lighted entry opposite. He pulled off his shoes, crossed the bridge in five quick steps.

Voices were audible above, and dark shadows moved on the pebble-glass ceiling. Retief went up, caught a brief glimpse of five richly draped Groaci under an ornate chandelier, fingering elaborate Yalcan wine glasses and clustering about the stooping, chinless figure of Minister Barnshingle.

"—pleasure to deal with realists like yourselves," the diplomat was saying. "Pity about the natives, of course, but as you pointed out, a little discipline—"

Retief knocked two Groaci spinning, caught Barnshingle by the arm, slopping his drink over the crimson cuff of his mess jacket.

"We've got to go—fast, Mr. Minister! Explanations later!"

Fiss hissed orders; two Groaci darted away and another rushed in to be stiff-armed. Barnshingle choked, spluttered, jerked free. His face had turned an unflattering shade of purple.

"What's the meaning of this outburst?"

"Sorry, Mr. Minister." Retief rammed a clean right cross to Barnshingle's jaw, caught the diplomat as he folded, stooped to hoist the weight to his shoulders, and ran for the door.

Suddenly Groaci were everywhere. Two bounced aside from Retief's rush; another ducked, swung a power gun up, fired just as Fiss leaped in and knocked his hand aside.

"To endanger the bloated one," he hissed—and went over backwards as Retief slammed him aside. A helmeted Groaci Peace-keeper tackled Retief from behind; he paused to kick him across the room, bowling over others. A blaster bolt rubbled glass above his head. The air hissed with weak Groaci shouts as Retief plunged down stairs. Behind him, there was a terrific crash; over his shoulder he caught a glimpse of glass chips showering from a fallen chandelier. He was at the bridge now; Barnshingle groaned and flapped his arms feebly. Retief stepped onto the narrow span, felt it sway under his weight. He took two steps, put a foot over the edge, teetered—

There was a crystalline tinkle, and a ten-foot spear of canary-yellow glass fell past him. He caught his balance, took another step, wobbled as the bridge quivered, leaped clear as the glass shattered into ten thousand glittering shards that sparkled as they fell.

He went up stairs three at a time. A sudden lurch threw him against the wall, where mosaic glass figures depicted glass blowers at work. A huge chunk of the scene fell backwards, letting in a gust of cool night air. Retief scrambled for footing, went up, felt a glass slab drop from underfoot as he gained the terrace. Wind beat down from the heli, hovering a few yards distant. The sparkling tower that had loomed nearby was gone. A sustained crashing, as of nearby surf, drowned the heli's turbos.

Retief lowered Barnshingle, now pawing weakly and blinking vague eyes, half lifted, half shoved him into the rear seat.

"Hurry, Mr. Retief! It's going!" The noise was deafening now. Retief grasped a strut to pull himself up, and suddenly he was hanging by one hand, his feet treading air. The heli surged, lifting. He looked down. The tower was dropping away below, a cloud of varicolored glass splinters puffing out as the upper stories thundered down into the depths. A slender sapphire spire, thrusting up almost alone now, rippled like a dancer, then broke into three major fragments and dropped gracefully from view. Retief hauled himself up, got a foot inside the heli, pulled himself into the seat.

"Mr. Retief, you're bleeding." He put a hand up, felt slickness across his cheek.

"A lot of splinters flying around. It was a little too close—"

"Mr. Retief!" Miss Braswell worked frantically at the controls. "We're losing altitude!"

There was a harsh droning noise. Retief looked back. A heavy armored heli with Groaci markings was dropping toward them.

"Make for the bog!" Retief called over the racket.

There was a buzz, and garish light glared across the struts above Retief's head, bubbling paint.

"Hang on!" Miss Braswell shouted. "Evasive action!" The heli tilted, whipped up in the opposite direction, spun, dropped like a stone, darted ahead. The futile buzzing of the Groaci's blaster rattled around the faltering vehicle.

"Can't do much more of that," Miss Braswell gasped. "Losing altitude too fast."

A vast, dark shadow flitted overhead.

"We're sunk," Miss Braswell squeaked. "Another one—"

There was a flare of actinic blue from above and behind, followed by a muffled clatter. Retief caught a glimpse of the Groaci heli, its rotors vibrating wildly, falling away behind them. Something huge and shadowy swept toward them from the rear in a rising whistle of air.

"Get set," Retief called. He brought up the blaster he had taken from Oo-Plif, steadied his hand against the heli—

The shadow dropped close; the running lights of the heli gleamed on thirty-foot canopies of translucent tracery spread wide above a seven-foot body. Oo-Plif's gaily painted face beamed down at them. He floated on spread wings, arms and legs folded close.

"Ah. Retief-Tic! Punch in thorax hasten metamorphis. Got clear of chrysalis just in time!"

"Oo-Plif!" Retief yelled. "What are you doing here?"

"Follow to warn you, dear buddy! Not want you to meet gods in lousy company like crowd of Five-eyes! Now on to bog for festivities!"

Below, the torch-lit surface of the swamp rushed up. Miss Braswell braked, threw herself into Retief's arms as the battered heli struck with a massive splatter at the edge of the mud. Painted Yalcan faces bobbed all around.

"Welcome, strangers!" voices called. "Just in time for fun!"

VII

Barnshingle was groaning, holding his head.

"What am I doing here, hip-deep in mud?" he demanded. "Where's Magnan? What happened to that fellow Fiss?"

"Mr. Magnan is coming now, Miss Braswell said.
"You bumped your head."

"Bumped my head? I seem to recall—"

Someone floundered up, gasping and waving
skinny, mud-caked arms.

"Mr. Minister! These primitives dragged me bodily
from the street!"

"I thought you were going to stay inside the Legation," Retief said.

"I was merely conducting a negotiation," Magnan
huffed. "What are you doing here, Retief—and Miss
Braswell!"

"What were you negotiating for? A private apartment just below the Ambassadorial penthouse?"

"Wha—whatever's happened?" Barnshingle burst
out. "Where's the shrine gone?" He stared across at
the glowing heap that marked the site of the fallen
towers.

"It seems to have—ah—been offered to the local
deities," Magnan said. "It seems to be the custom."

"And all those nasty little bug-eyes with it," Miss
Braswell put in.

"Really, Miss Braswell! I must ask you to avoid the
use of racial epithets!"

"It's really too bad about the towers; they were
awfully pretty."

Oo-Plif, perched like a vast moth on a nearby tree-fern spoke up. "Is okay. Re-use glass. Make
plenty bowl and pot from fragments."

"But—what about all those Groaci mixed in with the
pieces?"

"Impurities make dandy colors," Oo-Plif assured
her.

"My jaw," Barnshingle grated. "How did I fall and hit my jaw?"

"Retief-Tic arrive in nick of time to snatch you from sacrificial pile. Probably bump chin in process."

"What in the world were you doing there, Mr. Minister?" Magnan gasped. "You might have been killed."

"Why, ah, I was trepanned there by the Groaci. Quite against my will, of course. They . . . ah . . . had some fantastic proposal to make. I was just on the point of daring them to do their worst when you appeared, Retief. After that, my recollection grows a bit hazy."

"These head-blows often have retroactive effects," Retief said. "I'll wager you don't recall a thing that was said from the time they picked you off that perilous mountain."

"Don't remember? Why, I have perfect recall—"

"It's even possible that Oo-Plif has forgotten some of the things he overheard—about penthouses and gilt-edge stocks." Retief went on. "Maybe it was the excitement generated by your announcement that Yalc will be getting some large shipments of fine gray silica sand from Groac suitable for glass-making, courtesy of the CDT."

"Announcement?" Barnshingle gulped.

"The one you're going to make tomorrow," Retief suggested very gently.

"Oh . . . that one," the Minister said weakly.

"Time to go along now to next phase of celebration," Oo-Plif called from his perch.

"How jolly," Magnan said. "Come along, Mr. Minister."

"Not you, Magnan-Tic, and Barnshingle Tic-Tic," Oo-Plif said. Mating rites no place for elderly drones. You scheduled for cosy roost in thorn-tree as ceremonial penitence for follies of youth."

"What about us?" Miss Braswell asked breathlessly.

"Oh, time for you to get busy on youthful follies, so have something to repent later!"

"You said . . . mating rite. Does that mean . . . ?"

"Vomm festival merely provide time, place and member of opposite gender," Oo-Pliff said. "Rest up to you!"

WICKER WONDERLAND

I

CONSUL-GENERAL MAGNAN clutched his baggy chartreuse velvet beret against the blast of air from the rotor of the waiting heli and beckoned Retief closer.

"I'll be candid with you, Retief," he said from the side of his mouth. "I'm not at all happy about leaving you here as deputy chief under a Groaci superior. The combination of unpredictable elements is an open invitation to disaster."

"I've never known disaster to wait for an invitation, where our Groaci colleagues were concerned," Retief commented.

"Naturalizing a Groaci was irregular enough in itself," Magnan went on. "Tendering him an appointment in the Corps smacks of folly."

"Don't underestimate the boys at headquarters," Retief said cheerfully. "Maybe this is just the first step in a shrewd scheme to take over Groac."

"Nonsense! No one at HQ would want to go on

record as favoring such a policy . . ." Magnan looked thoughtful. "Besides, what does Groac have that we need?"

"Their cast-iron gall would be a valuable acquisition—but I'm afraid that's the sort of intangible that will elude the wiliest diplomacy."

Magnan pursed his lips. "Take care, Retief. If anything goes awry, I'll hold you fully responsible." The senior diplomat turned to the other staff members waiting nearby on the tower-top helipad, moved among them shaking hands, then scrambled into the heli. It lifted and beat its way eastward against a backdrop of vermillion-bellied clouds in a sky of luminous violet. Behind Retief, the voice of Vice-Consul Wimperton rose to a shrill bark.

"No want um basket! No need um beads! Want um heavy metal, you blooming idiot!"

Retief turned. A short-legged, long-torsoed local draped in a stiff lime-green garment stood round-shouldered before the Commercial Attache, dwarfed under a load of fancifully beaded baskets.

"No want um?" the Poon enquired in a voice that seemed to thrum in his chest. "Plenty too cheap—"

"Nobody want um! How many times do I have to tell you, you bug-eyed—"

A curtain twitched aside from a narrow doorway; a spindle-legged Groaci in Bermuda shorts, argyle socks and a puce and magenta aloha shirt peered out.

"Mr. Wimperton," he said faintly, "I must request that you refrain from abusing the locals so loudly. I have a splitting headache."

The deck lifted, creaking, and sank gently back. The Groaci put a hand against his midriff and clutched the doorframe. His name was Dools. He was new in his post—as well as in his citizenship.

"My, that was a dandy," Wimperton said. "Felt like my stomach came right up and bumped my chin!"

"I'm sure we're all aware of the motion, Mr. Wimperton. All too aware," Dools whispered.

"Say, you don't look at all well, Mr. Consul-General," Wimperton said solicitously. "It's this constant rocking, up and down, to and fro. You can never tell which way the tower will lean next."

"Yes, yes, a penetrating observation, Mr. Wimperton." The Consul-General tilted two eye-stalks toward Retief. "If you'd step inside a moment, Mr. Retief?" He held the curtain aside, let it drop behind Retief.

Late sunlight filtering through the open-work walls of the Consulate splashed a checkered pattern across colorful rugs of kelp fiber, low couches, desks and chairs of woven wicker work. Consul-General Dools looked at Retief nervously.

"Mr. Retief," he said in his faint voice. "Now that our previous chief, Mr. Magnan, has departed, I, of course, find myself in charge." He paused while the floor lifted and sank; his eye-stalks waved sickeningly.

"As a newcomer, perhaps you've noticed certain . . . oh . . . irregularities in our little organization here." Four of his eyes studied different corners of the room. Retief said nothing.

"I wished merely to caution you: It would be unwise to evince excessive curiosity . . ."

Retief waited. The tower leaned to the steady pressure of the rising gale. The floor slanted. Consul-General Dool clung to a desk, his throat-sacs vibrating.

"There are many ways," he started, "in which accidents could befall one here."

The floor sagged, rose abruptly. Dools gulped, threw Retief a last despairing glance and fled as Wimperton came in, still muttering. He looked after the departing Groaci.

"Consul-General Dools isn't a very good sailor," he commented. "Of course, in the week you've been here, you haven't seen a real blow yet—"

The native peddler poked his round head through the door hanging, padded across the room on large, bare webbed feet and paused before Retief.

"You want um basket?" The round, amber-and-olive patterned face gazed hopefully at him.

"I'll take that one," Retief said in the native language, pointing.

The wide lipless mouth stretched wide in the local equivalent of a delighted grin.

"A sale! I was beginning to think you High-Pockets—excuse me, sir—you Terries were tighter than weed-ticks in a belly-button." He lowered his wares, extracted the basket.

"You shouldn't encourage him," Wimperton said snappishly. "For months I've been indoctrinating him to bring in some gold nuggets. The land-masses are practically solid with them—but no, they build their town on a raft of seaweed in mid-ocean and weave baskets!"

"They evolved in the weed," Retief said mildly. "And if they lifted the embargo on gold, in six months the planet would be swarming with prospectors, dumping their tailings into the ocean. They like it the way it is."

The Poon caught Retief's eyes, jerked his head toward the doorway, then ducked out through the door hanging.

Retief waited half a minute, then rose lazily and stepped out on the wide observation deck.

All around, lesser towers, intricately patterned, rose from the miles-long mat of yellow-green seaweed far below, moving restlessly with the long ocean swells. Sea fowl with weed-colored backs and sky-blue undersides wheeled and screamed. Between the swaying pinnacles, a spiderweb complex of catwalks swung in hundred-yard festoons. A continuous creaking of rattan filled the air. Far away, the white-flecked surface of the open sea was visible.

Retief crossed to where the Poon waited by the stairwell entry.

"You seem like a good fellow," the peddler said as Retief came up. "So I'll give you some free advice." He glanced around at the color-drenched sky. "There'll be a Big Blow tonight. Get down below—don't waste any time." He hitched at his load of baskets and turned to the stairs. "And don't bother to tell those clowns." He jerked his head toward the Consular offices. "They're bad medicine." He bobbed his head and was gone.

Retief threw a sharp glance at the clouds, got out a cigar and lit up, turned from the rail.

A tall, broad-shouldered man in a somber uniform stood by the catwalk mouth, looking Retief over. He came across the close-woven deck and thrust out a large, well-tanned hand.

"My name's Klamper, Planetary Monitor Service. I guess you're the new man."

Retief nodded.

"Let me give you some advice. Watch out for the natives. They're sly, tricky devils." He paused. "You were talking to one just now. Don't let him lure you into going down into the native quarter. Nothing down there but natives and dark holes to fall into. A helluva place for a Terry. Knifings, poisonings—nothing there worth climbing down thirty flights of wicker steps to look at."

Retief puffed at his dope stick. The wind swirled the smoke away.

"Sounds interesting," he said. "I'll think it over."

"Plenty to do right up here in the Consulate tower," Klamper said. "I guess you've seen the Tri-D tank—a twenty-footer—and the sublimation chamber. And there's a pretty good auto-banquet. And don't overlook the library. They've got a few dandy sense-tapes there; I confiscated them from a Joy-boat in a twelve mile orbit off Callisto last year." The constable got out a dopestick and cocked an eye at Retief. "What do you think of your Groaci boss, Consul-General Jack Dools?"

"I haven't seen much of him. He's been seasick ever since I got here."

"First time I ever ran into a Groaci in the CDT," Klamper said. "A naturalized Terry, I hear. Well, maybe he hasn't got all five eyes on an angle—but I'd say watch him." Klamper hitched up his gun belt. "Well, I'll be shoving off." He glanced at the stormy sky. "Looks like I've got a busy night ahead."

Retief stepped back into the office. A small, round man with pale hair and eyebrows looked up from the chair by Wimperton's desk.

"Oh." Wimperton blinked at Retief. "I thought you'd gone for the day." He folded a sheaf of papers hurriedly, snapped a rubber band around them, turned and dropped them in the drawer of the filing cabinet.

Wimperton rose. "Well, I'll be nipping along to Dorm Tower, I believe, before the wind gets any worse. This breeze is nothing to what we get sometimes. I'd suggest you take care crossing the catwalk, Retief. It can be dangerous. In a cross-wind, it sets up a steady ripple." His limber hands demonstrated a steady ripple. "Other times it seems to float up and down." He eyed Retief. "I hope the motion isn't bothering you?"

"I like it," Retief said. "As a boy, I had a habit of eating candy bars—you know, the sticky kind—while standing on my head on a merry-go-round."

Wimperton's eyes stared fixedly at Retief. A fine sweat popped out on his forehead.

"Feels like it's building up, all right," Retief said genially. "Feel that one?"

A distant, thoughtful look crept over Wimperton's face.

"It's good and hot in here, too," Retief went on. "And there's that slight odor of fish, or octopus, or whatever it is . . ."

"Uh . . . I'd better see to the goldfish," Wimperton gasped. He rushed away.

Retief turned to the round-faced man.

"How was your trip, Mr. Pird?"

"Ghastly," Pird piped. His voice sounded like a rubber doll. "I visited continents One and Two. Bare rock. No life higher than insects, but plenty of those.

You know, it never rains on Poon. All five continents are deserts, and the heat—''

"I understood the Zoological Investigation and Liaison Council Headquarters had financed a couple of wild-life census stations over there," Retief said.

"To be sure, facilities were provided by ZILCH but unhappily, no volunteers have come forward to man them." Pird smiled sourly. "A pity. Consul-General Dools has expressed a passionate interest in wildlife." Pird grabbed at a paperweight as it slid across the desk-top. The walls creaked; wind shrilled, flapping the door hanging. The floor heaved and settled back. Pird swallowed, looking pale.

"I believe I'd best be going," he said, starting toward the door.

"Hold it," Retief called. Pird jerked. His eyes blinked.

"Aren't you going to warn me about anything?"

Pird stared for a moment, then scurried off.

Alone, Retief stood with braced feet in the Consular office, gloomy now in the eerie light of the stormy sunset. He crossed to the filing cabinet, took a small instrument from a leather case and went to work on the lock. After five minutes' work, the top drawer popped out half an inch.

Retief pulled it open; it was empty. The second contained a dry sandwich and a small green flask of blended whiskey. In the bottom drawer were four dog-eared copies of *Saucy Stories*, a prospectus in full-dimensional color illustrating Playtime on Paradise, the Planet with a Past, glossy catalogs describing the latest in two-seater sport helis and a fat document secured by a wide rubber band.

Retief extracted the latter and opened the stiff paper. It was an elaborately worded legal instrument. In the fifth paragraph he read:

". . . whereas such body is otherwise uninhabited, unimproved, and subject to no prior claim filed with the proper authorities as specified in paragraph 2 A (3) above, and;

Whereas claimant has duly established, by personal occupancy for a period of not less than six Standard Months, or by improvement to a value of . . ."

Retief read on, then removed the elaborately engraved cover sheet of the document, folded the rest and fitted it into an inside pocket.

Outside, the wind rose to a howling crescendo; the floor shuddered; the walls tilted precariously. Retief took a magazine from the drawer, fitted the document cover over it, folded it and snapped the red rubber band in place, then replaced it in the drawer and closed it. The lock seated with a snick. He left the consulate and crossed the swaying catwalk to the next tower.

II

Retief stood in the doorway of his room, smoking a cigar. Pird, just starting down the stairway, clucked. "Better hurry, sir. Everyone else has gone down. The wind is rising very rapidly."

"I'll be along." Retief looked down the empty corridor, undulating in the dim late-evening light, then went along to a curtain-hung doorway and stepped out onto a wind-swept balcony. From it a swaying wicker catwalk launched itself in a dizzy span to the Consulate Tower, a hundred yards distant.

A dim light winked on in the consular offices, moving about slowly. Retief watched for a moment, then turned up the collar of his windbreaker and stepped off into the dark tunnel of the wildly swinging passage. The gale buffeted at it with a ferocity that had increased even in the quarter-hour he had spent in the Dorm Tower. The sky had darkened to an ominous mauve, streaked with fiery crimson. Below, lights sparkled all across the lower levels.

The last fifty feet of the crossing was a steep climb up the sagging catwalk. Abruptly the catwalk dropped three feet and came to a stop with its floor canted at a sharp angle. Retief steadied himself, then went on, climbing now. Ten feet ahead, the yellow and blue hanging at the end of the passage was visible. It moved. The slight figure of Consul Dools appeared for a moment, wrapped in a dark poncho, then whisked back out of view.

Retief made another two yards against the bucking of the sloping passage. He could hear a rasping now, a harsh sawing sound. A wedge of electric-purple sky appeared through the wicker roof ahead. It widened . . .

With an abrupt crackling of breaking fibers, the end of the catwalk broke free and dropped like an express elevator. Retief locked his fingers in the twisted rattan and held on. The face of the tower flashed past. Retief slid two feet and caught himself with his torso half out the open end. Air shrieked past his face. A foot from his eyes, the severed end of the supporting cable whipped in the screaming wind—cut clean.

Retief looked down and saw the massed lights of the native section swooping up to meet him. A wall rushed close; Retief felt the whistle of air as he brushed it; then he was hurtling past low towers with lighted windows behind which alien faces gaped briefly. He swept low over a narrow street ablaze with colored lights, felt a shock as the catwalk brushed a building somewhere above; then the street was falling away below as the free-swinging catwalk cracked-the-whip, soaring upward in a wild zoom, slowing now . . .

A wall loomed before him with a narrow balcony before lighted windows. For an instant, it seemed to hang before his face—and Retief lunged, kicked his legs free of the twisted wicker. He caught the heavy rattan guard rail. He hung on, groping with his feet, with the gale tearing at him, shrieking in his ears . . .

Hands gripped him, hauling him up. He shook his head to clear it, felt a heavy hanging brush his face. Then he was standing on a yielding floor, blinking in the soft light of a primitive incandescent lamp, feeling the warmth and strange, spicy odor of an alien room.

A five-foot native stood before him, staring up anxiously with large protruding green eyes in a smooth, olive-colored face. The wide, almost human mouth opened showing a flash of pink interior.

"Are you all right, buddy?" a strangely resonant voice inquired in the bubbly local tongue.

Retief felt of his jaw, moved his shoulders gingerly. "A little dazed by the speed with which the boys work, but otherwise fine," he replied.

"You speak Poon like a native, by Hoop!" the alien said. "Here sit down. How about a drink of Yiquil?" He indicated a low couch heaped with varicolored cushions and turned to a cupboard, wide webbed feet in bright yellow sandals gripping the swaying floor.

"You fell off a catwalk, eh?"

"Something like that," Retief accepted a deep two-handled porcelain jug, delicately shaped. He sniffed the drink, then sipped.

"My name's Url Yum. I'm a netter for Matwide Fooderies."

"I'm Retief. I'm with the Terran Consulate." He glanced around the room. "Handsome apartment you have here."

"Oh, it's all right." There was a sharp whistle at the door.

"You feel like meeting a bunch of people? I guess they saw you fall, and they'll be crowding in now to take a look at you. We don't often see Terries here in town, you know."

"I'd rather not go on exhibit right now. Yum."

"Sure, I know how you feel. I had to go over to Dryport on business a few months back, and every damn do-gooder wanted to have me in for tea and look me over."

The whistle sounded again at the door. Url Yum padded across to the closet, brought out a large satchel and pulled out bright-colored gear of plastic and metal.

"I was just about to go for a swim. Why don't you join me? You don't want to go back up tonight in this wind. We can go down the back way. How about it?"

"A swim? In this weather?"

"The best time. Hunting's good. The small stuff shelters under the Mat, and the big stuff is in there hunting them—and we hunt the big stuff." He held up a polished spearhead.

"Look, Yum, I'm just a Terry. I can't hold my breath more than a minute or two."

"Neither can I. That's what the gear's for. You burn oxygen, same as we do, don't you?"

The whistle came again, more peremptory now. "Hey, Yum!" a voice called.

Retief finished his drink. "That yiquil's great stuff, Yum; it's already affecting my judgment. Let's go!"

They stood in a narrow way that wound between high walls hung with dights and signboards, studded with balconies from which pennants fluttered, crowded with brilliantly mantled and jeweled Pupoony, filled with the shriek of wind, the chatter of whistled conversation, and over all the polyphonic creaking of the city.

"I've heard of twisting roads," Retief called. "This is the first time I ever saw one that really twisted."

Yum put his mouth close to Retief's ear. "You know the whistle dialect?"

"I can understand it," Retief shouted back. "But I can't whistle it."

Yum motioned, led the way down a side alley to a sea-shell ornamented hanging and pushed into a low room with couches along one wall, open shelves on another. A portly Poon waddled forward.

"Oi, Yum! Oi, stranger."

"Oi," Yum said. "Gipp, this is Retief. We're going down. Can you fix him up with a spray job?"

"Lucky you came to my place, Yum. I happen to have a compound specially prepared for Terry requirements, a fresh batch, just concocted yesterday."

"Good. Retief, put your stuff over there." Yum opened his satchel, took out equipment and laid it out on a low table. He selected a pair of goggles, handed them to Retief. "These are a little big, but I think they'll seat all right." He handed over a heavy cylinder the size and shape of a beer bottle, added other items.

"Okay: propulsion, communication lights, breathing apparatus, emergency gear. Now, after you strip and get your equipment buckled on, Gipp will fit you with water-foils and spray you in."

Retief donned the gear and watched with interest while the portly proprietor shaped a putty-like material to his feet, forming large fins which stiffened to a rubbery consistency, then brought out a portable apparatus with a tank, compressor and hose with a wide nozzle.

"Give him a Striding Devil job, Gipp," Yum ordered.

Gipp hesitated, looking at Retief. "I suppose you've had a lot of experience—?"

"He'll be all right," Yum put in. "He catches on fast, and he's got a good arm."

"Whatever you say, Yum—but you ought to warn him that a Death Angel will jump a Strider on sight."

"Sure. That way we don't have to go looking for 'em."

"Well, if you get one remember I'm paying top sprud for stones."

"You'll get first crack."

Gipp started up the compressor, twiddled knobs, then directed a heavy spray of viscous, greenish fluid on Retief's chest, working it in a pattern that covered him to the knees. Then the Poon shut down and set about changing hoses.

"What's this stuff for?" Retief inquired, studying the thick, soft layer hardening on his skin.

"Protective covering. It's tough as yuk skin. And it has an osmotic action; passes oxygen in, and CO_2 out. The color disguises you so you don't scare off the game—and the finished job holds all your gear in place. It's a good insulation, too. That water's cold. It strips off easily when you come back in."

Gipp worked for another five minutes. Retief craned his neck to look at himself. His back, he saw, was a dull black, with red and white flecks, separated from the glossy green front by pale gray sides. Broad pink gill-flaps flared from throat to shoulders. The ankles and fin-covered feet were a vivid red.

"He's got the build for it," Gipp said, looking him over. "If I hadn't done the job myself, I'd swear he was a Strider, by Hoop!"

"That's the idea, Gipp. Now just give me a straight Big Mouth outfit." Yum took a flask from a side pocket and offered it to Retief, who took a generous pull, then passed it to Gipp, busy with his apparatus.

"No, thanks. I don't need any delusions of grandeur tonight. I hope to do a good volume of business before the storm hits its peak." He worked carefully, covered Yum with a uniform dull gray, added a peaked crest of garish yellow.

"All right, Retief." Yum handed him a light, short-barreled rifle from the muzzle of which a razor-edged spearhead protruded. "Let's go down."

Gipp led the way to a back room and opened a wide wicker cover set in the floor. Retief looked down to the sloping surface of a three-foot tube of close-woven strips.

"Follow me," Yum said, and dived, head first, out of sight. Retief gripped his spear-gun, waved Gipp a cheery farewell and dived after him.

III

The water was ink-black, alive with darting lights in red and yellow, ponderous-moving patterns of green and blue and, far below, dull gleams of violet. Retief kicked his feet, watched lights scatter before him in a boil of phosphorescence.

A dark shape darted from the gloom and hovered before him. He recognized Yum's yellow crest, waving gently in the moving water.

"Only peaceful place in town, when the wind's working," Yum's voice crackled in Retief's ears. "Let's work our way east to get clear of the activity around here; then we'll see if we can't bait an Angel up."

"How deep are we?"

"The Mat's twenty meters thick here. We're going to work Underside first; if that's no go, we'll move down."

Yum darted off with a flick of webbed feet. Retief followed. Above, the mass of the floating continent of weed was a fairyland tangle of waving fronds, fantastically shaped corals, coiling weed, and moving lights.

"Use the knob on your left hip as a jet control," Yum said. "Steer with your feet—and keep your rifle ready. If you see anything that looks like you, let him have it."

Retief tried the knob, felt water churn past his knees; he leaped ahead, driving through the water with a speed that blurred the weedscape above. A slight twist of the ankles sent him angling sharply toward the depths; a minute adjustment brought him back to Yum's side. His eyes adjusted to the darkness, picked out the shapes behind the lights now. Massive, sluggish swimmers cruised, wide jaws open. Slim torpedo shapes darted and wheeled. A nebulous form, glowing with a nacreous pink, rose up and reached out with feathery arms; Yum swerved away, Retief following fifteen feet to one side of his bubble-trail.

After a ten-minute run, Yum slowed, rose until he brushed the tops of the coral trees, then reached up with his feet, planted them in a swirl of smoky mud and stood, inverted. Retief came alongside, twisted, felt the soft ooze under his feet.

"It's a little confusing at first," Yum's voice came clear in Retief's ears. "But you'll get used to it."

Retief looked around. The undulating surface of the weed mass stretched away into deep gloom, studded with waving fronds, stiff-branched trees of red-violet, orange and chartreuse coral, feathery banks of leafy undergrowth set with multi-colored flowers as big as dinner plates, among which moving lights sparkled and played.

"I'll pace you, off to the left," Yum said. "Move along with big, leaping strides. Anything your size except another Strider will give you a wide berth. If you see one, hit him fast. Aim for the mid-section. Now, if we pick up an Angel, you'll notice the shadow first. Just keep moving; I'll get under him and hit him where it hurts. When he turns, give it to him near the big red spot on his back. Got it?"

"How many rounds in this rifle?"

"Five in the magazine, and a spare on your left shoulder."

"How do we know there aren't other hunters around? I'd hate to spear a friend of yours by mistake."

"You'll get a recognition tone in your phones if anybody gets within fifteen yards—maybe. That's part of the game. I got a nice barb cut out of my left leg last year. Some joker wanted a Big Mouth for cut bait." Yum waved and flicked away. Retief picked an open avenue between towering corals and started off. Walking was not too difficult after the first few steps; rather like tramping the dusty surface of an asteroid, he reflected—except that the diving gear was considerably less bulky than a spacesuit.

There was a movement to Retief's right. A tall biped stalked into view ten yards distant, barely visible in the glow of phosphorescence. Retief halted and brought the gun around. The newcomer moved on in great floating leaps. Retief turned to follow.

"Never mind the Strider," Yum said. "He didn't see you; he must have just fed. We'll work off to the right here and let him have this territory."

Retief watched as the biped bounded off into the gloom, then moved on.

Ahead, the darkness seemed deeper. A cow-sized creature with warts and glowing rings around wide eyes blundered past, rocking him with a surge of water. Tiny fish flashed by. The gloom deepened.

"Action!" Yum's voice came, tense in the earphones. "Keep going; we've got a big one coming up to take a look!"

Retief twisted to look toward the depths, like a black sky in which a dark cloud moved. He went on.

"That's the stuff. Act like you don't notice him;

otherwise he'll let fly with his musk, and we'll be working in the dark. . . ."

The shadow moved, spreading. All around, the scene darkened. At last a sluggish sea-creature humped past, raising a trail of mud-fog.

"Hey," Yum's voice came. "He's by-passing us, moving on."

"Maybe he's just not hungry tonight."

"It's that Strider we saw; he's after him. Let's go!"

Retief turned, saw a swirl of phosphorescence, jetted after it. The surface of the weed sloped, an inverted hill. Retief moved up beside Yum, following the immense shadow that fled across the rolling surface. The Strider came into view, leaning back toward the two hunters.

"Take him!" Yum barked. "I'll get under the big boy!" He swirled away. Retief brought the rifle to his shoulder, aimed—

A brilliant light flashed from the Strider's chest. The creature reached, grabbing at its back . . .

"Hold it!" Yum's voice snapped. "That's no Strider!"

The long greenish beam of the searchlight swung, flashing from coral trees, glowing through drifting mud-clouds.

"The damned fool! He'd better douse that light!"

The Death Angel closed, like a hundred-foot blanket of black jelly settling in; the stranger backed, working frantically to fit a magazine to his rifle, bringing it up—

The Angel struck. For a moment it hugged the surface of the weed, rippling its edge—then it heaved, recoiling violently—

"Good-oh!" Yum yelled. "I planted one fair and square! Move in and hit the hot-spot, Retief, and we'll be up half the night counting gold over a bottle of hundred-year yiquil!"

Retief hurled himself forward, kicked clear of the weed-bed, centered his sights on a foot-wide patch of luminous red at the center of the vast writhing shape, and fired, fired again, then went tumbling as the turbulence caught him and bowled him over.

Retief and Yum crouched by the prone body of the Angel's victim.

"He's a Terry, all right, Retief. I wonder what he was doing Underside—alone?"

"Probably a tourist, out to see the sights. Though I hadn't heard of any travellers registered with the Consulate."

"You may be right. We're not far from the Tap Root; he was headed that way, and he seemed to know where he was going."

Retief checked the man's equipment, noted his pulse and respiration.

"He seems to be all right."

"Sure. He just took a good jolt of current. We didn't give the Big Boy a chance to get his shredding hook into him."

"We'd better take him up."

"Sure. Soon as we stone out our Angel, before the Big Mouths get him. There's a public entry-well not far away; probably the one he used. We'll just tow him along with us. He'll be okay."

The vast bulk of the Angel drifted fifty yards from

the crowns of the coral trees. They swam to it, shooed off an inquisitive scavenger, moved around to the red spot on the expanse of black hide. A short spear stood, half its length buried dead center in the target. A second spear protruded a foot away.

Yum whistled. "You work close Retief. Nice shooting." He unclipped a slim-bladed knife, made an incision, plunged an arm into the rubbery body and brought out a lumpy organ the size of a grapefruit. He whistled again.

"This must be the beachmaster of all Angels! Look at the size of that pouch!" He slit the leathery body carefully, dipped in two fingers and extracted a black sphere as big as a large grape.

"Retief, we make a great team. Look at those stones!"

"What do you use them for?"

"We grind them up and sprinkle them on our food. A great delicacy."

"Yum, what's this Tap Root you mentioned?"

"Eh? Why, it's—well, it's the root that supplies the mat."

"Just one for all this weed?"

"Sure; it's all one plant—the whole Mat."

"I'd like to take a look at it. I can't picture a Terry swimming around down here at the height of a storm, just to rubberneck—not unless it's a pretty spectacular sight."

"It doesn't look like much. Just a big tough cable, running down into the Big Deep." Yum tucked the pearls into a pouch clipped to his leg and led the way along the sloping weed surface. He indicated a black mass ahead.

That's it—back in that tangle of rootlets there. The tap's a hundred feet in diameter and over a mile long. It anchors the Mat, and feeds it, too.''

"Let's take a closer look.''

Retief moved in among the waving rootlets.

"Say—what's that?'' Yum's voice came over the earphones. Ahead, a large dark shape nestled among the entwining roots. Retief swam up alongside.

"It's a scout boat—Terry designed.'' He swam to the entry port, found it locked. "Let's reconnoiter a little, Yum.''

The two moved over the waving mass of rootlets, cruising beside the moss-grown, barnacled wall of the immense root. Retief caught a glimpse of a white object, fluttering in the dark water. He headed for it.

It was a plastic tag, wired to a spike driven into the husk of the root. Below it hung a small box, metal covered, with an insulated cable projecting from one side.

"What is it? Who'd come here and tamper with the Root?'' Yum asked, puzzled.

"It's a detonator,'' Retief said. "The cable is designed to plug into a packaged explosive charge.''

"Explosive! Here, by the Root?''

"How long would the weed last with the root cut?''

"Last? It wouldn't last a day! You cut a sprig of the weed, it crumbles in a matter of minutes. Oh, the fruit, leaves, husks, are tough enough—but the main mass would disintegrate like a sugar lump in a mug of hot *roca*.''

"Somewhere there's a bomb to go with the detonator, Yum,'' Retief said. "Probably aboard the boat.

Our swimmer was on the way to get it, I'd guess. Let's check him for keys.

Yum fumbled over the limp body. ''He's clean, Retief. He must have lost them in the fight.''

''All right; let's get him to the surface and see what he has to say.''

IV

In the damp-smelling cavern of the public entry hall, Retief stood over the unconscious man. Water dripped from him, puddled on the heavy-duty rattan ramp that sloped up from the water. The attendant on duty came forward, clucked at the sight of the inert body.

''He left here, not fifteen minutes ago. Wouldn't accept my offer of a guide. I warned him . . .''

''Where are his clothes?'' Retief asked.

''On the shelf—there.'' The attendant pointed to a coat, trousers, boots, a tangle of heavy leather belts and an empty holster in a neat pile.

''A cop?'' Retief said. He examined the garments. ''No identification,'' he said. ''And no keys.''

''What happened?'' the attendant asked.

''An Angel hit him.''

''He'll be out for hours, then,'' the attendant said. ''A big Angel gives a pretty good shock. Hah! These tourists are all alike.''

''Yum, you don't have a police force here—or an army?''

''No. What would we need with those?''

''Can you get a few friends together—volunteers, to watch the patrol boat?''

"Sure, Retief. All you want."

"Station about a dozen in the underbrush around the boat. Tell them to keep out of sight—we don't want to scare anybody off. But be careful. A spear-gun is no match for a Mark IV blaster."

"I'll call the boys." Yum went into the attendant's office, emerged five minutes later.

"All set," he declared. "What about him?" He indicated the sleeping cop.

"Have the fellow on duty watch him until your friends get here. Meanwhile, he'd better put him somewhere out of sight."

"What about the bomb?"

"We'll have to try to stampede somebody. Whoever sent our friend here doesn't know he didn't make it."

Retief looked at Yum, frowning in thought. "Yum, peel out of that scare suit and put the uniform on." He began stripping off the Strider Devil disguise. "I'll borrow some local garb."

"You've got an idea?"

"Not much of one. Just a wild hunch."

Yum kicked free of the last of the diving gear, pulled on the shapeless Patrol outfit. It hung ludicrously on his squat frame.

"Retief, I wouldn't fool anybody in this."

"That's just the point, Yum. Now let's move!"

Yum stopped before a dark entry and pointed up at the lighted floor above.

"This is it," he called over the howling wind. Retief's long cloak whipped at his ankles; Yum held onto his patrolman's cap with one hand.

"All right," Retief leaned close to Yum and shouted. "You wait five minutes, Yum; then just move on down the street. Move as though you were in a hurry. Then you'd better go back and help out the boys. If anybody comes close, let him get the port open; then hit him fast.''

''Well—I guess you know what you're doing.''

Retief climbed the trembling wicker stairway, gripping the handrail as a violent gust bounced him against the swaying wall. Two flights up he pushed aside a hanging lettered TERRESTRIAL CONSULATE GENERAL—EMERGENCY QUARTERS.

Wimperton and Pird looked up from a table on which a meal of emergency rations was laid out in the bleak light of a feeble DC lamp. Wimperton's mouth opened wide. Pird scrambled up and stood wiping his fingers on his pink vest.

''Hi, boys,'' Retief said cheerfully. 'Damnedest thing happened to me. You'll never guess.''

''Ah . . . you fell out a window?'' Wimperton hazarded.

''Close, but no dope-stick; the catwalk broke under me. Quite a ride.'' He strolled to the window. ''Some wind out there. Say . . .''

''Yes, indeed, quite a wind, you're right,'' Pird piped.

''Look here,'' Retief said. ''Is that a Patrolman? Wonder what he's doing out in the storm!''

Wimperton and Pird jumped to the window, craned. Below, Yum's ungainly figure waddled briskly along the pitching street, turned a corner.

''Hey, that's—'' Wimperton started.

''Yes, that's strange, all right,'' Pird cut in. ''Poor weather for a stroll.''

''But that wasn't—''

"Wasn't anything for us to worry about, ha ha," Pird babbled. He pretended to yawn. "Well, about time to turn in, eh?" He patted his mouth, watching Retief.

"I'm glad you suggested that," Retief said. "I was afraid you'd want to sit up and talk."

"Just take that first room there," Pird said eagerly. "Lovely room. Just lie right down and drift right off. Wimperton, you show Mr. Retief the room and I'll just . . . ah . . . check a few things."

Retief glanced back from the door, caught a glimpse of Pird darting past the outer hanging. He stepped into the room. There was a tidy bunk, an easy chair, a rug, a tri-D set.

"This is dandy." He patted the bed. "Well, Wimperton, have a pleasant night."

"Yes, indeed. You too." Wimperton disappeared. Retief flipped the light off, lay back on the bed and waited. A minute passed. The door curtain twitched aside for a moment, dropped back. Lights winked off in the outer room.

Retief rose, glanced out. The shelter was deserted. He crossed to the outer hanging, went down the swaying wicker stairs three at a time, stepped out into the storm-whipped street. Pird and Wimperton, each dragging a suitcase, staggered out of sight around the corner. Retief wrapped the cloak close and followed.

Standing in the shadows by the straining, wicker-work wall of a Public Entry Well, Retief watched Wimperton and Pird as they paced the ramp. Pird glanced at a finger watch.

". . . any time now . . ." the words came faintly through the hammer of the wind and the groaning of wicker. Pird stopped before Wimperton, apparently asking a question.

Wimperton reached inside his coat, brought out a thick packet of papers restrained by a red rubber band, waved them at Pird, put them back. Retief edged somewhat closer."

". . . don't like it either," Wimperton's nasal voice stated. "Either the locals are wise—or they've got a deal with . . ." The wind whirled the words away.

Retief stepped back into the street, saw the pink glow of a public phone fifty yards distant. He fought his way to it through the wind, dialed and asked to speak to Yum.

"No action here yet," the native said. "How did the routine go over?"

"Our pigeons flew the coop, all right. They know they've got troubles, but they're not sure just what kind. They're at a Public Entry near the Consulate, waiting for a pickup."

"They'll have a long wait. Their driver's still asleep."

"Yum, I have a feeling the bomb's timed to go off at the peak of the storm. How long will that be?"

"Oh, about two hours, I'd say."

"What will conditions be like at the top of the Consulate Tower now?"

"Rough. The towers lean to the wind. The ceilings fold right down against the floors in a good blow—and this one's a dandy."

"We're about out of time, Yum—and there are two parties still unaccounted for. I'm afraid I have one more trip in this wind."

"You're coming back here?"

"I'm going up—and I'd rather get moving while there's still crawl space in the Consulate."

A howling gale struck Retief's head as he hauled himself up from a dark opening onto the thirtieth-floor balcony and looked up the long slant of the tower face. Forty feet above, the guard rail lining the terrace of the Consulate penthouse was dimly visible in the murk.

Under Retief, the tower was trembling and moved like a living thing. He reached for a handhold, started up the thirty-degree slope. Gusts tore at him. He rested, hugging the surface, then went on. Ten minutes later he pulled himself over and lay full length on the steep slope of the tower roof.

The wind was less, here in the shelter of the canted floor. Retief slid down, then jumped, tumbled through the wind-tattered entry hanging, caught himself and blinked through the gloom of the deserted office.

From the far wall, a grunt sounded. Retief made his way across the room and flicked a wall switch. Dim light glowed, showed him the trussed form of Consul-General Jack Dools huddled in the angle of wall and floor. Five blood-shot eyestalks quivered appealingly at Retief.

He went to a tilted desk, extracted a letter knife from a clip, came back and sawed at the cords binding the Groaci, then pulled the gag free of the mandibles.

"Ah, the shining of the sun on your ancestral egg-hill," Dools gasped in Groaci. "To express heartfelt gratitude; to vow eternal chumship. . . ."

"Think nothing of it, Mr. Dools. You feel well enough to travel? 'We'll have to go down the outside. The stairs are collapsed."

"How pleasant to see you alive, dear fellow," Dools

went on in Terran. "I feared the miscreants had done their worst. I tried to interfere, but alas—"

"I saw you. At the time, I had the idea you were doing the sawing, but then I got to thinking about the booze and girly-book supply in the filing cabinet. Alcohol would poison you and as for unadorned mammals—"

"Mr. Retief, take care!" Dools hissed. "My hearing is keen: someone comes. . . ."

Retief looked toward the doorway, then hastily tucked the cut ends of the rope out of sight under Dools' body. "Play 'em close to your thorax, Mr. Dools," he cautioned.

A tall figure climbed through the dripping door hanging, crouched on the sloping floor, braced by one hand. The other held a power pistol, aimed at Retief.

"Just stay where you are, bright boy," Klamper called over the screech of the wind. "Don't bother untying him. My errand won't take but a minute."

He half-slid, half-crawled to the filing cabinet, keeping both eyes on Retief, fumbled a key from a pocket. He opened the top drawer, then the next, rummaged, tried the last drawer, then turned on Retief, showing even white teeth in an expression that was not a smile.

"I ought to have my head examined. I let those two lightweights sell me a story. What an act! Wimperton gobbled like a turkey when he opened up that phoney cover and got a load of the funny-books inside. So I let 'em sucker me into a goose-chase . . . unless you've got it?" He came closer. "Turn out your pockets, hotshot."

Retief shook his head. "If you're looking for the papers, forget it. I left them in my other suit."

"You loused up six months' work, greenhorn. But I'll be back to fill out some fresh forms. Too bad you won't be here to watch."

He raised the power pistol; behind him, Dools lunged for the patrolman's ankle.

A bolt of blue fire crackled harmlessly past Retief's ear as he leaned aside, chopped at Klamper's gun hand, followed up with a knee to the face. Klamper rolled with the blow, scrambled over a sagging desk and dived for the doorway. Dools started after him.

"Let him go, Mr. Dools," Retief said. "I think I know where he's headed. Now let's get out of here before we get our clothes pressed—with us in 'em!"

V

At the Public Entry Well, Yum and a group of well-muscled locals met Retief.

"Our man was here about ten minutes ago," Yum said blandly. "Big fellow, in a big hurry."

"You let him through?"

"That's right."

"Then you warned the boys at the boat to stop him?"

"Well, no, Retief. I told them to let him go. As you pointed out, he had a blaster. He's several hundred miles out by now."

Retief folded his arms. "There's something funny going on here, Yum. What about the bomb? It's probably timed to go off at the height of the storm—say in another ten minutes."

"Oh, that. I found it. It's taken care of."

"Found it where? And how the devil do you take care of a sealed titanite charge?"

"It was aboard the boat. You were right about that—"

"Come on, Yum. Give!"

"Well, Retief, I was a little curious. You can't blame me, after meeting you under such—unusual circumstances. I took a look through your clothes. I found this." He held up the document Retief had extracted from the Consulate files. "A fancy piece of paper laying claim to the whole damned planet of Poon—which it states is uninhabited—which it would have been if the bomb idea had worked out. The Mat would have broken up in the wind, and when the sky cleared, it would look like just another natural disaster. And in a few months, all five continents would be one big gold mine."

"So?"

"So I held out on you. Our slumbering pal had keys, all right. I went back and opened up the boat. There sat the bomb—all labelled and ready to go."

"Except for the detonator. That was wired to the root."

"Uh-huh. A safety precaution. But I found another one. It wasn't hard to install. I had an idea the owner would be along to see about it before zero hour; but I didn't like the sight of the thing sitting out the middle of the floor, so I tucked it away."

"Where?"

"In the chart storage bin."

Retief whirled to the discarded Terran uniform, jerked the communicator from the lapel clip, keyed it on the official frequency.

"Klamper, if you can hear me answer—fast!"

After a moment, Klamper's voice came back, a thin piping in the miniature earphone. Yum and Dools leaned closer.

"Klamper here. Who're you?"

"This is Retief, Klamper—"

"Oh, yeah, the bright young official. Well, I predict a big change in the near future for you. In about thirty seconds, to be exact."

"Klamper, there's a bomb—"

"Well, well, so you found out about that, too. Sorry I can't help you. So long, su—" The earphones went dead.

"Klamper!"

Yum looked at his watch. "Right on the button," he said.

"At least," Dools said, "he lived long enough to exonerate Mr. Retief."

There was a patter of hurried footsteps. Retief and Yum turned. In the door, Wimperton and Pird stood like ruffled birds, staring.

"I'm afraid you lads missed the boat," Retief called. Yum signaled with his hand. Half a dozen local citizens fanned out to hem in the newcomers.

"Oh, why Mr. Retief . . . What are you doing out of bed?" Pird squeaked.

"Oh, I just dropped down to offer you boys a crack at a peachy new opportunity in the Achievement Corps. Consul-General Dools here has need of two volunteers to man the new wildlife census stations over on continents One and Two. I'm going to give you first grabs at it. We'll go over to the Shelter and type out your resignations from the CDT and a couple of five-year enlistment contracts in the A.C.—on a non-compensatory basis, of course.''

Wimperton's mouth sagged open.

''And I have a number of microtape recordings I'll contribute,'' Dools said. ''They're quite exciting. All about bombs and land claims and gold mines. You can play them over during your leisure time—during sand-storms, perhaps.''

''But—Mr. Retief,'' Pird cried. ''We—we've found conditions here somewhat less than congenial . . .''

''What if we refuse?'' Wimperton gulped.

''In that case, Yum and his associates would like to interview you on the subject of homesteading.''

''Your pen or mine for the signature?'' Pird said hastily.

''I'll ask a couple of the boys to help these two philanthropists over to the Consulate,'' Yum said. ''Let the business wait till morning. You and I have a bottle of Yiquil to finish, Retief.''

''Show Mr. Dools a few of those pearls we netted, Yum.''

Yum fished out the stones, handed them to Dools, who canted two pairs of eye-stalks at the lustrous one-inch spheres.

''Gentlemen—this is precisely the product I need to qualify Poon as a Class One commercial world! Can these be supplied in any volume? Say, a dozen a month?''

''I think it could be arranged,'' Yum said in heavily accented Terran. ''Why don't you join Retief and the boys and me in a snort?''

''Well, I really don't think . . .''

''I know a barman who can concoct a suitable booze

for any metabolism,'' Yum urged. ''And a hangover cure afterwards.''

Retief linked arms with the slender Groaci. ''Come along Mr. Consul-General,'' he said. ''We won't take no for an answer.''

THE BRASS GOD

I

THE HOOGAN chamberlain was tall, black-clad, and high-shouldered. He had an immense dome-shaped head sloping on to his massive shoulders. His eyes were like freshly shelled oysters in a leathery face and he had long, dangling arms.

He turned to face the party of Terrestrial diplomats who stood clutching suitcases under the lofty vaulted ceiling of the vast, dark hall. Shafts of eerily colored light filtered through stained-glass loopholes, which were high in the walls, shedding a faint glow on the uneven stone floor. The drab-colored murals and hangings depicted the specialities of the seven Hoogan Hells. The mouths of dark corridors radiated from the circular chamber with helmeted and kilted Hoogan pikemen spaced between them, immobile as the gargoyles that peered from high niches.

"His Arrokanze the Pishop has graziously blaced at your dispozal theze cozy quarters," the chamberlain said in a deep, hollow voice. "You may now zelect rooms on the floors above and array yourselves in the karments provided."

"Look here, Mr. Odom-Glom," Ambassador Straphanger cut in, "I've been thinking it over, and I've decided that my staff and I will just nip back over to our ship for the night."

"His Arrokanze will be egspectink you at the fete in the Ebiscobal Kardens in one hour's time," the Hoogan bored on. "His Arrokanze tizlikes to be kept waitink."

"Oh, we're all keenly aware of the honor His Arrogance has paid us in offering accomodations here in the Episcopal Palace, but—"

"One hour," Odom-Glom repeated, his voice echoing across the hall. He turned away, the symbolic chain attached to his neck clanking as he moved. He paused, turned back.

"By the way, you are instrugted to iknore any small ah . . . indruzions. If you zee anything . . . unusual, zummon a guard at onze."

"Intrusions?" Straphanger repeated querulously. "What kind of intrusions?"

"The balace," Odom-Glom said, "is haunted."

Four twisting turns of a stone staircase above the reception hall, Second Secretary Magnan tiptoed at Retief's side. They went along an echoing corridor, past black iron-bound doors and mouldy tapestries which were dimly visible in the light of a flambeau.

"Quaint beliefs these bucolics entertain," Magnan said in a tone of forced heartiness. "Haunted indeed! How silly! Ha!"

"Why are you whispering?" Retief inquired.

"Just out of respect for the Bishop, of course."
Magnan came to an abrupt halt, and clutched Retief's
sleeve. "Wha-what's that?" he pointed.

Along the corridor, something small and dark slipped from the shadow of a pilaster to the shelter of a
doorway.

"Probably just our imagination," Retief suggested.

"But it had big red eyes," Magnan protested.

"They're as easy to imagine as any other kind."

"I just remembered—I left my shower cap in my
hold baggage. Let's go back."

Retief moved off. "It's just a few doors farther. Six,
seven . . . here we are." He inserted the key Odom-
Glom's aide had provided. The heavy door swung open
with a creak that descended the scale to a low groan.
Magnan, hurrying forward, paused to stare at the
nearest wall-hanging which showed a group of Hoogans suspended head-down from spikes above leaping
flames, while goblins of various shapes prodded them
with long barb-tipped spears.

"Curious how similar religious art is from one world
to another," he commented. Inside the room, he stared
around in dismay at the damp stone walls, the two
spartan cots and carved devils which stood in the corners.

"What perfectly ghastly quarters!" He dropped his
suitcase and went over to prod the nearest bunk. "Why,
my spine will never endure this mattress! I'll be a
physical wreck after the first night! And the draft—I'm
sure to catch a chill. And . . . and . . ." He broke off.

Magnan raised a shaky finger to point at the darkest
corner of the narrow chamber where a tall, bug-eyed
demon carved from pale blue stone winked garnet eyes.

"Retief! Something moved over there—it was just like the devils in the pictures! All fuzzy red bristles and eyes that glow in the dark!"

Retief opened his suitcase. "If you see another one, throw a shoe at it. Right now, we'd better be getting into costume; compared with an aroused ambassador, a few devils are just friendly pets."

Half an hour later, after having sponged off at a stone sink, Magnan's eyes were still rolling nervously. He adjusted the folds of his Hoogan ceremonial sarong before the tarnished, rippled mirror.

"I suppose it *is* just nerves," he said. "It's all the fault of that Odom-Glom fellow and his quaint native superstitions! I confess his remarks quite unnerved me for a moment."

Across the room, Third Secretary Retief was loading match-head sized charges into the magazine of an inconspicuous handgun.

"Probably just his way of warning us about the mice," he said.

Magnan turned and caught a glimpse of the gun. "Here, Retief! What's that?"

"Just a quaint native cure for spooks—if they get too noisy." He tucked the gun out of sight under the Hoogan sarong. "Just think of it as a sort of good-luck charm, Mr. Magnan."

"A knife up the sleeve is an old diplomatic tradition," Magnan said doubtfully. "But a power pistol under the sarong . . ."

"I'll have it along in case something jumps out of the stonework and yells boo!" Retief said reassuringly.

Magnan sniffed, admiring himself in the dark glass.

"I was rather relieved when the ambassador insisted

on native dress for the staff instead of ceremonial nudity for tonight's affair.'' He turned to study the hang of the uneven hemline that exposed his bare shins. ''One of his finer moments, I fancied. He *does* cut an impressive figure, once his jowls get that purplish tinge. Not even Odom-Glom dared stand up to him. Though I do wish he'd gone just the one step further and demanded the right to wear trousers—'' He broke off, his eyes on the black drapes covering the high, narrow window.

The heavy cloth twitched.

''Retief!'' he gasped. ''There it is again!''

''Shhh,'' Retief watched as the curtain moved again. A tiny red-glowing bead appeared at its edge, a foot above the floor; a wire-thin leg emerged, and then another. A body like a ball of reddish fluff came into view, it's red-bead eyes on two-inch stalks which tilted alertly to scan the chamber. Its gaze fixed on Retief; it moved clear of the curtain, paused, then started toward him on skittery legs—

With a yell, Magnan dived for the door and flung it wide. ''Guards! Help! Goblins! Spooks!'' His voice receded along the hall, mingling with the clank of accoutrements, and the slap of wide Hoogan feet.

The intruder hesitated at the outcry, dithered for a moment, then, emitting a cry like a goosed fairy, fumbled with two of its limbs at something attached to its back.

Beyond the door, Magnan's voice supplied a shrill counterpoint to the rumble of Hoogan questions.

''Then get someone who speaks Terran!'' he yelped. ''At this moment my associate is being savaged by the monster!''

Retief crossed quickly to the window, pulled the

drapes aside and unlatched a panel, letting in a draft of damp night air.

"This way out, fellow," he said. "You'd better get going before the cops arrive."

The fluffball darted across the room and came to a shaky stop before Retief. He made quick, nervous motions. A folded square of paper fell to the floor at Retief's feet. Then the creature sprang for the opening and was gone as Hoogan feet clumped at the door.

"Where Spism?" a heavy voice demanded in thick Terran. A conical Hoogan head in a flaring helmet swivelled to scan the room.

Behind the guard, Magnan craned for a view. "Where is the beast?' he shrilled. "It was at least four-feet high, and its tusks were four-inches long at the very least!"

The Hoogan advanced into the room. He pointed to the open window with his broad-headed seven-foot pike.

"It was a mouse after all," Retief said. "It got away."

"You let Spism ko?"

"Shouldn't I have?" Retief inquired mildly, pocketing the paper.

"Spism bad imp from nether rechions; might bite Derry, get blood boizonink."

"I think you're being impertinent," Magnan said sharply. "Biting Terrans is perfectly safe—"

The Hoogan turned to him, his pike lowered ominously.

"You will gome with me," it ordered. "The benaldy for consortink with minions of Unterworlt is poilink in oil.''

"Here,'' Magnan said, backing up. "Stand back, my man—''

The Hoogan reached for Magnan with a long, snaky hand; Retief stepped up behind him, selected a spot, and struck a sharp blow with bunched fingertips. The guard stumbled, fell past Magnan, and hit chin first with a resounding slam. His pike shattered against the wall.

"Retief!'' Magnan gobbled. "What are you thinking of? You've laid hands on a member of the Episcopal Guard!''

"I had the distinct impression that this fellow hooked a toe on the rug and fell down. Didn't you notice?''

"Why, you know very well—''

"Just before he reached you, Mr. Magnan.''

"Ah . . . why yes, now that you mention it, he did trip,'' Magnan's tone was suddenly brisk. "Nasty fall. I rushed up to support him, but alas, too late. Poor fellow. Served him right, the brute. Shall we go through his pockets?''

"Why?''

"You're right; there isn't time. That crash was doubtless heard throughout the palace.''

A second Hoogan appeared at the open door, his helmet bearing the fanged angel, which was indicative of officer rank. He eyed the fallen pikeman.

"You addacked this one?'' he demanded.

Magnan glanced at the victim as though noticing him for the first time. "He seems to have fallen down,'' he observed brightly.

"Against rules to kill Hoogan," the captain said ominously.

"He . . . ah . . . broke his spear," Magnan pointed out helpfully.

"Very bad crime, defile ceremonial spear," the captain said sternly. "Require burification zeremony. Very expenzive."

Magnan fumbled in a money pouch at one hip. "I'd love to contribute a little something."

"Ten Hoogan gredits, forget the whole thing. For extra five dizpose of body."

The felled Hoogan stirred, mumbled, sat up.

"Ha!" the captain said. "Look like no teal. But for another extra five—" he lifted a short, ugly club from his belt, "—finish off unfortunate victim of Derry violence."

"Stop!" Magnan yelled. "Are you out of your mind?"

"Inzult to overseer castle briest cosd you two more gredits. For you I mage zpecial brice, three for five."

"Bribery?" Magnan gasped. "Corruption?"

"Three it is," the Hoogan nodded. "How about you?" he turned to Retief. "You sbort like other Derry?"

"Look here, I'm paying you nothing!" Magnan barked. "Just assist this unfortunate chap out of here, if you please, and we'll get on with our dressing!"

"Small religious contributions fine old Hoogan gustom!" the overseer protested. "You want to fiolate local tapoos?"

"We Terrans have a few customs of our own," Retief put in smoothly. "We feel that graft should only be paid voluntarily." He offered a note which the officer palmed deftly. The guard was on his feet now, swaying. The captain barked an order, his subordinate gathered up the spear fragments, shot Magnan a poisonous look and departed, followed by the captain.

Retief closed the door behind the departing visitors, fished out the scrap of paper dropped by the fleeing Spism and opened it.

BY THE OGRE FOUNTAIN AT SECOND MOONRISE; WEAR A YELLOW DUNG FLOWER.

Magnan, busy at the mirror again, heaved a deep sigh.

"Hardly an auspicious beginning," he commented. "Heavens! It's twenty-thirty! We're late!" He gave his sarong a final tug and smoothed a thinning lock across His forehead.

He led the way along the echoing hall and down a spiral stair to an archway debouching onto wide steps above a ragged lawn. Blue lanterns hanging in the branches of skeletal trees shed a wan radiance on the fungus-like ornamental plants. Sculptures representing souls in torment were placed near wide tables laden with Terran delicacies hastily unloaded from the Corps transport for the occasion. A dozen grotesquely shaped fountains spread a fine mist and an odor of sulphur across the festive scene.

Beyond the high spike-topped wall, the ominous shape of an immense brass-colored idol reared up half a mile away. Its ferocious sculptured grin glowing in the glare of spotlights, its right arm raised in the Hoogan royal salute—elbow straight out, forearm pointing upward with fingers spread, the left hand gripped the right biceps.

Magnan shuddered.

"That beastly idol—it's sub-Hoogan," Magnan commented. "Isn't that smoke coming out of its nostrils?"

Retief sniffed. "Something's burning," he agreed.

II

A dark figure stepped from dense shadow at Magnan's elbow. "Only old newsbabers you scent," it rumbled. "Our Hoogan Kods are uzeful; they serve as gommunity inzinerators."

"Odom-Glom! You startled me!" Magnan chirped. He slapped at an insect that buzzed about his face. "I do hope the evening is a big success. It was so thoughtful of his Arrogance to allow the Corps to act as host tonight; such a gesture of acceptance—sort of."

"Reverze hosbitality iz an old Hoogan gustom," Odom-Glom said. "It would be a kood itea to know all our old Hoogan gustoms, zo az not to end up lige the lasd Derran Tiplomat."

"Yes, it was unfortunate about Ambassador Straphanger's predecessor getting excommunicated, and all. But really, how was he to know he was supposed to fill the Episcopal begging bowl with hundred-credit notes?"

"It wasn't zo much not contributink; but pourink the canned beans in spoiled the bill His Arrokanze had planted as a hint."

"A bad scene," Magnan agreed. "But I'm sure this evening will smooth everything over."

The orchestra began tuning up and lugubrious notes groaned across the lawn. Armed Episcopal guards were taking up their posts, and sarong-clad diplomats were forming a receiving line by a stone arch opening through which the dignitaries would arrive.

"I must hurry alonk now and zee to the kun emplacements," Odom-Glom said. "One lasd suggestion: wordly goods of course mean nothing to His Arrokanze, but the deadliest of the zinz is Ztinchinezz. His Arrokanze detests a tightwad." He moved off, chains clashing.

"The ambassador's not out yet," Magnan noted nervously. "Gracious, I hope he puts in an appearance before Bishop Ai-Poppy-Googy arrives. I dread the prospect of having to engage His Arrogance in light chit-chat."

"According to the Post Report, dealing with the Bishop is very simple," Retief said. "Just give him everything in sight, and if that doesn't satisfy him, give him some more."

"I can see that you're finally getting the hang of diplomacy, Retief," Magnan said approvingly. "Still, I'm worried."

"Since it's your job as protocol officer to soften up difficult guests," Retief said, "why not meet the Bishop at the gate and try out a few racy stories on him?"

"I hardly imagine that the Chief of State of a Theocracy would react to biological anecdotes," Magnan said stiffly.

"Oh, biology is a perfectly clean subject here on Hoog; but don't bring up cooking in polite conversation. According to the handbook, there's an unspoken agreement among the cultured element that the stork brings the goodies."

"Really? Heavens, and all the cookies are stamped 'Made in Hong Kong'! I'll have to tell the cook to substitute blintzes. While I'm attending to that, you'd best take your post at the gate. You'll handle the first shift tonight. I'll send Stringwhistle along to relieve you in an hour."

"I could delay the Bishop a few minutes for you," Retief offered as they crossed to the gate. "Suppose I start by demanding to see his invitation."

"None of your ill-timed japes, Retief! After the last mission's fiasco, establishing a friendly rapport with the Bishop tonight could mean promotions all around."

"I think the traditional lawn party is a little too subtle for a fellow like the Bishop. We should have used a simple symbolism—like a few rounds of heavy artillery lobbed into the palace grounds."

"Hardly the diplomatic approach," Magnan sniffed. "For centuries now it's been understood that if enough diplomats go to parties, everything will come right in the end."

"I wonder if the Hoogans understand that tradition?"

"Certainly; after all, we're all fellow beings—brothers under the skin, as it were."

"In this case, the skin is an inch thick and tougher than armorplast. I'm not sure we can pentrate to the brotherhood layer in time to stop bloodshed."

"Actually, I rather look forward to matching epigrams with His Arrogance tonight," Magnan said loftily, turning to scan the gardens. "As you know, I'm always at my sparkling best with high-ranking guests—and, of course, mere size and strength fail utterly to intimidate me."

Magnan turned at a sound behind him, uttered a strangled yelp, and trampled a Hoog waiter's foot as he leaped back from the spectacle of a seven-foot high, six-foot wide Hoog wrapped in cloth of gold. The monster's gilded features included one-inch nose holes, huge, watery, reddish eyes and a wide mouth set in a formal grimace to display polished gold-capped teeth. Two clusters of ringed fingers gripped the hilt of an immense two-edged sword.

"Somethink smells pat!" the apparition bellowed. He leaned forward, sniffed vigorously at Magnan and snorted.

"Horriple!" he announced, elbowing Magnan aside. "Ko away, vellow! You're invested with an acute P.O.!"

"Why, Your Arrogance—it's just a touch of skin bracer in back of my ear."

"It smelts like pargain night in a choy house. Where's Ambassador Hapstrinker? I drust you have blenty of food reaty. I unterstant you Derries take a kreat interesd in gooking." The Bishop winked a damp, pink eye, rammed Magnan under the ribs, and guffawed comfortably.

"Oof!" Magnan said. "Why, Your Arrogance!"

The Bishop was already striding toward the nearest table, his escort of armed and helmeted guards trailing behind, fingering scimitars and eyeing the diplomats supiciously.

"I . . . I think I'll just scoot along and see to the refreshments," Magnan bleated. "Retief, you accompany His Arrogance and keep him amused until help arrives—I mean, until the ambassador puts in an appearance!" He fled.

The Bishop dipped a boneless finger into a large crystal container of cheese sauce, studied it at arm's length, sniffed it, then, with a flick of a limber wrist, spattered it across the ruffled shirt fronts and glassy smiles of the diplomats strung out in the receiving line.

"Who are these loavers?" he demanded loudly. "Bropaply relatives, waitink arount for handouts. I have the zame proplem. Or had the zame proplem, I should zay. Two weeks ako was Zelf-Denial Feztival. I made the subreme sagrifize ant offered the entire lot to the anzestral spirids."

"Giving up your relatives for Lent is quite an idea," Retief said. "It could catch on."

The Bishop picked up a plate of dainty sandwiches, spilled the food off, sniffed the plate, and took a small bite. "I've heard a kreat teal about Derran tishes," he said, chewing noisily. "A bit too crizp, but not pat." He took a second nip from the thin porcelain and offered it to Retief.

"Have a bite," he invited genially.

"No thanks, I filled up on a beer bottle just before Your Arrogance arrived," Retief countered. "Try the dinner plates. They're said to be an epicure's delight."

There was a sudden stir from the vicinity of the wide terrace doors. Ambitious diplomatic underlings sprang to positions of eager anticipation, their delighted smiles ready. The squat figure of Career Minister Straphanger, Terrestrial Ambassador Extraordinary and Minister Plenipotentiary to Hoog waddled into view, stylishly decked out in a short but heavily brocaded Hoogan longhi, a brilliant red sash which all but dragged the ground, and jeweled sandals. At his side puffed a companion of almost identical build and garb, distinguished only by a mop of vivid orange hair. Magnan trailed by two yards.

"Ah, the ambassador is twints?" the Bishop inquired, moving toward the approaching pair.

"No, that's Mrs. Straphanger," Retief said. "If I were Your Arrogance I'd ditch that saucer; she's fierce when aroused."

"Ah, the edernal female, ever conzerned with food gonzervation." The Bishop tossed a crust of the plate in back of a flowering bush.

"Ah, there, Ambassador Strakhumper!" he bellowed. "And your charmink cow! She will be litterink zoon, I trust?"

"Littering? How's that?" Straphanger stared around in confusion.

"I azzume you keep your cows pregnant?" the Bishop boomed. "Or possibly thiz one is over-aged. Bud no matter; doubtless she waz a gread broducer in her day."

"Well, I never!" Mrs. Straphanger snapped, bridling.

"By the way," Ai-Poppy-Googy went on, "I hate to diguss finanzes over food, zo I suggesd we deal with the broplem of an abbrobriate kift ad onze. I am of gourse quite brebared to vorget the drivial misunterstantink with the former ampassator ant agcepd any zum in egzess of one million gredits withoud quibblink."

"One million credits?" Straphanger babbled. "Gift?"

"Of gourse, if you wish to avoid aquirink a reputation az a piker, an egstra million would not be taken amiss."

"A million credits of Corps funds? But . . . but whatever for?"

"Ah, ah," the Bishop waggled an admonitory tactile member. "No pryink into Hoogan internal matters!"

"Oh, no, indeed. Your Arrogance! I only meant . . . what's the occasion? For the gift. I mean."

"It's Tuesday."

"Oh."

The Bishop nodded placidly. "Luggy you didn't throw thiz affair on Wentsday; thad's douple gifd day." He plucked a glass from a tray offered by a bearer, emptied the contents on the lawn and nipped a chip from the edge with his polished metallic teeth, munching thoughtfully.

"Lackink in flavor," he commented.

"My best crystal," Mrs. Straphanger gasped. "All the way from Brooklyn, yet, and like a goat he's eating it!"

"A koat?" The Bishop eyed her suspiciously. "I don't belief I know the term."

"It's a . . . a sort of gourmet," Straphanger improvised. Sweat was glistening on his forehead. "Known for its discriminating tastes."

"Now, about the matter of a bension," the Bishop continued. "I zee no neet of oztentation. A mere thousant a day would suvvize as a token of Corps ezteem."

"A thousand what a day?" The ambassador inquired around a frozen diplomatic grin which exposed old-fashioned removable dentures.

"Gredits, of gourse. And then there is the matter of zupzidies to Hoogan industry; zay vivty thousant a month. Ton'd give a thoughd to atminisdration; just make the cheggs payable to me perzonally—"

"Hoogan industry? But I was given to understand there are no industries here on Hoog."

"That's why we reguire a zupzidy," the Bishop said blandly.

Straphanger hitched his smile in place with an effort.

"Your Arrogance, I'm here merely to establish friendly relations, to bring Hoog into the mainstream of Galactic cultural life—"

"What coult be frientlier than money?" the Bishop inquired in a loud, final-sounding voice.

"Well," Straphanger conceded, "we might arrange a loan—"

"An oudright krant iz zo much zimpler," the Bishop pointed out.

"Of course, it would mean extra staff, to handle the administrative load." Straphanger rubbed his hands together, a speculative gleam in his eye. "Say twenty-five for a start."

The Bishop turned as a mediumsized Hoog in tight, black and silver vestments came up, growled in his ear and waved a rubbery arm toward the house.

"What?" the Bishop exploded. He swivelled on Straphanger. "You are harporink tapoo greatures? Givink aid and gomfort to untesirable elements? Sharink your zubstanze with minions of the opposition?"

"Your Arrogance!" Straphanger's voice quavered against the rising roar of the outraged cleric. "I don't understand! What did that fellow say?"

The Bishop bawled commands in Hoogan. His escort scattered and began beating the bushes which rimmed the garden. The ambassador trotting at his side, the guest of honor strode to the laden refreshment tables, and began stuffing in fragile china, muttering to himself.

"Your Arrogance," Straphanger panted. "If I could just have some explanation! I'm sure it's all just a ghastly mistake! What are these men searching for? I assure you—"

"Out of the gootnezz of my heart I welgomed you to Hoog!" the Bishop roared. "As a great gompliment to you, I abzorbed your language! I was even ready to agzept cash, the zubreme chesture! And now I find that you openly gonzort with the enemies of the Kods!"

Standing on the sidelines of the verbal fray, Retief glanced around the garden. He spotted a fountain in the shape of a two-headed Hoogan dwarf with oversized teeth and belly, and moved over to it.

There was a tug at his sandal lace. He looked down. Two bright eyes at the ends of wirelike stalks stared up appealingly from a clump of grass. He glanced around—all eyes were on the Bishop.

"Are you looking for me?" Retief asked softly.

"Right!" a squeaky voice piped. "You're a hard man to have a quiet chat with, Mr. . . . ahh."

"Retief."

"How do, Retief. My name's Jackspurt. The boys appointed me spokesman to tell you Terries about what's going on. After all, I guess us Spism's got a few rights, too."

"If you can explain what's going on in this filbert factory, I'll be forever in your debt, Jackspurt. Speak your piece."

"It's the Hoogans; they don't give us a minute's peace. Talk about persecution! Do you know those psalm-singing hippos are blaming us for everything from sour milk to loss of potency? It's getting where it's not safe to take a stroll after sundown.''

"Hold on, Jackspurt. Maybe you'd better fill me in on some background. Who are you? Why are the Hoogans after you? And where did you learn to speak Terran with that flawless enunciation of consonants?''

"I used to be a mascot on a Terry trader; I stowed away when she landed here for emergency repairs. It was a great life; but after a while I got homesick for good old Hoog—you know how it is—''

"You're a native of this charming world?''

"Sure—us Spism's have been around longer than the Hoogs. And we got along for thousands of years with no trouble. The Hoogs took the surface, and we settled in nice and comfy underground. Then they got religion and it's been hell ever since.''

"Hold on, Jackspurt. I always heard that religion exercised a beneficent influence on those fortunate enough to possess it.''

"That depends on which side you're on.''

"That's a point.''

"But I haven't given you the big picture yet. These Hoogan priests launched a full-scale propaganda campaign—painted up a lot of religious art with pictures of Spisms poking pitchforks at Hoogs, and pretty soon it got so even the average Hoog in the street started jumping and making X's in the air and mumbling spells everytime one of us came up for a breath of fresh air. The next thing we knew, it was full-scale war! I'm telling you, Retief, us Spisms are in bad shape—and it's gotta get worse!''

A guard was working his way toward the ogre fountain.

"Jiggers, the gendarmes," Retief said. "You'd better get out of sight, Jackspurt. They're beating the bushes for you. Why don't we continue this later."

The Spism whisked back under cover. "But this is important, Retief!" Jackspurt's voice emanated from the brush. "The boys are counting on me."

"Shh! Watch me and take your cue."

Magnan had turned and was eyeing Retief suspiciously. He stepped to his junior's side.

"Retief, if you're mixed up in this mix-up . . ."

"Me, Mr. Magnan? Why, I just arrived this afternoon the same time you did."

"Magnan!" Straphanger's voice cut through the hubbub. "The Bishop informs me that some sort of demonic creature was seen here on the Embassy grounds this evening! Of course we know nothing about it, but His Arrogance has drawn the unfortunate implication that we're consorting with denizens of the netherworld!" He lowered his voice as Magnan drew close. "Superstitious poppycock, but we've got to play along. You and the others spread out and go through a show of looking for this mythical imp. I'll pacify His Arrogance."

"Certainly, Mr. Ambassador. But . . . ah . . . what if we find it?"

"Then you're an even greater idiot than I suspect!" Straphanger twisted his working smile into position and turned back to the Bishop.

"Retief, you start along there," Magnan indicated the front of the house. "I'll go poke about in the bushes. And whatever you do, don't turn up anything—like that ghastly creature we encountered upstairs." A startled look spread across his face. "Good Lord, Retief! Do you suppose—?"

"Not a chance. I picture something more like a medium-sized dragon."

"Still . . . perhaps I'd better mention it to the ambassador."

"And confirm the Bishop's opinion? Very courageous of you. Mind if I stick around and watch?"

"On the other hand, he's a busy man," Magnan said hurriedly. "After all, why bother him with trivia?" He hurried off to take up a position near the Bishop and make a show of stooping and peering among the conifer-like hedges.

Retief sauntered back to the table deserted now except for a lone Hoogan bearer at the far end gathering empties onto a wide tray and tossing damp paper napkins into a capacious waste-paper receptacle. Retief picked up an empty sandwich plate, said "hsst!" The Hoogan looked up as Retief tossed the plate, dropped the big paper bag and caught the tossed crockery.

"Here's some more," Retief offered helpfully. He gathered up and handed over a pair of saucers, three empty glasses and a couple of cheese sandwiches each minus one bite. "You'd better hump along now and police up behind His Arrogance," he suggested. "He's leaving a trail of saucer rims behind him—doesn't seem to like the floral design."

"You dry dell me my chop?" the Hoogan demanded truculently as Retief fumbled a spoon and let it drop to the grass just under the edge of the hanging table cloth.

"Certainly not, old boy," Retief reassured the glowering local. He stopped for the spoon, caught a glimpse of an eye peering from the shadows.

"Get in the bag," he hissed from the corner of his mouth.

"Who you talg to?" the servant ducked and stared under the table. Behind him, the paper-trash container rustled softly as the Spism whisked into it.

"Just addressing a few words to the spoon god," Retief said blandly. "Bad luck to drop a spoon, you know."

"Yes?" the Hoogan said. He leaned against the table, got out a much-used toothpick and began plying it on his unpolished teeth. "You voreigners kot grazy iteas. Efrypoty know kood lug trob sboon, bat lug trob forg." He carefully examined the tip of the toothpick.

"Back home, falling from a ten-story building is considered an inauspicious omen," Retief rambled on, watching the armed Episcopal Guards as they worked closer. One came over to the table, gave Retief a sharp look, thrust his head under the table, and then reached down to check the paper-trash container.

"How about a little refreshment?"

Retief picked up a cup, dipped it full from a bowl of thick purple punch, took a step toward the warrior and seemed to trip; the sticky fluid struck the Hoogan just below the clasp holding the rainbow-hued cape, spread out in an interesting pattern across his polished breastplate. The bearer grabbed up his tray and bag and backed off hurriedly as the spluttering guard slapped limber fingers at the purple mess.

"Itiot! Clumpsy oaf!" he choked angrily.

"What? Boozink on tudy?" a vast voice boomed. The Bishop bellied past Retief, planted himself before the confused Hoogan. "The benalty is boilink in oil!" he roared. "Take him away!"

III

Other guardsmen closed in and grabbed their unfortunate fellow.

"That was my fault, Your Arrogance," Retief started. "I offered him—"

"You would inderfere with the Ebiscobal administration of justize?" the Bishop bellowed, turning on Retief. "You have the demerity to sugchest that the Ebiscobal judgment is fallible?"

"Not exactly; you're just wrong," Retief said. "I spilled the punch on him."

The Bishop's face purpled; his mouth worked. He swallowed.

"It's ben zo long zinze anyone condraticded me," he said mildly, "that I've vorkotten the bunishment." He waved two fingers in blessing. "You are apzolved, my zon," he said airily. "In vact, I apzolv you for the whole weekent. Have fun; it's on the house."

"Why, isn't that gracious of His Arrogance," Magnan chirped, popping up beside the Bishop. "What a pity we didn't find the demon; but I—"

"That reminds me," the Bishop said ominously. He fixed an eye on Ambassador Straphanger as the senior diplomat came up. "I'm still waitink for results!"

"Look here, Your Arrogance! How can we find a demon if there's no demon here?"

"That's *your* broblem!"

There was a yell from the gate. Two guards were man-handling the bearer with the waste-paper bag, who jerked away, making indignant noises. The bag fell, split open, spilling garbage from the midst of which the fugitive Spism burst, sending scraps flying in every direction.

With a bound, it was past the astonished guards and heading for the rear gate. More guards appeared in its path, jerking long-barrelled guns from tooled holsters. A shot seared a long gouge in the deep grass, narrowly missing other Episcopal retainers dashing up to get a crack at the action. The Bishop yelled, waving his boneless arms.

Cut off, the Spism veered, dashed from the house, but was met by a squad charging out from inside. A near-miss smashed dishes on the table behind Magnan, who yelped and hit the dirt.

The Spism skittered, took evasive action, headed for the flower-decked gate letting out onto the drive. The guards were all behind it now, the way clear. With a tremendous yell, Bishop Ai-Poppy-Googy whipped his giant sword out and leaped to intercept the fleeing creature. As he bounded past Retief, the latter pivoted, and thrust out a foot. He hooked the Espiscopal leg just above a flare-topped, bejeweled pink leather shoe. His Arrogance dived forward, struck medals-first, and skidded on his face under the table.

"Why, hi there," Magnan's voice piped under the muffling canopy of the drooping tablecloth. "Just a minute, and I'll scroonch over—"

The Bishop roared and rose up, the table lifting with him; dishes, glasses, and food cascaded off on Magnan, who was still crouching on the ground. With a surge, the Bishop hurled the board aside and roared again, while whirling to confront the dancing figure of

Ambassador Straphanger, who flapped a napkin at the mud on the ornate conicals of the guest of honor.

"Treazon!" Ai-Poppy-Googy bellowed. "Azzazzints! Murderers! Achents of the Unterworlt! Obstructors of chustist! Heretics!"

"Now, now, Your Arrogance! Don't get upset—"

"Upzet! This iz maybe a choke?" The Bishop dashed the muddied cloth from Straphanger's hand. He bent down, snatched up his sword and waved it overhead. The Episcopal Guard was closing in quickly now.

"I hereby eggsgommunigate the lot of you!" the Bishop yelled. "No food, no water, no bolice brotection! Alzo, you will be publicly eggsecuted! Boys, round zem up!"

Guns were suddenly leveled at the huddle of diplomats surrounding the ambassador. Magnan yelped. Straphanger's wattles quivered.

"Ton'd miss this one!" Ai-Poppy-Googy indicated Retief. "It was his foot I fell over!" A guard poked a gun into Retief's side.

"Ah, I think Your Arrogance is foregetting that Mr. Retief has an Episcopal dispensation," Straphanger said brightly. "Retief, if you'll just run along to my office and send out a code two-oh-three—or is it three-oh-two—or—anyway, a call for aitch ee ell pee—"

"He'll ko along with the rest of you scoundrels!" the Bishop yelled. Half a dozen armed Hoogans were herding the remainder of the staff up to join the group now.

"Any more insite?"

"No, Your Arrokants," the captain of the guard reported. "Only a few zervants."

"Poil them in oil for azzociatink with azzazzints! As for the rest of you—"

"Your Arrogance," Straphanger spoke up. "Naturally, I don't mind dying, if its Your Arrogance's pleasure, but then we won't be able to give you the gifts and things, will we?"

"Tamn!" Ai-Poppy-Googy threw his sword down, narrowly missing Magnan's foot. "I forgot about the gifts!" He looked thoughtful. "Look, zuppose I make arranchmends for you to write a few chegs in your zell before the eggzecution?"

"Oh, I'm afraid that wouldn't do at all, Your Arrogance. I need the Embassy seal, and the check verifying machine, and the code books and—"

"Well . . . bossibly I might make an egzeption; I'll defer punishment until the cash arrives."

"Sorry, Your Arrogance, but I wouldn't ask you to deviate from tradition just to accommodate me. No, we're all excommunicated, so I suppose we may just as well get comfortable and start starving—"

"Holt it! Don't rush me! Who's doing the eggsgommunigatink, you or me?"

"Oh, you are."

"Brecizely! And I zay you're not eggsgommunigated!" The Bishop stared around truculently. "Now, about the gifd! You can deliver the two million immediately; I juzt happened to pring an armored gar alonk—"

"TWO million? But you said one million!"

"This is touple-gift day."

"But you said Wednesday was double-gift day. This is only Tuesday."

"It's now Wentsday, by Ebiscobal decree," the Bishop said, raising his sword.

"But you can't—I mean, how can you?"

"Calendar reform," Ai-Poppy-Googy said. "Lonk overdue."

"Well, I suppose it could be arranged."

"Kood! I herepy grant you an Ebiscobal rebrieve. Put that toesn't inglude the resd of these untesireaples!" the Bishop waved a hand. "Drake them away, poys!"

"Ah . . . I'm grateful for the pardon, I'm sure," Straphanger said, gaining confidence rapidly; "but of course I won't be able to process the paper work properly without my staff."

Ai-Poppy-Googy glared with large, damp red eyes. "All right! Keep them! They're all rebrieved egzebd thad one!" He aimed a finger at Retief like a gun. "I have sbezial blans for him!" the guards shifted their attention to Retief ringing him in with aimed guns.

"Maybe His Arrogance would be just a teeny bit lenient this time," Magnan suggested, dabbing at a smear of liver paste along his bare arm, "if Mr. Retief apologized and promised never to do it again."

"Do whad akain?" the Bishop demanded.

"Trip you," Magnan said. "You know, like he did just now."

"He dribbed me?" Ai-Poppy-Googy choked. "On burpose?"

"Why, ah, it must have been a mistake—" Straphanger started.

"Your Arrogance has such a keen sense of humor,

I'm sure you'll see the comic aspect of it, if you just think about it," Magnan offered.

"Retief! Did you—I mean, surely you didn't." Straphanger choked.

"Well!" Magnan said indignantly. "I was lying right there."

"Zearch him!" the Bishop bellowed. Guards jumped forward; busy hands grabbing at Retief's kilt-pockets, almost at once came upon the folded paper the Spism had dropped as it fled his room.

"Ah-hah!" the Bishop pounced. He opened the paper and read the message.

"A gonsbirazy!" he yelled. "Unter my very nose! Put the ironts on him!"

"I must protest!" Straphanger spoke up. "You can't go about chaining up diplomats every time a little indiscretion is committed! Leave the matter to me, Your Arrogance; I'll see that a sharp entry goes in his record."

"The Kods will nod be denied their tue!" Ai-Poppy-Googy roared. "Domorrow is the Krant Vesti-fal of Wentstay—"

"Tomorrow's Thursday," Magnan interjected.

"Domorrow is Wentstay! Today is Wentstay! I herepy teclare a whole weeg of Wentstays, plast it! Now, as I was sayink—this Derran will bartizibate in the vestifal! Zuch is the holy will! No more arku-ments!"

"Oh, he'll be taking part in a ceremony!" Straphanger said in a relieved tone. "Well, goodness, I suppose we can spare him long enough for that." He offered a small diplomatic chuckle. "The Corps is always ready to promote worship in whatever form, of course.''

''The only drue Kods are the Hookan Kods, py the Kods!'' the Bishop boomed. ''Any more of your Derran heresy and I'll referse my tisbenzation! Now dake thiz one to the demple and brebare him vor the rides of Wentstay! The resd of you will remain unter arresd, undil the will of the Kods is known!''

''Mr. Ambassador,'' Magnan quavered, tugging at Straphanger's arm, ''do you think you should allow them—''

''Merely letting His Arrogance save face,'' Straphanger said in a confidential tone. He winked at Retief. ''Don't worry, my boy; good experience for you. You'll get an inside view of the Hoogan religious concept at work.''

''But—but, what if they . . . I mean, boiling in oil is so *permanent*,'' Magnan persisted.

''Quiet, Magnan! I'll have no whiners in my organization!''

''Thanks for thinking of me, Mr. Magnan,'' Retief said. ''I still have my good-luck charm.''

''Charm?'' Magnan looked blank.

''Witchgraft?'' the Bishop boomed. ''I zuzbegted as much!'' He turned a large, red eye on Straphanger.

''I'll pe zeeing you at the zeremony! Ton'd pe lade!'' He eyed Retief. ''Are you goming beazevully?''

''In view of the number of guns aimed at me,'' Retief said, ''I sincerely hope so.''

IV

The cell was narrow, dark, damp, and unfurnished except for a plain table with a bottle of bitter-smelling wine and a narrow bench on which Retief sat. His wrists were chained together, and he was listening to a muffled tapping which sounded faintly from beyond the walls. It had been going on now for twelve hours, he estimated—long enough for the Hoogans to have completed their preparations for the religious ceremonies in which he was to play a part.

The tapping abruptly changed tone and sounded louder, nearer. There was a light clatter, as of pebbles tossed on the floor. A moment later, there was a soft scraping sound, a rasping like fingernails on a blackboard; then silence.

"Retief, are you there?" a thin voice chirped through the pitch darkness.

"Sure, Jackspurt! Come on in and join the party. I'm glad to see you eluded the gendarmes."

"Those slobs! Hah. But listen, Retief, I've got bad news."

"Press on, Jackspurt; I'm listening."

"This is Festival Day—and Old Googy's scheduled the big all-out push for today, to tie in with the mumbo-jumbo. The Hoogs have been building this king-size fumigator for months—stacking it full of rubbish, old rags, worn-out tires, and what not. At the height of the big ceremony they set the stuff on fire and start the smoke-pumps going. They got a system of pipes laid out leading into the burrows, see? There won't be a safe spot for Spisms for miles around. Our boys will come stampeding out of their hideaways, some of which have been in the family for generations, and zowie! the Bishop's troops lower the boom! It'll be the finish of us Spisms!''

"That's a heart-rending story, Jackspurt—or it would be, if I weren't in such a heart-rending position myself at the moment.''

"Yeah, the Wednesday Rites. You scheduled for the matinee or the big evening spectacular?'' Jackspurt broke off as clankings sounded from beyond the door.

"Holy Moses, Retief! Time's up! They're here! Listen, I was supposed to brief you in, like, but it took longer'n I figured tunneling through that wall, and then I got to yakking—''

A key scraped in the keyhole.

"Listen! Did you drink any of what's in the bottle?''

"No.''

"Good! It's doped! When I leave, dump it! You'll have to pretend you can't talk or the jig's up! Put on a kind of zombie routine, see? Whatever they tell you—do it! If they get the idea you're putting something over, it's zkkk! for every Terry on Hoog! And remember! Keep your head down and your arms and legs tucked in—''

The lock turned with a rasp of rusty tumblers.

"Gotta go! Good luck!'' Jackspurt scrambled and was gone.

Retief took a step, grabbed up the bottle, poured it down the three-inch hole through which his visitor had fled.

Light blazed as the heavy door swung inward. Three hooded Hoogan pikemen came into the cell, followed by a black-robed priest. Retief stood holding the empty bottle, his body concealing Jackspurt's escape route.

"How to you veel, Derry?" the priest inquired, looking Retief over. He stepped in, thumbed Retief's eyelid up, grunted, and took the empty bottle from his hand.

"Goked to the eyeprows," he stated.

"Are you zure?" a pikeman challenged. "I ton'd drust these voreigners."

"Nadurally I'm zure; the hypervasgulations of the subraoccibital whatchamagallids is dypical; a glassic gase. Dake him alonk."

Hemmed in by pikes, Retief followed along a torch-lit passage, up winding stone stairs, to emerge abruptly into blinding light and the susurrus of a multitude of voices, above which one rose like the boom of surf:

". . . azzure you, my tear Ampassador Hipstinker, our brinzibal tiety, Uk-Ruppa-Tooty, is nod only a hantzome degoration and a gonstand reminter to the bobulaze that the nexd tithe is tue—he also broduzes oragular stadements rekularly effry Wentstay at one B. M. Of gourse, it is nod always kiven to us to untersdant what he's dalkink apout, bud the evvegd on the beasandry is most zaludory."

Squinting against the sudden sunlight, Retief made out the resplendently robed figure of the Bishop, seated under a vast parasol on a massive throne of dark wood carved with designs of intertwined serpents. He was flanked on the left by the Terran Ambassador and on the right by a huddle of lesser diplomats. The group was ringed in by stony-faced Hoogan guards with bared scimitars.

The priest who had accompanied Retief bowed unctiously before the Episcopal throne. "Your Arrokanze, the Zoon-to-pe-Alefated One is here," he indicated Retief with a wave of the hand.

"Is he . . . ah . . . ?" Ai-Poppy-Googy looked inquiringly at the escort.

"A glassig gase of hypervasgulations of the think-amapops," a pikeman spoke up.

"Poil thad one in oil," the Bishop said, frowning. "He dalgs doo mudge."

"You appear a bit peaked, Retief," Straphanger commented. "I trust you slept well last night? Comfortable quarters and all that?"

Retief stared absently past the ambassador's left ear.

"Retief, the ambassador's addressing you," Magnan said sharply.

"Brobably he's losd in metitations," Ai-Poppy-Googy said hastily. "On with the zeremony."

"Perhaps he's sick," Magnan said. "Here, you'd better sit down."

"Ah-ah," Ai-Poppy-Googy held up a limber hand. "The mosd imbortand bortion of the zeremony yed remaints to pe zeleprated."

"Ah, yes, of course," Straphanger sat back. "I'd quite forgotten, Your Arrogance." He glanced around. "We'll have a magnificent view of the proceedings from here."

At a prod from an Episcopal Guard, Retief turned—and found himself staring directly into the vast brass smile of the Hoogan idol.

From Retief's elevated viewpoint atop the two-hundred foot high ziggurat, the head of the god reared up another fifty feet. It was an immense stylized Hoogan face of polished yellow metal, the vast hand upraised beside it. The eyes were deep hollows at the back of which a sullen red glow gave an impression of malignant intelligence. The noseholes, a yard each in diameter, drooled a thin trickle of smoke which coiled up past soot-streaked cheeks to dissipate in the clear air. The mouth which split the massive head, gaped in a crocodile smile set with spade-shaped teeth with spaces between them beyond which was visible a curve of polished esophagus agleam with leaping reflections from inner fires below.

Two lesser priests stepped forward to hang assorted ornaments on Retief's shoulders and neck. Another taking up a position before him, intoned a repetitious chant. Somewhere, drums commenced a slow tattoo. A murmur passed over the crowd packing the slopes of the ziggurat and the plaza below. Standing at ease, apparently ignoring his surroundings, Retief noted a two-foot wide trough cut in the stone platform at his feet, deepening and slanting down as it ran to the abrupt drop-off ten yards distant. An acolyte was busy pouring oil into the hollow and spreading it with swipes of his hands.

"Just what does this phase of the ceremonial involve?" Straphanger inquired in a tone of synthetic diplomatic interest.

"Waid and zee," Ai-Poppy-Googy said shortly.

"Mr. Ambassador," Magnan whispered hoarsely. "His hands are chained!"

"Part of the ceremony, no doubt."

"And that groove," Magnan went on. "It runs from Retief right over to the edge . . . just above that horrible ig-bay outh-may."

"Yes, yes, you needn't play the part of a tourist

guide, Magnan. By the way," Straphanger lowered his voice, "you didn't happen to bring along a hip flask, I suppose?"

"Why, no, Mr. Ambassador. I have a nice antiviral nasal spray, if that would help. But about that chute—"

"Warm, isn't it, Your Arrogance?" Straphanger turned to the Bishop. "A bit dry, too."

"You ton'd lige our Hoogan weather?" the Bishop asked in an ominous tone.

"No, no, it's fine. I love it when it's nice and hot and dry."

"Ah, Your Arrogance," Magnan spoke up. "Just what is it you have in mind doing with Retief?"

"Iz kreat honor," the Bishop said.

"I'm sure we're all delighted at this opportunity for one of our group to get an inside view of the Hoogan religious philosophy," Straphanger said sharply. "Now kindly sit down and stop that infernal chattering," he added behind his hand.

The Bishop was speaking quickly in Hoogan; the attendant priests urged Retief forward a step, grasped his arms and deftly placed him face-down in the oiled channel. The rattle of the drums rose to a crescendo. Flabby Hoogan hands shoved Retief forward down the steepening slope.

"Mr. Ambassador!" Magnan's voice rose to a shrill bleat. "I do believe they're feeding him to that monster!"

"Nonsense, Magnan!" Straphanger's suety voice countered. "It's all symbolic, I'm sure. And I might point out that you're hardly conducting yourself like a seasoned diplomat."

"Stop!" Retief, sliding rapidly toward the edge,

heard Magnan's yelp and the scuffle of rapid footsteps.

There was a wet splat! and bony elbows slammed against him. He twisted, caught a glimpse of Magnan's white face, open mouth and clutching hands as together they shot over the edge and out in a graceful arc toward the waiting jaws of Uk-Ruppa-Tooty.

V

Keep your arms and legs tucked in, Jackspurt had said; Retief had time to grit his teeth—then he was hurtling past the tombstone-sized fangs, Magnan's hands still clutching his legs. They dropped down into a blast of searing heat and light, then suddenly, stunningly, they slammed against and through a yielding, shredding network of filaments as fine as spiderwebs. Retief came to a stop, rebounded, caught at a heavier cable that brushed his hand, and was clinging to a coarse rope ladder, Magnan's weight dangling from his heels.

"Bullseye!" a tiny voice screeched almost in his ear. "Now let's get out of here fast, before they dope out what happened!"

Retief found a foothold in the snarl of rope, reached down and hauled the rag-limp second secretary to his side. The heat from below was scorching, even here in the shelter of a bulge in the god's throat.

"Wha-what-bu-bu—" Magnan babbled, groping for a handhold.

"Hurry up, Retief!" Jackspurt urged. "Up here by the tonsils! It's a secret passage!"

Retief assisted Magnan in scrambling up. He

boosted him into the narrow, circular burrow that ran back through the solid metal. The Spism in the lead, they moved hurriedly away from the sound of priestly voices raised in puzzled inquiry, reached a set of cramped steps leading down.

"We're okay now," Jackspurt said. "Take a breather, and then we'll go down and meet the boys."

Later they were in a cavern floored with rough masonry, and lit by a burning wick afloat in a shallow bowl of aromatic oil. All around, twitching Spism eye-stalks stared at the intruders; the close-packed red goblin-forms of Jackspurt and his clan moved restlessly, like giant fiddler crabs on some subterranean beach. Behind them, tall, pale-blue cousins poised on yard-long legs, watched from shadowy corners. In niches and crannies in the walls, tiny green Spisms and sluggish orange forms with white spots clung, gazing. Dark purple Spisms, dangling from the ceiling like tumorous stalactites, waved their free legs hypnotically, studying the scene.

Magnan's fingers dug into Retief's arm. "G-great heavens, Retief!" he gasped out. "You—you don't suppose we've died and that my Aunt Minerva was right all along?"

"Mr. Retief, meet the boys," Jackspurt clambered up to perch on a ledge overlooking the gathering. "A lot of them are pretty shy, but they're a good-natured bunch, always a thousand laughs. When they heard you was in trouble, they all joined in to help out."

"Tell them Mr. Magnan and I said thanks," Retief said. "It was an experience we wouldn't have missed. Right, Mr. Magnan?"

"I'd certainly never miss it," Magnan swallowed

audibly. "H-how is it you can talk to these hobgoblins, Retief?" he hissed. "You haven't . . . ah . . . made some sort of pact with the powers of darkness, I trust?"

"Hey, Retief," Jackspurt said. "Your friend got some kind of race prejudice or something?"

"Heavens, no," Magnan said in a strangled voice. "Some of my best friends are fiends—I mean, in our profession, one meets—"

"Mr. Magnan is just a little confused," Retief put in. "He didn't expect to be playing such an active role in today's events."

Speaking of active, we better get you gents back to the surface fast," Jackspurt said. "The pumps will be starting up any minute now."

"Where are you going when the fumigation begins?"

"We got an escape route mapped out through the sewers that ought to bring us out in the clear a couple miles from town. We're just hoping the Hoog don't have the outfall staked out."

"Where are these smoke pumps located?" Retief asked.

"Up above—in Uk-Ruppa-Tooty's belly."

"Who's manning them?"

"A couple of priests. Why?"

"How do we get there from here?"

"Well, there's a couple passages—but we better not waste any time sight-seeing."

"Retief, are you out of your mind?" Magnan blurted. "If the priests see us, our goose will be cooked, along with the rest of our anatomies!"

"We'll try to make it a point to see them first. Jackspurt, can you get a couple of dozen volunteers?"

"You mean to climb up in that brass god? I don't know, Retief. The fellas are pretty superstitious."

"We need them to make a diversion while Mr. Magnan and I carry out the negotation—"

"Who me?" Magnan squeaked.

"Negotiation?" Jackspurt protested. "Jumping Jehosophat, how can you negotiate with a Hoog?"

"Ahem," Magnan cleared his throat. "That, Mr. Jackspurt, is after all one's function as a diplomat."

"Well . . ." Jackspurt buzzed briefly to his fellows, then hopped down from his perch as a dozen Spisms of assorted sizes and colors came forward.

"We're game, Mr. Retief. Let's go!"

The dull gleam of the metal walls of the vast chamber that was the interior of the god Uk-Ruppa-Tooty loomed out of dense shadow where Retief and Magnan crouched with their hobgoblin crew. At the center of the gloomy chamber, low-caste Hoogans labored before the open door of a giant, red-glowing furnace, tossing in armloads of rubbish, old shoes, bundled magazines, and broken plastic crockery. A layer of harsh, eye-watering smoke hung in the air. Jackspurt snorted.

"Boy, when they start pumping that stuff into the burrows . . ."

"Where are the priests?" Retief inquired in a whisper.

Jackspurt pointed to a small cubicle at the top of a flight of steps. "Up there, in the control room.

"Retief studied the layout. "Jackspurt, you and your men spread out around the room. Give me five minutes. Then take turns jumping out and making faces."

Jackspurt gave instructions to his crew; they faded away into the darkness.

"Maybe you'd better wait here," Retief suggested to Magnan.

"Where are you going?"

"I think I'd better have a chat with the ecclesiastics up in the prompting box."

"And leave me here alone, surrounded by these ghoulish Spisms?"

"All right, but keep it quiet or the smoke of burning diplomats will be added to the other fumes."

Fifty feet above the floor, Retief gripped narrow handholds, working his way around to the rear of the control box. Through the dusty windows a blue-robed Hoogan priest could be seen lounging in a bored attitude, studying a scroll. A second Hoogan, in the familiar black, stood nervously by. Suddenly the silence below was broken by a mournful wail.

"What's that!" Magnan jumped, slipped and grabbed for a secure grip on a projecting angle-iron supporting a narrow catwalk.

"Our co-workers going into action." Retief said softly. Beside the furnace door, the Hoogan workers were staring around nervously. There was another doleful moan. One of the Hoogans dropped his shovel and muttered. Retief ducked back as the blue-robed priest came to the window and peered down below. He then motioned to the other, who went to the door of the tiny chamber, opened it, stepped out on the catwalk and shouted down to the workers. One answered in defiant tones. Two of the workers started toward a door dimly visible at the far side of the furnace room. The priest shouted after them; as his bellow faded and echoed, the thin hoot of a Spism sounded, like the last wail of dying hope.

The priest jumped and whirled to dart back inside the control room. He slipped, fell from the catwalk and found himself staring directly into Magnan's startled face. He opened his mouth to roar—

Magnan whipped off his mauve cummerbund and thrust it into the gaping mouth. With a muffled grunt, the Hoogan lost his grip, fell, and slammed into the heaped rubbish with a tremendous slam. The stokers fled, shouting. The lone priest flattened his face against the window, peering down into the gloom. With a quick movement, Retief gained the catwalk, and stepped through the door. The priest whirled and leaped for a microphone-like device on the corner table. Retief eased the power pistol from his sarong and aimed it at the priest.

"I wouldn't make any announcements just yet," he said. "The results aren't all in."

"Who are you?" The Hoogan sidled toward a corner cabinet.

"If that's where you keep your prayer books, better let them lie for a while yet."

"Look here, berhabs you are unaware thad I am His Voracity, the Deacon Um-Moomy-Hooby, ant I have gonnegtions—"

"Doubtless. And don't try for the door; I have a confederate out there who's noted for his ferocity," Retief said.

Magnan came through the door, panting. Um-Moomy-Hooby backed away.

"Whad—whad do you wand?"

"I understand the god is about to utter oracular

statements, as the high point of the Wednesday services," Retief said.

"Yez—I waz jusd goink over my sgribt. Now if you'll eggsguze me I have to—"

"It just happens that it's the script we want to talk about. There are a couple of special announcements I'd like to see inserted."

"Whad? Damper with holy sgribture?"

"Nothing like that; just a good word for a group of associates of ours and possibly a short commercial for the CDT."

"Plasphemy! Herezy! Refishionizm! Nefer will I pe a barty to zuch zagrileche!"

Retief clicked off the pistol's safety catch.

"—Put, on the other hant, bosiply somethink gould pe arranched," the Deacon said hastily. "How much did you hafe in mind offerink?"

"I wouldn't think of attempting to bribe a man of the cloth," Retief said smoothly. "You're going to do this for the common welfare."

"Jusd whad is it you hafe in mind?"

"The first item is the campaign you've been waging against the Spisms."

"Ah, yez! And a wontervul jop our lats hafe peen toink, doo. Uk-Ruppa-Tooty willink, zoon we will zee them ztambed oud endirely, and virtue driumvant!"

"The CDT takes a dim view of genocide, I'm afraid. Now, my thought was that we could agree on a reasonable division of spheres of influence."

"A teal with the Bowers of Tarknezz? Are you oud of your mind?"

"Now, now," Magnan put in, "a more cooperative attitude would do Your Voracity greater credit."

"You zugchesd that the jurch should gombromize with zin?"

"Not exactly compromise," Magnan said placatingly. "Just work out a sort of peaceful coexistence plan."

"Nefer will I, as deacon, gome oud in vafor of dogetherness with Zatan'z Impz!"

"There, there, Your Voracity; if you'd just sit down across the table from them, you'd find these imps weren't bad fellows at all."

There was a soft sound from the door. Jackspurt, a jaunty, two-foot sphere of red bristles, appeared, waving his eyestalks exultantly. A looming blue Spism behind him.

"Nice going, Relief!" he called. "I see you caught one. Pitch him down after the other one, and let's clear out of here. This little diversion will give us time to get clear before the smoke starts."

"Jackspurt, do you suppose your fellows could do a fast job of shifting a few hoses around? You'll have to block off the sewers and feed the smoke off in some other direction."

"Say, that's an idea!" Jackspurt agreed. "And I think I know just the direction." He gave instructions to the big blue Spism, who hurried away.

The Deacon had retreated to a corner, eyes goggling, his hands describing mystic passes in the air. More Spisms were crowding into the room now, tall blue ones, tiny darting green ones, sluggish purple varieties—all cocking their eyestalks at the prelate.

"Help!" he croaked weakly. "The minions of the netherworlt are ubon me!"

Magnan drew out a chair from the table. "Just have a

seat, Your Voracity," he said soothingly. "Let's just see if we can't work out a *modus vivendi* suitable to all parties."

"Come to termz with the enemy? Id will mean the ent of the jurch!"

"On the contrary, Your Voracity; if you ever succeeded in eliminating the opposition, you'd be out of a job. The problem is merely to arrange matters in a civilized fashion so that everyone's interests are protected."

"You may hafe somethink there," Um-Moomy-Hooby seated himself gingerly. "But the nevariouz agtifities of these goplins musd pe kebt unter sdrigd gondrol—Ebiscobal gondrol, thad is."

"Look, my boys got to make a living," Jackspurt started.

"Zellink a vew love-botions, zerdainly," the Deacon said. "And the jurch is willink to zmile at a modezd draffic in aphrodisiags, dope, and raze-drack tips. But beddling filthy menus to teen-agers, no!

"The zame goez vor sdealing withoud a licenze, and the zale of algoholic peferaches, with the eggzebtion of small amounts of broberly aged sduff for medicinal use py the glerchy, of gourse."

"Okay, I think we can go along with that," Jackspurt said. "But you priests will have to lay off the propaganda from now on. I want to see Spisms getting better billing in church art."

"Oh, I think you could work out something lovely in little winged Spisms with haloes," Magnan suggested. "I think you owe it to them, Your Voracity, after all this discrimination in the past."

"Tevils with winks?" Um-Moomy-Hooby groaned.

"It will blay hop with our zympolizmz—put I zubboze it can pe done."

"And you'll have to have guarantees that everything from two feet under the surface on down belongs to us," Jackspurt added. "We'll leave the surface to you, and throw in the atmosphere, just so you dedicate a few easements so we can come up and sightsee now and then."

"Thad zeems egwidaple," the Deacon agreed. "Supchegd to vinal abbrofal py His Arrokanze, of gourze."

"By the way," Jackspurt asked casually, "who's next in line for the Bishop's job if anything happens to Ai-Poppy-Googy?"

"Az it habbenz, I am," Um-Moomy-Hooby said. "Why?"

"Just asking," Jackspurt said.

A loud thumping started up from the wide floor below.

"What's that?" Magnan yelled.

"The pumps," the Deacon said. "A bity so many Spisms will tie, but it is manivezdly the will of Uk-Ruppa-Tooty."

"I guess old Uk-Ruppa-Tooty had a last-minute change of heart," Jackspurt said callously. "We shifted the pipes around to feed the fumes back up into the city plumbing system. I guess there's black smoke pouring up out of every john in town by now."

"Touple-grozzer!" the Deacon leaped up, waving his arms. "The teal'z off—"

"Ah, ah, you promised, Your Voracity," Magnan chided. "And besides, Mr. Retief still has a gun."

"And now, if you'll just pick up the microphone,

Your Voracity,'' Retief said. ''I think we can initate the era of good feeling without further delay. Just keep our role quiet, and take all the credit for yourself.''

VII

''A pity about poor Ai-Poppy-Googy falling off the ziggurat when the smoke came boiling out of Uk-Ruppa-Tooty's mouth,'' Ambassador Straphanger said, forking another generous helping of Hoogan chow mein onto his plate. ''Still, one must confess it was a dramatic end for a churchman of his stature, shooting down the slide and disappearing into the smoke as he did.''

''Yez, alreaty the canonization papers are peing brebared.'' His newly installed Arrogance, Bishop Um-Moomy-Hoopy, shot a nervous glance at the Spism seated beside him. ''He'll pe the batron zaint of rehapilidated tevilz, impz, and koplins.''

''A pity you missed all the excitement, Magnan,'' Straphanger said, chewing. ''And you, too, Retief. While you absented yourselves, the Hoogan philosophy underwent a veritable renaissance—helped along, I humbly assume, by my modest peace-making efforts.''

''Hah!'' the Bishop muttered under his breath.

''Frankly, what with all the smoke, I hadn't expected the oracle's pronouncement to be quite so lucid,'' Straphanger went on, ''to say nothing of its unprecedented generosity—''

''Chenerosity?'' interrupted Um-Moomy-Hoopy,

his heavy features reflecting rapid mental recapitulation of his concessions.

"Why, yes, ceding all mineral rights to the formerly persecuted race here on Hoog—a charming gesture of conciliation."

"Mineralts rightz! Whad mineralts?"

Jackspurt, splendid in the newly tailored tunic of Chief Representative for Spismodic Affairs to the Episcopal court, spoke up from his place along the table set up on the palace terrace.

"Oh, he's just talking about the deposits of gold, silver, platinum, radium, and uranium, plus a few boulders of diamonds, ruby, and so forth that are laying around below ground. The planet's lousy with the stuff. We'll use our easements to ferry it up to the surface where the freighters will pick it up, so we won't put you Hoogs out at all."

The Bishop's alligator-hide features purpled. "You—you knew apout theze mineralts?" he choked.

"Why, didn't His former Arrogance mention it to you? That was what brought the mission here; the routine minerals survey our technical people ran from space last year showed up the deposits."

"Ant we puilt our Brincible Kod oud of prass—imborted prass at thad," the Bishop said numbly.

"Too scared of a few Spisms to dig," Jackspurt said in a stage whisper.

There was a flicker of lightning in the sky to the east. Thunder rolled. A large raindrop spattered on Straphanger's plate, followed by another.

"Oh-oh, we'd better head for cover," Jackspurt said. "I know these flash squalls; lightning out the kazoo—"

A brilliant flash cast the looming figure of the god Uk-Ruppa-Tooty into vivid silhouette against a blue-black sky. Dishes rattled on the table as sound rumbled across the sky on wooden wheels. The Bishop and his guests rose hastily, as a third jagged electrical discharge ripped across the sky—striking the giant idol full on the shoulder.

A shower of sparks flew; the Hoogan gesture of salute, pivoted slowly at the elbow. The yards-wide hand, seen edge-on with the fingers extended, swung slowly in a great arc, came to rest with the extended thumb resting firmly against the snub nose. Sparks flew as the digit was welded firmly in place.

The Bishop stared, then tilted his head back and looked up at the sky, long and searchingly.

"Chusd pedween uz men of the worlt, " he said hoarsely, "do you zubboze thad phenomenon haz any sbezial zigniviganze?"

"I think if I were you, Your Arrogance, I'd watch my step," Jackspurt said in an awed tone. "And, uh, by the way, on behalf of the Spisms, I'd like to make a contribution to the Episcopal treasury."

"Hmmm. Have you ever thought aboud tagink inzdruction?" the Bishop inquired. "I'm sure it could be arranged, and as for the little contribution you sboge of, dwenty bercend of the take would zuvvice."

They strolled off along the corridor, deep in conversation. Ambassador Straphanger hurried away to prepare his dispatches to Sector HQ, Magnan at his heels.

Retief stepped back out onto the terrace and lit up a dope-stick. Far away, Uk-Ruppa-Tooty loomed, solemnly thumbing his nose at the Episcopal Palace.

Cheerfully, Retief returned the salute.

MECHANICAL ADVANTAGE

I

"TWENTY THOUSAND years ago," said Cultural Attache Pennyfool, "this, unless I miss my guess, was the capital city of a thriving alien culture."

The half dozen Terrans—members of a Field Expeditionary Group of the Corps Diplomatique Terrestrienne—stood in the center of a narrow strip of turquoise-colored sward that wound between weathered slabs of porous, orange masonry, rusting spires of twisted metal to which a few bits of colored tile still clung, and anonymous mounds in which wildflowers nodded alien petals under the light of a swollen orange sun.

"Imagine," Consul Magnan said in an awed tone, as the party strolled on through a crumbling arcade and across a sand-drifted square. "At a time when we were still living in caves, these creatures had already developed automats and traffic jams." He sighed. "And now they're utterly extinct. The survey's life detectors didn't so much as quiver.''

''They seem to have progressed from neon to nuclear annihilation in record time.'' Second Secretary Retief commented. ''But I think we have a good chance of bettering their track record.''

''Think of it, gentlemen,'' Pennyfool called, pausing at the base of a capless pylon and rubbing his hands together with a sound like a cicada grooming its wing-cases. ''An entire city in pristine condition—nay, more, a whole continent, a complete planet! It's an archeologist's dream come true! Picture the treasures to be found: the stone axes and telly sets, the implements of bone and plastic, the artifacts of home, school and office, the tin cans, the beer bottles, the bones—oh, my, the bones, gentlemen! Emerging into the light of day after all these centuries to tell us their tales of the life and death of a culture!''

''If they've been dead for twenty thousand years, what's the point in digging around in their garbage dumps?'' an assistant Military Attache inquired *sotto voce*. ''I say Corps funds would be better spent running a little nose-to-ground reconnaissance of Boge, or keeping an eye on the Groaci.''

''Tsk, Major,'' Magnan said. ''Such comments merely serve to reinforce the popular stereotype of the crassness of the military mind.''

''What's so crass about keeping abreast of the opposition?'' the officer protested. ''It might be a nice change if we hit them first, for once, instead of getting clobbered on the ground.''

''Sir!'' Magnan tugged at the iridium-braided lapels of his liver colored informal field coverall. ''Would you fly in the face of six hundred years of tradition?''

"Now, gentlemen," Pennyfool was saying, "we're not here to carry out a full-scale dig, of course, merely to conduct a preliminary survey. But I see no reason why we should not wet a line, so to speak. Magnan, suppose you just take one of these spades and we'll poke about a bit. But carefully, mind you. We wouldn't want to damage an irreplacable art treasure.''

"Heavens, I'd love to," Magnan said as his superior offered him the shovel. "What perfectly vile luck that I happen to have a rare joint condition known as Motorman's Arm—"

"A diplomat who can't bend his elbow?" the other replied briskly. "Nonsense." He thrust the implement at Magnan.

"Outrageous," the latter muttered as his superior moved out of earshot, scanning the area for a likely spot to commence. "I thought I was volunteering for a relaxing junket, not being dragooned to serve as a navvy.''

"Your experience in digging through Central Files should serve you in good stead, Mr. Magnan," Second Secretary Retief said. "Let's just pretend we're after evidence of a political prediction that didn't pan out by someone just above you on the promotion list.''

"I resent the implication that I would stoop to such tactics," Magnan said loftily. "In any case, only an idiot would go on record with guesswork." He eyed Retief obliquely. "I, ah, don't suppose you *know* of any such idiot?''

"I did," Retief said. "But he just made Ambassador.''

"Aha!" Pennyfool caroled from a heavily silted

doorway flanked by a pair of glassless openings. "A well-nigh intact structure, quite possibly a museum. Suppose we just take a peek." The diplomats trailed their enthusiastic leader as he scrambled through into a roofless chamber with an uneven, dirt-drifted floor and bare walls from which the plaster had long since disappeared. Along one side of the room a flat-topped ridge projected a foot above the ground. Pennyfool poked a finger at a small mound atop it, exposing a lumpy object.

"Eureka!" he cried, brushing dirt away from his find. "You see, gentlemen? I've already turned up a masterpiece of the Late Meretricious!"

"I say, sir," a plump Third Secretary addressed the expedition's leader. "Since Verdigris is a virgin world, and we're the first beings to set foot here since its discovery, how does it happen the era already has a name?"

"Simple, my boy," Pennyfool snapped. "I just named it."

"Look here, sir," an eager information Agency man who had been poking at the find said, "I think there's been an error. This place isn't a museum, its a lunch counter. And the masterpiece is a plate of petrified mashed potatoes and mummified peas."

"By jove, I think you've got something there, Quagmire," a portly Admin Officer said. "Looks just like the stuff they served at the Testimonial Dinner for Ambassador Clawhammer—"

"He's right," Magnan announced from his position farther down the line. "Here's a side-order of french fries."

"Dunderheads!" Pennyfool snapped. "I'm not in

need of uninformed conjectures by amateurs in order to properly classify priceless antiquities. Kindly leave such matters to experts. Now come along. There seems to be an adjoining room with an intact roof—a room unvisited for twenty centuries! I'll wager my fig-leaf cluster to my *Grand Cordon* of the Legion d'Cosme that a thrilling discovery awaits us there!'' His staff followed him past the edge of a metal door standing half open, into a dark chamber. The next moment, pale yellowish light flooded the room.

"To stop where you are!" A weak voice hissed the words in a breathy alien tongue from behind the delegation. "To raise your digital members above your cephalic nodules or to be incinerated on the spot!"

II

A spindle-legged creature in a flaring helmet and sequinned greaves emerged from the deep shadow of the door, aiming a scatter gun carelessly at Magnan's knees.

"What's this?" Pennyfool's voice cracked on the words. "Groaci? Here?"

"Indeed, Soft One," the alien confirmed. "To comply at once with my instructions or to add your osseous components to those already interred here!"

Other gun-toting creatures appeared from alcoves and behind columns, closed in, clacking horny mandibles threateningly.

"See here, Captain," Pennyfool said in a high nervous voice to a larger than average Groaci in jeweled eye-shields who carried no weapon but an ornamental side arm. "What's the meaning of this unwarranted interference with a peaceful party of duly authorized official personnel of the Corps Diplomatique Terrestrienne?"

"The meaning, Mr. Pennyfool," the officer replied in accent-free Terran, "is that you are anticipated, forestalled, preceded." He casually waved a dope-stick in a foot-long ivory holder. "You are interlopers, trespassers on Groacian real estate. You note that out of delicacy I refrain from use of the term 'invaders.' "

"Invaders? We're scientists! Artlovers! And—"

"To be sure," the captain cut him off curtly. "However, it will be necessary for you to indulge these fancies elsewhere. Verdigris, as an unoccupied planet, has been claimed by my government. Unfortunately, we are at present unable to issue tourist visas to the curious. You will therefore repair at once to your vessel, pay the accumulated landing fees, demurrage, fines for illegal parking and lift-tax and be on your way."

"This is an outrage, you five-eyed bandit!" the assistant military attache yelled, thrusting to the fore. "This planet was discovered by a Corps scouting vessel! It belongs to us!"

"I shall overlook your tone, Major," the Groaci whispered acidly, "induced no doubt by envy at my race's superior optical endowments and simply inquire whether any Terran claim to the world was ever registered with the appropriate tribunals?"

"Of course not," Pennyfool snapped. "We didn't want every claim-jumping Tom, Dick and Irving in this end of the Arm swarming in here to see what they could loot!"

"An unfortunate oversight."

"But the Survey boat planted a claim beacon. You must have seen it."

"Dear me, now that you mention it I seem to recall my chaps vaporizing some sort of electronic noise-maker which was interfering with radio reception. Too bad that not a trace remains."

"That's a gross violation of Interplanetary Rules!"

"So? Possession is nine points of the law, Mr. Pennyfool. But enough of these pleasantries; at the moment, the matter of accounts receivable requires our attention. I'm sure you're eager to clear up the trifling indebtedness and be about your no doubt legitimate activities elsewhere."

"How . . . how much," Pennyfool asked, "is this going to cost us?"

"If one of you will hand over twenty-two thousand six hundred and four galactic credits—cash, no checks, please—you can be on your way."

"Twenty-two thousand!" Pennyfool choked on the words. "That's highway robbery!"

"Plus an additional thousand penalty fee for each insult," the captain added in an ominous whisper. "And of course I need not remind you that the demur-rage charges are piling up minute by minute."

"That's out of the question," Pennyfool gasped. "I have no such amount in my possession! We're a scientific expedition, not a party of bank messengers!"

"Too bad," the captain whispered. "In that case . . ." He made a curt gesture; armed troops stepped forward, guns at the ready.

"Stop!" Magnan yelped. "You can't just shoot diplomats down in cold blood!"

"Since higher organisms such as myself employ no vascular fluids, I am under no such restraint," the captain pointed out. "However, I agree it would be less than couth to fail to observe the forms. Accordingly, I shall refer the matter to my chief." He murmured a word to a soldier, who slung his weapon and hurried away. The captain sauntered off, humming a gay little tune to himself.

"Verdigris was supposed to be the best-kept secret of the year," Pennyfool muttered brokenly to Magnan. "Who would have dreamed the Groaci would be here ahead of us?"

"They couldn't have found it by accident," the Information Agency man said glumly. "Coincidences like that don't happen."

"You're right, Crouchwell," Pennyfool said, staring around at his staff. "Gentlemen—somebody leaked!"

"Well, gracious, don't look at me, sir," Magnan said, an indignant expression pinching his narrow features. "*I* hardly breathed a word, except to a few highly respected colleagues."

"Colleagues?" Pennyfool raised a pale eyebrow.

"Fellow diplomats; high-type chaps like Ambassador P'Yim-Yim of Yill and Slunk the Fustian Minister, and . . . and . . ."

"And?" Pennyfool prompted.

"And Consul-General Shilth," Magnan finished weakly.

"Planetary Director Shilth, if you don't mind," a voice susurrated from the doorway.

There was a stir among the troops ringing in the Terrans. A tall Groaci in an elaborately ribbed hip-cloak strolled forward, waved jauntily at Magnan, nodded to Pennyfool.

"Well, gentlemen, good of you to pay a courtesy call," he said smoothly.

"Consul-General Shilth," Magnan said in a hurt tone. "I never dreamed you'd be so uncouth as to betray a confidence."

Shilth frowned, an expression he achieved by crossing two pairs of eyes. "No?" he said in a surprised tone. "Why not?" He vibrated his throat sac in a manner analogous to throat-clearing. "By the way, Pennyfool, just what was it you expected to find here?" His whisper was elaborately casual.

"You're standing in the center of a treasure house," Pennyfool said sourly, "and you have the confounded gall to ask me that?"

"My chaps have devoted the better part of the past ten hours to fruitless scrabbling in these ruins," Shilth hissed. "They've turned up nothing of the remotest utility."

"You've allowed your troops to dig here at random?" Pennyfool yelped.

"Aha!" Shilth wagged an accusatory tentacle. "In spite of your subtle dissembling, your reaction proves that treasures do indeed lie beneath this wilderness." His tone became crisp. "Kindly specify precisely what it is we're looking for, and I might—*might* mind you—find a way to reduce your port fees."

"You . . . you assassin!" Pennyfool yelled. "You have no right to so much as set foot on this hallowed ground!"

"Still—I am here," Shilth said blandly. "And I see nothing in these rubble-heaps to excite CDT interest."

He stirred a heap of potsherds, bottle caps and broken phonograph records with a horny foot. "Ergo, there must be a subtler prize awaiting the lucky finder."

"Shilth, you Vandal!" Pennyfool yelped. "Have you no reverence for anything?"

"Try me with gold," the Groaci said succinctly.

"You're out of your mind, you Philistine! I've told you I don't have any cash on hand!"

"You refuse to speak?" Shilth turned to the captain. "Thish, I tire of the Soft One's lies and his insults. Take him out and execute him." Pennyfool squealed as the guards laid hold of him.

"Execute him?" Magnan bleated. "Couldn't you just strike him off the invitation list for cocktail parties or something?"

"If it's gold you're interested in," Retief suggested, "I'm sure CDT Sector HQ will come through with a tidy sum in return for Mr. Pennyfool's hide, unbroken."

"Splendid notion," a member from the Commercial Section piped up. "I'm sure the ransom money—that is to say, the port fees—will be forthcoming the minute they see us all back to Sector HQ."

"Indeed?" Shilth said in a bored tone. "And if I allowed you to depart, what surety would I then have that the just indemnities will be paid?"

"You have the word of a diplomat," Magnan said promptly.

"I admire your coolness, Magnan," Shilth said with a little bow, "essaying jests at such a moment."

"I suppose I might consent to go alone," Pennyfool said, blinking his eyes rapidly. "Although of course I'd prefer to stay on as hostage myself, my rank will undoubtedly be helpful in expediting payment.''

"One may go," Shilth said in a chilling whisper. "That one." He pointed at Retief. Thish stepped forward, pointing his over-decorated hand-gun at the victim.

"Watch him closely, Captain," Shilth admonished. "He has a reputation as a trouble-maker. As well have him off our hands."

As Thish, close beside Retief, waved the gun toward the entrance, Retief, with a swift motion, swept the weapon from the other's grip, took a step, caught Shilth by the neck and backed against the wall, the muzzle of the pistol pressed against the hostage's ventral carapace.

III

"Tell your boys to stand fast," he said in a conversational tone as the Groaci official writhed and kicked futily, while the soldiers looked on as if paralyzed. "Mr. Pennyfool, if you're ready to board ship, I don't think Planetary Director Shilth will voice any objection."

"My soldiers will shoot you down like nesting nidfowls!" Shilth hissed.

"In which case I'd be forced to pump your thorax full of soft-nosed slugs," Retief said. "I've heard they penetrate the exo-skeleton and then just ricochet around inside until they lose momentum. Be interesting to find out if it's true."

"I remind you, Pennyfool," Shilth cocked his oculars at the Terran, who had not moved, "my lads' scatter-guns are highly disruptive to flimsy organisms such as yourselves. Disarm your misguided colleague, and spare the CDT the expense of a mass funeral, no less costly for lack of any identifiable remains!"

"Better get moving, sir, before some bright lad gets ideas," Retief suggested.

"They . . . we . . . I . . ." Pennyfool gasped.

"By no means," Retief said soothingly. "They hold Shilth in far too high esteem to see him converted into a boiled pudding in the half shell."

Cautiously, the Terrans sidled toward the door. Pennyfool went through in a scrambling leap, followed closely by his associates.

"Retief," Magnan, at the rear of the party said "How are *you* going to get clear? If one of them gets behind you—"

"Better get aboard, Mr. Magnan," Retief cut in "I have an idea Mr. Pennyfool won't dawdle around waiting for stragglers."

"But—but—"

"Captain Thish, perhaps you'd be kind enough to act as escort," Retief said. "Just in case any of the boys on the outside leap to conclusions."

"To comply," Shilth whispered in Groaci as the officer hesitated. "Later, to visit this miscreant's crimes upon him in a fashion devised at leisure. Our leisure, that is."

Magnan made a gobbling sound and disappeared, Thish at his heels. Shilth had stopped struggling. The Groaci soldiery stood in attitudes of alert paralysis, watching for an opening.

It was ten minutes before the sound of the Corps vessel's drive rumbled briefly, faded, and was gone.

"And now?" Shilth inquired. "If you contemplate a contest of endurance, I remind you that we Groaci can carry on for upward of ten standard days without so much as nictating a membrane.

"Send them outside," Retief said.

Shilth remonstrated, but complied. A moment later, a shrill but unmistakably human yelp sounded from beyond the door. Magnan appeared in the entry, his arms gripped by a pair of Groaci while a third held a scatter gun to his head.

"They . . . they didn't wait," the diplomat wailed.

"Release me!" Shilth hissed. "Or would you prefer to wait until after my lads have blown your superior's head off?"

"Sounds like an even trade," Retief said. Magnan gasped and swallowed.

"Much as I should dislike to see the Planetary Director's internal arrangements hashed in the manner you so vividly describe," Thish said from behind Magnan, "I assure you I would make the sacrifice in the interest of the Groaci national honor."

"In the interest of his next promotion, he means," Shilth hissed. "What does he care if I'm diced in the process?"

Retief thrust Shilth away, tossed the gun on the floor. "If I didn't know you wanted both of us alive, I'd have called your bluff, Thish," he said.

"Oh? And do I want you alive, Soft One?" Thish took aim with a borrowed rifle.

"Of course you do, litter-mate of genetic inferiors!" Shilth snapped, massaging the point of his back where the gun muzzle had dug in. "At least until they divulge the secret of what they sought here!" He turned to Retief. "And now let us to business, eh?"

Retief plucked a cigar from his breast pocket, puffed it alight, blew scented smoke past the alien's olfactory orifices, which cinched up tight at the aroma of Virginia leaf.

"Certainly, Shilth. Who's for sale now?"

"You are, my dear Terry," the Groaci said ominously. "The price of your life is a complete description of the nature and location of the riches hidden here."

Retief waved the stogie at the blotched walls, the dirt-drifted corners, the broken tilework. "You are looking at them."

"Ah, so we are to have the pleasure of assisting you in developing a more cooperative attitude, eh? Capital. Easy babblers are such bores."

"You wouldn't dare torture us," Magnan said in squeaky tone. "Our colleagues know where we are. If we aren't returned unharmed, they'll extract a terrible vengeance!"

"A sharp note to the Ambassador, no doubt," Shilth said, with an amused snap of the mandibles. "Still, there are subtler methods of persuasion than living dismemberment. Now, we Groaci are quite at home in enclosed spaces; but you Terries, it is rumored, are claustrophobes, an allegation I've often yearned to test. And I know just the setting in which to conduct the experiment." He gestured to Thish, who urged the two Terrans at gun point along a wide passage to a metal door. Two soldiers came forward to wrestle the heavy panel aside, exposing a tiny chamber no more than six feet on a side, windowless, unfurnished.

"Gentlemen, your cell. A trifle cramped, perhaps, but well protected from excessive wind and rain, eh?"

Retief and Magnan stepped inside. The two soldiers forced the heavy sliding door shut.

In the total darkness, a dim spot of light glowed on one wall. Retief reached out and pressed a thumb against it.

With a grinding of ancient gears, a groaning of antique cables, the elevator started down.

IV

Magnan emitted a shrill cry and attempted to climb the wall "Retief! What's happening?"

"No, no, Mr. Magnan," Retief said, "Your line is, 'Ah, just as I planned.' That's the way reputations for forethought are built."

"Shilth was quite right about the claustrophobia," Magnan said in a choked voice. "I feel that the walls are going to close in on me!"

"Just close your eyes and pretend you're at a Tuesday morning staff meeting. The relief when you find yourself here should carry you through anything short of utter catastrophe."

With a shudder and a clank, the car came to a halt.

"N-now what?" Magnan said in a small voice. Retief felt over the door, found the stub of a lever. He gripped it and pulled. Reluctantly, the door slid aside on a large, column-filled room faintly lit by strips of dimly glowing material still adhering to the ceiling and walls, which were adorned with murals depicting grotesque figures engaged in obscure rites.

"Tomb paintings," Magnan said in a hushed voice. "We're in the catacombs. The place is probably full of bones—not that I actually believe in the curses of dead kings or anything."

"The curses of live Ambassadors are far more potent, I suspect," Retief said, leading the way across the room and into one of the many passages debouching from the chamber. Here more cabalistic scenes were etched in still-bright colors against the ancient walls. Cryptic legends in an unknown script were blazoned across many of them.

"They're probably quotations from the local version of the Book of the Dead," Magnan hazarded, his eye caught by a vividly pigmented representation of a large alien being making what seemed to be a threatening gesture at a second alien from whose ears wisps of mist coiled.

"This one, for example," he said, "no doubt shows us the God of the Underworld judging a soul and finding it wanting."

"Either that, or it's a NO SMOKING sign," Retief agreed.

The passage turned, branched. The left branch dead-ended at an ominous-looking sump half filled with a glistening black fluid.

"The sacrificial well," Magnan said with a shudder. "I daresay the bottom—goodness knows how far down *that* is—is covered with the remains of youths and maidens offered to the gods."

Retief sniffed. "It smells like drained crankcase oil."

They skirted the pit, came into a wide room crowded with massive, complex shapes of corroded metal, ranked in rows in the deep gloom.

"And these are the alien idols," Magnan whispered. "Gad, they have a look of the most frightful ferocity about them."

"That one," Retief indicated a tall, many-armed monster looming before him, "bears a remarkable resemblance to a hay-baler."

"Mind your tongue, Retief!" Magnan said sharply. "It's not that I imagine they can hear us, of course, but why tempt fate?"

There was a sharp *click!*, a whirring and clattering, a stir of massive forms all across the gloomy chamber. Magnan yipped and leaped back as a construct the size of a fork-lift stirred into motion, turned, creaking, and surveyed him with a pair of what were indisputably glowing amber eyes.

"We're surrounded," Magnan chirped faintly. "And they told us the planet was uninhabited!"

"It is," Retief said, as more giant shapes moved forward, accompanied by the squeak of unlubricated metal.

"Then what are these?" Magnan came back sharply. "Oversized spooks?"

"Close, but no kewpie doll," Retief said. "This is the city garage, and these are maintenance robots."

"R-r-robots?"

"Our coming in must have triggered them to come to alert status." They moved along the row of giant machines, each equipped with a variety of limbs, organs, and sensors.

"Then . . . then they're probably waiting for us to give them orders," Magnan said with returning confidence. "Retief! Don't you see what this means? We can tell them to jump in the lift and ride up and scare the nether garments off that sticky little Shilth and his army—or we could have done," he added, "if they understood Terran."

"Terran understood," a scratch bass voice rasped from a point just opposite Magnan's ear. He leaped and whirled, banging a shin smartly.

"Retief! They understand us! We're saved! Good lord, when I first planned our escape via the lift, I never dreamed we'd have such a stroke of luck!"

"Now you're getting the idea," Retief said admiringly. "But why not just add that extra touch of *savoir-faire* by pretending you'd deduced the whole thing, robots and all, from a cryptic squiggle on the contact party's scopegram?"

"Don't be crude, Retief," Magnan said loftily. "I fully intend to share the credit for the coup. In my report I'll mention that you pushed the lift button with no more than a hint from me."

"Maybe you'd better not write up that report just yet," Retief said, as a robot directly before them shifted position with a dry squeal of rusty bearing to squarely block their advance. Others closed in on either side; they turned to find retreat similarly cut off.

"My, see how eager they are, Retief," Magnan said in a comfortable tone. "There, there, just stand aside like a good, er, fellow," he addressed the machine before him.

It failed to move. Frowning, Magnan started around it, was cut off by a smaller automaton—this one no bigger than a commercial sausage grinder, and adorned with a similar set of blades visible inside a gaping metallic maw.

"Well! I see they're in need of re-programming," Magnan said sharply. "It's all very well to fawn a little, but—"

"I'm not sure they're fawning," Retief said.

"Then what in the world are they doing?"

"Terran are surrounded," a voice like broken glass stated from behind the encircled diplomats.

"We are judging Terran," an unoiled tenor stated from the rear rank. *"And finding you wanting."*

"Frightful oversized robots will jump on your smoking remains," chimed in a third voice, reminiscent of a file on steel.

"We are eager for crude contact," Broken Glass agreed.

"They have a curious mode of expressing themselves," Magnan said nervously. "I seem to detect an almost ominous note in their singular choice of words."

"I think they're picking up their vocabulary from us," Retief said.

"Retief—if it wasn't so silly, I'd think that one intended us bodily harm," Magnan said in a tone of forced jocularity, as a ponderous assemblage of sharp edges came forward, rumbling.

"We intend you bodily harm," File-on-Steel said.

"But—but you can't attack *us*," Magnan protested. "You're just machines! We're alive! We're your rightful masters!"

"Masters are better than robots," Broken Glass stated. *"You are not better than us. You are not masters. We will certainly harm you."*

"You will not escape," a red-eyed monster added.

"Retief, I suspect we've made a blunder," Magnan said in a wavering tone. "We were better off at the tender mercies of the Groaci!"

"What's it all about, boys?" Retief called over the gathering creak and clank as the machines closed in.

"This planet is not your world. We are programmed to give no mercies to you fellow."

"Just a minute," Magnan protested. "We're just harmless diplomats. Can't we all be friends or something?"

"Who gave you your order?" Retief asked.

"Our masters," replied a voice like a sand-filled gearbox.

"That was a long time ago," Retief said. "Matters have changed somewhat."

"Yes, indeed," Magnan chimed in. "You see, now that your old masters are all dead, we're taking over their duties."

"Our duties are to see you dead," Red-eye boomed, raising a pair of yard-long cleavers.

"Help!" Magnan yelped.

"We wouldn't want to stand in the way of duty," Retief said, watching the poised cutting edges, "but suppose we turned out to be your masters after all? I'm sure you wouldn't want to make the mistake of slicing up your legitimate owners."

"You see, we took over where they left off," Magnan said hastily. "We're, ah, looking after all their

affairs for them, carrying out their wishes as we understand them, tidying up—"

*"There is no mistake, Terran. You are not our
masters."*

"You said masters are better than robots," Retief
reminded the machine. "If we can prove our superiority, will you concede the point?"

V

Silence fell, broken only by the whir and hum of
robotic metabolisms.

*"If you could so prove, we will certainly concede
your status as our masters,"* Sand-in-the-gears said at
last.

"Gracious, I should think so! Magnan jerked his
rumpled lapel into line. "For a moment, Retief I confess I was beginning to feel just the teeniest bit apprehensive."

"You have one minute to prove your superiority,"
Broken Glass said flatly.

"Well, I should think it was obvious," Magnan
sniffed. "Just look at us."

*"Indeed, we've done so. We find you little, silly,
crude, tender, apprehensive and harmless."*

"You mean—?"

"It means we'll have to do something even more
impressive than standing around radiating righteous
indignation, Mr. Magnan."

"Well, for heaven's sake," Magnan sniffed. "I
never thought I'd see the day when I had to prove the

obvious ascendancy of a diplomat over a donkey engine.''

"We are waiting," File-on-Steel said.

"Well, what do they expect?" Magnan yelped. "It's true they're bigger, stronger, faster, longer-lived, and cheaper to operate; and of course they have vast memory banks and can do lightning calculations and tricks of that sort—which, however, can hardly compare with our unique human ability to, ah, do what we do," he finished in a subdued tone.

"What do you do?" Red-eye demanded.

"Why, we, ah, demonstrate moral superiority," Magnan said brightly.

"Shilth was right about your sense of humor," Retief said admiringly. "But I think we'd better defer the subtle japes until we discover whether we're going to survive to enjoy the laugh."

"Well for heaven's sake *do* something, Retief," Magnan whispered, "before they make a terrible blunder." He rolled his eyes sideways at a scythe-like implement hovering as if ready to shear at any instant through the volume of space he occupied.

"Time is up," Broken Glass said.

The machines surged forward. The scythe, sweeping horizontally, clanged against the descending cleavers as Retief and Magnan jumped aside from the rush of a low-slung tree mower with chattering blades. The latter swerved, collided with a massive punch-press, one of whose piston-like members stabbed through the side of a ponderous masonry wrecker. It wobbled, did a sharp right turn and slammed into the cast-concrete wall, which cracked and leaned, allowing a massive beam to drop free at one end, narrowly missing Magnan as he rebounded from the flank of a charging garbage shredder. The falling girder crashed across the mid-section of the latter machine with a decisive *crunch!* pinning the hapless apparatus to the spot. It clashed its treads futilely, sending up a shower of concrete chips. The other machines clustered around it in attitudes of concern, the Terrans for the moment forgotten.

"Hsst! Retief! This is our chance to beat a strategic withdrawal!" Magnan stage-whispered. "If we can just make it back to the elevator—"

"We'll find Shilth waiting at the top," Retief said. "Mr. Magnan, suppose you find a comfortable spot behind a packing case somewhere. I'm not quite ready to leave yet."

"Are you insane? These bloodthirsty bags of bolts are ready to pound us to putty!"

"They seem to be fully occupied with another problem at the moment," Retief pointed out, nodding toward a post-hole digger which was fruitlessly poking at the end of the beam which had trapped its fellow. The scythe-armed robot was as busily scraping at the massive member, without result. The ranks parted to let a heavy-duty paintchipper through; but it merely clattered its chisel-tips vainly against the impervious material. And all the while, the pinioned machine groaned lugubriously, sparks flying from its commutator box as it threshed vainly to pull free.

Retief stepped forward; Red-eye swiveled on him, raising a large mallet apparently designed for pounding heavy posts into hard ground.

"Before you drive home your argument," Retief said, "I have a proposal."

"What proposal?"

"You don't seem to be having much luck extricating your colleague from under the beam. Suppose I try."

"One minute. I will lift the beam," a deep voice boomed. A massively built loading robot trundled forward, maneuvered deftly into position, secured a grip on the concrete member with its single huge arm and heaved. For a moment, nothing happened; then there was a sharp *clonk!* and a broken duralloy torque rod dangled from the lifter's forged-steel biceps. The girder had not stirred.

"Tough luck, old fellow," Retief said. "My turn."

"Good heavens, Retief, if that cast-iron Hercules couldn't do it, how can you hope to succeed?" Magnan squeaked from his corner.

"You have the ability to help our colleague?" Broken Glass demanded.

"If I do, will you follow my orders?"

"If you can do that which we cannot do, your superiority is obvious."

"In that case, just pull that bar out of there, will you?" Retief pointed to a four-inch diameter steel rod, twenty feet long, part of a roller assembly presumably once used in loading operations. A stacking machine gripped the rod and gave it a firm pull, ripping it free from its mountings.

"Stick one end under the edge of the beam, like a good fellow," Retief said. "You there, jack-hammer: push that anvil under the rod, eh?" The machines complied with his requests with brisk efficiency, adjusting the lever as directed, with the fulcrum as close as possible to the weight to be lifted.

"Retief—if you couldn't even lift the lever how are

you going to. . . ." Magnan's voice faded as Retief stepped up on the treadskirt of a sand-blaster and put a foot on the up-angled long arm of the jury-rigged pry-bar. Steadying himself, he let his full weight onto the rod. Instantly, it sank gracefully down, lifting the multi-ton beam a full half-inch from the depression it had imprinted in the garbage shredder. The latter made a clanking sound, attempted to move, emitted a cascade of electrical sputterings and subsided.

"He's ruptured himself!" Magnan gasped. "Poor thing. Still, we've done our part."

The other machines were maneuvering, making way for a squat cargo-tug, which backed up to the victim, but was unable to get in position to attach its tow-cable. A dirt-pusher with a wide blade tried next, but in the close quarters failed to get within six feet of the disabled machine. The others had no better luck.

"Mr. Magnan, find a length of cable," Retief called. Magnan rummaged, turned up a rusting coil of braided wire.

"One of you robots with digits tie one end of the cable to the patient," Retief said. "Cinch the other up to something that won't give."

Two minutes later the cable was stretched drum tight from a massive stanchion to the cripple, running between closely-spaced paired columns.

"Next, we apply a transverse pull to the center of the cable," Retief directed.

"They can't," Magnan wailed. "There's no room!"

"In that case, Mr. Magnan, perhaps you'd be good enough to perform the office."

"I?" Magnan's eyebrows went up. "Perhaps you've forgotten my Motorman's Arm."

"Use the other one."

"You expect me, one-handed, to budge that ten-ton hulk?"

"Better hurry up. I feel my foot slipping."

"This is madness," Magnan exclaimed, but he stepped to the cable, gripped it at mid-point, and tugged. With a harsh squeak of metal, the damaged machine moved forward half an inch.

"Why—why, that's positively astonishing!" Magnan said with a pleased look.

"Tighten the cable and do it again!" Retief said quickly. The machines hurried to take up the slack. Magnan, with an amazed expression, applied a second pull. The wreck moved another centimeter. After three more nibbles, the tug was able to hook on and drag its fellow clear. Retief jumped down, letting the beam drop with an incredible floor-shaking *boom!*

"Heavens!" Magnan found his voice. "I never imagined I was such a brute! After all, the diplomatic life *is* somewhat sedentary. . . ." He flexed a thin arm, fingering it in search of a biceps.

"Wrestling with the conscience is excellent exercise," Retief pointed out. "And you've held up your end of some rather weighty conversations in your time."

"Jape if you must," Magnan said coolly. "But you can't deny I *did* free the creature. Er, machine, that is."

"You have freed our colleague," Sand-in-the-gears said to Magnan. *"We are waiting for your orders, Master."*

"To be sure," Magnan placed his fingertips together

and pursed his lips. "You won't fit into the lift," he said judiciously, looking over his new subjects. "Is there another way up?"

"To be sure, Master."

"Excellent. I want all of you to ascend to the surface at once, round up and disarm every Groac on the planet, and lock them up. And see that you don't squash the one called Shilth in the process. I have a little gloating to do."

VI

On a newly excavated terrace under a romantically crumbling wall of pink brick, Magnan and Retief sat with Shilth, the latter wearing a crestfallen expression involving quivering anterior mandibles and drooping eye-stalks. His elaborate cloak of office was gone, and there were smudges of axle grease on his once-polished thorax.

"Dirty pool, Magnan," the Groaci said, his breathy voice fainter than ever. "I was in line for the Order of the Rubber Calipers, Second Class, at the very least, and you spoiled it all with your perambulating junk-yard. Who would have dreamed you'd been so sly as to secretly conceal a host of war-machines? I suspect you did it merely to embarrass me."

"Actually," Magnan began, and paused. "Actually, it *was* quite shrewd of me, now that you mention it."

"I think you overdid the camouflage, however," Shilth said acidly as a street-broom whiffled past, casting a shower of dust over the party. "The confounded things don't appear to be aware that the *coup* is over. They're still carrying on the charade.''

''I like to keep my lads occupied,'' Magnan said briskly, nodding grandly at a hauler trundling past along the newly cleaned avenue with a load of newly uprooted brush. ''Helps to keep them in trim in case they're needed suddenly to quell any disturbances.''

''Never fear, I've impressed on Thish that he will not long survive any threat to my well-being.''

''Company coming,'' Retief said, gesturing toward a descending point of sun-bright blue light. They watched the ship settle into a landing a quarter of a mile distant, then rose and strolled over to greet the emerging passengers.

''Why, it's Mr. Pennyfool,'' Magnan said. ''I knew he'd be along to rescue us. Yoo-hoo, Mr. Pennyfool!''

''That's Mr. Ambassador, Magnan,'' Pennyfool corrected sharply. ''Kindly step aside. You're interfering with a delicate negotiation.'' The little man marched past Retief without a glance, halted before Shilth, offering a wide smile and a limp hand. The Groaci studied the latter, turned it over gingerly and examined the back, then dropped it.

''Liver spots,'' he said. ''How unesthetic.''

''Now, Planetary Director Shilth, we're prepared to offer a handsome fee in return for exploratory rights here on Verdigris.'' Pennyfool restored his smile with an effort. ''Of course, anything we find will be turned over to you at once—''

''Oh, ah, Mr. Ambassador,'' Magnan hazarded.

''We Groaci,'' Shilth said sourly, ''are not subject to such pigmentational disorders. We remain a uniform, soothing puce at all times.''

"Sir," Magnan piped up. I'd just like—"

"Now, naturally, we're prepared to underwrite a generous program of planetary development to assist your people in settling in," Pennyfool hurried on. "I had in mind about a half a billion to start . . ." He paused to gauge reaction. "Per year, of course," he amended, judging the omens, "with adequate bonuses for special projects, naturally. Now, I'd say a staff of say two hundred to begin with . . . ?"

"Pennyfool, I have a dreadful node-ache," Shilth hissed. "Why don't you go jump down an elevator shaft?" He patted back a counterfeit yawn and stalked away.

"Well, I can see that this is going to be a challenge," Pennyfool said, staring after the alien. "The tricky fellow is going to hold out for two billion, no doubt."

"Mr. Ambassador, I have good news," Magnan said hastily. "We can save the taxpayers those billions. Verdigris belongs to me!"

"See here, Magnan, the privation can't have scrambled your meager wits already! You've only been here seventy-two hours!"

"But, sir—there's no need to promise Shilth the moon—"

"Aha! So that's what he's holding out for. Well, I see no reason the negotiation should founder over a mere satellite." Pennyfool turned to pursue Shilth.

"No, no, you don't quite grasp my meaning," Magnan yipped, grabbing at his superior's sleeve.

"Unhand me, Magnan!" Pennyfool roared. "I'll see to your release after other, more vital matters are dealt with. In the meantime, I suggest you set a good example by cobbling a record number of shoes or whatever task they've set you—"

"Master, is this person troubling you?" a torn-metal voice inquired. Magnan and Pennyfool whirled to see a rust covered hedge-clipper looming over them, four-foot-clippers at the ready.

"No, that's quite all right, Albert," Magnan said acidly. "I *like* being bullied."

"You're quite certain you don't wish him trimmed to a uniform height?"

"No. I just want him to listen to what I have to say."

Albert clacked the shears together with a nerve-shredding sound.

"I—I'd love to listen to you, my dear Magnan," Pennyfool said rapidly.

Magnan delivered a brief account of his capture of the planet. "So you see, sir," he concluded, "the whole thing is Terran property."

"Magnan!" Pennyfool roared; then with a glance at Albert lowered his voice to a whisper. "Do you realize what this means? When I reported the Groaci here ahead of us, I was appointed as Terran Ambassador Extraordinary and Minister Plenipotentiary to the confounded place! If we own it, then pfft! There goes my appointment!"

"Great heavens, sir," Magnan paled at the announcement. "I had no idea!"

"Look here, do you suppose we could get the Groaci to take it back?"

"What, stay here, surrounded by these mobile moldy monstrosities?" Shilth, who had returned silently, hissed. "Never! I demand repatriation!"

Retief caught Magnan's eye as Pennyfool turned to soothe the Groaci.

"What is it, Retief? Can't you see I'm at a critical point, careerwise?"

"I have a suggestion," Retief said. . . .

As Magnan rejoined Pennyfool, Shilth was still hissing imprecations.

"Master, what say I prune this fellow a bit?" Albert proposed. "He seems to have sprouted too many eyes."

"Not unless he says another word," Magnan said. He turned to Pennyfool with a thoughtful look. "I say, sir, suppose I should come up with a scheme which will insure you confirmation, and which will at the same time reflect favorably on the Terran image? You know, the kindly, selfless, helping-hand sort of thing?"

"Yes, yes?"

"I daresay once established here, you'd want to surround yourself with a staff widely versed in local problems—"

"Naturally. There are plenty of reliable team-men available doing Underground research work in subterranean libraries back at Sector. Get on with it, Magnan."

"I want the Counsellorship," Magnan said crisply.

"You, number two man in my Embassy? Ridiculous! I'd have to jump you over the heads of men with vast experience under their belts!"

"Most of my experience has been at a somewhat higher level," Magnan said loftily. "No Counsellorship, no scheme."

"What's this, Magnan, blackmail?" Pennyfool gasped.

"Precisely," Magnan said.

Pennywise opened his mouth to yell, then closed it and nodded.

"Magnan, it's apparent you're more familiar with the techniques of diplomacy than I suspected. I accept. Now, just what do you have in mind?"

VII

"It's a bit unusual," Ambassador Pennyfool said complacently, glancing out the window of his freshly refurbished office on the top floor of a newly excavated tower of green-anodized aluminum serving as CDT chancery. "But on the other hand, it is a challenge."

"Gracious, yes," Counsellor Magnan said, nodding. "The first Terran envoy to present credentials to a mechanical Head of State.

"I don't know," the Military Attache said darkly. "Freeing these inaminate objects and letting them set up in business for themselves may create a dangerous precedent. What if my cybernetic military equipment, for example, should start getting ideas about pensions and promotions?"

"And office machines," the Budget and Fiscal Officer said worriedly. "If my bookkeeping computers took it into their transistors to start agitating for civil rights I shudder to contemplate the consequences in terms of, say, late pay checks."

"I'm already having trouble with my Motor Pool picking up liberal ideas," the Admin Officer wagged his head, frowning. "I've had to enact strict rules against fraternization with the natives."

There was a musical chime from the desk screen. The square-cornered sense-organ panel of Planetary Secretary Albert Sand-in-the-Gears appeared.

"Ah, there, Pennyfool," the robotic Chief of State said in a tone as genial as his vocal equipment would allow. "I hoped I'd find you in. I was just ringing up to ask whether you'd care to join me on the links this afternoon for a few holes of ballistic golf."

"I'm sorry, Mr. President," the Terran said shortly. "A game in which one is required to score eight holes-in-one out of ten from a tee seven miles from the green is not my strong suit."

"Of course. I keep forgetting you're not equipped with telescopic sights. A pity." The President sighed, a sound like tearing steel. "It was difficult enough grasping the idea of the superiority of my inferiors; trying to behave as equals is even more trying. No offense intended, of course."

"Mr. President—who's that sitting behind you?" Pennyfool asked sharply.

"Ah, forgive me. This is Special Trade Representative Shilth, of Groac. His government has sent him along to assist in getting the Verdigrian economy rolling."

"How long has he been here?"

"Long enough to demonstrate my indispensability," Shilth leaned forward to leer at the Terrans. "I've already concluded Trade Agreements with a number of hard currency markets for export of Verdigrian antiquities."

"You didn't," Pennyfool gasped.

"Oh, have no fear, they're not the real thing." Shilth waggled an eye at Magnan, who pretended not to notice. "Though we let it be noised about that they're all bootleg National Treasures."

"Oh, I see. Reproductions?" Pennyfool grunted.

"Just so you don't ship any irreplacable objets d'arte off-planet."

"We won't. We require them as patterns for the matter duplicators."

"Eh?"

"The locals are digging them out by the truckload; they sort them, discard the rejects—broken pots and the like—then scrub up the choice items and send them along to the duplication centers. We already have a dozen plants in full swing. Our ceramic fingering-knobs are already a sensation with the cultured set. In a year Verdigris will be known as the antique capital of the Eastern Arm."

"Matter duplicators? You're flooding the Galaxy with bogus antiques?"

"Bogus? They're identical with the real thing, to the last molecule."

"Hah! The genuine articles are priceless examples of Verdigrian art; the copies are just so much junk!"

"But, my dear Pennyfool—if one can't distinguish a masterpiece from a piece of junk . . .?"

"*I* can detect the genuine at a glance!"

"Show me," the Groaci said, and whipped out a pair of seemingly identical shapes of lumpy blue-glazed clay the size and approximate shape of stunted rutabagas.

" . . . but unfortunately, I have something in my eye," Pennyfool subsided, poking at the offending organ.

"A pity. I would have enjoyed a demonstration of your expertise," Shilth cooed.

"Well, gentlemen, that tears it," the Ambassador said to his staff after the screen had blanked. "After all my delicate maneuvering to secure self-determination for these unfortunate relics of a by-gone age, and to place the CDT in a position of paternal influence vis-a-vis their emergent nation, the infernal Groaci have stolen a march on us again. Fake antiques, indeed!''

''Goodness, I see what you mean, Mr. Ambassador,'' Magnan said sympathetically. ''Why didn't *we* think of doing that?''

In the Chancery corridor ten minutes later, Magnan mopped at his thin neck with a large floral-patterned tissue.

''Heavens, who'd have thought he'd fly into such a passion?'' he inquired of Retief. ''After all, it isn't as if those silly little gobs of mud possessed an intrinsic merit.''

''Oh, I don't know,'' Retief said. ''They're not bad, considering that the locals have to mass-produce them and bury them at night when nobody's looking.''

''Retief!'' Magnan stopped dead. ''You don't mean . . . ?''

''It seemed like a good idea to sidetrack the Groaci away from the genuine stuff,'' Retief pointed out, in a completely serious voice. ''Just in case any of it had any sentimental value.''

''Fake fakes,'' Magnan murmured. ''The concept has a certain euphony.''

They paused beside a pair of double doors opening onto an airy balcony two hundred feet above the freshly scrubbed city. As they stepped out, a small copter with a saddle and handlebars came winging in across the park to hover just beyond the balustrade.

''Hope aboard, Retief, we're late,'' the machine called in a cheerful baritone.

"Retief, where are you going?" Magnan barked as the latter swung over the rail. "You have the quarterly Report of Redundant Reports to compile, to say nothing of the redundant reports themselves!"

"Duty calls, Mr. Magnan," Retief said soothingly. "My additional assignment as Wildlife Census Officer makes it incumbent on me to cement relations with the locals. I'm off to a game of sky polo with a couple of Cabinet Ministers." He waved and set spurs to his mount, which launched itself with a bound into the wide green sky.

DAM NUISANCE

I

JAME RETIEF, Second Secretary of the Terrestrial Embassy to South Skweem, turned at a shrill hail from the low doorway of one of the squat grass huts lining the dusty main street of the capital village.

"Good mornings, Terry," a knobby, brown-mottled, four-foot alien with a bewildering variety of appendages waved a couple of the latter at the diplomat. "How's trick? Say, I've been meaning to ask ones of you fellow a question: any chance of you Terry supplying a little economic aid in the forms of a new roofs for my pad here?" the Skweeman gesticulated with half a dozen limbs. "Every time it rain, all the squish goes out of my mud pack."

"Sorry, Mr. Uptakapacheenobufers, but you know the ground-rules. Much as we Terries want to impress you people with a Public Works Project, it can't be anything useful. According to the Underground Deep-Think Teams back at Sector, that might be taken as an implied criticism of your culture."

The Skweeman made a rubbery noise indicating mild disappointment. "Yous know I'd likes to throw my weights behind the Terry program, but without a few goody to show for it, what's the percentage?"

"I see what you mean, Mr. Uptakapacheenobufers. I'd better start by installing a couple of new transistors in that language teacher I lent you. It seems to have imparted a faulty grasp of the plural."

"Hecks, Retief, call me 'takapacheenobufers for shorts. I guess we're chum now, after those snort we had together last night. Wows, what a hangovers!"

"Speaking of headaches, I have to hurry along to Staff Meeting. Too bad about the roof, but if you think of something spectacularly superfluous the town needs, hasten to let Ambassador Treadwater know. He's sweating out his next E.R."

Retief went along to the large hut which served as the Terran Chancery; inside, he took a camp stool among the staff assembled before a low split-bamboo podium which sagged visibly under the bulk of the chief of Mission.

"Now, then," the Ambassador opened the meeting briskly. "First this morning we'll take a look at the challenge which confronts us, gentlemen." He signalled and the lights dimmed. A projector hummed. On the rostrum, a life-sized, three-dimensional, vividly colored image of a stubby, boxy Skweeman appeared under a glowing legend reading KNOW YOUR ENEMY. Treadwater tapped the solidogram with his rubber-tipped pointer.

"This, gentlemen," he stated, "might appear to some of you to bear a superficial resemblance to our great allies, those valiant freedom fighters, the South

216

Skweemans. However, to a practiced eye it's at once apparent that it is, in fact, a *North* Skweeman. Note the sly expression, the general air of inscrutability, the fierce cast of eye . . .'' The pointer rapped each feature in turn.

"Ah . . . Mr. Ambassador.'' Colonel Pluckwyn, the Military Attache, raised an interrogatory finger from his seat in the front row. "I don't believe that last organ was precisely an eye. More of an ear, I think you'll find.''

"Whatever it is, it has a fierce cast!'' Treadwater snapped. "Now let's move along to the coloration.'' He studied the simulacrum. "Hmm—an offensive greenish purple with clashing dun rosettes.''

"Golly, Mr. Ambassador,'' the Cultural Attache's voice piped from the rear. "Maybe I'm mixed up, but aren't *our* Skweemans the same color?''

"Certainly not! Quite the opposite! The South Skweeman is characterized by a soothing overall tannish tone, tastefully set off with purply-green rosettes. Not the same at all.''

"Yes, but—''

"Now, about the warts.'' The Ambassador pursued his point. "Note that this fellow has large blue ones, with tufts of yellowish hair.''

"But, sir—isn't that what the South Skweemans have?''

Treadwater smiled patronizingly. "A common mistake, Dimplick. Actually, the South Skweeman is adorned with somewhat smaller warts, bearing attractive tufts of *golden* hair.''

"Oop, my mistakes, boss,'' a thin South Skweeman voice chirped from the direction of the projector.

"Looks like I accidentally slipped in a shots of the South Skweeman Minister of Eats and Drinks. A nice likeness, too, made just before the mob got him." The image flicked out of existence and another, obscurely different, took its place.

"Well, I'm sure we all get the general idea, anyway," the Cultural Attache offered breathlessly, as Treadwater's face took on a dangerous shade of purple.

"Yeah—*these* are a shot of the common foe," the projectionist announced. "Boy, will you look at those look of ferocity?"

"Take it away!" Treadwater bellowed. "And I suggest you look to your labels, sir, before you create an international incident!" He yanked his pale violet lapels back in line. "Now, it's time to get on to the substantive portion of today's briefing." He beetled his brows at his audience.

"You're all aware that the success of our mission here depends on establishing the legitimacy of the government to which I—that is, we—are accredited. Namely, that of Free Skweem, formerly known as South Skweem. We are similarly aware that next month's plebiscite will determine once and for all whether the mantle of planetary leadership falls on the shoulder of our sturdy allies, the South Skweemans, or on the bowed backs of the North Skweeman insurgents, the satellites of the unprincipled Groaci."

"I have a suggestion," the Political Officer broke in excitedly. "We could hire some of the rougher local patriots to patrol the polling places, weeding out undesirables, distributing special disappearing ballots among the opposition and making a few minor adjustments to the counting machines to insure a victory for democratic processes!"

"This is no time for subtlety," Treadwater stated flatly. "We must impress the locals of both political persuasions with our superior capacity to bestow largesse. We need, gentlemen, a large and impressive symbol of Terran generosity and technical virtuosity. The floor is now open for your suggestions."

The Ambassador waited. The silence was profound.

"Gentlemen," Treadwater said ominously, "a full week has passed since I first requested suggestions from the staff—and as of today, the net response has been nil!"

A shuffling of feet greeted the accusation.

"A curious lethargy seems to have afflicted you, gentlemen." The Ambassador stared around belligerently. "This, while a certain foreign mission daily entrenches itself more securely, prestige-wise, by virtue of a certain probably illegal but nonetheless highly effective propaganda device. I refer, of course, to the dam the Groaci have bestowed on their North Skweeman toadies."

"I propose we build a dam too," someone said quickly.

"Wonderful notion," the Economic Officer rumbled. "About to suggest it myself—"

"Say, Charlie. you're hitting right in there this morning," a First Secretary offered. There were clucks and chuckles of admiration from the rest of the staff. Treadwater waited for the approbation to die down.

"The dam constructed by the Groaci engineers at the point where the river loops briefly into North Skweem," he purred, "has not only crippled South Skweeman commerce, but has effected a drought which is rapidly starving our brave allies into an advanced state of malnutrition, complicated by dust storms. Add to this the unfortunate flooding of that portion of the nation's farmland lying above the dam and we see, gentlemen, a striking example of creative public relations—unhappily, in the service of the opposition. Now—'' he smiled thinly at the group— ''will someone kindly tell me what possible detriment would accrue to our rivals if I were so ill-advised as to construct still another navigational hazard in what was once this nation's main artery of communication!'' His voice rose to an apoplectic bellow on the last words. No one volunteered a reply.

A junior Third Secretary raised a hand timidly. Treadwell blinked expectantly.

''Ah . . . sir. The dam is creating a sizable lake, I understand. What do the Groaci have in mind doing with all that water?''

''Eh? Do? Nothing, of course!'' the Ambassador snapped. ''The entire project was designed merely to harass me! Or rather, us! The proud and independent populace of South Skweem, that is to say!''

''Oh.'' The young man subsided.

''Well, then,'' the Ambassador went on, icily calm now. ''Let us try again, gentlemen, avoiding, if possible, the idiotic.''

''Well, Mr. Ambassador, Project Proposals are a tricky proposition,'' the quavering voice of the elderly Press Attache offered. ''There was quite a row kicked up in certain journals concerning that hundred-man bird bath the CDT built for the Quornt before we discovered they were allergic to water. And it will be quite a while before we live down the shoe factory we gave the Jaq, since they seem to have no feet to speak of. And there was a certain amount of criticism of—''

"I'm well aware of the history of the fiasco, as practiced by my colleagues," Treadwater cut him off glacially. "It is precisely for that reason that I am determined to present to Sector Headquarters a Proposal which will bear microscopic scrutiny, farce-wise. Now, thinking caps, men! I needn't remind you that we are caught between the mortar of Groaci expansionism and the pestle of Corps policy. If the government to which we are accredited is not starved out from under us, we still face an unfilled Project Quota."

"Damned awkward, sir," Colonel Pluckwyn murmured. "Couldn't we just give the beggars a touch of the old quirt? A small fractional megatonner, say, just to teach 'em their manners."

"Bomb Headquarters?" Treadwater looked astonished.

"Actually I was thinking of the North Skweemans, sir, but your suggestion has merit—"

"Colonel, I think you'd better report to the dispensary after Staff Meeting, for skull X-rays," Treadwater said bleakly. "I suspect the plates will come out blank. Now, let's move along to Mr. Magnan's report." The Ambassador glanced expectantly over the seated diplomats.

"Magnan? Where is the fellow, drat it!" The Ambassadorial eye fixed on Retief. "You, there. What's-your-name. Magnan's your chief, I believe. Where the devil is he?"

"Mr. Magnan failed to confide in me, Your Excellency," Retief said.

"Didn't your Excellency send him over to call on the Groaci Ambassador?" Dimplick queried.

"Of course," Treadwater agreed. "I instructed him

to unobtrusively scout out the effects of the new dam under cover of the protocol visit. It is that on which I wish his report."

"Mr. Magnan went across the line into North Skweem, alone?" Retief inquired casually.

"I believe that is where his Groacian Excellency is usually to be found," Treadwater replied testily, glancing at his finger watch. "And he was distinctly directed to be back before tiffin time."

"The present crisis may have thrown off the tiffin schedule," Retief conjectured.

Treadwater frowned ominously. "Are you suggesting the scoundrels may have so far forgotten their protocol as to have *detained* an accredited diplomat in the performance of his duty?"

"*Something* seems to have detained him," Pluckwyn offered.

"I hope he didn't go sniffing too closely around the dam," the Political Officer said soberly. "Those North Skweemans can be pretty nasty. I saw some atrocity photos our visual aid people mocked-up, based on reliable rumors—"

"Oh, boy." The Press Attache doddered to his feet. "This'll make great copy, chief. 'TERRY ENVOY MURDERED . . .' "

"Who said any thing about murder, you cretin!" Treadwater roared. "I merely noted that the man is late for Staff Meeting!"

"Yes, I suppose you're right." The Press Attache sat down reluctantly. Then he brightened. "Still, if he hasn't shown up by sundown . . ." He began jotting notes on his scratch pad.

"Well, if there are no further follies with which to

waste our time, that's all for this morning, gentlemen,'' the Ambassador growled. "But I shall be looking for results—prompt, dramatic results!'' He swept the group with a final expectant glare, moved ponderously down from the shaky platform.

"Say, Mr. Retief,'' the young Third Secretary came up beside him as they stepped out into the hot, dusty sunlight. "What really *is* the difference between North Skweeman's and South Skweemans?''

"Very simple, Teddy. South Skweemans are natural democrats.''

"Oh . . .'' The youth fell back as Treadwater beckoned Retief over.

"About Magnan,'' the Ambassador said off-handedly. "It's occurred to me the situation might bear looking into. Never can tell what these unprincipled foreigners might take a fancy to perpetrate—not that I think Magnan is in any difficulty, of course. But I've been thinking possibly we might just dispatch someone to make sure.''

"Excellent idea, sir,'' Retief agreed.

"Actually, I've been wondering whom I could spare long enough to attend to the chore.'' Treadwater put a thoughtful finger to his chins.

"Indeed, sir?'' Retief encouraged.

"Frankly, *your* name popped into my mind.''

"Very flattering, Mr. Ambassador. A pity you assigned me to do the liquor inventory. Ottherwise I'd be delighted.''

"Never mind the inventory—if you're sure you really feel you should go . . .''

"Well . . .''

"Very well, then, if you insist. Though personally I

think you young fellows spook too easily. Well, I must hurry along, Retief. Let me hear from you." He turned and strode away.

"How'd it go, Retief?" Uptakapacheenobufers called from his doorway.

"Predictably," Retief said.

II

The once-purple and verdant countryside of Skweem was a wan, sun-baked expanse of water-starved fields criss-crossed with the dusty gulleys of empty irrigation ditches. Tinder-dry stalks of mudwheat stood in endless, arid rows across the cracked, concrete-like clay.

Retief studied the view as he steered the official ground-car with the CDT pennant flapping from the prow along the rocky road that paralleled the dry river bed, where stranded boats rested high and dry, their formerly bright paint and rigging as bleached and sere as the land. A few listless South Skweeman peasants waved spiritless greetings from the shade of their huts as he passed. Others merely stared with drooping visual organs.

It was an hour's drive to the heavy barbed-wire fence that marked the North Skweeman border. Retief pulled to a stop at the gate. A large, warty North Skweeman in official loops of braid decorated by dangling straps and medals undulated over, fingering a blast rifle of unmistakable Groaci manufacture.

"What's your problem, Two-eyes?" he inquired in Skweemish.

"Just a courtesy call," Retief replied in the same tongue. "Tell me, did you see another Terry pass here early this morning?"

The Skweeman's eyes shifted. "Naw, nothing like that," he said flatly.

"This fellow would be hard to miss," Retief persisted. "Twelve feet tall, flaming red hair all over, three eyes—"

"Frinkle-fruit! The guy wasn't as big as you, and . . ." His voice trailed off.

"I see," Retief nodded. "Well, he was taking a birthday cake to the Groaci Ambassador, and it seems he lost the cherry off the top of it. We Terries are pitching in to help locate anyone who might have delayed him."

"Not me, Terry! I waved him through and he headed straight for town—thataway." He pointed along the road.

"Fine. I'll tell them you're clean, then."

"Gee, thanks, fella." The guard set his gun aside and opened the gate.

"Think nothing of it." Retief waved cheerily and drove through.

A mile and a half past the gate he encountered a small village, identical with its South Skweeman equivalent. Rows of grass huts, of various sizes depending on the status of their occupants, were arranged around a small grassed plaza in the center of which the public structures were grouped. As Retief pulled up to the tall, conical buildings which presumably housed the town officials, half a dozen uniformed North Skweemans came to the alert. One, more elaborately decorated than his fellows, wobbled forward and looked the car over with the air of a Customs officer tipped off to a load of contraband.

"What brings *you* here?" he demanded.

"I'm looking for the Groaci Consulate General," Retief said.

"Yeah? Where'd you lose it?" the Skweeman came back snappily.

"The last I heard it was neck-deep in North Skweeman internal affairs," Retief replied breezily. "But that's for you fellows to worry about." He looked around the somnolent town square. "I don't suppose you know where I might find a fellow Terry who wandered over the line while chasing a promotion?"

"You got that one right," the Skweeman nodded.

"Well, in that case I'll just move along and take a look at the dam the Groaci suckered you into letting them build on your property." He glanced along the line of the arched river-bed to the looming wall of concrete half a mile distant. "I see it's still holding. Water's about halfway to the spillway now, eh?" He looked thoughtful.

"Whattaya mean, suckered? That's the finest dam on Skweem!"

"Um," Retief said. "What's it for?"

"Huh? To hold back the water, whattaya think?"

"Why?"

"On acount of . . . so we can . . . I mean, it's for . . ." The Skweeman broke off. "Listen, you better talk to old Five-eyes personal; I mean, what's the big idea trying to pump me for military secrets?"

"Military secrets, eh? Well, that's interesting. Just

what sort of illegal military plans are you concocting over on this side of the line?"

"We got no illegal plans!"

"Any military plans are illegel," Retief said flatly.

"Who says so?"

"The CDT."

"Oh, yeah?"

"Uh-huh. And we have the military resources to back it up, if you'll goad us far enough. Starting a war ought to do it. And now, if you'll just sort of slither to one side, I'll get on with my business."

"Hey, you can't—" The North Skweeman's words were drowned in a cloud of dust as Retief gunned the car off toward the massive pile of the dam.

Retief parked the car on a stretch of bulldozed gravel on the shoulder of the hill against which the abutment was anchored. Carrying a pair of miniaturized 100x9 binoculars, he moved up in the shelter of a small shed housing the dam's power controls, looked over the scene below.

To the right of the massive concrete barrier a parched valley wound away toward the North Skweeman border. Patches of mud gleaming here and there at the bottom of the gorge were all that remained of the former river. To the left stretched a broad lake of blue-black water, its breeze-riffled surface reflecting the greenish late-morning sun. Under it lay a hundred square miles of South Skweem's best farm land, now forty feet deep in backed-up river water.

A narrow catwalk lined with pole-mounted polyarcs for night operations crossed the top of the dam. On the far side a crew of Skweeman construction workers in baggy ochre overalls toiled under the supervision of a spindle-legged Groaci engineer, putting the finishing touches on the job. Other Skweeman's, heavy-laden, struggled up a trail across the steep slope from below like a column of ants. A touch of color met Retief's eye. He fine-focused the glasses, picked out the sagging shape of a small hut half-concealed in the brush near the base of the dam. Through its open door he saw the edge of a coil of wire, shelves, the corners of packing cases.

A Groaci supervisor stepped into the field of vision, closed the door, hung a lock on it, followed the workers up the trail. Retief lowered the glasses thoughtfully. Then, keeping low, he moved off in the concealment of deep brush.

It was a stiff climb down to the floor of the ravine. Retief completed it without arousing unwelcome attention. He came up on the supply hut from the rear. Nothing moved near it now. The lock looked stout enough, but the warped boards of the door were riddled with dry rot. At a sharp kick it bounced rattlingly open.

Inside, Retief looked over a stock of tools, reinforcing steel fittings, detonator caps, mechanical spares for the pumps—and a generous supply of compressed smashite: three-inch rods of a bilious yellow color, each capable of excavating a hundred cubic yards of hard rock in one blast. Quickly, Retief selected materials and set to work.

III

He left the shed ten minutes later, unreeling a coil of two-conductor insulated wire behind him. The ascent to the cliff-top took half an hour, by which time the

228

workmen had completed the task at hand and were busily packing up their tools. Retief made his way up-slope to the control shed.

Its corrugated metal door stood half open. Inside, the floor was littered with snipped-off bits of wire, empty cartons that had contained switching gear and the butts of several dozen Groaci dope sticks. An inspection of the panels showed that the wiring was complete. Five more minutes' study indicated that the large white toggle switch beside the door controlled the polyarcs atop the dam.

Retief brought the ends of his wires into the shed, linked them into the lighting circuit. Against the gray floor, the insulated lines were almost invisible.

Back outside, he brushed loose sand over the wires leading up from below, then headed back to the car. He topped the rise, halted at sight of two bile-green cars bearing the crossed-oculars insignia of the North Skweeman Home Guard, parked across the bumpers of the CDT vehicle. There were eight armed Skweemans in sight, patrolling alertly around the blocked car, while a pair of Groaci stood by, dapper in Bermuda shorts and solar topis, deep in conversation.

As Retief strolled down to meet the reception committee, the locals swiveled to cover him with their guns. The two Groaci stared, their eye-stalks twitching hypnotically. Retief recognized one as a member of the Groaci diplomatic staff.

"Good morning, Lith," Retief greeted the Groaci Councillor as he came up. "Keeping busy, I see."

"To depart instantly," the Groaci diplomat hissed in his faint voice. "To explain at once this illegal intrusion on North Skweeman soil!"

"Which would you like first, the explanation or the departure?" Retief inquired interestedly.

"To make no jest of this red-handed crime, Terran interloper!"' Lith whispered urgently. His multiple eyes fell on the miniature binoculars in Retief's hand.

"As I thought." He motioned to his Skweeman aides. "Your presence explains itself." He stepped back to allow the gun-handlers to close in. "Cover him," he ordered. "At the first false move, fire."

"You're in a devil-may-care mood this morning," Retief noted. "Given up all hope of advancement, I suppose, and want to go out in a blaze of notoriety by making an even bigger mistake than usual."

"What did you observe up there?" The second Groaci indicated the top of the rise.

"Just what's there," Retief replied easily.

The two Groaci exchanged glances, a feat they accomplished with one pair of eyes while keeping two on Retief and another on the Skweemans. Retief whistled in admiration.

"No signalling," one of them warned.

"To poke your long Terry nose in once too often," Lith said. He made a curt gesture with a pair of arms. "Take him," he commanded the Skweemans.

"Before you do that—" Retief held up an admonitory hand—"maybe it would be a good idea to ask Lith what the future plan for North Skweem might be—if North Skweem has a future."

"Silence!" Lith keened. "To take care, Terry, not to tempt me too far!"

"Hey, talk Skweemish," one of the guards objected. "What are you two foreigners cooking up, anyway?"

"We're merely nattering of trivialities," Lith explained. "Now do your duty, fellows."

"Yeah . . . but I been thinking: this sapsucker *is* a Terry diplomat."

"Enough," Lith cut him off. "I assure you no complaints will be lodged by his associates."

The Skweemans closed in on Retief. "All right, big boy, let's go," the lieutenant said, poking his gun at the prisoner.

Retief glanced at the weapon. It was a heavy-duty power pistol, a Groacian copy of an early Terran type.

"Have you ever fired that thing?" he inquired interestedly.

"Who, me?" the Skweeman rotated a number of sense organs in a gesture expressing astonishment. "Heck, no. We got orders to only shoot at live targets." He looked meaningfully at Retief.

"A wise precaution. I understand that model blows up rather easily. That's why the Groaci sold them to you at bargain prices."

"To make no attempt to subvert my minions!" Lith hissed.

"I wouldn't dream of it," Retief assured the ruffled diplomat. "I prefer minions who change sides on their own."

"You will have long to wait for that eventuality," Lith snapped. "In a cell which, alas, lacks most of the amenities."

"That's all right," Retief said. "Perhaps I won't be in it long enough to need them."

Lith vibrated his throat-sac, expressing amusement.

"You may be right, my dear Terran," he commented blandly. "Now, into your vehicle, and drive as directed, remembering that guns are upon you!''

Escorted by the two police cars, Retief drove the CDT Monojag at a sedate pace along the indicated route to the village, pulled it in before a low mud brick building with one small window set with metal bars. Lith and the Skweeman police surrounded him as he stepped out into the street. One of the cops stared into the interior of the Monojag.

"Hey, this is a fancy job," he commented. "What's that?'' He pointed at a short red-handled lever labeled EMERGENCY LIFT. At his side, Lith goggled, then whirled on Retief.

"To explain at once!" he hissed. "Our intelligence reports have indicated that vehicles so equipped are capable of VTO and supersonic speeds! Why, then, did you permit yourself to be so docilely convoyed?''

"Well, Lith, maybe those reports you read were exaggerated,'' Retief smiled deprecatingly. "After all, your gumshoe brigades have to report *something*.''

Lith snorted. "So much for the vaunted Terry technology.'' He turned to his troops.

"Lock him up.''

The Skweemans closed in to box Retief, like alert, waist-high goblins modelled in blotchy clay; their guns prodded him along an alley to a small metal door set in the side of the brick building. The lieutenant opened it with a clumsy electrokey, waved him inside. The door clanked shut and a shadowy figure rose up, its face pale in the dim light.

"Retief!'' First Secretary Magnan gasped. "You mean they captured you, too?''

"It seemed the simplest way to solve the problem of

finding you," Retief said. "Now all we have is the problem of getting out."

III

The Skweeman sun was low in the sky now. A brisk, hot wind had sprung up from the north, whirling streamers of dust into the cell through the barred window from which Retief watched the activity in the street. Behind him, Magnan turned away, coughing.

"They're as busy as Verpp in moulting season," he sniffed. "No one is paying us the slightest attention. I suppose we may rot here for hours more before Ambassador Treadwell secures our release."

"There's just one cop patrolling the jail now," Retief said. "The rest of them have trooped off, arm in arm with their friends the Groaci. I think we picked a bad time for our calls; they're up to something."

"I can't think what's keeping him!" Magnan eyed his watch fretfully. "I'm missing my afternoon coffee break, to say nothing of dinner." He sighed heavily, settled himself on the floor.

"I simply can't grasp it," he muttered. "The Groaci are famed for their chicaneries, but open diplomat-napping broaches an entirely new field of rascality. Why, an honest diplomat won't even be able to run around to trouble areas, picking up eye-witness impressions, without the risk of being treated as a mere spy."

"On the other hand, if we join in the spirit of the thing—" Retief turned from the window—"we might find that it opens up new avenues to us, too." He went across to the narrow door, leaned over the barred, waist-high opening, and shouted for the guard.

"Good idea." Magnan got to his feet. "I think it's time we spoke sharply to these brigands. Just step aside, Retief, and I'll drop a few broad hints." His voice faded as the fierce visage of the police lieutenant appeared beyond the aperture. Retief spoke first:

"Do you have any idea what a blaster would do to you if I fired from this range?" he inquired. "Don't give any alarm," he went on as the speechless cop goggled into the dark cell. "Just quietly unlock the door—and be sure no one notices anything unusual going on."

"B . . . b . . . b . . ." the Skweeman said.

"You can express your astonishment later," Retief said briskly. "Open up now, before I have to demonstrate how well armed I am."

"I . . . I didn't see any weapon on you when we brought you in," the jailer expostulated.

"Naturally; it's the sort of thing a fellow likes to keep secret. Hop to it, now. My trigger finger is twitching."

"I had to be a wise guy and volunteer to be a big shot," the Skweeman muttered to himself. Retief heard the scrape of the key in the lock. Tumblers clicked over. The door swung in with a dry squeak.

"Shhh!" Magnan put a finger to his lips, looked severely at the native as he sidled out past him. He looked both ways.

"The coast seems to be clear," he whispered as Retief lifted the cop's pistol from its holster. "Maybe you'd better let me have one of the guns."

"Hey!" The Skweeman waved several sensory or-

gans in an agitated way. "I don't see any blaster—
except mine!"

"Nothing wrong with your vision, anyway," Retief
congratulated him. Now we have to be running along."
He looked thoughtfully at the local. "I really should
shoot you . . ." he said judiciously.

"Sh . . . shoot me?" the Skweeman gulped. "But
I've got a couple of dozen chicks ready to break through
the shell any day now! Those little devils will have the
hide off the old lady in five minutes flat if I'm not there
to protect her when they hatch out!"

"On the other hand," Retief went on, "I *could* give
you a break."

"Yeah!" the Skweeman breathed. "Now you're
talking, Terry!"

"You just carry on as though nothing had happened.
We'll go about our business and trouble you no more. I
don't think you'll want to bother Uncle Lith by men-
tioning our departure; he might take the unreasonable
attitude that you're in some way to blame. Just play
them close to your medals and act innocent when they
notice the cell's empty."

"You bet, boss. I always knew you Terries were
gents. Between us, I never went much for that two-
legged slicker—"

"Mind your derogatory references to the number of a
being's limbs, sir," Magnan said stiffly. "Two legs
appears to me to be an admirable endowment of such
members."

"Sure, no offense, gents. Now, how's about beating
it quick, before somebody comes along? And you better give me back my gun. Somebody might get nosy if I
don't have it."

Retief ejected the power cylinder from the butt of the gun, dropped it into his pocket, handed the empty weapon over.

"We can't reach the car," he said to Magnan. "They towed it away to tinker with at leisure. We'll have to ease out the back way and see how far we get."

Keeping to the narrow alley, Retief and Magnan safely traversed a block of ragged grass dwellings, emerged at the end of a long avenue that meandered down a slope toward the mile-distant fence marking the South Skweeman border, barely visible now in the late twilight.

"If there were just some way to cover that ghastly open stretch," Magnan muttered, "we could be safe in a matter of minutes . . ." He broke off, pointed at a flickering glow, a smudge of smoke rising lazily from a point near the gate where the road crossed the international line. "What's that? Dust, perhaps? Or smoke?"

"The wind's from the north," Retief said. "And there's nothing but twenty miles of dry mud-wheat between here and those haystacks housing our friends, the South Skweeman leaders. Something tells me that's a fire, Mr. Magnan—and not an accidental one."

"Fire?" Magnan gasped. "Great heavens, Retief—the capital is directly down-wind! They'll be roasted alive—the Ambassador, the staff, the South Skweemans—and no water anywhere to fight the blaze!"

"That's one way of influencing an election," Retief pointed out.

"Why, there's nothing to keep it from burning off the prairie all the way to the sea," Magnan blurted. "The entire country will be incinerated! There'll be nothing left of our allies but a pall of smoke!''

There was a scratchy Skweeman shout from behind the Terrans. They turned to see a policeman approaching up the alley on the run—a spectacle not unlike a cubic yard of olive-drab noodles rolling up-hill.

''Let's go,'' Retief snapped. He turned and ran for it, with Magnan pelting at his heels and a gathering force of pursuers baying on the trail.

''It's . . . no . . . use,'' Magnan gasped as they toiled up the last hundred yards toward the mighty flank of the dam. ''They're . . . gaining.'' He cast a look back at the mob of half a hundred North Skweeman patriots strung out in a torch-waving line-halfway to the village.

''Just a little farther,'' Retief caught Magnan's arm and hauled him along. ''You're doing fine.''

They reached the top of the dam, massive and ominous in the darkness. A blaster bolt crackled blue nearby, from extreme range.

''Retief, we're not going to cross *that!*'' Magnan stared in horror at the narrow unrailed catwalk that led out to disappear in darkness, the great black void on one side, the lapping waters slapping at the concrete on the other.

''Unless we want to be shot, we are.'' Retief started out at a trot. Magnan bleated, then followed, edging along flat-footed. Another shot chipped concrete behind him. He yelped and broke into a nervous canter.

They reached the far side, scrambled up the dry slope, lit only by the blaster that peppered them with flying gravel as the shots struck around them.

''Where are they?'' a Skweeman voice sounded. ''I

can't see a thing; those Terries must have eyes like a weenie-bug!''

"Lights," someone else called. "Don't let 'em get away, boys!''

Retief stood, cupped his hands beside his mouth.

"Lith," he called. "A word of advice: don't light up!''

"We can't . . . hide here," Magnan gasped out. "No cover . . . and those shots . . . getting close!''
He dived flat as a shot kicked up dirt almost at his feet.

"They won't find us in the dark," Retief said.

"But—they'll switch on the lights.''

"There is that chance—but they were warned.''

There was a shock through the mound that bounced both men three inches into the air. Then a deep-throated *tooom!* rolled from the abyss like chained thunder, as brilliant light flooded the entire length of the dam.

Retief raised his head, saw great chunks of masonry rising with languid grace high in the air. Atop the stricken dam, the few bold Skweemans who had started across dithered momentarily, then pelted for safety as the walkway subsided with dream-like majesty under them. Most of them reached the far side as the immense bulk of the dam cracked with a boom like a cannon; the rest dived for the glistening surface of the pent-up water, splashed desperately for shore as dust boiled up from the gorge, obscuring the scene of destruction.

Polyarcs still blazing bravely, the great dam crumbled, sinking from sight. Wave after wave of sound rolled across the slope. Rocks and pebbles thudded down near the diplomats. They gained their feet, sprinted for the top of the hill, then turned, watched as the surface of the artificial lake heaved, recoiling ponderously from the blast, then bulged toward the broached dam, formed a vast spout like translucent black syrup that arched out, out, over, and spilled down, foaming white now, plunging into the boiling dust. The ground shook as the incalculabe tonnage of water struck far below. A roaring like caged dinosaurs bellowed upward from the gorge as the river poured back into its bed in a torrent that shredded concrete and steel from the broken rim of the dam like water dissolving dry mud. In a scant five minutes, nothing remained of the great Groaci Dam but the denuded abutments, studded with the stripped ends of clustered reinforcing rods.

"Retief!" Magnan piped over the roar of the waters. "The . . . the dam broke!"

Retief nodded judiciously. "Yes, Mr. Magnan," he said. "I think you could say that."

IV

Retief and Magnan waded past the tattered remains of the soggy huts thrusting up from the swirling, mud-brown waters that covered the site of the South Skweeman capital, inundated by the flood that had swept down so abruptly an hour earlier. Ambassador Treadwater stood with his staff before the remains of the Chancery hut, waist deep in the flow. "Ah, there you are, Magnan." He turned to look disapprovingly at the new arrivals. "Remind me to speak to you about punctuality. I'd almost begun to wonder if you'd met with foul play. Even considered sending someone after you."

"Mr. Ambassador—about all this water—"

"Hark!" Someone raised a hand torch, shot its blue-white beam out across the water, picked up the low silhouette of an inflated dinghy on which a number of bedraggled, knobby-kneed Groaci crouched. Several Skweemans splashed forward to intercept the craft.

"Well, nice of you to drop in, my dear Shish," Treadwater called. "Most unfortunate that your engineers have apparently proved unequal to their task. Possibly their slide-rules were out of adjustment. Still their timing was good, conflagrationwise."

He smiled sourly as the staff chuckled dutifully.

"Bah, the design was flawless," Shish whispered as the raft bobbed on the ripples. "We were sabotaged!"

"Sabotage?" Treadwater surveyed the Groaci Ambassador as haughtily as his sodden puce cutaway would allow. "I think you are as aware as I that import of explosives to an emergent planet like Skweem is quite impossible, but for certain industrial types allocated to massive engineering projects."

"You suggest that Groaci detonants were employed in this dastardly fashion? Why, the very idea . . ." Shish fell sulkily silent.

"Confidentially, Retief," Magnan whispered behind his hand, "Just what do you suppose *did* happen to the dam?"

"Possibly someone got their wires crossed," Retief murmured.

"Now, Mr. Ambassador," Treadwater said. "I fear I shall have to expropriate your conveyance for official CDT use. I find it necessary to remove to my hill station at once to prepare my dispatches." He broke off as a muddy scarecrow faintly recognizable as the Agricultural Attache splashed up to join the group.

"Did you notice the current change, Mr. Ambassador?" he cried gaily. "The water's draining off into the river bed now—and the new channel cut by the flood is just this side of the border. I fancy we'll have no more interference from these meddlesome Groaci—oh, Ambassador Shish," he nodded to the sodden dignitary. "Nice night Your Excellency."

"Bah," Shish replied.

The attache was rubbing his hands together. "My preliminary study seems to indicate that the inundation has deposited a good six inches of new topsoil over a large portion of South Skweem. All scoured off Northern Skweem, of course, but then, they *will* allow defective dams to be built on their land . . ." His voice trailed off. He pointed across the rapidly receding waters. Amid much splashing, a large party of Skweemans was approaching at a rapid clip.

"Gad!" Colonel Pluckwyn boomed. "We're being invaded!"

"Here, do something!" Treadwater turned to Shish. "They're your allies! Tell them to go along quietly and we'll see about a handsome CDT reparation for any inconvenience—"

"I claim sanctuary!" Shish whistled in agitation. "Treadwater, it's your duty to protect me and my chaps from these soreheads!"

"They *do* appear somewhat irate." Magnan began backing away. "Don't lose your heads, gentlemen!" Treadwater croaked. "We'll demand the privileges of honorable prisoners of war—"

"We haven't lost, yet," Retief pointed out.

"An excellent point, Mr. Retief." The Ambassador reached for the Groaci raft. "I hereby appoint you as a special committee to meet with these fellows and study their grievances. If you can drag the talks out for an hour, the rest of us will go for help."

"Quite an honor, my boy," Colonel Pluckwyn said, as he tumbled a faintly protesting Groaci over the side. "And you merely a Second Secretary."

"I don't think we should do anything hasty," Retief said. "Now that the North Skweemans have had a taste of Groaci sponsorship, they may be ready for our program."

Councillor Lith, showing signs of wear and tear, surfaced beside Retief, having been replaced by a Terran aboard the raft. "Some day, Terry, the truth of this affair will out," he hissed in faint Groaci ferocity.

"Why be pessimistic?" Retief responded. "If you play your cards right, the North Skweemans may never learn that the dam was placed so that when the basin was full you could open the flood gates and wipe out their capital along with anything that might have been left of South Skweem, leaving an open field for a Groaci take-over."

"What? Are you suggesting—"

"I'd suggest dawn as a reasonable deadline," Retief went on. "If you wade along with Ambassador Treadwater, you can get off a 'gram and have a ship in here to pick you up by then. I can't guarantee that I can keep it quiet much longer than that."

"Hey!" Dimplick shouted suddenly. "Look at the placard they're waving!" Retief glanced toward the approaching North Skweemans, coming up rapidly now.

"Why, those appear to be hastily lettered pro-Terry slogans," the Political Officer burst out.

"Have you lost your wits?" Treadwater rumbled. He peered through the gloom. "Hmmm. It appears you're right." He straightened his back. "Just as I expected, of course. I knew that my policies toward these fellows would bear fruit, given time." He shot Magnan a reproving look. "A pity you chose to go junketing just at the climactic point of the finesse. You missed a valuable lesson in diplomatic sublety."

Magnan opened his mouth, caught a look from Retief, closed it again.

"I'm sure we were all fooled by Your Excellency's apparent total inactivity, sir," he gulped.

"Exactly." Treadwater beamed around at the others as the front-runners of the North Skweeman delegation arrived, uttering cries of delight and pledging eternal friendship. "It appears we'll have a solid electorate behind us, gentlemen! My job—that is to say, the future of Terran-Skweeman relations seems secure. Now, if we just had an adequate Project Proposal to offer Sector Headquarters, our cup would be brimming." He stepped forward, began shaking members left to right. "Sir!" Secretary Dimplick bounded forward. "I've a dandy notion! Why not build a new capital for United Skweem to replace the former city swept away by the flood?"

"Of course!" Colonel Pluckwyn chimed in. "My idea exactly; just waiting for an appropriate moment to mention it. I'd also suggest a massive aid program to rectify the other ravages of the disaster."

"Food!" the Agricultural Attache shouted. "I think I can justify a schedule of deliveries under the Chrunchies for Lunchies program that will keep two dozen

Corps bottoms in use for the next fiscal quarter!''

"Superb, gentlemen!" Treadwater warbled. "I can see promotions all around—to say nothing of extra staff, monuments to Skweeman independence and democratic solidarity, larger operational budgets, and a magnificent new Terran Chancery rising from the ruins!''

"Say, Mr. Retief." The junior Third Secretary plucked at his sleeve. "I thought these North Skweemans were little better than dacoits and brigands; suddenly they're welcomed as bosom friends.

"True, they're a shifty lot," Retief confided as he accepted a moist Skweeman handshake. "But who are we to be choosy?"

GRIME AND PUNISHMENT

I

THE VOICE of Consul General Magnan, Terran envoy to Slunch, crackled sharply through Vice-consul Retief's earphones as he steered the slab-sided mud-car up the slope through the dense smog issuing from the innumerable bubbling mud-pockets in the rocky ground.

"Retief, this whole idea is insane! We're likely to bog down or be blown up; we'll have to turn back!"

"It's just a few hundred yards now," Retief replied.

"Look here! As chief of mission, I'm responsible for the safety of all Terran personnel on Slunch, which means, specifically, you and me. It's not that I'm timid, you understand, but—Look out!" he shouted suddenly, as Retief cut hard at the wheel to avoid the uprearing form of a twenty-foot tangleworm. Magnan chopped with his machete as the blind creature swung its capacious jaws toward him. Brown juices spattered as the severed, football head tumbled into the car, still biting the air.

He kicked it away and wiped a mud-stained sleeve across his face, peering ahead through the smoky air.

"There it is now," Retief pointed. Through the murky atmosphere, a dull glow swam into visibility. Half a minute later the mud-car came to a halt at the brink of a vast sinkhole, from which choking, sulphurous fumes rose in ochre billows, reflecting the fitful play of light from below.

Retief swung over the side of the car, went forward to the precipitous edge. Magnan advanced cautiously behind him.

"You see those openings down there?" Retief pointed through the swirling vapors. "I think we can work our way down along the ledge on this side, then—"

"Great heavens, Retief!" Magnan broke in. "You seriously propose that we explore this—this subterranean furnace—on foot?" His voice rose to the breaking point.

"We'll be all right inside our thermal suits," the junior diplomat said. "If we can discover which vents are the ones—"

"Mark!" Magnan raised a hand. A new, deeper, rumble was rising to drown the fretful murmurings from underfoot.

"Is that—could that be high tide coming?" he gasped.

Retief shook his head. "Not due for six hours yet. You're not by any chance expecting a ship today?"

"A ship? No, I wasn't—but yes—it could be . . ." Far above, a faint bluish light flickered through the clouds, descending. "It is!" Magnan turned toward the car. "Come along, Retief! We'll have to go back at once!"

Ten minutes later, the car emerged from the fumes of the field onto an expanse of of waving foot-high stems which leaned to snatch at the car's oversized wheels with tiny claws. Retief shifted to low gear, to the accompaniment of ripping sounds as the strands of tough grabgrass parted. Beyond the town, the newly arrived vessel stood, a silvery dart against the black clouds rolling slowly upward from the tar pits in the distance.

"Retief, that's a Corps vessel!" Magnan said excitedly. "Heavens! You don't suppose Sector has decided to cut the tour of duty on Slunch to three months, and sent our relief along a year and a half ahead of schedule?"

"It's more likely they're shipping us a new ping-pong table to soften the blow of the news the tour's being extended to five years."

"Even ping-pong equipment would be a shade nearer the mark than the six gross of roller skates the Recreational Service sent out, Magnan sniffed.

"They're running out the VIP pennant," Retief called.

Magnan shaded his eyes. "Damn it! No doubt it's a party of junketing legislators, out to be wined and dined out of our consular luxury allowance."

Five minutes later, the car pulled up in the lee of the gleaming vessel with the ornate crest of the *Corps Diplomatique Terrestrienne* blazoned on its prow. Already, a few questing runners of creeper vine had found the ship and were making their way rapidly up the landing vanes and twining over the access lock. As Magnan descended, machete in hand, to clear the entry, the ship's exit lock swung open and extruded a landing ramp. Half a dozen Terrans, resplendent in pearl-gray pre-tiffin sub-informal coveralls and lime green seersucker dickeys emerged, drawing deep, healing lungfuls of air and immediately coughing violently.

"No time to waste, gentlemen," Magnan called, his voice muffled by his breathing mask. "Everybody out and into the car!"

A stout man with the look of a senior attache shied violently as Magnan confronted him. Those behind recoiled toward the lock.

"Good Lord! Dacoits!" The fat man raised his hands, backing away. "Don't strike sir! We're merely harmless bureaucrats!"

"Eh?" Magnan stared at the newcomers. "Look here, I don't wish to alarm you, but unless you come along at once, you're all going to be in serious danger. The air. . . ."

"Ransom!" the fat man cried. "I have a doting auntie, sir, who'll pay handsomely! The old minnie has more money than she knows what to do with."

"What's going on here!" A tall, broad-shouldered man had appeared at the lock, staring down at the tableau with a stern look.

"Look out, sir!" a small, wispy staffer chirped. "He has a dreadful-looking sword!"

"I'll handle this!" The big man pushed forward, stared down at Magnan. "Now then, what was it you wanted, fellow?"

"Why, ah," the consul general temporized, backing a step. "I just came out to welcome you to Slunch, sir, and to offer you transportation back to the consulate—''

"You're from the consulate?" the big man boomed.

"Of course."

"I'll have a word to say to the consul about sending a sweeper to welcome an arriving trade mission," the fat attache said, pushing forward. "I knew the moment I laid eyes on him."

Magnan gobbled. "A full-scale trade mission? But I've only been here three months! There hasn't been time—''

"Ha!" the big man cut him off. "I'm beginning to understand. You're a member of the diplomatic staff, are you?" He looked Magnan up and down, taking in the hip boots, the gauntlets, the battered poncho, the black smudges of soot under his eyes.

"Of course. And—''

"Yes, you'd be that fellow Whatshisname. They told me about you back at Sector. Well, there are a number of matters I intend to set you straight on at the outset." The big man's steely eye transfixed the astounded Magnan. "I'm putting you on notice that I have no sympathy with undisciplined upstarts!"

"I . . . I think your excellency has the wrong upstart," Magnan stammered. "That's Retief over there, in the old horse blanket. I'm Magnan, the principal officer."

"Wha . . . ?"

"It's not really a horse blanket," Magnan amended hastily. "Actually it's an urze-beast blanket. It's for the mud, you understand; and the rain, and the soot, and the nitmites—''

"Well, anyone could have made the mistake," the

fat staff member said. "This chap certainly *looks* ferocious enough."

"That's enough!" The new arrival thrust out his lower lip. "I'm Rainsinger. Just pass along what I said to the proper party."

He smoothed his features with an effort. "Mr. Magnan, you'll be delighted to know I've brought along a number of items for you."

"How grand!" Magnan beamed. "Gourmet foods for the consulate larder, I suppose? A nice selection of wines, of course—and possibly—" he winked playfully—"a library of racy sense-tapes?"

Rainsinger blinked. "Nothing so frivolous," he said flatly. "Actually, it's an automatic tombstone factory, complete, adequate to serve a community of one hundred thousand souls." He rubbed his hands together briskly. "After we've gotten the natives started on proper interment, we can expand into the casket and embalming end. The possibilities are staggering." His eye fell on the mud car. "What's *that?*"

"You gentlemen will have to excuse the limousine," Magnan said. "Freddy didn't have time to dust it up after the little shower we had this morning. Mind your trousers, now."

"This is a Marx IX diplomatic issue limousine?" The fat man gaped at the conveyance. "Why, it's made of baling wire and clapboards!"

"The mud crabs ate the other body," Magnan explained. "They found the plastic highly palatable. I saved the cigar lighters, though."

"By golly, speaking of eating, I could do with a bite of lunch," the fat man said to no one in particular.

Rainsinger gave Magnan a hard stare. "Well, under

the circumstances, I suppose a case could be made for a Report of Survey. By the way, how is the berp-nut crop?'' He looked around the mud-coated port. ''How many bottoms will you require for the first shipment?''

''Ah . . . none, to be precise,'' Magnan said faintly. ''There isn't any shipment.''

''No berp-nuts?'' Rainsinger's left eyebrow went up as the right came down in a ferocious scowl. ''As I understand your instructions, Magnan, your sole mission here is to flog up a little enthusiasm among the Slunchans for Terry goods. Since berp-nuts are the sole Slunchan source of foreign exchange, I fail to see how we can succeed without them!''

''Unfortunately, the mud seems to have a corrosive effect on most everything we manufacture,'' Magnan said. ''Like shoes, for example.'' He eyed Rainsinger's feet. The visitor followed his gaze.

''My shoes!'' he yelped. ''Magnan, you idiot, get me out of this mud at once!''

Coughing, the newcomers sloshed across to the vehicle, mounted the rude ladder, stared with dismay at the mud-coated benches.

''Hold tight,'' Magnan called with an attempt at gaiety. ''We'll have to hurry to get you in out of the weather. Don't be alarmed. We should get through with no more than a few mud burns, and maybe the old firebug bite.''

At the wheel, he gunned the car in a wide circle, inadvertently sending a sheet of mud sluicing over the polished stern of the vessel and the crisp whites of the crewmen peering from the lock. There were shrill cries as the passengers went reeling to form an untidy heap at the rear of the car. Of the visitors, only Inspector

Rainsinger remained on his feet, gripping the upright that supported the sheet-metal awning.

"You'll soon catch on," Magnan called over his shoulder. "Gracious, you already look like old veterans, and you've only been here ten minutes!"

II

Magnan steered the car across the soft, black half-inch mud of the plaza, pulled up before an entry where a paunchy, splay-footed little humanoid with a flattened skull and a loose, liver-colored hide leaned on a combination broom-rake, humming to himself.

"Drive on, Mr. Magnan," Rainsinger barked. "We can tour the slum areas later, after my staff and I have had an opportunity to freshen up a bit."

"But—but this is the consulate," Magnan explained with a glassy smile.

Rainsinger stared with a darkening expression at the scorched, chipped and discolored facade, banked with drifted muck from which tufts of greenery sprouted.

"This is the new building, completed only ninety standard days ago at a cost of one hundred thousand credits of Corps funds?"

"Ah, that's right, sir." Magnan climbed down from his seat.

Rainsinger looked down at the sea of oleaginous black mud in which the car rested hub-deep. "I'm supposed to walk through that?" he demanded.

"Retief could carry you," Magnan proposed brightly.

Rainsinger shot him a sharp look. "If there's any

carrying to be done, I'll do it.'' He stepped down, followed by his staff, squelched through the ankle-deep mud that coated the ornamental tile steps. As they passed, Magnan beckoned to the native sweeper.

"See here, Freddy, let's see a little more spit and polish,'' he whispered. "Don't just knock those mud-puppy nests down; sweep the extra mud into neat little piles or something. We don't want our visitors to imagine we've grown slovenly, you know. And you'd better dig out the entrance to the snack bar and squirt a little more deodorant around; the stench-fungus is getting the upper hand again.''

"Mud smooth nice my up messing are fellows these, Magnan Mister, hey!'' the local protested in his scratchy voice.

"It's all right, Freddy,'' Magnan soothed. "Ah . . . headquarters from shots big, they're,'' he added in an undertone.

Inside, Rainsinger stared about incredulously at the runners of vine poking in through shattered windows, the dried and caked mud through which footpaths led to the grand staircase, itself well nigh buried under a luxuriant growth of coiling green weed. He started as a sharp-nosed rat scurried into view, scuttled away into the shelter of a pile of brush heaped carelessly beside the balustrade.

"Shall we have a look at the chancery wing?'' he inquired in ominous tones.

"Say, where do we eat lunch?'' the portly attache looked around curiously.

"Maybe we'd better not go up just yet. . . .'' Magnan broke off as a cascade of brown water came surging down from the landing above, bearing with it a flotsam of papers, twigs, vigorously swimming small animals and other odds and ends. The stream struck the floor, sluiced its way across to the exit and poured out into the street, eliciting a loud cry from Freddy.

"Conception esthetic whole my up loused they've!" his voice was hoarse with indignation. "On going what's?"

"Unplugged drains those got I, Magnan Mister Oh!" a cheery Slunthan voice called from above.

"Hmmm. Unfortunate timing," Magnan said. "But at least it scoured a path for us." He led the way up the stairs and along a corridor, the walls of which were obscured by a ragged growth of vines, through which discolored wallpaper was visible. He ducked under a festoon of creepers undulating in a doorway, waved the team members into his spacious office. Rainsinger stopped dead as his eye fell on the mud-clotted weeds layering the floor, the slab of rough ironwood spanning two upended oil drums serving as a desk, the clustered stems crowding the glassless windows.

There was a moment of profound silence. Then:

"Gentlemen!" The trade mission chief's voice had something of the quality of a volcano preparing to erupt. "During my career I've encountered slackness, inefficiency and disorder at many a station. A little dust on the filing cabinets, a few dope-stick burns in the upholstery, gum wrappers in the john—even some minor discrepancies in the voucher files—all these are normal concomitants of life at a remote post. But this!" His voice rose. "This model town, built with CDT funds as a gift to the Slunchan people less than six months ago—a perfect example of civic design produced by the most skillful Deep Think teams on the departmental payroll! Look at it! A blighted area! A pest hole! And the consulate general itself! Two inches of mud in the main lounge! Broken drains flooding the halls! Rats, mice and vermin swarming in every nook and cranny! Weeds sprouting in the corridors! Broken glass! Vanished furnishings! Vandalism! Dereliction of duty! Destruction of Corps property! And withal—no berp-nuts!''

With an effort he pulled his voice back into the lower registers and directed a chilling gaze at Magnan.

''Sir, as of this moment you may consider yourself suspended, relieved of duty and under close house arrest! Under emergency powers vested in me under Article Nine, Section Four, Title Two of Corps Regulations, I'm taking personal command!''

''But—but, sir!'' Magnan protested. ''I haven't yet had time to settle in, as it were. The mud crabs ate the furniture; and the conditions here—the mud tides and the cinder storms, and the shortage of local labor and . . . and. . . .''

''Say, I was wondering—how about a sandwich,'' the fat attache put in.

''No excuses!'' Rainsinger bellowed. ''We built the town to point these benighted natives the way to higher living standards and an increased consumption of Terry-manufactured goods! A fine example you've set, sir! But I'll do what I can in the eleventh hour to retrieve the situation!''

He whirled on his staff.

''Blockchip, you'll take a detail and attend to the broken plumbing. Horace—'' he addressed the stout attache— ''you'll see to shovelling out the mud from the ground floor. Poindexter will seal off the upper floors and fumigate. As for you, Mr. Magnan—I'm suspending your arrest long enough for you to round up an adequate labor force to unload the cargo I brought in." He looked at his old-fashioned strap watch.

"I'll expect to see this building spotless by sundown, in time for a reception to be held this evening at eight o'clock sharp. Full formal attire, including clean fingernails! I'll show these natives how civilized Terrans live—and inspire the wish to emulate us!"

"Ah—there might be a little trouble about the local labor," Magnan spoke up. "The Slunchans have rigid taboos against working on weekdays."

"This is Sunday!"

"How true, sir. Unfortunately, they don't work on Sundays, either."

"Offer them double wages!"

"They don't use money."

"Then offer them what they want!"

"All they want is for us to go away."

"Mr. Magnan." Rainsinger cut him off with an ominous tone. "I suggest you discontinue your obstructionism at once, or the word 'insubordination' will be cropping up in my report, along with a number of other terms non-conducive to rapid advancement in the service!" He broke off to grab up a bound volume of Corps regulations from the improvised desk and hurl it at an inquisitive vine rat which poked its snout above the window sill.

"Oh, I wouldn't do that, sir," Magnan blurted. "In about five hours—"

"Save your advice!" Rainsinger raored. "I'm in charge here now! You may make yourself useful by ringing up the Slunchan Foreign Minister and making me an appointment. I'll show you how to handle these locals! In an hour I'll have him begging for Terran imports!''

"Ah, about lunch," the stout attache began.

"I'll have him here in a jiffy," Magnan said. He stepped to the door. "Oh, Freddy," he called. A moment later a Slunchan appeared in the doorway.

"It is what; boss, yeah?" the local looked around the office. "Mat floor a for sneakweed the using, effect snazzy a that's, say!" he exclaimed.

"Mr. Rainsinger, may I present—" Magnan started.

"Here, isn't this the fellow who was raking mud at the front door as we came in?" Rainsinger demanded.

"Yes, indeed. Of course Freddy is just filling in for the regular man. As I was saying, may I present Sir Frederik Gumbubu, K.G.E., L. deC., N.G.S., Slunchan Minister of Foreign Affairs."

"A Foreign Minister? A part-time janitor?" Rainsinger took the proffered hand gingerly.

"Know you, do to ministering foreign my got I've," the Slunchan said defensively. "Janitor time full a be to me expect couldn't you, all after, well." He rolled a ball of dried mud between his fingers, lined up on a framed photo of the sector undersecretary and scored a bull's-eye.

"Mr. Magnan, I stand astounded at your ingenuity," Rainsinger said in a voice like broken crockery. "Not content with failing in your mission while violating every regulation in the book, you invent a unique offense by demeaning an official of a friendly foreign power to the performance of menial tasks in your own Consulate!"

"But, sir! Freddy's one of the few locals with a taste

for Pepsi. And the only way he can get it," he added behind his hand, "is to work here. I pay him off with a case a week."

"Get somebody else!"

"Job my me lose to trying you are—hey?" Freddy broke in.

"I can't!" Magnan wailed. "Scout's honor, sir—they won't work!"

"Union labor the with beef a for looking you're maybe," Freddy said. "Action fast you promise can I, member sole and president the be to happen I as and!"

"Look here, ah, Sir Frederik." Rainsinger faced the foreign minister. "I'm sure we can work out a mutually agreeable arrangement. You round up and send along about a hundred good workers, and I'll see to it that Slunch is given full Most Favored Nation status in the new Trade Agreement I'm about to propose."

"It do can't, nope," the Slunchan said shortly.

"Now, don't be hasty, Mr. Minister," Rainsinger persisted. "I'm prepared to promise you prompt shipment of any items you care to name. What about a nice line of genuine machine-loomed antimacassars, inscribed with patriotic and inspirational mottos? I can make you an attractive price on lots of a hundred thousand."

Sir Frederik shook his flat head sadly. "Items luxury afford can't we, bringing nuts-berps prices the at—nix!"

Rainsinger took the minister's elbow in a fatherly grip. "Now, Freddy. . . ."

"It's no use, sir," Magnan interposed glumly. "Lord knows I've tried. But they're incurably content. They already have everything they want."

"That's enough of your defeatism," Rainsinger snapped. "You'd best be on your way, and take Mr. Retief with you. I'll pitch in myself, as soon as I've given a few more instructions. We have a great deal of ground to cover if we're to be ready to receive our guests in four and a half hours!"

III

"Well, Magnan," Rainsinger complacently surveyed the chattering conversational groups of Slunchans and Terrans dotted across the gleaming ballroom floor, newly ornamented along one wall by a tasteful display of engraved headstones and funerary urns. "I must say we've acquitted ourselves creditably. And I've taken measures to insure conditions don't deteriorate again." He lifted a glass from a passing tray borne by a Slunchan who limped heavily.

"Hmmm. Chap seems to have a cast on his foot," the Inspector remarked. "Couldn't you have secured able-bodied personnel to staff the catering function, Magnan?"

"He's not actually injured, sir," Magnan said. "He just happened to step in some, er, material."

"Say, isn't that a lump of powdered tombstone adhering to his foot?" Rainsinger demanded suspiciously. "I hope you haven't handled my cargo carelessly!"

"Say, when are the sandwiches coming?" the stout attache inquired testily.

"Ah, here comes the premier," Magnan cut in as a loose-hided local approached, rotating a hula-hoop with his torso. "Hi, there, your Excellency. May I present Mr. Rainsinger our new, er, ah. Sir, Mr. Blabghug, the leader of the Slunchan people in their fight against, ah, whatever it is they're fighting against.''

Rainsinger nodded curtly, eyeing the muddy tracks across the floor left by the chief executive. ''See here, Blabghug,'' he said in a no-nonsense tone. ''I'd like to request that you have your people step up the street-cleaning program. Those pavements are a gift of the Terrestrial taxpayer.''

''Too, was it gesture nice a and,'' Blabghug acknowledged cheerfully. ''Them see to get never we bad too.''

''Yes. My point exactly. Now, Mr. Prime Minister; I've been here for only five hours, but I've already gotten a firm grasp of the situation and I see what the source of our problem is. Once we've cleared up the more active vermin—''

''Vermin what?''

''That little monster, for one!'' Rainsinger nodded sharply toward an inquisitive rodentoid nose poking around the nearest door.

''Kidding be must you,'' Balbghug said. ''Rats-vine the for wasn't it if—''

''As soon as we've completed dusting with fast-acting pesticides, we'll see no more of the creatures,'' Rainsinger bored on. ''Meanwhile, a few zillion tons of weed killer will control these man-eating vines you've been tolerating so complacently.''

''About talking you're what know don't you,'' Blabghug protested.

''I know how to conduct a clean-up campaign!'' Rainsinger came back hotly. ''This state of affairs is an insult to the Slunchan people and a reflection on the Terran Consulate! I've already set wheels in motion—''

He broke off as a low rumble tinkled the newly polished glass of the chandelier. A deep-throated *ba-rooom!* sounded, like a distant cannonade, followed by a vast, glutinous *smooosh!*

Magan glanced at his watch. "Right on time," he said.

The Slunchan premier cocked his head thoughtfully. "Usual than fluid more little a sounds that," he commented. "High early an for ready get better we'd."

"What the devil's he saying, Magnan?" Rainsinger muttered in an aside. "I can't make out one word in three."

"High mud in a few minutes," Magnan translated, as a second shock rocked the ballroom. A heavy splattering sounded, as of moist material raining against the building.

"Up button to time, oh-oh," Blabghug warned. He stepped to the nearest window and slammed shut a set of improvised shutters.

"What's this, Mr. Retief?" Rainsinger inquired. "Some sort of religious observation? Tribal taboo sort of thing?"

"No, it's just to keep the worst of the soot and mud out of the building during the eruption."

"What's this about an eruption?"

"It's a sort of mud geyser. Shoots a few million tons of glop into the air every twenty-seven hours."

Rainsinger blinked. "A million tons of glop?"

A third, even more vigorous tremor caused the ballroom to sway drunkenly. Rainsinger braced his feet, thrust out his chin, glared at Magnan, who was staring anxiously toward the door.

"Glop or no glop, this is an official diplomatic function, gentlemen! We'll carry on, and ignore the disturbance!"

"Frankly, I don't like the sound of that mud, sir." Magnan turned to the window, peered through a crack in the shutter.

"No doubt the consulate has weathered such conditions before," Rainsinger said uncertainly. "No reason why. . . ."

His voice was drowned by an ominously rising bubbling sound swelling outside. At the window, Magnan emitted a sharp yelp, leaped back as something struck the side of the building with an impact like a tidal wave. Jets of ink-black mud squirted into the room like fire hoses through every cranny around the shutters. One stream caught Rainsinger full in the flowered weskit, almost knocked him down.

"One bad a is this!" Blabghug called over the hissing and splattering. "Look a have and roof the for head better we'd think I!"

"He's right, sir!" Magnan raised his voice. "This way!" He led the excited party along a hall, up a stair splattered with steaming mud from a shattered window on the landing. Emerging on the roof, Rainsinger ducked as a head-sized cinder slammed down beside him, bounded high and disappeared over the side. A rain of mud splattered down around them. The air was thick with tarry soot. Coughing, Rainsinger hastily donned the breathing mask offered by Magnan.

"This must be the worst disaster ever recorded

here," he shouted over the groaning and squishing of the mud welling along the street below them.

"No, actually, by the sound of it, it's a rather mild one, as eruptions go," Retief leaned close to shout. "But the mud seems to be running wild."

"There look!" Blabghug shouted, pointing. "Seven-sixty in back made mark mud-high record the over it's!"

"There's something wrong," Retief called over the still-rising roar of the flowing mud. "The tide's not acting normally. Too fluid—and too much of it."

"Why on Slunch, with an entire planet to choose from, was the town situated in a disaster area?" Rainsinger frowned ferociously as sounds of massive gurglings and sloshing sounded from below.

"It appears this was one of the rush jobs," Magnan called. "The entire city was erected in four days which happened to be during a seasonal lull in the underground coolery."

"See here, Magnan, why didn't you report the situation?"

"I did. As I recall, my dispatch ran to three hundred and four pages!"

"A three hundred page dispatch? And nothing was done?"

"We received a consignment of twelve brooms, six dust-pans and a gross of mops. They must have been overstocked on mops back at Sector."

"And that's *all?*" Rainsinger's voice almost cracked.

"I think that's about as far as Headquarters could go without admitting a mistake had been made."

Across the street, the swelling, bubbling surface of

the mud flow was rising past the first row of windows. Shutters creaked and burst inward. Refugees were crowding onto roofs all along the streets now. Retief stepped to the edge of the roof, looked down at the heaving bosom of the sea of mud, dotted with small, sodden forms, floating inertly. A great mass of dead creeper vine came sweeping along on the flood. A tongue of mud sluicing in from a side street struck a wall, sent a great gout thundering upward to descend on the crowded consulate roof. Diplomats and locals alike yelped and slapped at the hot, corrosive muck.

"Look there!" Magnan pointed to the feebly struggling body of a large vine-rat, which gave a final twitch and expired.

"Trouble in we're, oh-oh!" Premier Blabghug exclaimed, as other Slunchans gathered about, talking rapidly.

"Why all the excitement about a dead animal?" Rainsinger barked.

"It's a vine-rat," Magnan blurted. "What could have killed it?"

"I imagine the vigorous application of pest-killer I ordered had something to do with it," the inspector snapped. "I suggest we defer grieving over the beggar until after we've taken steps to extricate ourselves from this situation!"

"You . . . you ordered *what?*" Magnan quavered.

"Ten tons of rodenticide, from your own consulate stores," Rainsinger said firmly. "I don't wonder you're astonished at the speed with which I went into action—"

"You . . . you didn't!"

"Indeed I did, sir! Now stop goggling at a purely

routine display of efficiency, and let's determine what we're to do about this mud."

"But—" Magnan wailed. "If you killed off the vine-rats—that means the creeper-vine was allowed to grow all afternoon, uncontrolled—"

"Uncontrolled?"

"By the rats," Magnan groaned. "So the vines got the upper hand over the grab-grass—and it's the grass, of course, which suppresses the tangleworms—"

"Tangleworms?"

"And the young worms eat the egg-nit grubs," Magnan yelped. "The egg-nits being the only thing that keeps the firebugs under control—though of course the vine-rats need them for protein in the diet; while their droppings nourish the sneak weed which provides a haven for the nit-mites which prey on the mud-crabs—"

"Here, what's all this nonsense!" Rainsinger roared over the roar of the rising mud-flood. "You'd chatter on about the local wildlife, with disaster lapping at our ankles?"

"That's what I've been trying tell you!" Magnan's voice broke. "With the ecological cycle broken, there's nothing to control the mud! That's why it's rising! And in another hour it will be up over roof level and that—" he shuddered—"will be a very sticky ending for all of us!"

IV

"Why, I don't believe it," Rainsinger said hoarsely, as he stared over the roof's edge at the steadily rising mud, its surface hazed with sulphurous fumes. "You mean to tell me that these worms were all that kept the mud in check?"

"That's an oversimplification—but yes." Magnan dabbed at the mud on his chin. "I'm afraid you've upset the blance of nature."

"All right, men!" Rainsinger turned to face his staff, huddled in the most protected corner of the roof. "It seems we've painted ourselves into a bit of a corner, ha-ha." He paused to square his shoulders and clear his throat. "However, there's no point in crying over spilled mud. Now, who has a suggestion for a dynamic course of action from this point onward? Horace, Poindexter?"

"I suggest we write out our wills and place them in mud and heatproof jackets," a lean accountant type proposed in a reedy voice.

"Now, men! No defeatism! Surely there's some simple way to elude our apparent fate! Mr. Premier." He faced the Slunchan contingent, muttering together at a short distance from the Terrans. "What do your people have in mind?"

"Opinion of difference a there's," Blabghug said. "Mud the into you pitching for out holding are extremists the but. Limb from limb you tear to want fellow the of few a."

"It's hopeless!" a trembling Terran blurted, staring down at the heaving surface of the tarry mud. "We'll all be drowned, scalded and eaten alive by acid!"

"Magnan!" Rainsinger whirled on the former chief of mission. "You chaps must have had some sort of plan of action for such an eventuality!"

"Nothing." Magnan shook his head. "*We* never interfered with Nature's Plan." His eyes strayed across the steaming bog now washing about the fourth story windows of the model town. On high ground half a mile distant, the slim form of the vacated Corps Vessel stood. Beyond it rose the rugged peaks from which the mud-flow issued.

"Retief *did* have some sort of mad notion of diverting the gusher at its source," he said, "but of course that's hopeless—especially now. I daresay it's all under mud."

"Retief!" Rainsinger hurried across to where the young man was prying a board from a ventilator housing. "What's this about a scheme to dam off the mud?"

Retief pointed to a rickety construction of boards, afloat in the mud below.

"It's the body off the car. It won't make the best boat in the world, I'm afraid, but as soon as it gets within reach I'll give it a try."

"You'll sink," Magnan predicted, standing at the fifth floor window through which Retief had climbed to secure the makeshift skiff. "You can't possibly row that contrivance with a board across half a mile of mud!"

"Maybe not," Retief said. He dropped down into the boat. "But if it sinks, I won't have to row it."

"Maybe the mud won't come this high," someone offered. "Maybe if we just wait here—"

"If we don't go now, it will be too late," Rainsinger cut off the discussion.

"We?" Magnan said.

"Certainly." Rainsinger threw a leg over the sill,

lowered himself down beside Retief. "It will take two men to row this thing. Cast off, Mr. Retief, whenever you're ready."

V

For ten minutes the two men paddled in silence. Looking back, Retief saw the consulate tower rising from the bubbling mud, almost obscured by the wafting vapors. In a bundle at his feet were the two thermal suits and a number of small packets previously prepared but unused.

"Better get your suit on, Mr. Rainsinger," he said.

"I give them another half hour," Rainsinger called, his voice muffled by his breathing mask. "How much farther?"

"Ten minutes," Retief said, "until we ground on the hill. Then five minutes walk." He paddled as Rainsinger pulled on the bulky thermal suit.

Beside him, a loose board creaked; mud slopped over the low gunwale. A sudden bulging of the mud almost swamped the boat; a bursting gas bubble threw a stinging spray across both men.

"When we get there—what?"

"We hope it's not already flooded out."

Five minutes later, just as Retief had pulled on his heat-suit, the overloaded boat emitted a sudden massive creaking and disintegrated.

"Jump!" Retief called; he grabbed the bundles and went over the side, landing in knee-deep muck, turned to lend a hand to Rainsinger, who floundered after him. They fought their way up-slope, emerged on a rocky shore at which the surging mud lapped like a sea of chocolate pudding.

"It's pretty deep," Retief said. "Let's hope it's not into the main bore yet."

Rainsinger followed Retief up the steep slope. Ahead, a ruddy glare lightened the murky scene. They reached the edge of the great circular vent from which smoke and cinders boiled furiously, whirling glowing embers high in the air. Rainsinger stared down into the white-hot pit.

"Ye gods, man," he shouted over the din. "That's an active volcano! What in the world do you plan to do here?"

"Climb down inside and pull the plug," Retief said.

"I forbid it!" Rainsinger yelled. "It's suicide!"

"If I don't, the consulate will go under with all hands—to say nothing of a few thousand Slunchans."

"That's no reason to throw your life away! We'll head for higher ground and try to work our way around to the ship. We might be able to summon help—"

"Not a chance," Retief said. He started forward. Rainsinger stepped in his way, a bulky figure in the mud-coated heat-suit. They faced each other, two big men, toe to toe.

"That's an order!" Rainsinger grated.

"Better stand aside, Mr. Rainsinger," Retief said.

"I've warned you," Rainsinger said, and drove a short, sledge-hammer right to Retief's mid-section. Retief grunted and took a step back.

"You throw a good right, Mr. Rainsinger," he said through his teeth. "How are you at catching?"—and he slammed a straight left that spun the other around, sent him to his knees. Retief started past him, and

Rainsinger dived, tackled him from the side. Retief twisted, drove a knee to Rainsinger's chin. He went down on his face.

"Sorry," Retief said. He went forward, picked his spot and lowered his feet over the edge. Behind him, Rainsinger called out. Retief looked back. The trade mission chief struggled to his feet, stood swaying back and forth.

"You'll probably need a little help down there," he said blurrily as he started forward. "Wait for me. . . ."

Roped together, the two men worked their way from one precarious foothold to the next, descending toward the smoky surface bubbling beneath them. A hundred feet below the crater's rim, Retief gripped Rainsinger's arm, pointed through the swirling clouds of soot.

"The level's risen about a hundred feet," he said. "If it reaches that series of vents along the north side before we can block them, the volume of the flow will double, and fill the valley in no time. We have to reach them and plug them before the mud covers them."

"What good will that do?" Rainsinger's voice came thinly through Retief's earset. "It will just keep rising until it goes all the way over the top!"

"That brings us to part two," Retief said. "You see that dark patch there, on the south wall, a little higher up? That's an old vent, silted up a long time ago. If we can blast it clear in time, the flow will go down the other side, away from the town."

Rainsinger studied the aspect below.

"We'll never make it," he said grimly. "Let's get started."

Another ten minutes' climb brought Retief and Rainsinger to the set of side-channels leading to the valley and the town. Working rapidly, Retief placed the charges of smashite so as to collapse the four six-foot-wide openings.

"All set," he called. "We'll take shelter from the blast in the other cave."

"It will be close," Rainsinger said. "The mud's risen ten feet in the last five minutes. Another ten feet and we're out of luck!"

"Come on!" Retief followed a ledge that led halfway around the seventy-foot throat of the volcano, then used a series of cracks and knobs to cover the remaining distance. The boiling muck was a bare six inches from his feet when he reached the dark conduit. Twenty feet inside its mouth, their progress was halted by an obstructing mass of hardened mud and volcanic ash.

"We'll fire our other charges first," Retief said. "As soon as they blow, we'll set another one here and head for the surface."

"I don't like the looks of this, Retief! All this rock is full of fractures!"

"I'm not too fond of it myself," Retief said. "Better turn off your earset. Here goes!"

He pressed the button on the detonator in his hand. White light winked; the crash that followed was deafening even over the shrieking of the volcano. Rock fragments rained down past the cave opening, sending geysers of steaming lava fountaining high. There was a deeper rumble, and the floor shook under them. A giant slab of stone dropped into view, lodged across the throat of the volcano. Others slammed down, packing themselves into place with impacts like mountains falling. Trapped smoke and dust recoiled, thickening into opacity.

"That does it!" Rainsinger shouted. "We've blocked the main passage! We can't get out!"

"It looks that way—" Retief started. His voice was cut off by a thunderous boom as the cave's roof fell in.

"Retief!" Rainsinger's voice was a hoarse croak in the relative silence after the last rattle of falling rock had died away. "Are you still alive?"

"For the moment," Retief reassured his companion.

"Well—if there was any doubt about whether we'd get out, this finishes it," Rainsinger said grimly.

"Let's take a look," Retief suggested. Using hand-lamps, they scanned their surroundings. The original cave was now a rubble-choked pocket, blocked at one end by the lava plug, at the other by multi-ton fragments of fallen rock, through which small trickles of mud were already finding their way.

"The only remaining question is whether we broil in hot mud, drown in lava or die of asphyxiation," Rainsinger said grimly.

"It would be interesting to know whether our blast did any good," Retief said. "Will the lava go over the top, or will the dam hold?"

"Let's tell ourselves it wasn't all in vain," Rainsinger grunted. "Don't misinterpret my remarks," he added. "I'm not complaining. I have only myself to blame. I started the whole thing with my misplaced zeal." He laughed hollowly. "And I was going to make a name for myself by putting Slunch on the map, businesswise."

"Let's just blame it on local conditions and let it go at that," Retief suggested. He looked at the gauge on his wrist. "The temperature in here is ninety-one and a half degrees Centigrade. It looks as if drowning is out."

"Look, the mud's hardening as it comes through the barrier," Rainsinger said. "The trickle's choking off." He looked thoughtful. "By now the level outside our door is up to the blockage. If the lava that squeezes through that hardens as fast as this did. . . ."

A tremor went through the cave's floor. "Oh-oh!" Rainsinger rocked on his feet. "Looks like this is it, Retief. . . ."

"Set your suit air on maximum pressure!" Retief said quickly. "Then lie down and wrap your arms around your knees and hold on!" His voice was drowned in an end-of-the-universe boom as the side of the mountain blew out.

VI

Retief's first impression, as he came back to consciousness, was of a gentle rocking motion, which ended rudely as something hard gouged him in the back. He rolled over and got to his feet. He was standing in shallow mud at the shore of a placid expanse of brown, already stiffening into hardness. A few yards distant, a lumpy mansized object stirred feebly. He went to it, assisted Rainsinger to his feet.

"Quite a view, eh?" He indicated the cone rising from the mists wreathing the expanse of mud. The entire wall of the volcano was gone, and from the vast rent a glistening river of gumbo poured.

"We're alive," Rainsinger said groggily. "Remarkable! And it looks as though we succeeded in diverting the mud." He pulled off his suit helmet, revealing a face puffed and bruised. "My apologies to you, Mr. Retief—for a number of things."

"And mine to you, Mr. Rainsinger, for an equal number of things. And I suggest we get these suits off before we harden into statues."

The two men stripped off the suits, thickly coated with rapidly hardening mud.

"Well, we may as well be getting back, I suppose," the trade mission chief said glumly. "I'll transmit my resignation to Sector, then gather up my chaps and be on my way."

They tramped along the lake shore in silence for half an hour. Rounding the curve of the mountain, the valley came into view. Where the town had been, a pattern of building tops reared up above a glossy expanse of eggplant brown.

"I came here to make commercial history," Rainsinger muttered. "Instead I destroyed a city, including enough Corps property to keep me in debt for six lifetimes. . . ."

"I wonder what's going on down there?" Retief said, pointing. On the level mud surrounding the buried buildings of the town, small figures darted and swooped.

"They look like giant water-bugs," Rainsinger said wonderingly. "What do you suppose it means?"

"Let's go down and see," Retief said.

"It's remarkable!" Magnan rubbed his hands together and beamed at the lively group of Slunchans disporting themselves on the mirror-flat surface of the hardened mud flow that occupied the former town plaza, brightly illuminated by the light from the surrounding windows. "It was Blabghug who discovered the crates stores in the consulate attic. He opened them, imagining they might contain something to eat—and discovered roller skates!"

"Rainsinger Mr., Hey!" One of the gracefully cavorting locals came whizzing across the newly formed rink, executed a flashy one-toe reverse spin and braked to a halt before the trade mission chief. "Footwheels these of shipment a get we can soon how?"

"They've had to set up a rotation system," Magnan said. "Every Slunchan who sees them simply goes mad for them!"

"With start to, sets thousand hundred a about take we'll," Blabghug cried. "More take we'll, ready rinks more get we as soon as!"

"I . . . I don't understand," Rainsinger said. "The mud—what's happened to it? It feels like top-quality asphalt, worth fifty credits a ton!"

Magnan nodded happily. "Just after the mud began to recede, Freddy was doing a little foraging—for salvage, of course—and accidentally got into the powdered tombstones. When the mud contacted the plastic, it started hardening up. It must have had some sort of catalytic action, because the whole plaza froze over."

"So that's why the volcano plugged up so quickly," Rainsinger said in wondering tones. "And it's still hardening, just as fast as it's exposed to the air and the, er, catalyst!''

"You've brought off a real coup, sir!" Magnan caroled. "The Slunchans have never had anything but squishy mud underfoot before. Now that they see the possibilities, we'll be able to sell them on all the court games: tennis, volleyball, badminton—then on to the whole gamut of wheeled vehicles! I can see it now: Round-the-planet motorcycle races! The Grand Prix to end all Grand Prixes!"

"Grands Prix," Rainsinger corrected absently. "But not only that, Magnan, my boy! This new material—I'll wager we can corner the paving market for the entire Galactic Arm! And it's virtually free!"

"Ah, am I to understand then, sir, that your report won't place as much emphasis on certain apparent custodial deficiencies as your earlier remarks might have indicated?" Magnan inquired smoothly.

Rainsinger cleared his throat. "My first impressions were a bit wide of the mark," he said. "I was just wondering if you'd find it necessary in your report of my visit to detail the *precise* circumstances surrounding the discovery—or should I say invention?—of this new product."

"No point in burdening Sector with excess detail," Magnan said crisply.

"Now, about transport," Rainsinger mused aloud. "I'd estimate I could place ten million tons at once on Schweinhund's World—and another ten or twenty million tons on Flamme. . . ."

"I think it would be wise to place immediate orders for pogo sticks, croquet sets and bicycles," Magnan thought aloud. "We'll want to work through the small items before bringing on the heavy equipment. . . ."

The two strolled away, deep in conversation.

"Say, all this excitement has given me an appetite," the fat attache said. "I believe I'll go get myself a sandwich. Possibly two sandwiches." As he hurried off, Sir Frederik Gumbubu scooted up to Retief, executing a speed-braking stop.

"Terry, us join and pair a grab!" he shouted.

"Good idea," Retief said, and swung off across the plaza, arm in arm with the foreign minister.

THE FORBIDDEN CITY

I

AN EVENING BREEZE bearing the fragrance of ten-thousand year old Heo trees in bloom moved across the Embassy dining terrace. In the distance pipes sounded softly, picking out a haunting melody, like fairy feet retracing a forgotten path through an enchanted forest. The setting sun, vast and smoky red, cast crimson shadows along the leaf-shaded streets below.

"A pity all this is dying." First Secretary Magnan of the Terran Mission to Sulinore waved a hand toward the fragile, crumbling towers silhouetted against the dusk. "In spite of a million years of civilization and a reputation for immortality, the Sulinorians seems impotent to stem the population decline. I suppose in a century or less they'll all be gone."

"With ninety-nine per cent of the planetary surface devoted to cemeteries, historical shrines and monuments to the past, there's not much room for the living," Second Secretary Retief commented. "And you can tie up a lot of minerals in a planet-wide graveyard.''

"I suppose you're referring to their belief that the world's supply of Divine Effluvium is exhausted,'' Magnan sniffed. "Mere folklore, of course. Still, one might almost be tempted to look into the matter of depletion of essential elements—except that Corps policy forbids poking into local religious doctrine. And in any event, they won't permit any deep-mining operations which might disturb the hallowed dead—or the sleeping heroes, as they prefer to put it.''

Magnan cocked an eye at the small humanoid waiter standing at a discreet distance, apparently lost in thought. "One can't help thinking that the modern Sulinorian is a far cry from his legendary ancestors,'' he said behind his hand. "Just compare these civilized little chaps with those ghastly statues you see everywhere.''

The local turned, approached the table, a polite expression on his elfin features.

"You wished something, sir?''

"Why, ah, tell me.'' Magnan cleared his throat. "How does the Sulinorian in the street feel about all this? Wouldn't you be willing to see a modest rock-mining operation set up here to unlock some of those scarce elements that are tied up in the planetary crust?''

"Modest, my lord? The figure I heard was a million metric tons per day per unit, and Great Tussore knows how many units.'' He looked toward the ruin-crowned skyline. *"Rather the easy erosion of eons/than eaten by industry's engines insatiable,"* he quoted. "At least that's what the poet Eulindore said a couple of millenia ago. Me, I wouldn't know.''

"But what about importation?'' Magnan persisted.

"Why, your Administrative Council turned thumbs down flatly on the CDT proposal that we haul in a few million cubic miles of useful minerals and establish raw material dumps that all could draw on freely!"

"I guess we'd rather look at the landscape the way it is, sir," the Sulinorian said. "And besides, rooting in a dump isn't our style. You know, a race of heroes and all that." He flicked an imaginary crumb from the table. "How about another flagon of ancient wine, my lords? Laid down by Yodross in the year 574,635. That would be about 3600 B.C., old Terry reckoning."

"I think not—" Magnan broke off as the table-side P.A. unit pinged and lit up. The plump features of Ambassador Shindlesweet snapped into mirror-bright focus on the one-way screen.

"Ah, gentlemen," the portly diplomat beamed. "It's my pleasure to inform the staff that the Blug delegation has, after all, been prevailed upon to be present at the Peace Conference here on Sulinore."

"What, *those* bloodthirsty little killers?" Magnan gasped. "With their armor and their opaque atmosphere helmets and their sneaky ways? Why, everybody knows they're the Groaci's proteges, and responsible for all the fighting!"

"At least that's a dozen or so Blugs that won't be off plundering somewhere—as long as the conference is on anyway," Retief pointed out.

". . . a gesture which reflects their sincere desire to see peace restored to the Sector," Shindlesweet was rumbling on. "And with all due modesty, I think I may say—"

A pale visage sporting five stalked eyes crowded

onto the screen, thrusting the Terrestrial ambassador aside.

"As you're perhaps aware," the Groaci ambassador whispered in his faint voice, "it was through my efforts as co-sponsor of the present talks that this happy eventuality was brought about. And—"

"Look here, Mr. Ambassador," Shindlesweet muttered from the side of his mouth, turning a glassy smile to the camera. "I was on the air first!"

"Hogging the limelight, as usual, George," the Groaci hissed. "An unfortunate habit of yours. But as I was saying," he addressed the screen, "I was able, through deft handling of a number of sensitive issues—"

"Now just a minute, Shith!" The Terran forced his way back to center screen. "When I agreed to lend the weight of Terran participation to your confounded gabfest, I—"

"Ha! You begged me on bended anterior ginglymus joint to be permitted to crowd in!"

"Why, you little—"

"Ah-ah," Ambassador Shith admonished. "No racial epithets, George. Open mike, remember?"

Retief and Magnan had a last quick glimpse of Shindlesweet's rage-flushed features as he reached to blank the screen.

"Well, the peace talks are off to a rousing start," Retief said cheerfully. Magnan shook his head, looking grave.

"I foresee no good to come of this gathering." He rose and looked at his watch. "We've time for a constitutional before dinner, Retief. And if we're to dine cheek by mandible with our Groaci colleagues at to-night's banquet, I for one have need of a hearty appe-tite.''

II

A block from the renovated palace housing the Ter-ran Chancery, Magnan plucked at Retief's arm.

"Look there; another party of Groaci Peacekeepers, in full armor. You'd think they were expecting full scale rioting to break out at any moment.''

A block away, a squad of constabulary, in grotesque flaring helmets and black hip-cloaks, side-arms at knobby hips, minced briskly along the empty avenue.

"Shith was quite insistent that the Groaci be as-signed responsibility for the security arrangements for the Conference,'' Magnan muttered. "They have the only guns on the planet.''

"For alleged police, those fellows have a suspicious look of regular infantry about them,'' Retief said.

"Good lord, you don't imagine they're planning anything foolish?'' Magnan gasped. "Everybody knows the Groaci secretly covet Sulinore. They've even tried to have it officially declared a deserted world, open to colonization.''

"It's a little hard to see how they could swing it, with a full squadron of CDT Peace Enforcers standing by off-planet,'' Retief said.

"You're right. We're imagining things.'' Magnan shook his head briskly. "A few dozen blasters can't take over a world. Still, I'd as soon avoid these bravos. In their arrogance they might attempt some sort of harassment.'' He angled across toward the entrance to a side street.

''That's the route to the Forbidden City, off-limits to foreigners,'' Retief said. ''How badly do you want to miss the fuzz?''

''Not that badly.'' Magnan shuddered, veered in the opposite direction. ''If even half the stories are true, not even our gnawed bones would ever be found.''

Fifteen minutes later they were in a narrow, crooked street where age-weathered carved griffins, satyrs and nymphs adorned the steep facades of the deserted buildings lining the way.

''This isn't the most cheerful route for a stroll,'' Magnan commented uneasily. ''At least not after sundown.'' He cocked his head. ''One almost imagines one can hear stealthy footsteps behind one.''

''Not so stealthy at that,'' Retief said. ''They've been getting pretty careless the last five minutes, as if they didn't care whether we heard them or not.''

''You mean someone's really following us?'' Magnan turned to stare back along the shadowy late-evening street.

''Two someones,'' Retief corrected. ''Non-humans, I'd say, weighing in at under a hundred pounds, and wearing padded shoes.''

''That could mean anything! There are forty-six non-human species on-world this week for the conference, and I can think of at least ten of them that wouldn't be above assaulting a pair of peaceful Terran diplomats for their own nefarious ends.''

''Or for the iridium in their teeth,'' Retief amplified.

''I think I recognize the street ahead,'' Magnan muttered. ''Coriale's Comestible Counter is just around the corner. I was there last week—in daylight—making some arrangements for the Reception. We can nip inside and 'phone the Embassy for transportation back. . . ." He broke off as they came in view of a high, narrow shop-front displaying the cranium and crossed thighbones, the Sulinorian symbols of a caterer's establishment. Beneath the deeply incised device, the windows were dark, the massive stonewood door shut tight.

"It's closed!" Magnan put his nose against the glass. "But there's someone inside. I heard a sound."

Retief tried the heavily patinaed bronze door latch, cast in the form of fanged jaws clenched on a leg.

"Perhaps—great heavens, Retief! What are you doing?" Magnan blurted as Retief gripped the knob in both hands and twisted hard. There was a sharp tinkle of breaking metal.

"Retief, stop!" Magnan gasped. "You can't—"

"I think it might be a good idea to get in off the street—now!" Retief thrust his protesting senior through into the gloomy interior, whirled to ease the door silently shut.

"We found the door unlocked," he said briskly, looking around the room. "And stepped inside to see if everything was okay."

Magnan peered from the window, made a choking sound. "Two Sulinorians in artisan's headdress just came around the corner! They'll find us here!"

"Let's check the back room." Retief led the way past tables heaped with displays of Sulinorian pastries, stuffed fowls and candied nutmeats, thrust aside a curtain. The dim shapes of stacked cartons bulked in the darkness. He sniffed the air, took a tiny handlight from his pocket, played the pencil-thin beam across the floor.

"What's that?" Magnan hissed, pointing. From behind a wall locker, a pair of narrow high-arched, long-toed feet protruded. Retief went across, flashed the light on a small, crumpled body. The bright robes were bedraggled and torn. A wound in the narrow chest oozed ochre blood.

"A Sulinorian," Magnan breathed. "He's been shot!" His lips moved in a faint whisper. Retief knelt beside him.

"Who did it?" he asked urgently. "Why?"

"He was not . . . what he seemed." Retief caught the whispered words. Then the luminous eyes closed; the last tinge of vital color drained from the small face, leaving it an unattractive shade of waxy green.

"It looks like Coriale, the caterer," Magnan groaned. "How terrible!"

"Listen!" Retief raised a hand. From the far corner of the storeroom a faint rustle sounded. He motioned Magnan to the left, started around the right side of the stacked boxes. There was a hurried scuttling sound.

"Why—*there* you are, Coriale," Magnan's voice squeaked. "We, er, just stepped in to increase our order. We'll have twelve gross of the bean and kidney pies and six dozen jellied bramble-hens—under glass, of course. . . ." Magnan backed into view, keeping himself between the small local and the body in the corner. The Sulinorian pulled free of Magnan's grip on his elbow. His bright eyes flicked around the room.

"But if you're busy," Magnan went on hastily, "we'll just toddle along now. . . ."

"Ummm. You are Terrestrials, isn't it?" the alien piped in a piercingly high voice.

"I'm, er, why, ah. . . ." Magnan swallowed audibly. "I was here just the other day, Mr. Coriale. Don't you remember me?"

"Yes. Quite so, I recalled now." The Sulinorian moved toward the door. "Six dozen jellied kidney-beans and glass hens under mud, I'll make notes of it. And now, you wish to leave, are you? To be sure. Goodby quickly, please."

Magnan reached the door ahead of the local, fumbled it open. "Well, it was jolly seeing you, Coriale. By, now . . ." He tugged at Retief's sleeve. "Come along!" he hissed. "We're in a frightful rush, remember?"

"I'm not sure Mr. Coriale got the order just right." Retief eased Magnan aside, glanced out the door. The dark street was empty. Pale flames burning in blue glass globes high on the walls cast wavering shadows along the ancient cobbles.

"It doesn't matter! I'm sure he can cope." Magnan's voice faltered as his eye fell on the Sulinorian, from whose nostrils brown smoke was filtering.

"Say, isn't that brown smoke filtering from your nostrils?" he blinked. "I didn't know you Sulinorians smoked."

Coriale edged sideways, eyeing the door. "A new vice, acquiring this week only. And now, reluctance, farewell."

Magnan frowned. "Curious," he said. "A few days ago you spoke perfect Galactic."

"Duck!" Retief snapped and dived past Magnan as the undersized alien made a lightning-fast motion.

Something flashed in his hand; a plate of hors d'oeuvres beside Magnan exploded in a shower of antipasto. With a yelp, Magnan leaped sideways, collided with the alien as the latter bounded aside from Retief's charge.

For a moment, there was a wild tangle of threshing limbs. Then Magnan staggered back, sat down hard. His head wobbled. He fell sideways and lay still.

The Sulinorian had whirled, bringing the gun up—

Retief swept a pie from a table, slammed it full into the pinched faced. The alien shrieked; the gun barked sharply, twice. One slug ripped the gilt epaulet from the shoulder of Retief's wine-red mid-evening semi-official blazer. The second *thunk!*ed into a pewter tureen; thick purple soup spurted from paired holes. Then Retief was on the gunner. He twisted the alien's gun-hand behind him, reached to seize his quarry's other arm . . . and felt the room expand suddenly to three times its former size.

He snorted hard, held his breath, threw the alien across the room. His legs felt like piano wire. He grabbed at a table for support, sent it crashing over on its side.

Magnan sat up, spluttering, as a cascade of icy green punch sluiced over him.

"Yes, yes, I'm coming, Mother," he gasped.

To Retief, Magnan's voice seemed to be filtered through an echo chamber. As in a dream, he saw the other totter to his feet.

"Wha . . ." Magnan gobbled. "What happened?"

His eyes focused on the room, took in the smashed crockery, the overturned furnishings the spilled viands—and the crumpled figure against the wall.

"Retief—he isn't . . .?"

Retief shook his head to clear it. He went across to the fallen alien. The creature lay on his back, eyes wide open, glassy. A great shard of broken punch-bowl protruded from his chest. His dead face was a livid purple.

"Coriale!" Magnan choked. "Dead again!"

"We'd better get out fast," Retief said. "And sort out the Coriales in the morning."

"By all means!" Magnan whirled to the door, pulled it wide—and backed into the room, prodded by the gleaming barrel of a crater gun in the hands of a spindle-legged Groaci in the uniform of a Peacekeeper.

"To make no move, vile miscreants," the helmeted and greaved Shore Patroller hissed in his native tongue as his five stalked eyes scanned the shambles. "To have you red-handed this time, Soft Ones."

"You're making a frightful mistake," Magnan choked as half a dozen more Groaci pushed into the shop, all with levelled weapons. "We didn't—that is, I didn't—I mean, Retief only—"

"Ah, Mr. Magnan, is it not?" the Patrol captain whispered in his faint voice. "The acceptance of your complete innocence, of course, dear sir. Provided only the testimony against the true criminal!"

"True criminal?" Magnan stuttered. "You mean Retief? But—"

"What other?" the Groaci inquired in a reasonable tone.

"But . . . but. . . ."

"To have no need to make a statement now," the captain soothed. "To come along quietly and to leave us to deal with the killer." He motioned sharply and his subordinates closed in, hustled the protesting Magnan away. Then the Groaci turned to Retief.

"To remember me, perhaps, Retief? Shluh by name, formerly of the Groacian Planetary Police, once deeply wronged by you. Tonight, in the cells of a Groaci prison, to even at last the bitter score."

III

The jeweled eye-shields of Captain Shluh gave back brilliant glints from the dazzling white Interrogation lights rigged at the center of the dusty room.

"Once more, my dear Retief," he whispered in accent-free Terran. "What was your motive for your atrocious crimes against the peace and order of Groac? Or Sulinore, if you prefer. Was it perhaps your plan to introduce subtle impurities into the provender to be supplied to the delegates? Or did your schemes run deeper? Was it your full intent to secrete illegal monitoring devices in the serving vessels—devices of the kind which I will testify were found on your person when you were searched?"

"A couple of years pounding a beat have done wonders for you, Schluh," Retief said conversationally. "You've lost that fat-behind-the-ears look. Unfortunately, you still sound about the same."

"And you, unlucky Terry, still indulge your penchant for flippancy! It will be amusing to watch the evolution of your japes into pleas for mercy, as our acquaintance ripens.''

"You Groaci must be planning something a little more elaborate than usual,'' Retief mused aloud. "Conning Ambassador Shindlesweet into lending CDT backing to these phony peace talks took a lot of time and groundwork—and you lads don't waste credits on empty gestures.''

"You imply that our motives are less than selfless?'' Shluh inquired in a careless tone. "Ah, well, what matter your thoughts, Soft One? You may share them freely with your executioner.''

"Let's look at it analytically,'' Retief went on. "What have you accomplished with all this effort, other than getting representatives of every important world in a CDT dominated sector of the Arm together in one room? But maybe that's enough, eh, Shluh? If some unfortunate incident occurred and wiped out the lot of them, whoever was responsible would find himself in a most unenviable position, public-relations-wise. And I have a feeling it wouldn't be you Groaci who'd be left holding the satchel. Which leaves the CDT, the other sponsor of the gathering.''

"Enough, presumptuous Terry!'' Shluh's eyestalks were whipping in an agitated manner. "In your panic, you rant nonsense!''

"And with the CDT discredited,'' Retief continued, "Groac would have to step in to straighten out the confusion; and they just might find it necessary to call on someone like their friends the Blugs to help keep the peace during the emergency. And maybe, before things got back to normal, the few remaining Sulinorians might just sort of go into a decline and die off, leaving an empty world for an enterprising power like Groac to latch onto.''

''What fever fancies are these?'' Shluh hissed. ''It is known to all that you Terries, ever suspicious of the pure motives of others, have installed Mark XXI surveillance devices at the port and throughout the Conference rooms, thus making impossible the introduction of any weapons other than the handful alloted to my Security patrols!''

''A good point, Shluh. The Mark XXI's will frisk every attender from socks to hair-piece. Of course, a little poison in the caterer's salt-shaker wouldn't trip the detectors, but the metabolic monitors would catch that on the routine analysis that's run on food to be sure it's safe for alien consumption. So the Borgia approach is out, too.''

''I tire of your theorizing!'' Shluh was on his feet. ''Think what you will! I tell you in confidence: Even now your Chancery is surrounded by my troops— ostensibly as honor guard—but none can leave or enter! By this hour tomorrow no Terry will dare to show his naked face in any capital in the Sector—''

''Tomorrow, eh?'' Retief nodded. ''Thanks for giving me your timetable.''

''Have done, infamous meddler in the destinies of Groac! But before you die, tell me the name of the spy who sold you our secrets, and I shall personally supervise his impalement on the wall of one thousand hooks!''

''Secrets, eh? I guess that confirms my guesswork,'' Retief said. ''One more question: What pay-off do the Blugs get—''

''Silence!'' Shluh keened. ''Be assured your brief

remaining hours will be devoted not to questioning matters of policy beyond your grasp, but to supplying detailed answers to a number of queries of my own!''

''Wrong again,'' Retief said and took a step toward the desk on which the police officer leaned, shaking a gloved fist. Shluh jumped back, motioned to the armed guard standing by, who swung his power gun to the ready, aimed at Retief's face.

''Haven't your lads been told that you can't fire a blaster in an enclosed space like this without incinerating everything in it, including the shooter?'' Retief asked casually, and took another step. The guard lowered the gun hesitantly, his eyes twitching in confusion.

''He lies, cretinous hive-mate of broodfoulers! Fire!'' Shluh screeched, and ducked to snatch at an open drawer. Retief reached him in a bound, caught the unfortunate captain by the neck, sent him skidding toward the guard as a belated shot lit the room like a photoflash. As the two Groaci went down in a heap, Retief caught up the dropped gun.

''Well, another myth exploded,'' he said. ''Shluh, take off your belt and strap him up.'' With the gun covering the two aliens, he seated himself at the desk, flipped up the OUT key on the desk field-phone, punched in a number. A moment later, the glum face of Counsellor of Embassy Clutchplate appeared on the screen. He gaped.

''Retief! What—how—Do you realize—? Did you actually—? How could you have . . .'' his voice faltered as he took in the scene in the background. ''Isn't that Chief Shluh? What's he doing?''

''He just ran into an old acquaintance,'' Retief

soothed, ignoring a sharp rap at the door. "Mr. Clutch-plate, how far along are the arrangements for Blug participation in the Conference?"

"Why, their delegation will arrive within the hour. The convoy just 'vised Port Authority for landing clearance. But see here—"

"Convoy?" Retief glanced up as pounding sounded at the door.

"Just fifty first-class cruisers; as escort for the trans-port. The Blug never travel unarmed, you know. But—"

"See if you can get the ambassador to turn them down," Retief rapped. "Failing that, meet 'em with an armed guard and—"

"Mr. Retief!" the counsellor barked. "I don't know what mad scheme you've embarked on, but it won't work! I know how you feel about the Blugs, and the Groaci too, for that matter. But taking the law into your own hands—"

"No time for any long discussions, Mr. Clutch-plate," Retief cut in as a heavy thud rocked the door. "I'd ask you for a squad of Marines if I knew where I was, but—"

"Turn yourself in," Clutchplate blurted. "It's the only way. You can plead guilty due to temporary insan-ity brought on by outraged political convictions, and get off with no more than half a dozen years on a penal satellite."

"It's an interesting proposal." Retief ducked as splinters of door whined past his head. "What am I guilty of?"

"Murder, of course," Clutchplate yelped. "Two Sulinorians, remember?"

"It slipped my mind," Retief said. "But see if you can hold the charge open a little longer. I may have a few Groaci to add to it." He flipped off the screen as the door shuddered and bulged inward.

"Time for you to talk fast, Shluh," he said crisply. "I've decided to slip out the back way to avoid the autograph hounds. There are three doors I could use. You'll tell me which one's the best route."

"Never!"

Retief fired a bolt from the hip past the Groaci.

"On the other hand," Shluh hissed quickly, "what matter if you temporarily elude my overzealous troops? Our plans will proceed—and the measures you sought to set in motion will avail naught to stop them!" He darted to a side door, keyed it open.

"Go, then, Retief! But take what path you will, a dreadful end awaits you!"

"In that case, you'd better go first." Shluh hissed and tried to dart aside, but Retief caught him, propelled him ahead with a foot in the seat. He slammed and barred the panel behind him, as the outer door fell in with a crash.

IV

They followed dim, dusty passages, ascended winding stairways, moved silently along dark, lofty halls lined with ancient armor and hung with rotted banners. Half a dozen times Retief eluded Groaci search parties by a hair's breadth. In a wide room decorated with painted murals showing centauroids cavorting on purple grass, Shluh gestured toward a high-arched, doorless opening through which pale moonlight gleamed.

"There is your exit to the night, Retief!" he keened sardonically. "Make what use of it you will! The way is clear!"

Retief crossed the room, stepped out onto a tiny balcony, thick with the droppings of the tiny bat-like creatures that wheeled and *skree!*ed at his appearance. Ragged vines grew over a low balustrade, beyond which darkness spread to a skyline of tower-encrusted hills. He looked down. The wall dropped sheer into inky shadows far below.

"Thanks for everything, Shluh." He threw a leg over the stone railing. "I'll see you at your trial—if your bosses let you live that long, after the way you've botched your assignement."

"Stop, impetuous outworlder!" Shluh keened, as Groaci feet clicked in the room behind him. "Even should you survive the descent, you know not what you do! Not even you would I urge on to to what waits in the darkness below!"

"You mean your short patrols?"

"Not my patrols, nor the Marines of your own embassy which even now seek you, warrant in hand, will ever find you, if once you set foot in those demon-haunted byways!"

"So *that's* where you set up your jail-house?" Retief looked thoughtful. "Still, I'd rather mingle with spooks than go back to your little party. Ta-ta, Shluh. Stay as sweet as you are." Shluh hit the deck as Retief raised the gun and fired a burst toward the approaching search party, slung the blast rifle over his shoulder and started down toward the silent streets of the Forbidden City.

It was an easy climb. Once a pair of Groaci heads appeared over the balcony rail above, but they drew back quickly. The wall was deeply carved, and the stout vines provided ample hand- and foot-holds. It was less than ten minutes before Retief swung down and dropped the last few feet into a mass of unpruned shrubbery from which he emerged in an avenue of marble mansions like abandoned funeral homes. The two pale moons of Sulinore came from behind a cloud and shone down ghostly white. Something small and dark flitted overhead, emitting thin cries. Far away, a mournful wail sounded. Retief set off at a brisk walk, his footsteps echoing hollowly on the worn mosaics that paved the way.

Ahead, a lofty obelisk reared up. The inscription, nearly effaced by time, seemed to commemorate a battle fought with giants. At the next corner, the carved heads of ogres peered blindly down at him from an ornate cornice. He passed a fountain, dry and silent, where finned and tailed maidens of stone disported themselves amid marble waves. The dank wind blew dead leaves along the street. As Retief paused, a sound as of small feet pattered for a moment, then fell silent.

"Come on out," Retief called. "There's some news you ought to hear."

There was a ghostly laughter—or perhaps it was only the wind, searching among the fluted columns of a temple. Retief went on. Rounding an abrupt angle, he caught a glimpse of movement—a darting shape that disappeared into a gaping doorway. He followed, found himself in a hall, open to the sky. From its walls, giant frescoed figures stared down with empty eyes.

"I need a guide," Retief called. "Any volunteers?"

"Tears . . . tears . . . tears," the echoes rolled back from every side.

"There's a small matter of an invasion to deal with right now."

"Now . . . now . . . now . . ." the sound faded and died, and as if the word were a signal, a creak sounded from the high doors through which Retief had entered.

He spun in time to see them clash shut with a dull *boom* that echoed and re-echoed. He went to them, found them jammed tight, immovable. He turned back to the interior of the roofless room. A wide passage was visible at the rear. Skitting a black pool that reflected a shattered moon, he entered the passage, emerged after twenty paces on a terrace above a flight of wide, shallow steps. Below a dark and wild-grown park spread out, a wilderness of untrimmed shrubs and lofty, black-leaved trees.

He descended to the foot-high sward; soft rustlings from the shadows retreated as he advanced along a weed-obscured path winding among the buttressed trunks of patriarchal trees. Carved faces leered at him from the shadows. The eerie shapes of stone monsters gleamed through the unpruned foliage. He emerged onto a broad mall along the center of which a double rank of what appeared to be painted statues of heroic size were drawn up along an aisle that led away into the night. Near at hand, a small collonaded shrine was almost hidden among the low-sweeping boughs of a giant conifer. Silently, Retief approached the building from the side.

Through a latticed opening, faint moonlight fell on the vine-entwined effigy of an oversized Sulinorian in the armor of an ancient warrior. In the darkness behind the graven hero, something moved minutely. Retief tossed a pebble through the window, flattened himself against the wall by the doorway. A moment later, a head poked cautiously from the entry—and Retief's hand clamped on the slender Sulinorian neck.

"Pardon my interrupting the game," he said. "But it's time we had a talk."

V

"The price of entrance into the Sacred Grove of Heroes is death, Terran!" the tenor voice of the alien shrilled.

"So I understand," Retief said holding his catch at arm's length to avoid the wildly kicking feet. "However, my little intrusion is nothing compared with what the Groaci have scheduled. Maybe you'd better listen to what I have to say before you carry out the sentence."

"Tomorrow is nothing; the past is all," the Sulinorian declaimed. "Why struggle against Destiny, outworlder?"

"We can give destiny a run for her money if you'll spread the word that I need a few hundred able-bodied Sulinorians to distract the Groaci patrols long enough for me to get through to the Terry Embassy—"

"Offer your final devotions to your gods, man of Terra," the Sulinorian cut in. "Your fate is sealed."

"You're consistent, I'll concede that," Retief said. "It looks as though I'll have to look a little farther for a public-spirited citizen." He released the native, who jerked his varicolored toga straight and faced him defiantly.

"Not so, Terran!" The local folded his knobby arms. "Never will you leave these hallowed precincts!"

Rustlings sounded behind Retief. He turned. From every shadowed clump of shrubbery, a Sulinorian emerged; light winked from the foot long stilettoes in their hands. Silently, the ring of aliens closed in. Retief backed to the shrine, unlimbered the blast rifle, swung it to cover the throng which halted, facing him.

"Welcome to the party," he said. "Now that we've got a quorum, maybe we'll get somewhere."

"You outrage the glorious past, Terran," a wizened Sulinorian quavered, staring up at Retief. "You heap outrage on outrage!"

"The outrage the Groaci are planning is the one I'm concerned with," Retief said. "You people don't seem to care much, but from the Terry viewpoint, it might set an unfortunate precedent for other budding empire-builders."

"Terry, gone are the days when we of Sulinore were mighty warriors. If now it falls our lot to die, we face our fate in dignity."

"There's nothing dignified about being scragged by the Groaci, or strung up by the heels by a platoon of Blugs," Retief cut in. "I hear they have a curious sense of humor when it comes to dealing with anyone who's proved his inferiority by getting conquered by them."

"Kill this alien at once, isn't it?" a scratchy-voiced Sulinorian in the front rank called. "After, everybody die nicely, as scheduled."

"Enough talk," the elderly Sulinorian declared.

"Let the disturber of the sleep of heroes suffer the penalty!"

The Sulinorians eyed the gun in Retief's hands, shuffled their feet. No one advanced.

"Maybe you'd better call the penalty off," Retief suggested. "Then you can divert your righteous indignation into doing something about the invasion."

"Hmmmm." The elderly spokesman beckoned to a couple of his fellows; they put their heads together.

"We have decided," the oldster stated as the conference ended, "that the matter must be referred to the Old Ones for decision." He raised a trembling hand. "Not that we fear to fall under your murderous weapon, Terran—but it is a death which lacks elegance." He waved a hand and an avenue opened up through the dense ranks of armed locals.

"Terran, I give you temporary safe-conduct and the honor of confrontation with the Ancient Lords of Sulinore, who will themselves dispose of this case. Come, if you fear not!"

"Fair enough," Retief said. "When you want fast action, there's nothing like going direct to the top brass. Where do we find them?"

"Behold the Lords of Sulinore!" the ancient piped feebly. The locals made sweeping bows to the ranks of still figures about them. Retief inclined his head respectfully.

"They cut an impressive figure," he said. "I'll be interested to see how they go about dealing with the problem at hand."

"Simplicity itself," the old Sulinorian said. "One waft of the sacred incense, and a faint shadow of their vanished vitality will energize them. Then will they hear our pleas and hand down justice in the ancient way.''

Retief walked slowly along the row of motionless effigies, noting the worn trappings, the realistically scarred limbs and fierce visages, the tarnished armor of the ancient warriors. In spite of their size and varied forms, all bore some resemblance to the shrunken Sulinorians who followed, silent and awed.

''Once the races of Sulinore were many,'' the ancient said as he noticed Retief's questing gaze. ''And mighty was their prowess.

''There stands Zobriale the Intense, Requiter of Wrongs. Beyond, we see proud Valingrave, victor at Har and Jungulon and Spagetwraithe. Here—'' he indicated the modest crypt ''—behold the shrine of Bozdune the Restial, known also as Bozdune the Baresark, of ferocious memory. And there—'' he pointed to a four-legged barrel-chested creature with a typical Sulinorian torso and head ''—stand the mortal remains of Great Tussore, he who single-handed vanquished the hordes of Doss, on a world so distant that even now the sunlight of his day of battle has not yet reached the face of Sulinore!''

''He looks like a tough boy,'' Retief commented. ''Too bad he's not still around. He might take a dim view of the way things are going.''

''Did I not say Mighty Tussore would give his judgment? Aye, and Cranius the August, and Maglodore the Swift, and Belgesion, and Vare, and High Pranthippo, King of Kings—''

''A most august assemblage,'' Retief conceded. ''But they seem a rather taciturn group.''

''You jape at the Lords of Sulinore, Terran?'' The

oldster drew himself up, made an imperious gesture. A pair of locals nearly as old as himself came forward, bearing a large case which they placed on the grass, opening the lid. Inside was a cylindrical tank fitted with valve and a coil of flexible plastic tubing. The dodderer lifted the nozzle of the hose, advanced to the pedestal on which the centauroid stood.

"Awaken, Great Tussore!" he cried in his cracked voice. "Rouse from thy long dreams to render judgment on one who comes unbidden to the Place of Heroes!" He raised the hose and waved it under the flared nostrils. Retief heard a faint hiss of escaping gas.

"Give us of thy ancient wisdom, as in days of old, O Tussore," the old fellow exhorted. He shoved the hose closer. "Almost is the sacred effluvium exhausted," he muttered. "I'll bet a pretty some of these backsliders tave been tapping it on the sly."

Suddenly one pointed ear of the statue twitched. The flared nostrils quivered. The eyelids fluttered. As Retief watched the lips parted.

"Glop," the mighty figure said, and fell silent. "Drat it, what a time for the tank to run out," someone beside Retief muttered.

"How does he work it?" Retief inquired softly as the Keeper of the Sacred Fumes waved the hose agitatedly, vainly invoking the unmoving demigod.

"We work nothing, interloper," the Sulinorian said sullenly. "A good shot of sacred gas, and their metabolism starts ticking over fast enough to start them talking, that's all."

Abruptly Tussore stirred again. "The devil take the blackguards," a deep voice suddenly rumbled from his chest. "Where's my greaves? Where's my fetlock powder? Where's my confounded mace? Blast that butter-fingered squire. . . ."

"Great Tussore, wake from thy dreams!" The hosewielder redoubled his efforts. "Hear me! Even now there stands in our midst a stranger who violates the honored rest of the Lords of Sulinore with his presence!"

"Oh . . . it's you, Therion," Tussore mumbled. His eyes were open now, bleary and dull. "You look terrible. Been a long time, I guess. And it's not the stranger who disturbs my rest—it's you, with your infernal babbling!" He reached, plucked the hose from the oldster's hand, jammed it under his nose, drew a deep breath. "Ahhhh! That's what the doctor ordered."

"Even so, Great Tussore!" The Sulinorian proceeded to relate the circumstances surrounding Retief's presence. Halfway through the recital, Tussore's eyelids drooped. The hose fell from his hand. He snored.

"So the problem, Great One, is how to administer the prescribed rituals without suffering the indecorum of being mowed down like ripe beer-corn by the condemned one," the oldster concluded. "Great Tussore? Mighty one?" He waved the hose frantically, but his efforts this time were unavailing. The still figure stood, unmoving as a sphinx.

"So much for the wisdom of the ages," Retief said. "Nice try, Therion, but it looks like the oracle's not interested. Let's go."

"Make silent this one, plenty quick!" a small Sulinorian rasped—the same one, Retief thought, who had spoken up earlier. "No more time for pulling string

on wooden god! Cut away the head of this Terry, yes!
And soon after, fates proceed on schedule!''

"Silence, imperinent oaf!" Therion rounded on the
speaker. "Your cacophonous squeakings impugn the
majesties of Sulinore! Give me your name, for later
disciplining!"

The one addressed backed away, looking flustered,
as if suddenly conscious of being conspicuous. Retief
studied his face.

"Well, if it isn't my old friend Coriale," he said.
"You ought to be an expert on the subject of dying.
Seems to me I've seen you expire twice already this
evening."

The Coriale-faced alien whirled suddenly, plunged
for the rear rank.

"Seize him!" Therion called. The quarry ducked,
dodged, dived through a gap in the suddenly surging
ranks, scuttled sideways as his retreat was cut off, made
a dash for the shrubbery. The chase pounded off into
the underbrush. Retief seated himself on a convenient
pedestal and lit a dope-stick. Five minutes passed before the crowd again surged into view, the darting
quarry still in the lead. He put on a sprint, scuttled to the
shrine, dived inside.

"His impiety passes all bounds!" Therion puffed,
coming up to Retief. "Now the mad creature seeks
shelter in the very crypt of Bozdune!"

"Let him be fetched out and dealt with!" someone
shrilled.

"Stay!" Therion piped as the aroused crowd closed
in. "We'll not bring dishonor to the hero by scuffling
about his feet. Come! Let us withdraw and leave this

fevered maniac to regain his sense among the shadows
of the greatness which was his race's!''

Retief took out his pocket light and played the beam
between the columns of the refugee's hiding place.
Between the great steel-toed boots of Bozdune, a
smaller pair of feet was visible. He directed the light
higher.

"Correction," he said. "Not *his* race's; that's no
Sulinorian. Look." The light revealed a cloud of brown
mist coiling upwards around the rigid features of the
preserved hero. "The meeting's been infiltrated by a
masquerading alien—an alien who exhales brown gas
when he gets excited."

"What's this? Brown gas—?" Therion's question
was interrupted by a startled cry from a Sulinorian near
the temple entry, followed a moment later by a snort
like a teased bull.

"He stirs! Bozdune rouses!" Suddenly Sulinorians
were running in every direction. Retief caught Therion's arm as the elder turned to follow the general
flight.

"Unhand me, fellow!" the oldster screeched as a
bellow sounded from the shrine. "Death I face with a
proud smile—but there's something inappropriate
about being ripped limb from limb by an ancestor!"

"Is that the kind of fellow you make a hero of?'
Retief inquired as smashing sounds emanated from the
crypt, followed by the hurtling body of the Coriale
double, which skidded to Retief's feet and lay moving
feebly.

"Unfortunately Bozdune lost his wits as a result of
three month's exposure to the Tickling Torture at the

hands of the infamous Kreee,'' Therion explained hastily. ''He's prone to rages, when suddenly aroused, and prudence demands my swift removal hence!'' He pulled free and bounded away with an agility remarkable in a being of his age. Retief turned as a rumble of falling stone sounded from the shrine. A mighty figure had appeared between the columns, stood with hands pressed against them. Great cords of muscle stood out on his neck; his biceps bulged; his *latissimi dorsi* strained. The column buckled and went over, bringing down a section of the arhictrave. Bozdune roared as the marble slab bounced from his back. With a final thrust he toppled a second column, stepped forth as stone collapsed behind him. Eight feet high, massive as a buffalo, he stood in the moonlight, snarling. His wild gaze fell on Retief.

''Kreee!'' he bellowed. ''I have you now!'' and charged the lone Terran.

VI

Retief stood his ground as Bozdune closed in.

''You've got me confused with someone else. Bozdune,'' he called. ''I'm just a Terry doing a little job of planet-saving.''

With a bellow, the ancient fighter thundered past the spot where Retief had stood a moment before. He fought his way clear of the underbrush into which the momentum of his dash had carried him, rounded up his elusive prey.

''And in that connection, I'd like to ask a little favor

of you,'' Retief continued. ''A group of opportunists called the Groaci are planning to massacre all the foreign diplomats in town—''

''Arrrrghhh!'' Bozdune roared and closed in swinging roundhouse swipes sufficient to decapitate a horse. Retief leaned aside from one wild swing, ducked under another, planted his feet and drove a solid left-right to the giant's stomach, an effect like punching a sea-wall. He jumped aside as Bozdune grunted and made an ineffective grab, landing a blow in his own midriff that staggered him.

''Now, the Groaci have the streets cordoned off,'' Retief went on. ''And since it's important that I get through to the Embassy with the news, I'd like to ask you to lend a hand.'' He stepped back as Bozdune ripped his six-foot blade from its sheath, whirled it overhead. Retief tossed the last rifle aside, plucked a wrist-thick spear from the grip of a horned warrior which loomed immobile beside him. Bozdune made a bound, brought the massive claymore down in a whistling arc that cleaved air an inch to Retief's right as he faded aside.

''Now, if you'd just say a word to your descendants, I think they might consent to lend a hand.'' Retief poked the spear hard against Bozdune's breastplate. ''How about it?''

Bozdune dropped his sword, grabbed the spear shaft with both hands, and gave a prodigious pull—and as Retief let go, tottered backward, tripped over a fragment of shattered column and went down like a fallen oak. Retief heard the dull *thonk!* as his head struck the marble steps of his erstwhile shelter. He stepped quickly forward, used the warrior's own harness straps to bind his wrists together, then his ankles. At that moment, the bushes parted and Therion's aged faced appeared.

"What transpires?" he piped. His eye fixed on the prone giant. "What, Bozdune the Bestial, felled by a mere outworlder?"

"I'm afraid I can't claim the glory," Retief said. "He ran out of gas." He glanced toward the spot where the false Coriale had lain. "But if you can find the ringer, I may be able to remedy that."

"He's here, the infamous dastard," a Sulinorian called, dragging the unfortunate imposter from a clump of gorse. Retief got a grip on the captive's collar, assisted him to Bozdune's side.

"Breathe on the nice man, Shorty," he ordered.

A great gout of brown gas puffed obediently forth. "Again."

The prisoner huffed and puffed, exhaling the vapor past the fallen fighter's snoring visage. In a moment, Bozdune twitched, jerked and opened his eyes.

"You're still here, eh?" he said to Retief. "I thought I dreamed you." He sniffed again.

"Gadzoons, first good air I've breathed in a couple hundred years. More!" He raised his voice as Retief withdrew the pseudo-Coriale.

"Not unless you agree to lend a hand," Retief countered. "Then I promise you all the sacred essence you want."

"Are you kidding? Just let me get my hands on these Gruckles or whoever they are that think they can carve my home town up, and I'll grind them into library paste!"

"It's a deal." Retief turned to Therion. "How about it? You in or out?"

"If Bozdune approves the enterprise, then who are we to demur?" the oldster inquired of the cool night air. "Rise, loyal Sons of Sulinore! For this night at least, the ancient glories live again!"

Retief gave Bozdune another shot of gas, then passed the captive to Therion.

"Don't squeeze him too hard," he cautioned. "We've got to make him stretch as far as we can; if this caper's going to succeed, we'll need all the ancient glory we can muster."

From a shadowy arch half a block from the carved gates of the Terran Embassy, Retief, seated astride Tussore's broad back, watched as the fifty-Groaci guard detail sauntered past, their stemmed eyes scanning the street alertly, their blast rifles ready at port arms. Behind him, the tread of booted Groaci feet approached relentlessly.

"Get ready," he said softly. "Another ten seconds. . . ."

There was a chorus of weak shouts from the rear, a slapping of running feet, the *buzzzz-whapp!* of power guns firing; then a pair of Groaci troopers appeared, pelting along in advance of a mighty figure in ancient armor. In full stride, he overtook them, snatched them up by their necks and tossed them aside. Behind him, a crowd of Sulinorians, toga skirts hitched high, brandished their ceremonial knives as they followed their massive leader toward the gate. A moment later, the giant was among the patrollers, flailing with a spike-studded mace before the gun was fired.

"Let's go!" Retief kicked his heel into Tussore's sides, and the mighty centauroid bounded forward. In an instant, they were in the thick of the melee, Retief swinging a yard-long club as Tussore reared and struck out with iron-hard hooves.

"Cut your way through!" Retief called to his mount. We can mop up later, after we've taken care of the main event!"

"Aiii! What a lovely squishing sound these Gruckers make beneath my hooves!" the old warrior yelled, but he wheeled and charged the gate. Half a block away, Retief caught a glimpse of Bozdune, tossing Groaci troopers aside like straw dummies. From every dark alleymouth and byway, Sulinorians were pouring. A lone Groaci in the gatehouse brought up his blast-rifle, loosed a round that missed by inches; then Retief's club felled him, and they were through, crossing the lawn toward the lighted entry at full gallop. A startled Marine guard let out a yell and reached for the lever which would slam the grill in the faces of the invaders, but a sweep of Tussore's arm sent the sentry sprawling. Inside, Retief swung down, started up the grand staircase, five steps at a time. Suddenly Counsellor Clutchplate appeared on the landing above.

"Retief!" His eyes took in the massive, sweaty, horse-bodied Tussore, helmeted and sword-girded, the motley horde of Sulinorians swarming behind.

"Good lord! Treason! Treachery! Hallucinations!" He whirled to run as Retief caught him, spun him around.

"Has the banquet begun yet?" he demanded.

"J . . . j . . . just starting now," the counsellor choked. "It happens I don't like Groaci iodine chowder, so I just stepped out for a breath of air." He stumbled back as Retief dashed on.

At the high double doors to the banquet hall, a

Marine in dress blues, polished helmet and chrome-plated ceremonial .45 departed from his rigid position of attention sufficiently to roll his eyes as the newcomers surged down on him. At what he saw, he grabbed for the holster at his hip. Retief slammed a side-handed blow at his wrist. "Sorry, son," he snapped and sent the doors flying open on the roomful of startled diplomats. From both sides of a long U-shaped table, oculars of every description goggled at the spectacle that burst upon them. Retief pointed to the impassive Sulinorian servitors standing behind the diners, spaced all along the room, one to a customer.

"Get 'em" he commanded and reached for the nearest as the troop at his heels boiled past to carry out his instruction.

VII

"You've gone out of your mind, Retief!" Counsellor Clutchplate gazed, white-faced and shaken, from the broken doorway at the scene of carnage after the capture of the last of the servitors. "What can it mean, leading this party of dacoits to violate the Embassy? I must protest, even at risk of my life, whatever atrocities you plan to visit on these poor chaps! They're under CDT protection!"

"They'll survive—some of 'em," Retief said, and plucking a steak knife from the table, he stooped over one of the fallen waiters and with a quick stroke, laid him open from chin to navel. Clutchplate uttered a strangled yelp; Ambassador Shindlesweet turned pale and quietly collapsed under the table as Retief reached, extracted a limp, two-foot-tall creature resembling a shelled lobster from the interior of the pseudoflesh costume.

"They're not Sulinorians; they're Blugs." He reached again, pulled out a small pressure-tank. "This is his air supply; liquid nitrogen."

"Blugs?" Clutchplate gaped at the unconscious creature, from whose breathing orifice a brown exhalation now was issuing. "But what—how—? See here, Retief! even if these are, er, Blugs, what harm could they have done unarmed, which would warrant your outrageous behavior?"

"Blugs are rock-eaters," Retief explained. "And they seem to have a remarkable degree of control over their metabolism. Normally, they exhale innocuous gases; under stress, they start exhaling nitrogen trioxide. But when occasion demands, they can switch to production of any one of three or four poisonous oxides of nitrogen. Here in this closed room, all it would have taken was one good whiff down each guest's neck, on signal, and bingo! Clean sweep."

"But why?" Clutchplate wailed.

"I have an idea Ambassador Shith can tell us how they happened to be here, instead of Coriale's regular table-waiting staff," Retief suggested.

Shith, still dangling in Tussore's grasp, emitted a harsh bleat. "Gloat while you can, Mr. Retief!" he hissed. "True, every word! I commend your cleverness! But while you spent your efforts in thwarting this feint—yes, feint!—the squadron of Blug warships which you Terries so naively permitted to pass your blockade were discharging fifty thousand picked troops, the cream of the Bluggish navy! Even now these diminutive but doughty doughboys are spreading out over the town, breathing their deadly halitosis on every living creature in their paths! By morning, no Sulinorian will be alive to dispute the Groaci claim to planetary ownership!''

"Shith—have you taken leave of your senses?" Shindlesweet had revived sufficiently to crawl forth, spluttering. "When this is known you'll be hauled before a Galactic tribunal and dealt with in a manner that will make the name of Groac a byword to replace that of Doctor Mush!''

"Mud," Shith corrected. "Permit me to contradict you, my dear George! Not one word of the coup will be noised abroad. My constabulary have already taken the precaution of securing the only communications facilities on the planet capable of contacting CDT naval forces; in a matter of moments my chaps will arrive to put an end to your illusions of success! Don't fret, however. I promise you a swift and painless demise.'' He paused, aiming several eyes at Retief. "Why do you shake your head, sir! My scheme is flawless! My invasion is an accomplished fact!''

"True—but you missed one small point," Retief said. "The Sulinorians were gradually fading off the scene due to the exhaustion of the planet's supply of a certain element vital to their well-being. But instead of dying, after about the age of five hundred, they'd drift off into a comatose state. You and your nitrogen-fixing Blugs have changed all that, Mr. Ambassador. Thanks to you, Sulinore has a new lease on life.''

"You seek even in the eleventh hour to delude yourself!'' Shith hissed. "Hearken! Even now my occupation forces approach the door!''

There was a noisy clump of feet from the hall outside.

Then the mighty figure of Bozdune the Bestial, broad and bronzed, appeared in the entry. He plucked a shattered door from its hinges with one hand and tossed it aside.

"Nice going, Retief," he boomed. "I don't know how you worked it, but the place is swarming with those lovable little guys you called Blugs. All the boys are catching 'em and making pets of 'em. I've got one in my pocket, and he's keeping me supplied like a tall glunthound!" The behemoth's ochre eyes fell on the laden table. "Chow!" he bassooned. "I haven't had a square meal in eight hundred years!"

"Then—this means my invasion has failed?" Shith wailed. "My so meticulously planned invasion, spoiled in the eleventh hour by one trivial oversight?"

"Oh, your invasion is a huge success," Retief said comfortingly. "But this time the invadees are the winners."

VIII

"I really must protest this flagrant interference in the internal affairs of a sovereign world, George," Ambassador Shith whispered vehemently from his position on the platform where the group of local and foreign dignitaries stood, awaiting the appearance of the parade organized by the Sulinorians to celebrate the invasion. "I demand the immediate return of the impounded units of the Blug navy and the repatriation of all Blug nationals!''

"Spare me your threnodies, my dear Shith.'' Ambassador Shindlesweet raised a remonstrative hand. "We'd have a sticky time of it were we to attempt to dislodge the Blugs now. You're aware, I'm sure, that as their breathing tanks ran low, they escaped their captors and burrowed their way down half a mile to a nitrogen-rich stratum and are busily digesting rock and releasing free radicals—that, and reproducing. I think you might be said to be fortunate to be sharing the honors today as co-sponsor of the Blug Immigration Plan, rather than languishing in the VIP suite of a CDT brig, awaiting trial.''

"Pah!'' the Groaci envoy vibrated his throat-sac in indignation. "In that case,'' he changed tack, "I see no reason why Groac should share credit for this enlightened program under which, at no cost to these ungrateful locals, their atmosphere is being so rapidly renewed!''

"Really, Shith,'' the Terran chief of mission said in a low voice, "it's only the fact that a full disclosure of the events leading up to the present *rapprochement* might tempt certain petty critics at Sector to the faulty conclusion that I had been in some way remiss, that prevents me from releasing the transcript of the rather excited pronouncement which you so providently delivered into the recorders set up to capture the after-dinner speeches. . . .'' He cupped an ear as distant bugles sounded. "Gentlemen, I think I hear them coming now.''

Along the ancient street, a procession was advancing, banners awave. In the front rank were Tussore and Bozdune, grim and gigantic, CDT-supplied nitrogen tanks slung at their hips, their armor sparkling in the red rays of the swollen sun.

Behind them, rank on rank, marched the revived immortals of Sulinore, a column that stretched away out of sight along the shadowy street.

"This matter of allowing these chaps to seize the Blug ships as spoils of war and set off on a raiding expedition is an irregularity that I'm going to have difficulty glossing over in my report," Shindlesweet said behind his hand to Therion. "But off the record," he added, "I suppose I'll manage—so long as you're sure they'll do their raiding in Groaci-mandated territory."

"Indeed, I hope you'll interpose no obstacles to the ruffians departing Sulinore as expeditiously as possible," the elder whispered loudly.

"We're well rid of the smelly brutes. They have no conception of the dignity appropriate to legendary heroes."

Tussore, catching sight of Retief, broke ranks and cantered over to the group, puffing smoke from the cigar clamped in his mouth.

"Well, we're off," he called heartily. "And glad to be going! The old place isn't the same any more. I can't even step on the grass without some whisk-broom handler jumping out and giving me a hard time. And that dying sun! Paugh! It gives me the Deep Willies!" He puffed out a great cloud of smoke, raised an eyebrow at Retief.

"Say, why don't you change your mind and join us, Retief?" he demanded. "We'll have a lot more fun out there chasing across the universe than you will staying back here with these stick-in-the-muds.''

''It's a temptation,'' Retief said. ''Maybe some day I'll take you up on it. I have an idea your trail will be easy to follow.''

THE PIECEMAKERS

I

"GENTLEMEN," Undersecretary for Extraterrestrial Affairs Thunderstroke announced in tones of doom, "it looks like war."

"What looks like war?" a stout man in plainly tailored civvies asked blurrily, as one just awakened from a pleasant nap. "War, you say?" He slapped the conference table with a well-manicured hand. "Well, it's about time we taught the beggars a lesson!"

"You've leaped to a faulty conclusion, Colonel," the undersecretary said sourly. "We are not on the point of embarking on hostilities—"

"Naturally not," the military advisor said, rising. "Not your job. Civilians all very well—but time now for military to take over. You'll excuse me, Mr. Secretary? I must rejoin my regiment at once—"

"Sit down, Henry," the chief of the Groaci Desk said tiredly. "You haven't got the big picture. No

318

Terran forces are involved on Yudore at all. Strictly an Eetee affair.''

"Sound thinking.'' The colonel nodded approvingly. "Why throw away the lives of Terran lads when plenty of native lives are available for the purpose? To be given selflessly in defense of sacred Terran principles, that is to say. By the way, which is our side?''

"Try to grasp the point, Colonel,'' the undersecretary said acidly. "We're neutral in the affair.''

"Of course—but whom are we neutral in favor of? Or in favor of whom, I should say, are we—''

"No one. And we intend to keep it that way.''

"Umm.'' The colonel resumed his seat and his nap.

"It appears,'' the undersecretary resumed, "that our old friends the Groaci are locked in an eyestalk-to-eyestalk confrontation with the Slox.''

"What are these shlocks called, sir?'' the acting assistant deputy undersecretary inquired in a tone of deep synthetic interest.

"Slox, Magnan, S-l-o-x. Inveterate trouble-makers from the Slox System, half a dozen lights in-Arm. It appears both they and the Groaci are claiming mandate-ship of Yudore, an unexceptional planet of a small Class G sun well off the trade routes.''

"Well, why doesn't one of them just go mandate somewhere else?'' a commerce man demanded. "There are scads of avilable planets out that way.''

"The Groaci state that Yudore falls within their natural sphere of influence,'' Thunderstroke said. "As for the Slox, their position is that they found the place first.''

"They could flip a coin for it,'' the commerce man snapped. "Then we could all get back to matters of importance, such as the abnormal rate of increase in the rate of decrease of the expansion of the trend toward reduction of increasing berp-nut consumption among unwed fathers ages nine through ninety on backward worlds of the Nicodeman group; a development which I just detected this morning through the use of refined psychostatistical techniques.''

''Good lord, Chester—'' a political forecast specialist picked up the cue—''what will be the projected impact of this downturn in the upturn?''

''Upturn of the downturn, if you must use layman's language,'' Chester corrected. ''Why, at the present rate it appears that by fiscal ninety-seven there'll be a record high in unwed fathers.''

''To return to the subject at hand, gentlemen,'' Thunderstroke cut in ominously, ''both parties to the dispute have dispatched battle fleets to stand by off Yudore, primed for action.''

''Hmm. Seems to me there's a solution of sorts implicit in that datum,'' someone murmured.

''Let us hope not. An outbreak of hostilities would blot our copybooks badly, gentlemen.'' Thunderstroke glared at the offender. ''Unfortunately the Groaci ambassador has assured me privately that his government's position is unalterable. Groaci doctrine, as he explained matters, makes accommodation with what he terms 'vile-smelling opportunists' impossible, while a spokesman for the Slox has announced they refuse to yield an inch to the 'five-eyed sticky fingers—' as he calls the opposition party.''

''It sounds like a major policy blunder on the part of the Groaci,'' Magnan observed contentedly. ''How refreshing that for once the CDT is not involved.''

"We could hardly be said to be uninvolved, Mr. Magnan," Thunderstroke pointed out sternly, "if we undertake to mediate the dispute."

"No, I suppose not—but why be pessimistic? Who would be idiot enough to suggest poking our nose into that bag of annelids?"

"As it happens," Thunderstroke said in a voice like an iceberg sliding into an Arctic sea, "I did!"

"You, sir?" Magnan croaked. "Why, what a splendid notion—now that I've had time to consider it in depth, I mean."

A fragile-looking acting section chief sprang to the undersecretary's support.

"After all, our function as diplomats is to maintain interplanetary tensions at a level short of violence."

"Would you want to make that 'reduce tensions,' Chester?" the information agency representative inquired, pencil poised. "Just in case you're quoted out of context."

"No reporters," Thunderstroke decreed. "I shudder to think what critics of the Corps might make of any little slip in our part in this affair."

"I suppose you'll be sending along a hundred-man Conciliation Team with a squadron of Peace Enforcers to deal with the matter," Magnan said, a speculative look on his narrow features.

"Hardly," Thunderstroke said flatly. "This is a job for finesse, not brute diplomacy. In a situation of this nature, a single shrewd, intrepid, coolly efficient negotiator is the logical choice."

"Of course, sir, how shallow of me not to have seen it at once." Magnan pursed his lips thoughtfully.

"Naturally, the task calls for a man of wide experience—"

"With a total contempt for deadly personal danger," someone put in.

"Preferably without a family," Magnan added, nodding.

"Too bad that lets me out," a deputy assistant undersecretary said briskly. "As you know, I'm the sole support of twelve cats and a most demanding parakeet—"

"I wasn't thinking of you, Henry," Thunderstroke said severely. "I had in mind a senior diplomat, a man of lofty IQ, unshakable principle and unquestioned dexterity in the verbal arena."

"Good lord, sir," Magnan blurted. "I appreciate your confidence, but my duties here—"

"Unfortunately," Thunderstroke bored on, "the files have failed to produce the name of any such paragon. Hence I must make do with the material at hand."

"Well!" Magnan muttered under his breath, then paled as Thunderstroke fixed him with an imperious eye.

"I assume your inoculations are in order?" the undersecretary inquired coldly.

"Mine, sir?" Magnan said, pushing his chair back and rising hastily. "Actually, my hayfever shot is due in half an hour—"

"I suggest you ask for a heavy dosage of anti-radiation drugs while you're there," the assistant for ET affairs said cheerfully. "And of course a tetanus shot wouldn't do any harm."

"Kindly be seated, Magnan," Thunderstroke

barked. "Now, you'll be going in in a plainly marked courier vessel. I suggest you exercise caution as you approach the battle flotillas. The Slox are said to be even more trigger-happy than the notoriously impetuous Groaci."

"I'm to go into that hornet's nest, sir—in an unarmed boat?"

"You'll be armed with instructions, Magnan. Buck up, man. This is no time to show the white feather."

Magnan sank into his chair. "As for myself, I'm delighted, of course," he said breathlessly. "I was just thinking of all those innocent crew members."

"I'd considered that aspect, Magnan. And of course you're right. It would be folly to risk the lives of an entire crew."

Magnan brightened.

"Therefore, you'll be dropped a fractional A.U. from the scene of action in a fast one-man scout."

"A one-man boat? But—" Magnan paused. "But unfortunately," he went on in tones of relief, "I don't know how to pilot one."

"Why not?" Thunderstroke demanded.

"Sector regs discourage it," Magnan said crisply. "Only last month a chap in my department received a severe dressing down for engaging in acrobatics over Lake Prabchinc—"

"Oh? What's this fellow's name?"

"Retief, sir. But as I said, he's already received a reprimand, so it won't be necessary—"

"Retief." Thunderstroke made a note. "Very well. Make that a two-man scout, Magnan."

"But—"

"No buts, Magnan. This is war—or it will be if you

fail. And time is of the essence. I'll expect you and this Retief fellow to be on the way to the battle zone within the hour.''

"But sir—two diplomats against two fleets?''

"Hm. Phrased in that fashion, it does sound a bit unfair. Still—they started it. Let them take the consequences.''

II

Strapped into the confining seat of the thirty-foot skiff, waiting in the drop-bay of the Corps transport, Magnan watched the launch clock nervously.

"Actually," he said, "the undersecretary had his heart set on a one-man mission—but at my insistence he agreed to send me along with you.''

"I wondered who my benefactor was," Retief said. "Nice to know you were thinking of me.''

"Retief—are you implying—'' Magnan broke off as the voice of the captain of the mother ship rang from the panel speaker.

"Fifteen seconds, gentlemen. Say, I hope your policies are all paid up. From what my translator tells me about the transmissions those boys are exchanging up ahead, you're going to arrive just in time for M minute.''

"I wish he'd trip the launch lever," Magnan snapped. "I'll be profoundly happy to depart this hulk, if only to be away from that gloating voice.''

"I heard that," the captain said. "What's the matter, no sense of humor?''

"I'm convulsed," Magnan said.

"Better unconvulse," came the swift suggestion. "This is it. Happy landings—"

There was a slam of relays, a thud, a jolt that dimmed the passengers' vision for a long, dizzying moment. When it cleared, black space dotted with fiery points glared from the screens. Astern, the transport dwindled and was gone.

"I'm picking them up already," Retief said, manipulating the controls of the R-screen. "Our daredevil captain dropped us practically in their midst."

"Has the shooting started?" Magnan gasped.

"Not yet. But from the look of those battle formations it won't be long."

"Maybe we ought to transmit our plea for peace from here," Magnan said hurriedly. "Something eloquent to appeal to their finer natures, with just a smidgin of veiled threat on the side."

"I have a feeling it's going to take more than sparkling conversation to stop these fellows," Retief said. "Anybody who owns a new battlewagon has a natural yen to see if it works."

"I've been thinking," Magnan said abruptly. "You know how short the CDT is of trained personnel—now that we've seen the hopelessness of the task, it's our duty to salvage what we can from the debacle. Besides, an eyewitness report will be of inestimable value to the undersecretary when the board of inquiry starts digging into the question of how he allowed a war to start right under our noses."

"I'm with you so far, sir."

"That being the case," Magnan went on quickly, "if you should insist on withdrawing from the scene at this point, I hardly see how I could prevent you."

"You're in command, Mr. Magnan," Retief pointed out. "But I have a distinct feeling that our reception back at Sector would be less then enthisiastic if we don't have at least a few blast burns on the hull to show for our trouble."

"But, Retief!" Magnan pointed at the screen on which the long, deadly-looking shape of a Groaci cruiser was growing steadily. "Look at that monster, bristling with guns from stem to stern. How can you reason with that kind of firepower?"

At that moment a crackle of static blared from the screen. A pale, alien visage with five stalked eyes stared out at the Terrans from under a flared war helmet.

"To identify yourselves at once, rash interlopers," a weak voice hissed in sibilant Groaci. "To be gone instantly or suffer dire consequences—"

"Why, if it isn't Broodmaster Slith!" Magnan cried. "Retief, it's Broodmaster Slith. You remember Broodmaster Slith of the Groacian Trade Mission to Haunch Four?"

"Is it you, Magnan?" the Groaci grated. "When last we met you were meddling in Groaci affairs under the guise of selfless uplifter, disrupting peaceful commerce. In what role do you now intrude in Groacian space?"

"Now, Slith, you have to confess it was a bit much, selling plastic frankfurters to those poor backward hot-dog lovers—"

"How were we to know their inferior metabolisms were incapable of assimilating wholesome polystyrenes?" Slith snarled. "Enough of this chatter.

Withdraw at once or take full responsibility for precipitation of a regrettable incident.''

"Now, don't be hasty, Broodmaster—''

"You may address me as Grand Commander of Avenging Flotillas Slith, if you please. As for haste, it is a virtue I recommend to you. In sixty seconds I order my gunners to fire.''

"I suggest you reconsider, Commander,'' Retief said. "At the first shot from your guns, three will get you five the Slox open up on you with everything they've got.''

"What matter? Let the miscreants invoke the full wrath of outraged Groacihood.''

"At a rough count, they have thirty-one ships to your twenty-four,'' Retief pointed out. "I think they've got you out-wrathed.''

"But what's all this talk of shooting?'' Magnan cried. "What could possibly be gained by gunfire?''

"Certain parcels of real estate, for a starter,'' Slith said crisply. "Plus the elimination of certain alien vermin.''

Magnan gasped. "You confess you're here to take Yudore by force?''

"Hardly—not that the matter is of any concern to Terran spies. My mission here is to prevent the invasion of hapless Yudore by the insidious Slox—''

"I hear this,'' a rasping, high-pitched voice cut in from the auxiliary screen. It was accompanied by a hissing of background noise. A wavering image formed on the tube, steadied into the form of a shiny, purplish-red cranium, long and narrow, knobbed and spiked. A pair of yellow eyes were mounted on outriggers that projected a foot on either side. "I outrage! I do not endure! You are gave one minutes, Eastern Standard Time, for total abandon of vicinity! Counting! Nine, twelve, two, several—"

"What—what is it?" Magnan gasped, staring at the newcomer to the conversation.

"Aha—collusion between Soft One and Slox!" Slith keened. "I see it now! You thought to distract my attention with an exchange of civilities while your vile cronies executed a sneak attack—"

"I—Chief General Okkyokk—chum to these monstrositaries?" The Slox spokesman screeched. "Such indignant my language lack! Insufficient you threaten to lowly benefits of Slox Protectorate—but addition of insults! My goodness! Drat! Other obscenity as required!"

"It will not avail you to rant," Slith whispered in a venomous tone. "My guns stand ready to answer your slurs—"

"Only incredible restrains of high-class Slox general intrudes herself to spare those skinny neck!" Okkyokk yelled in reply.

"Gentlemen, don't get carried away," Magnan called over the hiss of static. "I'm sure this can all be worked out equitably—"

"Unless this pernicious meddler in the Groaci destiny disperses his flimsy hulls at once, I'll not be responsible for the result," Slith declared.

"My frustrate!" Okkyokk yelled and brandished a pair of anterior limbs tipped with complicated shredding devices. "Gosh, such wish to know sensation of plait all five eyes into single superocular, followed by pluck like obscene daisy—"

"To wait in patience until the happy moment when I officiate at your burial, head-down, in the ceremonial sand-box," Slith countered.

"Well, at least they're still speaking to each other," Magnan said as the exchange raged on. "That's something."

"We may get through this without any hull-burns after all," Retief said. "They have each other bluffed. It looks like talk rather than torpedoes will carry the day. I suggest we execute a strategic withdrawal while they slug it out, vocabulary-to-vocabulary."

"Hmm. Scant points in that for Terran diplomacy. Duty demands that we play a more creative role in the *rapprochement*." Magnan put a finger against his narrow chin. "Now, if I should be the one to propose an equitable solution—"

"Let's not remind them we're here, Mr. Magnan," Retief suggested. "Frustrated tempers are often taken out in thrown crockery and we'd make a convenient teacup—"

"Nonsense, they'd never dare." Magnan leaned forward. "Gentlemen," he called over the din of battle. "I have the perfect solution. Since there seems to be some lack of confidence on the part of each of you in the benign intentions of the other, I propose that Yudore be placed under a Terran Protectorate." Magnan smiled expectantly.

There was an instant of total silence as two sets of alien sense organs froze, oriented toward the interruption. Slith was the first to break the paralysis.

"What? Leave the fruits of Groaci planning to Terran harvesting? Never."

"I convulse!" Okkyokk howled. "I exacerbate! I

froth at buccal cavity! How are you invite? Mercy! Heavens to Marmaduke! Et cetera!''

"Gentlemen," Magnan said. "We Terrans would only remain on Yudore until such time as the aborigines had been properly educated in modern commercial methods and sexual hygiene, after which we'd withdraw in favor of local self-determination!''

"First to pervert, then to abandon!" Slith hissed. "Bold threats, Soft Ones! But I defy you! General Okkyokk! I propose a truce while we band together to confront the common enemy.''

"Done! Caramba! I effronterize! I mortal insult! I even annoy! First destruction we the kibitzer! Then proceedure to Slox-Groaci quarrel!''

"Wait!" Magnan yelped. "You don't understand—''

"I'm afraid they do," Retief said as he reached for the controls. "Hang on for evasive action, Mr. Magnan.'' The tiny craft leaped ahead, curvetting wildly left and right. There was a flash and the screens went white and blanked out. The boat bucked wildly and flipped end-for-end. A second detonation sent it spinning like a flat stone skipped over a pond.

"Retief—stop! We're headed straight for no-man's land!'' Magnan gasped as a lone screen flickered back to life, showing a vast Groaci battlewagon swelling dead ahead.

"We're going in under their guns,'' Retief snapped. "Running away, we'd be a sitting duck.''

"Maybe they'll let us surrender,'' Magnan bleated. "Can't we run out a white flag or something?''

"I'm afraid it would just give them an aiming

point." Retief wrenched the boat sideways, rode out another near miss, dove under the big ship's stern.

"Look out—" Magnan screamed as a vast, mottled bluegreen disk slid onto the screen. "We'll crash on Yudore—"

"If we're lucky," Retief agreed. Then the rising keening of splitting air made further conversation impossible.

III

Except for the fading hiss of escaping air and the *ping* of hot metal contracting, the only sounds audible in the shattered cockpit were Magnan's groans as he extricated himself from the wreckage of his contour chair. Through a rent in the hull, yellow sunlight glared on the smoking ruins of the scout boat's control panel, the twisted and buckled floor plates, the empty pilot's seat.

"Glad to see you're awake," Retief said. Magnan turned his aching head to see his companion leaning in the open escape hatch, apparently intact but for a bruise on the cheekbone and a burned patch on the front of his powder-blue blazer. "The air's a little thin but the O$_2$ content seems adequate. How do you feel?"

"Ghastly," Magnan confided. He fumbled his shock harness free and groped his way through the hatch to drop down shakily on a close-cropped peach-colored sward. All around, tall, treelike growths with ribbed red-orange trunks rose into the pale sky, supporting masses of spongy tangerine-toned foliage.

Clumps of yellow, amber and magenta blossoms glowed in the shade like daubs of fluorescent paint.

"Why are we still alive?" the senior diplomat inquired dazedly. "The last thing I remember is a pale pink mountain sticking up through a cloud bank directly in our path."

"We missed it," Retief reassured his chief. "There was just enough power left on our plates to cushion touchdown. That and a lot of springy foliage saved our necks."

"Where are we?"

"On a small island in the northern hemisphere, which seems to be the only land on the planet. That's about as specific as I can be, I'm afraid—and I designated the north pole arbitrarily at that."

"Well—let's get it over with." Magnan sighed, looking around. "Where are they? I suggest we throw ourselves on Slith's mercy. Frankly, I don't trust that Okkyokk—there's something shifty about those cantilevered oculars of his."

"I'm afraid we son't be able to surrender immediately," Retief said. "Our captors haven't yet arrived."

"Hmm. Doubtless they're making a somewhat less precipituous approach then we. I suppose we might as well make ourselves comfortable."

"On the other hand," Retief said reasonably, "why wait around?"

"What other hope of rescue have we?"

"I don't think either party would make the ideal host—assuming they bother with live prisoners in the first place."

"You're implying that Slith—a fellow bureaucrat—a being with whom I've shared many a convivial cup—would acquiesce to our execution out of hand?'' Magnan gasped.

"He might. If he didn't do the job himself.''

"Heavens, Retief, what are we to do? How far do you suppose it is to the nearest native village?''

"I didn't see any signs of civilization on the way down—no towns, no roads or cleared fields. Let's give a listen on the long-wave bands.'' Retief climbed back into the wrecked craft, investigated the shock-mounted TRX, spliced a number of broken wires and twirled the knob. Nothing but faint static. He switched to the ship-to-ship frequency.

"—blundering two-eyed incompetent!'' Slith's furious voice came through loud and clear. "Your broken-down excuse for a flagship was closer to them than my own superb standard-bearer. It was your responsibility to blast them from space—''

"My indignant! My furious! Heck! Darn! This accuse from a Five-eyes margarine-fingers! I intolerate! Too bad!''

"Have done! These vituperations avail us not at all. If the Soft Ones survive to make known that we fired on a Terran vessel—in self-defense, of course—a horde of their execrable Peace Enforcers will descend on us like bim beetles in grub-harvest time.''

"I proposterate! My laughter! Your numbskull! Alive, oh! After such crashing, entirely! No, unpossible; I rediculate! Au contraire, I suggestion my resumption our dispute. Where were? Indeed, yes—my descriptioning your ancestry—''

"Hark, mindless one! Like other low forms of life, the Soft Ones are tenacious of vitality. We must make sure of their demise. Hence, I shall descend to administer the coup de grace to any survivors, while you stand by off-planet—or, preferably, withdraw to neutral space—"

"So you enable to theft these planet, unoppositioned? My amuse! My hylerical! Goodness me! I accompanate, quite so!"

"Very well—if you insist. You may accompany me aboard my personal gunboat. I'll designate a modest destroyer escort to convoy us down to the surface."

"Nix. I preference to my own vessel, gratitudes anyhow. And my bring few Slox cruiser in order to not lonesome."

"Cruisers?" Slith said harshly. "In that case I think a pair of Groaci battleships would be in order—just to balance the formation, you understand."

"Combination operate incompletion—unless Slox battlewagon also include."

"Actually," Slith hissed, "I see no reason not to bring my entire fleet along—just in case you should entertain ideas of a sneak attack during my absence."

"My agreeness! I, too! The more the merriment! Gracious me! Full speed ahead! Devil take the hind parts!"

"Agreed! Roger and out," Slith snapped.

"Good heavens, Retief," Magnan muttered, "those two madmen are going to stage a full-scale invasion just to keep an eye on each other."

"No one could accuse us now of having failed to influence the course of Slox-Groaci relations," Retief said calmly. "Well, let's be off. We have about an hour before they arrive."

Quickly he detached the compact radio from its

mountings, extracted an emergency ration pack from the debris.

"Which way?" Magnan queried worriedly, staring at the deep orange shade of the forest all around.

"Take your choice, Mr. Magnan," Retief said, indicating the four points of the compass. "Eeenie, meenie, miney or moe."

"Hmm. I think perhaps due meenie. It looks a tiny bit less forbidding. Or possibly just a few points to the miney of meenie."

"Meenie by miney it is," Retief said and led the way into the tall timber.

"Retief—I'm utterly exhausted," Magnan panted three quarters of an hour and three miles from the wrecked scout boat.

"We're not yet clear," Retief said. "We'd better keep going and rest later."

"I'd as soon face a Groaci firing squad as die of heart failure and heat prostration." Magnan sank down on the yielding turf, lay breathing in great gulps.

"How about a Slox skinning party?" Retief suggested. "I understand they start with the scalp and work downward—like peeling a banana."

"Jape if you must." Magnan groaned. "I'm past caring." He sat up suddenly, staring suspiciously at a small, bell-shaped blossom with petals of a delicate shade of coral pink.

"Bees," he said distastefully. "Allergic as I am even to Terran insects, a sting from an alien form would probably be instantly fatal."

"Still, as you pointed out, one demise is pretty much like another," Retief consoled his superior. "If it actually was a bee you saw, it's the first native animal life to make its presence known."

"I didn't see it but I heard it distinctly," Magnan said severely. "It buzzed practically in my ear."

"This is a rather curious forest," Retief observed. "Only one variety of tree, one kind of grass, one type of flower—in assorted sizes and colors. But no weeds. No parasitic vines. No big trees crowding out smaller ones, no stunted growth. Not even any deadfalls."

Magnan grunted.

"Retief, suppose for the nonce we succeed in eluding capture—what then? Nobody knows we're here. How will we ever be rescued?"

"Interesting question, Mr. Magnan."

"Not that it matters a great deal," Magnan went on morosely. "With my mission a failure—worse than a failure—my career is in ruins. Do you realize that if it hadn't been for our meddling this invasion would probably never have come to pass?"

"The thought had occurred to me," Retief conceded.

"To say nothing of the loss of the scout-boat. If the undersecretary holds me responsible—holds us responsible, I should say—that is, in the event he doesn't hold you personally responsible, Retief, as pilot—why, you'll be years paying it off," he went on more cheerfully. "Still, I'll put in a word for you. After all, Slith was shooting at us."

"There is that."

"And actually, who's to say it was my friendly attempt to offer a compromise that precipitated the invasion? I daresay the hotheads would have embarked on their conquest in any event."

"Possibly," Retief agreed.

"By engaging them in conversation I doubtless delayed the inevitable for a—a length of time."

"Several seconds at least."

"Retief, by offering myself as a sacrifice on the alter of inter-being chumship I may have saved countless lives."

"I suppose a certain number of bacteria were lost in our crash landing," Retief sarcastically pointed out.

"You scoff," Magnan charged. "But history will vindicate my stand. Why, I wouldn't be surprised if a special posthumous medal were struck—" He broke off with a start. "There it is again—" He scrambled up. "It sounded like an enraged hornet. Where did it go?"

Retief cocked his head, listening, then leaned over to examine the clump of apricot-colored flowers nodding on long stems, beside which Magnan had been sitting.

"Don't waste time plucking nosegays," Magnan yelped. "I'm under attack—"

"Mr. Magnan, I don't think there are any insects in the vicinity."

"Eh? Why, I can hear them quite plainly." Magnan frowned. "It sounds like one of those old fashioned hand-crank telephones still in use out on Jawbone. When you leave it off the hook."

"Close, Mr. Magnan," Retief said and leaned down to put his ear close to the trumpet-shaped bloom.

"Well, I thought you'd never speak," a tiny voice said distinctly in his ear.

IV

"Buzzing blossoms is quite fantastic enough," Magnan said wonderingly. "But talking tulips? Who'd ever believe it?"

". . . somebody to converse with," the cricket-sized voice was saying. "I'm dying to know all the news. Now, just tell me all about yourself—your hopes, your dreams, how you happened to be here—everything—"

Retief held a blossom to his lips as if it were indeed the mouthpiece of a phone.

"I'm Retief. This is my colleague, Mr. Magnan. Whom have we the honor of addressing?"

"Well, nice to know you, Retief. And Mister Magnan, too. May I call you Mister for short? First names are so much more sort of informal. I'm Herby. Just a nickname, of course. Actually I don't have a name. At least I didn't have until dear Renfrew came along. You have no idea what a sheltered life I'd led until then. Why, do you know I had the idea I was the only sentient intelligence in the Galaxy?"

"Who are you?" Magnan blurted. "Where are you? Why is the microphone camouflaged to look like a plant?"

"Camouflage? Why, there's no camouflage, Mister. You see me just as I am."

"But I don't see you at all," Magnan complained, looking around warily. "Where are you hiding?"

"You're squeezing me at this very moment," Herby said.

"You mean—" Magnan held the faintly aromatic blossom at arm's length and stared at it.

"You mean—I'm—you're—we're—"

"Now you're getting the idea," the voice said encouragingly.

"Talking flowers—here, in the middle of nowhere—and speaking Terran at that? I must be hallucinating. I've been driven mad by hardship."

"I doubt it, Mr. Magnan," Retief said soothingly. "I hear it, too."

"If I can imagine I hear voices coming out of posies I can imagine your hearing them too," Magnan retorted tartly.

"Oh, I'm real enough," the voice said reassuringly. "Why should you doubt me?"

"Who taught you to speak Terran?" Retief asked.

"Renfrew. I learned so much from him. Curious—but before he came, it never occurred to me to be lonely."

"Who is Renfrew?"

"A friend. A very dear friend."

"Retief, this is fantastic," Magnan whispered. "Are there—are there many like you?" he inquired of the bloom.

"No—just me. After all, there'd hardly be room, you know—"

"A coincidence," Magnan exclaimed. "One talking plant on the entire world and we stumble on it in the first hour. I'm beginning to think our luck is still holding."

"Now, where are you from, if you don't mind my asking?" the plant inquired.

"We're Terrans," Magnan said. "And I'm sure we're going to get on famously, Herby."

"But—I understood Terra was the name of Renfrew's home planet."

"Quite so. Marvelous place. You'd love it, now that all the jungles have been cleared and replaced by parking lots—" Magnan caught himself. "Ah, no offense intended, of course. Some of my best friends are plants."

"Heavens—all three of you from one planet? No wonder you left. Such overcrowding—"

"Yes—now, Mr. Herby, if you could just tell us the way to the nearest native settlement—"

"Buildings, you mean? Streets, spaceports, that sort of thing?"

"Yes. Preferably not one of these dismal provincial towns. Something in a modest metropolis will do."

"Sorry, there isn't one—though Renfrew told me about them."

Magnan groaned. "No towns at all? Then—"

"Just jungle."

"If this fellow Renfrew has a ship we may be able to catch a ride with him. I wonder—could we meet him?"

"Well—I suppose so, Mister. He's quite nearby as it happens."

"He's still here, then?"

"Oh, yes indeed."

"Saved," Magnan breathed in relief. "Can you direct us, Herby?"

"Certainly. Just press on meenie, bearing a little to the miney after you cross the stream, then hard moe at the lake. You can't miss him."

Magnan looked startled. "How did you know?" He frowned at Retief in puzzlement. "I thought we named the local directions."

"Oh, indeed," Herby spoke up. "I merely employed your own nomenclature."

"You must have a fantastic ear," Magnan said wonderingly. "That discussion was held miles from here."

"I don't miss much," Herby said complacently.

"He's remarkably sophisticated for such a modest bloom," Magnan commented as they started off.

"I suspect most of Herby is underground, Mr. Magnan," Retief pointed out. "There's no room for a speech center in the part we saw."

"Gad—a subterranean cerebrum—like a giant potato?" Magnan said uneasily, treading lightly. "A spooky thought, Retief."

Twenty minutes' brisk hike brought the two Terrans to the shore of a small, gurgling brook overhung with majestically arching foliage. They followed the bank to the right for a quarter of a mile, at which point the waters spilled down in a foaming amber cataract into a placid pond a half-mile across.

"So far so good," Magnan said uncertainly. "But I see no signs of habitation, not even a hut, to say nothing of a ship."

Retief moved past Magnan toward a dense thicket that obtruded somewhat from the smooth line of trees edging the lakeshore. He parted the broad, copper-colored leaves, revealing a surface of rust-pitted metal curving away into the dimness.

"Lousy Ann Two," he read the corroded letters welded to the crumbling hull plates. "Looks like we've found Renfrew's ship." He pulled a low-growing branch aside. "And here's Renfrew."

"Splendid!" Magnan hurried up halted abruptly to stare in horror at the heap of mouldering bones topped by a grinning skull still wearing a jaunty yachting cap.

"That's Renfrew?" he quavered.

"Quite so," said a deep voice from somewhere overhead. "And take my word for it, Mister—it's been a long, lonely time since he sat down there."

"Two hundred years, give or take a decade or two," Retief said as he climbed out through the derelict's sagging port, brushing the dust and rust scale from his hands. "She was a Concordiat-registered racing sloop, converted for long-range cruising. What's left of the crew quarters suggests she was fitted out for one-man operation."

"That's right," agreed the resonant baritone— which, the Terrans had determined, emanated from a large, orchid-like blossom sprouting amid the foliage twenty feet above their heads. "Just Renfrew. It was a small world he inhabited but he seemed content with it. Not that he was stand-offish, of course. He was as friendly as could be—right up until the difficulty about his leaving."

"What sort of difficulty?" Magnan inquired.

"He seemd quite upset that his vessel was unable to function. I did my best to console him—regaled him with stories and poems, sang merry songs—"

"Where did you learn them?" Magnan cut in sharply. "I understood Renfrew was the first Terran to visit here."

"Why, from him, of course."

"Good lord—imagine having your own chestnuts endlessly repeated back at you," Magnan whispered behind his hand.

"Did you ever tell a joke to an ambassador?" Retief inquired.

"A telling point," Magnan conceded. "But at least

they usually add a little variety by garbling the punch-line.''

''How did Renfrew happen to crash-land here?'' Retief inquired.

''Oh, he didn't. He came to rest very gently.''

''Then why couldn't he take off again?'' Magnan demanded.

''I believe he described it as foreign matter in the warpilator field windings,'' the voice replied vaguely. ''But let's not talk about the past. The present is so much more exciting. Heavens, there hasn't been such activity here since the last glacial age.''

''Retief—there's something slightly piscine about this situation,'' Magnan murmured. ''I'm not sure I trust these garrulous gardenias. Herby said he was the only one of his kind on the planet—yet here's another equally verbose vegetable.''

''Oh, that was quite true,'' the voice above spoke up promptly. ''Why in the world would I lie to you?''

''Kindly refrain from eavesdropping,'' Magnan said coldly. ''This is a personal conversation.''

''Not as personal as calling me a potato brain,'' the orchid said a trifle coolly.

''Goodness—I hope you don't listen to irresponsible gossip,'' Magnan replied with dignity. ''Do I appear the type to employ such an epithet?'' He put his mouth to Retief's ear. ''The grapevine here surpasses anything I've encountered even at a diplomatic reception.''

''Now, let me see,'' the voice from on high mused. ''You mentioned something called a parking lot. I'd like to know more about that and—''

''I suppose Herby told you that, too,'' Magnan snapped. ''If I'd known he was such a blabbermouth I'd never have confided in him! Come, Retief—we'll withdraw to where we can have a modicum of privacy.''

"As to that, Mr. Magnan—" Retief started.

"Not here," Magnan interrupted. He led the way a hundred feet down the shore, halted under a spreading bough. "It's apparent I was indiscreet with Herby," he said from the corner of his mouth, without moving his lips. "I see now he was a rumormonger of the worst stripe, in addition to being of questionable veracity. Sole representative of his race, indeed! Why, I suspect every shrub in sight has a wagging tongue."

"Very probably," Retief agreed.

"There's nothing to do now, quite obviously," Magnan said, "but select an honest-looking plant and approach the problem afresh, impressing the vegetable with our sincerity and benign intentions. When we've wormed our way into its confidence we can determine how best to make use of it to our own best advantage. How does it sound?"

"Familiar," Retief said.

"Excuse me." Magnan jumped a foot as a voice squeaked the words almost in his ear. "What does 'sincerity' mean in this context?"

Retief addressed a cluster of small, russet buds almost invisible among the roan leaves overhead.

"Very little."

"Is there no privacy to be found anywhere in the confounded wilderness?" Magnan inquired with asperity.

"I'm afraid not," the miniature voice piped. "As I was telling you a while ago, there's not a great deal I miss."

"A while ago?" Magnan repeated with a rising inflection. "Why, we've only just met—"

"I don't understand, Mister. I'm Herby. You know me."

"Nonsense. Herby is a little chap growing a mile from here."

"Of course. I grow everywhere, naturally. After all, it's my island, isn't it? Not that I'm not willing to share it with a few friends."

"Utter nonsense," Magnan sputtered. "I might have known a potato was incapable of coherent thought."

"Herby's telling the truth," Retief said. "It's all one plant—the trees, the grass, everything. Like a banyan tree, only more so." He examined a flower closely. "There's a tympanic membrane that serves as both microphone and speaker. Very ingenious of mother nature."

"In that case—they—or it—"

"He," Retief amended.

"He's overheard every word that's been spoken since we landed." Magnan addressed the blossoms directly. "Look here, Herby—you're aware that we're distressed diplomats, marooned here by an unfortunate accident—"

"I thought Slith and that other fellow—Okkyokk—were responsible," Herby corrected. "They seem dreadfully argumentative chaps. I do wish they'd lower their voices."

"Quite—now, you're aware of their hostile intentions toward Mr. Retief and myself—"

"Oh, my," Herby interrupted, "they do seem upset. Such language—"

"Yes. As I was saying—" Magnan paused. "What do you mean, 'such language?' "

"I was referring to Grand Commander Slith's rather

graphic use of invective," Herby explained. "Not that General Okkyokk isn't holding his own, of course. I must say my vocabulary is expanding rapidly."

"You speak as though you could hear them now."

"I can. On the ship-to-shore band."

"But—you don't have a radio—do you?"

"A what?"

"If he has organs for detecting sound," Retief said, "why not organs for picking up short wave?"

"Why—that's remarkable," Magnan exclaimed. "But short wave? It would be rather too much to hope that you can send as well as receive?"

"Why, I suppose I could transmit via my snarf-nodes—if there were any reason to."

"Retief—we're saved! Herby—send the following message at once: Special Priority-Z Mayday, CDT Sector HQ, Aldo Cerise. CDT eight-seven-nine-oh-three, subject unprovoked attack—no, make that unwarranted attack—resulting in emergency planetfall and—"

"Oh, I'm sorry, Mister," Herby cut in. "I couldn't send that."

"Why not?"

"Why, if I did, some nose parker might come and take you away."

"I sincerely hope so."

"I've waited two hundred standard years for someone to talk to," Herby said in a hurt tone. "Now you're talking of rushing off. Well, I won't have it."

"The SOS is our sole hope," Magnan cried. "Would you stand in the way of our rescue?"

"Please clam yourself, Mister. Look at Retief. He's not making a scene. Just resign yourself to the fact that

346

you'll spend the rest of your life here and we'll get on famously—just as Renfrew and I did right up until the last few days."

"The rest of our lives?" Magnan gasped. "But that's unthinkable. We may linger on for another fifty years."

"Not if Slith has his way," Retief said. "Where are they now, Herby?"

"I was about to say," Herby began. "They'll be arriving any—"

The vegetable voice was drowned by a rising drone that swelled swiftly to a bellowing roar. A sleek, shark-nosed shape swept overhead, followed by another, two more, then an entire squadron. Sonic booms crashed across the jungle, laying patterns of shock ripples across the still water of the lake. Treetops whipped in the turbulent wakes as two battle fleets hurtled past at low altitude, dwindled, were gone.

"You see?" Herby said a trifle breathlessly into the echoing silence. "Two's company but a crowd is altogether too much."

Retief twisted the knob of the radio slung at his belt.

". . . pinpointed our quarry!" Slith's breath voice was keening. "If you will employ your units in encircling the south shore of the island, General, I shall close the pincer to the north."

"Looks like they've spotted us," Retief said. "Slith must carry better optical and IR gear than I gave him credit for."

Sunlight winked on distant craft circling back to spread out on the far side of the lake, sinking down out of sight behind the massed foliage of the forest. Other vessels were visible to left and right.

"Not much point in running cross-country," Retief said thoughtfully. "They've got us surrounded."

"What are we going to do?" Magnan yelped. "We can't just stand here."

"Ouch!" Herby said suddenly. "Ooh! Ahh!"

"What's the matter?" Magnan leaped in alarm, staring around him.

"Why that hurts like anything!" Herby exclaimed indignantly.

"It's the landing blasts." Retief indicated the smoke rising from points all around the compass. "The Groaci still use old-style reaction motors for atmospheric maneuvering. Must be scorching Herby quite painfully."

"You see what sort of uncouth ruffians they are?" Magnan said indignantly. "Now wouldn't you like to change your mind, Herby, and assist us?"

"And collect a new crop of third-degree burns when your friends arrive? No, thank you. It's out of the question."

A deep-toned whickering sound had started up, grew quickly louder.

"A heli," Retief said. "They're not wasting any time."

In the shelter of the tree the two Terrans watched the approach of the small, speedy craft. It swung out over the lake, riffling the water, and hovered two hundred feet in the air.

"Attention, Terran spies!" an electronically amplified voice boomed out from it. "Surrender at once or suffer a fate unspeakable—"

"Herby—if those barbarians get their hands on us our usefulness as conversationalists will come to an abrupt end," Magnan said urgently.

"He's not talking about that, Mr. Magnan," Retief said. "He's talking about his use of Yudore as a red herring to cover an attack on the Slox Empire."

"Silence, verbose one," Slith said; but Okkyokk, whose image on the conference screen had been quietly occupying a complicated perch in the background, spoke up.

"Who this? My fascinate! Gosh! Tell more!"

"Fool." Slith leaped to his feet, vibrating his throat sac at Retief. "Your groundless insinuations deprive you of life's last sweet moments." He signaled the guards. "On with the executions."

"Not so hurry, Five-eyes!" Okkyokk snarled. "Conversation me, Terry; my interest, oh, yes! Tell on!"

"Keep out of this, Okkyokk!" Slith snapped as the guards started forward eagerly.

"My listen!" Okkyokk yelled. "Your forgot, Slith—I guns train on you! My chat there Terry—blow your in fragmentation, or!"

"Better humor him, Slith," Retief said. "Inasmuch as your fleet consists of disguised barges with dummy guns, you're in no position to call his bluff."

Slith made spluttering sounds.

"No gun?" Okkyokk chortled. "Good new tonight! Tell Terry!"

"It's quite simple," Retief said. "Slith lured you out here to get your gunboats out of the way so he could proceed to attack the Slox home planets with minimal interference. The bombardment is probably underway right now."

"Lies!" Slith found his frail voice. "Okkyokk—he seeks to set us at odds, each with the other!"

"I grateful you extreme, Terry!" the Slox commander grated in a voice like a steel girder shearing, ignoring Slith's appeal. "Preparation you for dead, Groaci big-shot! Fake up big war, eh, you tell. Make fool allbody, eh? Then join force and invasion Terries, eh? Fruits and nuts! You never delusion me for every! Hold on hats, kids—"

"Don't fire. The Soft One lies—as I can prove in most dramatic fashion—by blasting your cancerous aggregation of derelicts into their component atoms—"

"Retief—say something," Magnan yelped. "If they shoot—"

"Then you Soft Ones will die!" Slith piped. "If they prevail you die with my flagship—and if I prevail—then long shall you linger under the knives of my virtuosi!"

"How you plan do so big shoot with empty gun?" Okkyokk inquired warily.

"Retief!" Slith cried. "Confess to him you lied—else will I decree torments yet uninvented to adorn your passing!"

"Better open fire quickly—if you can," Retief said. "As for you, General," he addressed the screen, "it always pays to get in the first lick."

"Retief, what are you saying?" Magnan yelped. "Why goad them to this madness? No matter who wins, we lose!"

"My confuse!" Okkyokk stated. "Splendor idea, shoot up unarmed Five Eyes—but what if Terry big lying?"

"Don't let him get the jump on you, Slith," Retief advised.

"Gunnery Officer!" the Groaci commander piped

in sudden, agonized decision. "All batteries—open fire."

The response was instantaneous. A series of hollow clicking wounds came over the intercom. They were followed by the dumfounded voice of the Gunnery officer.

"Exalted one—I regret to report—"

"Sabotage," Slith yelled.

On the screen Okkyokk paused, one digital member poised above a large puce button.

"How, no explosing? Gun fails operationing, just as Terry inform? Splendor!" the Slox leader waggled his ocular extremities. "Now time procedure to you with leisurely! Master Gunner—procedure blow picture window in Five Eyes flagship, give Commander Slith good viewing of eventuals!"

Slith hissed and sprang for the door, where he fought for position with the guards who had reached the portal before him. Magnan covered his ears and screwed his eyes shut.

"Whats?" Okkyokk's puzzled voice was coming from the screen. "Hows? Malfunctionate of firepower at times like these? My intolerate! Caramba! Oh, heck!"

"I suggest both you gentlemen relax." Retief raised his voice slightly over the hubbub. "No one's going to do any shooting."

"So—your spies have infiltrated my flagship," Slith said. "Little will it avail you, Retief. Once in space, my most creative efforts will be lavished on your quivering corpori." He scrabbled on the rug, came up with his command mike. "Engineer—lift off, emergency crash procedures."

"Another disappointment in store, I'm afraid, Slith," Retief said as no surge of acceleration followed. "Herby's particularly sensitive to rocket blasts," he explained gently. "Ergo—no gunfire."

"Herby?" Slith keened, waggling his eyes from which the jeweled shields had fallen in the tussle. "Herby?"

"Herby," Okkyokk muttered. "What Herby, which?"

"Herby," Magnan gasped. "But—but—"

"Undone?" Slith whispered. "Trapped here by the treachery of the insidious Soft Ones? But briefly shall you gloat, my Retief."

The Groaci jerked an elaborately ornamented gun from the plastic holster at his bony hip, took aim.

"Three and out," Retief said as Slith stared in goggle-eyed paralysis at the small coral-toned flower growing from the barrel of the weapon. "Herby appreciates my conversation far too much to let you blow holes in me. Right, Herby?"

"Quite so, Retief," a cricket-sized voice chirped from the dainty blossom.

"My departure, golly whiz!" Okkyokk's voice blasted from the screen. "Navigationer—full fast ahead!"

"No use, General," Retief said. "Everybody's grounded. Your field windings are full of vines, I'm afraid."

"So that's why Renfrew couldn't leave." Magnan gulped. "I knew it all along, of course."

"What does this mean?" Slith whispered.

"It means you've been conquered single-handed by

a population of one," Retief addressed the alien leaders. "So—if you're ready, gentlemen, I'm sure Herby will be willing to discuss the terms of your surrender."

"Heavens, Retief," Magnan said, adjusting the overlapping puce lapels of his top formal mid-morning cutaway in the gilt-framed mirror outside the impressive mahogany doors of the undersecretary for extraterrestrial affairs. "If we hadn't seized a moment to transmit a distress call on Slith's TX while Herby was busy taking the surrender, we might still be languishing in boredom on that dismal island."

"I doubt if we'd have been bored," Retief pointed out. "With several hundred grounded sailors roaming the woods and blaming us for their troubles."

"What a ghastly experience, with every bush and bough jabbering away in colloquial Slox and accentless Groaci, carrying on twelve hundred scrambled conversations at once!"

"In time I think Herby would have mastered the knack of segregating his dialogues," Retief said. "Even with a slice missing from that four-mile brain the soundings showed he should be a fast learner."

"He certainly mastered the technique of creative negotiation with record speed," Magnan agreed. "I can't help feeling a trifle sorry for poor Slith and Okkyokk—their fleets consigned to moulder on the ground, the while they supply teams of conversationalists in relays in perpetuity to entertain their conqueror."

Retief and Magnan turned as the elevator doors opened behind them. An orderly emerged, pushing a tea cart on which rested a handsome teak tub containing a tall, lily-like plant topped by a six-inch flower, glowing a healthy pink and yellow.

"Ah, gentlemen," the blossom greeted them in a mellow tenor voice. "I'm happy to report that new scenes seem to stimulate me—or at least this slice of me."

Magnan shuddered delicately.

"Imagine sprouting a bureaucrat from a wedge of frontal lobe," he said behind his hand. "It makes my head ache just to think of it."

A slender man with thick spectacles thrust his head from the secretarial suite.

"The secretary will see you now," he announced and held the door as the orderly wheeled the cart through.

"Mr. Secretary," Magnan said grandly, "I have the honor to present his excellency the Herbaceous Ambassador."

"Delighted to meet you, sir or madam," Thunderstroke rumbled inclining his head graciously to the bloom, which nodded in reply. "Now—do tell me all the details of how you captured two fully armed war fleets—"

Retief and Magnan withdrew, leaving the undersecretary listening attentively to his visitor's account of the sapless victory.

"Lobotomy seems to agree with Herby," Magnan observed complacently. "Well, I must hurry along, Retief. I have a modest cutting I plan to infiltrate into the flower bed under the Groaci ambassador's window." He hurried off.

"Tsk," said a tiny voice from the pink buttoneire

adorning Retief's topmost lapel. "The segment of me you left with the undersecretary is being regaled with a rather gamy anecdote about cross-fertilizing tea-rose begonias. The punch line is—"

"It's not considered polite to listen in on private conversations, Herby," Retief pointed out.

"How can I help it?" the blossom protested. "After all, it's me he's talking to."

"Just don't repeat what you hear. Unless," Retief added as he strolled off toward the chancery bar, "it's something you think I really ought to know."

BALLOT AND BANDITS

I

SECOND SECRETARY RETIEF of the Terran Embassy emerged from his hotel into a bunting-draped street crowded with locals: bustling, furry folk with upraised, bushy tails, like oversized chipmunks, ranging in height from a foot to a yard. A party of placard-carrying marchers, emerging from a side street, jostled their way through the press, briskly ripping down political posters attached to shop walls and replacing them with posters of their own. Their move was immediately countered by a group of leaflet distributors who set about applying mustaches, beards and crossed eyes to the new placards. The passersby joined in cheerfully, some blacking out teeth and adding warts to the tips of button noses, others grabbing the brushes from the defacers and applying them to their former owners' faces. Fists flew; the clamor rose.

Retief felt a tug at his knee; a small Oberonian dressed in blue breeches and a spotted white apron looked up at him from wide, worried eyes.

"Prithee, fair sir," the small creature piped in a shrill voice, "come quick, ere all is lost!"

"What's the matter?" Retief inquired, noting the flour smudge on the Oberonian's cheek and the dab of pink icing on the tip of his nose. "Are the cookies burning?"

"E'en worse than that, milord—'tis the Tsuggs! The great brutes would dismantle the shop entire! But follow and observe!" The Oberonian whirled and darted away.

Retief followed along the steeply sloping cobbled alley between close-pressing houses, his head level with the second-story balconies. Through open windows he caught glimpses of doll's-houselike interiors, complete with toy tables and chairs and postage-stamp-sized TV screens. The bright-eyed inhabitants clustered at their railings, twittering like sparrows as he passed. He picked his way with care among the pedestrians crowding the way: twelve-inch Ploots and eighteen-inch Grimbles in purple and red leathers, two-foot Choobs in fringed caps and aprons, lordly three-foot-six-inch Blufs, elegant in ruffles and curled pink wigs. Ahead, he heard shrill cries, a tinkle of breaking glass, a dull thump. Rounding a sharp turn, he came on the scene of action.

Before a shop with a sign bearing a crude painting of a salami, a crowd had gathered, ringing in a group of half a dozen giant Oberonians of a type new to Retief: swaggering dandies in soiled silks, with cruelly cropped tails, scimitars slung at their waists—if creatures of the approximate shape of ten-pins can be said to have waists. One of the party held the bridles of their mounts—scaled, spike-maned brutes resembling gaily painted rhinoceroses, but for their prominent canines and long, muscular legs. Two more were busy with crowbars, levering at the lintel over the shop doorway. Another pair were briskly attacking the adjacent wall with sledge-hammers. The sixth, distinguished by a scarlet sash with a pistol thrust through it, stood with folded arms, smiling a sharp-toothed smile at the indignant mob.

" 'Tis the pastry and ale shop of Binkster Druzz, my grand uncle twice removed!" Retief's diminutive guide shrilled. "A little lighthearted destruction in the course of making one's political views clear is all very well—but these pirates would reduce us to penury! Gramercy, milord, canst not impede the brutes?" He swarmed ahead, clearing a path through the onlookers. The red-sashed one, noticing Retief's approach unfolded his arms, letting one hand linger near the butt of the pistol—a Groaci copy of a two-hundred-year-old Concordiat sliver-gun, Retief noted.

"Close enough, off-worlder," the Tsugg said in a somewhat squeaky baritone. "What would ye here? Ye'r hutch lieth in the next street yonder."

Retief smiled gently at the bear-like Oberonian, who loomed over the crowd, his eyes almost on a level with Retief's own, his bulk far greater. "I want to buy a jelly doughnut," the Terran said. "Your lads seem to be blocking the doorway."

"Aroint thee, Terry; seek refreshment elsewhere. Being somewhat fatigued with campaigning, I plan to honor this low dive with my custom; my bullies must needs enlarge the door to comport with my noble dimensions."

"That won't be convenient," Retief said smoothly.

"When I want a jelly doughnut I want it now." He took a step toward the door; the pistol jumped at him. The other Tsuggs were gathering around, hefting crowbars.

"Ah-ah," Retief cautioned, raising a finger—and at the same moment swung his foot in a short arc that ended just under the gun-handler's knee-joint. The victim emitted a sharp yap and leaned forward far enough for his jaw to intersect the course of Retief's left fist. Retief palmed the gun deftly as the Tsugg staggered into the arms of his companions.

"Aroint thee, lads," the giant muttered reproachfully to his supporters, shaking his head dazedly. "We've been boon drinking chums these six Lesser Moons and this is the first time ye've give me any of the food stuff . . ."

"Spread out, lads," one of the Tsuggs ordered his companions. "We'll pound this knave into a thin paste."

"Better relax, gentlemen," Retief suggested. "This gun is messy at short range."

"An' I mistake me not," one of the crowbar wielders said, eyeing Retief sourly, "ye'r one of the outworld bureaucrats, here to connive in the allocation of loot, now the Sticky-fingers have gone."

"Ambassador Clawhammer prefers to refer to his role as refereeing the elections, nothing more," Retief corrected.

"Aye," the Tsugg nodded, "that's what I said. So how is it ye're interfering with the free democratic process by coshing Dir Blash in the midst of exercising his voice in local affairs?"

"We bureaucrats are a mild lot," Retief clarified,

"unless someone gets between us and our jelly doughnuts."

Red-sash was weaving on his feet, shaking his head. " 'Tis a scurvy trick," he said blurrily, "sneaking a concealed anvil into a friendly little six-to-one crowbar affray."

"Let's go," one of the others said, "ere he produces a howitzer from his sleeve." The *banditi* mounted their wild-eyed steeds amid much snorting and tossing of fanged heads.

"But we'll not forget ye're visage, off-worlder," another promised. "I wot well we'll meet again—and next time we'll be none so lenient."

A hubbub of pleased chatter broke out among the lesser Oberonians as the party passed from sight.

"Milord has saved Great-uncle Binkster's fried fat this day," the small being who had enlisted Retief's aid cried. The Terran leaned over, hands on knees, which put his face on a level only a foot or two above that of the little fellow.

"Haven't I seen you before?" he asked.

"Certes, milord—until an hour since, I eked out a few coppers as third assistant pastry cook in the inn yonder, assigned to the cupcake division, decorative icing branch." He sighed. "My specialty was rosebuds—but no need to burden your grace with my plaint."

"You lost your job?"

"Aye, that did I—but forsooth, 'tis but a trifling circumstance, in light of what I o'erheard ere the hostler bade me hie me from the premises forthwith!"

"Let's see, your name is—"

"Prinkle, milord. Ipstitch Prinkle IX, at your service.'' The Twilpritt turned as a slightly plumper, grayer version of himself bustled up, bobbing his head and twitching his ears in a manner expressive of effusive gratitude. ''And this, Milord, is Uncle Binkster, in the flesh.''

''Your servant, sir,'' Uncle Binkster squeaked, mopping at his face with a large striped handkerchief. ''Wouldst honor me by accepting a cooling draft of pring-lizard milk and a lardy-tart?''

''In sooth, Uncle, he needs something stronger than whey,'' Prinkle objected. ''And in sooth, *The Plump Sausage* offers fine ale—if your Grace can manage the approaches,'' he added, comparing Retief's six foot three with the doorway.

''I'll turn sideways,'' Retief reassured the Oberonian. He ducked through, was led across the crowded room by a bustling eighteen-inch tapman to a corner table, where he was able to squeeze himself onto a narrow bench against the wall.

''What'll it be, gents?'' the landlord inquired.

''Under the circumstances, I'll stick to small beer,'' Retief said.

''Ale for me,'' Uncle Binkster said. '' 'Tis vice, perhaps to tipple ere lunchtime, but with Tsuggs roaming the Quarter and battering down walls, one'd best tipple while opportunity presents itself.''

''A sound principle,'' Retief agreed. ''Who are these Tsuggs, Uncle Binkster?''

''Lawless rogues, down from the high crags for easy pickings,'' the elderly baker replied with a sigh. ''After you Terrans sent the Groaci packing, we thought all our troubles were over. Alas, I fear me 'tis not the case. As soon as the ruffians got the word the Five Eyes were pulling out, they came swarming down out of the hills like zing-bugs after a jam-wagon—'tis plain they mean to elect their ruffianly chief, Hoobrik the Uncouth. Bands of them roam the city, and the countryside as well, terrorizing the voters—'' He broke off as the landlord placed a foaming three-inch tankard before Retief.

"Away with that thimble, Squirmkin!" he exclaimed. "Our guest requires a heartier bumper than that!"

" 'Tis an Emperor-sized mug," the landlord said, "but I allow his dimensions dwarf it. Mayhap I can knock the top out of a hogshead . . ." He hurried away.

"Pray don't mistake me, milord," Uncle Binkster resumed. "Like any patriot, I rejoiced to see the Sticky-finger go, leaving the conduct of Oberonian affairs to Oberonians. But who'd have guessed we normal-sized chaps would at once be subjected to depradations by our own oversized kith and kin exceeding anything the invaders ever practiced!"

"A student of history might have predicted it," Retief pointed out. "But I agree: being pushed around by local hoodlums is even less satisfying than being exploited from afar."

"Indeed so," Prinkle agreed. "In the case of foreigners one can always gain a certain relief by hurling descriptive epithets, mocking their outlandish ways and blaming everything on their inherent moral leprosy—an awkward technique to use on one's relatives."

The landlord returned, beaming, with a quart-sized wooden container topped by a respectable head. Retief raised it in salute and drank deep.

"And if what my nephew o'er-heard be any indication," Uncle Binkster went on, wiping foam from his whiskers, "the worst is yet to come. Hast related all to our benefactor, lad?"

"Not yet, Uncle." Prinkle turned to Retief. "I was sweeping up crumbs in the VIP breakfast room, my mind on other matters when I heard the word 'Tsugg' bandied among the company still stitting at the table. I cocked an auricle, thinking to hear the scoundrels roundly denounced, only to catch the intelligence that their chief, that brawling bravo Hoobrik, representing himself to be spokesman and natural leader of all Oberon, withal, hath demanded audience of His Impressiveness, Ambassador Clawhammer! 'Twas but natural that I undertook to disabuse their Lordships of this impertinent notion, accidentally overturning a pot of chocolate in process thereof—"

"Alas, my nephew is at times too enthusiastic in his espousal of his views," Uncle Binkster put in. "Though 'tis beyond dispute, in this instance he was sorely tried."

"In sooth, so was his honor, Mr. Magnan, when the cocoa landed in his lap," Prinkle admitted. "Happily, 'twas somewhat cooled by long standing."

"A grosteque prospect," Uncle Binkster ruminated. "Those scapegrace villains, lording it over us honest folk! Perish the thought, Sir Retief! I trow I'd sooner have the Five-eyes back!"

"At least they maintained a degree of control over the ne'r-do-wells," Prinkle said, "restricting them to their hills and caves."

"As will we, lad, once the election is consummated," Uncle Binkster reminded the youth. "Naturally, we Twilpritt stand ready to assume the burden of policing the rabble, as is only right and natural, as soon as our slate is elected, by reason of our supervisor virtues—''

"Hark not to the old dodderer's maunderings, Giant," a tiny voice peeped from the next table. A miniature Oberonian, no more than nine inches tall, raised his one-ounce glass in salute. "We Chimberts, being nature's noblemen, are of course divinely appointed to a position of primacy among these lumbering brutes, saving your presence, milord—''

"Dost hear a dust-cricket chirping in the woodwork?" a medium-sized Oberonian with black circles resembling spectacles around his eyes inquired loudly from three tables away. " 'Twere plain e'en to an outworlder that we Choobs are the rightful inheritors of the mantle of superiority. Once in office we'll put an end to such public rantings."

"You in office?" Prinkle yelped. "O'er my corpse, varlet!" He leaped up, slopping beer as he cocked his arm to peg the mug at the offender.

"Stay, nephew!" Uncle Binkster restrained the youth. "Pay no heed to the wretch, doubtless he's in his cups—''

"Drunk, am I, you old sot!" the Choob yelled, overturning the table as he leaped up, grabbing for the hilt of his foot-long sword "I'll ha' a strip o' thy wrinkled hide for that allegation—'' His threat was cut off abruptly as a tankard, hurled from across the room, clipped him over the ear, sending him reeling into the next table, whose occupants leaped up with indignant shouts and flailing fists.

"Gentlemen, time, time!" the landlord wailed, before diving behind the bar amid a barrage of pewter.

Retief finished his beer in a long swallow and rose, looming over the battle raging about his knees.

"A pleasure, gentlemen," he addressed the room at large. "I hate to leave such a friendly gathering, but Staff Meeting time is here."

"Farewell, Sir Retief," Prinkle panted from under the table, where he grappled with a pale-furred local of about his own weight. "Call around any time for a drop and a bit of friendly political chat."

"Thanks," Retief said. "If things get too slow in the front line trenches I'll remember your invitation."

II

As Retief entered the conference room—a converted packing room in the former warehouse temporarily housing the Terran Mission to the newly liberated planet Oberon—First Secretary Magnan gave him a sour look.

"Well—here you are at last. I'd begun to fear you'd lingered to roister with low companions in your usual manner."

"Not quite my usual manner," Retief corrected. "We'd barely started to roister when I remembered Staff Meeting. By the way, what do you know about a fellow called Hoobrik the Uncouth?"

Magnan looked startled. "Why, that name is known only to a handful of us in the inner security circle," he said in a lowered tone, glancing about. "Who leaked it to you, Retief?"

"A few hundred irate locals. They didn't seem to know it was a secret."

"Well, whatever you do, act surprised when the

Ambassador mentions it," Magnan cautioned his junior as they took seats at the long table. "My," he went on as the shouts of the crowd outside the building rose to a thunderous level, "how elated the locals are, now they realize we've relieved them of the burdens of Groaci overlordship! Hear their merry cries!"

"Remarkable," Retief agreed. "They have a better command of invective than the Groaci themselves."

"Why, Wilbur," Magnan said as Colonel Saddlesore, the Military Attaché slipped into the chair beside him, avoiding his glance. "However did you get that alarming discoloration under your eye?"

"Quite simple, actually." The colonel bit off his words like bullets. "I was struck by a thrown political slogan."

Magnan sniffed. "There's no need for recourse to sarcasm."

"The slogan," Saddlesore amplified, "was inscribed on the rind of a *bham-bham* fruit of the approximate size and weight of a well-hit cricket ball."

"I saw three small riots myself on the way in to the office," the Press Attaché said in a pleased tone. "Remarkable enthusiasm these locals show for universal suffrage."

"I think it's time, however," the Counselor put in ponderously, "that someone explained to them that the term 'political machine' does not necessarily refer to a medium tank."

The chatter around the long table cut off abruptly as Ambassador Clawhammer, a small pinkfaced man with an impressive paunch, entered the room, glowered at his staff as they rose, waved them to their seats as he waited for silence.

"Well, gentlemen," he looked around the table. "What progress have you to report anent the preparation of the populace for the balloting?"

A profound silence ensued.

"What about you, Chester?" Clawhammer addressed the Counselor. "I seem to recall instructing you to initiate classes in parliamentary procedure among these riffraff—that is to say, among the free citizens of Oberon."

"I tried, Mr. Ambassador. I tried," Chester said sadly. "They didn't seem to grasp the idea quite. They chose up sides and staged a pitched battle for possession of the chair."

"Ah—I can report a teentsy bit of progress in my campaign to put across the idea of one man, one vote," a slender-necked Political Officer spoke up. "They got the basic idea, all right." He paused. "The only trouble was, they immediately deduced the corollary: one *less* man, one *less* vote." He sighed, "Luckily, they were evenly matched, so no actual votes were lost."

"You might point out the corollary to the corollary," Retief suggested, "the lighter the vote, the smaller the Post Office."

"What about your assigned task of voter registration, eh, Magnan?" the Chief of Mission barked. "Are you reporting failure too?"

"Why, no indeed, sir, not exactly failure; at least not utter failure; it's too soon to announce that—"

"Oh?" The Ambassador looked ominous. "When do you think would be an appropriate time? *After* disaster strikes?"

"I'd like to propose a rule limiting the number of political parties to P minus 1, P being the number of voters," Magnan said hastily. "Otherwise we run the risk that no one gets a majority."

"No good, Magnan," the Counselor for P R Affairs spoke up. "We don't want to risk a charge of meddling. However," he added thoughtfully, "we might just up the nomination fee to a figure sufficiently astronomical to keep the trash out—that is, to discourage the weakly motivated."

"I don't know, Irving," the Econ Officer ran his fingers through his thinning hair in a gesture of frustration. "What we really need is to prune the ranks of the voters more drastically. Now, far be it from me to propose strong-arm methods—but what if we tried out a modified Grandfather Rule?"

"Say—a touch of the traditional *might* be in order at that, Oscar," the Political Officer agreed tentatively. "Just what did you have in mind?"

"Actually I haven't worked out the details—but how about limiting the franchise to those who have grandfathers? Or possibly grandchildren? Or even both?"

"Gentlemen!" Ambassador Clawhammer cut short the debate. "We must open our sights. The election promises to degenerate into a debacle of ruinous proportions, career-wise, unless we break through with a truly fresh approach." He paused impressively. "Fortunately," he continued in the modest tones of Caesar accepting the crown, "I have evolved such an approach." He raised a hand in kindly remonstrance at the chorus of congratulations that broke out at his announcement.

"It's clear, gentlemen, that what is needed is the emergence of a political force that will weld together the strands of Oberonian political coloration into a unified party capable of seating handy majorities. A force conversant with the multitudinous benefits which would stem from a sympathetic attitude toward Terran interests in the Sector.''

"Yes, Chief," an alert underling from the Admin Section took his cue. "But, gosh, who could possibly produce such a miracle from the welter of divergent political creeds here on Oberon? They're practically at swords' points with each other over each and every question of policy, both foreign and domestic.''

Clawhammer nodded acknowledgment. "Your question is an acute one, Dimplick. Happily, the answer is at hand. I have made contact, through confidential channels, with a native leader of vast spiritual influence, who bids fair to fulfill the role to perfection." He paused to allow the staff to voice spontaneous expressions of admiration, then raised a palm for silence.

"While 'Golly!' and 'Wow!' are perhaps less elegant effusions than one might logically expect from an assemblage of senior career diplomats," he said sternly, but with a redeeming twinkle in his small, redrimmed eyes, "I'll overlook the lapse this time on the basis of your obvious shock at receiving such glad tidings after your own abysmal failures to produce any discernible progress.''

"Sir, may we know the name of this messiah?" Magnan chirped. "When do we get to meet him?"

"Curious that you should employ that particular term with reference to Hoobrik," Clawhammer said complacently. "At this moment, the guru is meditating in the mountains, surrounded by his chelas, or disciples, known as Tsuggs in the local patois.''

"Did you say—Hoobrik?" Magnan queried uncertainly. "Goodness, what a coincidence that he should have the same name as that ruffian of a bandit chief who had the unmitigated effrontery to send one of his strong-arm men to threaten your Excellency!"

Clawhammer's pink features deepened to a dull magenta which clashed sharply with his lime-green seersucker suit.

"I fear, Magnan," he said in a tone like a tire-iron striking flesh, "that you've absorbed a number of erroneous impressions. His Truculence, Spiritual Leader Hoobrik, dispatched an emissary, it's true, to propose certain accommodations sphere-of-influence-wise; but to proceed from that circumstance to an inference that I have yielded to undue pressures is an unwarranted speculative leap!"

"Possibly I just misinterpreted his messenger's phraseology, sir," Magnan said with a tight little smile. "It didn't seem to me that 'foreign bloodsuckers' and 'craven paper-pushers' sounded all that friendly."

" 'IPBM's may fry our skins, but words will never hurt us,' eh, sir?" the Econ Officer piped brightly, netting himself a stab of the Ambassadorial eye.

"Still, it's rather strong language," Colonel Saddlesore spoke up to fill the conversational gap. "But I daresay you put the fellow in his place, eh, Mr. Ambassador?"

"Why, as to that, I've been pondering the precisely correct posture to adopt vis-a-vis the Tsuggs, protocol-wise. I confess for a few moments I toyed with the idea of a beefed-up 804-B: Massive Dignity, with overtones of Leashed Ire; but cooler counsels soon prevailed.''

''How about a 764, sir?'' the Econ Officer essayed. ''Amused Contempt, with just a hint of Unpleasant Surprise in the Offing?''

''Too subtle,'' Colonel Saddlesore grunted. ''What about the old standby, 26-A?''

''Oh, the old 'Threat to Break Off Talks' ploy, eh? Embellished with a side-issue of Table-Shape Dispute, I assume?''

''Gentlemen!'' Clawhammer called the conference to heel. ''You forget that the date of the elections is rushing toward us! We've no time for traditional ploys. The problem is simple: how best to arrive at a meeting of the minds with the guru.''

''Why not just call him in and offer to back him in a takeover, provided he plays ball?'' the PR Chief proposed bluntly.

''I assume, Irving,'' Clawhammer said into the shocked silence, ''that what you actually meant to suggest was that we give His Truculence assurances of Corps support in his efforts to promote Oberonian welfare—in the event of his securing the confidence of the electorate, as evinced by victory at the polls, of course.''

''Yeah, something like that,'' Irving muttered, sliding down in his chair.

''Now,'' Clawhammer said, ''the question remains, how best to tender my compliments to His Truculence, isolated as he is in his remote fastness—''

''Why, simple enough, sir,'' Magnan said. ''We just send a messenger along with an invitation to tea. Something impressive in a gold-embossed, I'd suggest."

"I understand this fellow Hoobrik has ten thousand blood-thirsty cutthroats—ah, that is, wisdom-hungry students—at his beck and call," the Econ Officer contributed. "They say anybody who goes up there comes back with his tail cropped."

"Small hazard, since we Terries have no tails," Magnan said.

"I've got a funny feeling they'd figure out something else to crop," Oscar retorted sharply.

"Am I to infer, Magnan, you're volunteering to convey the bid?" Clawhammer inquired blandly.

"Me, sir?" Magnan paled visibly. "Heavens, I'd love to—except that I'm under observation for possible fourth-degree cocoa burns."

"Fourth-degree burns?" Colonel Saddlesore wondered aloud. "I'd like to see that. I've heard of first, second, and third degree, but—"

"The symptoms are invisible to lay inspection," Magnan snapped. "Additionally, my asthma is aggravated by high altitudes."

"By Gad," Colonel Saddlesore whispered to his neighbor, "*I*'d like a chance to confront these fellows—"

"Better wear your armor, Wilbur," his confidant replied. "From all reports, they weigh in at three hundred pounds and wear six-foot cutlasses with which they lay about them freely when aroused. And they say the sight of a Terry arouses them worse than anything."

"—but, as I was about to say, my duties require that I hole up in my office for the forseeable future," the colonel finished.

"Cutlasses, you say?" the Econ Officer pricked up

his ears. "Hmm. Might be a market here for a few zillion up-to-date hand-weapons—for police use only, of course."

"Capital notion, Depew," the Political Officer nodded approvingly. "Nothing like a little firepower to bring out the natural peace-loving tendencies of the people."

"Now, gentlemen—let us avoid giving voice to any illiberal doctrines," Clawhammer said sharply. "Our only motive, let us remember, is to bring the liberated populace to terms with the political realities—in this case, the obvious need for a man on horseback—or should I say a Tsugg on Vornchback?" The Terran envoy smiled indulgently at his whimsy.

"I have a question, Mr. Ambassador," Retief said. "Since we're here to supervise free elections, why don't we let the Oberonians work out their own political realities?"

Clawhammer looked blank.

"Just—ah—how do you mean?" the Political Officer prompted uneasily.

"Why don't we let them nominate whomever they want, vote for any candidate they like?" Retief explained.

"I suggest you forget these radical notions, young fellow," Clawhammer said sternly. "These free elections will be conducted in the way that free elections have always been conducted. And now that I've considered the matter, it occurs to me it might be valuable experience for you to pay the proposed call on His Truculence. It might serve to polish your grasp of protocol a trifle."

"But, sir," Magnan spoke up. "I need Mr. Retief to

help me do the Consolidated Report of Delinquent Reports—''

''You'll have to manage alone, I fear, Magnan. And now, back to the ramparts of democracy, gentlemen! As for you, Retief—'' The Ambassador fixed Retief with a sharp eye: ''I suggest you comport yourself with a becoming modesty among the Tsugg. I should dislike to have to report any unfortunate incident.''

''I'll do my best to see that no such report reaches you, sir,'' Retief said cheerfully.

III

The green morning sun of Oberon shone down warmly as Retief, mounted on a wiry Struke, a slightly smaller and more docile cousin of the fierce Vorch tamed by the Tsuggs, rode forth from the city gates. Pink and yellow borms warbled in the tree tops; the elusive sprinch darted from grass tuft to grass tuft. The rhythmic whistling of doody-bugs crying to their young supplied a somnolent backdrop to the idyl.

Retief passed through a region of small, tidy farms, where sturdy Doob peasants gaped from the furrows. The forest closed in as the path wound upward into the foothills. In mid-afternoon he tethered the Struke and lunched beside a waterfall on paté sandwiches and sparkling Bacchus Black from a coldflash. He was just finishing off his *mousse éclaire* when a two-foot steel arrow whistled past his ear to bury itself six inches in the dense blue wood of a Nunu tree behind him.

Retief rose casually, yawned, stretched, took out a vanilla dope stick and puffed it alight, at the same time scanning the underbrush. There was a quick movement behind a clump of Foon bushes; a second bolt leaped past him, almost grazing his shoulder, to rattle away in the brush. Appearing to notice nothing, Retief took a leisurely step toward the Nunu tree, slipped suddenly behind it. With a swift motion he grasped a small, limber branch growing out at waist height on his side of the two-foot bole, bent it down and pegged the tip to the shaggy, porous bark, using the match-sized dope stick to pin it in place. Then he moved quickly away, keeping the tree between himself and the unseen archer, to the concealment of a dense patch of shrubbery.

A minute passed; a twig popped. A bulky, tattooed Tsugg appeared, a vast, dumpy figure clad in dirty silks, holding a short, thick, recurved bow clamped in one boulder-like fist, a quarrel nocked, the string drawn. The dacoit tiptoed forward, jumped suddenly around the tree. Finding his quarry fled, he turned, stood with his back to the tree peering into the undergrowth.

At that moment, the bent branch, released by the burning of the dope stick, sprang outward, ramming the astounded bowman in the seat of his baggy green velveteen trousers. The arrow smacked into the dirt at his feet as he jumped, then stood rigid.

"Don't strike, sir!" he urged in a plaintive tenor. "The older lads put me up to it—"

Retief strolled from his shelter, nodded easily to the Tsugg, plucked the bow from his nerveless grip.

"Nice workmanship," he said, inspecting the weapon. "Groaci trade goods?"

"Trade goods?" the Tsugg said with a note of indignation. "Just because yer partner has a dirk at me back's no cause to make mockery of me. I plundered it from the Five-eyes all open and aboveboard, so help me."

"Sorry," Retief said. He withdrew the arrow from the loam, fitted it to the bow experimentally.

"You're not by chance a member of Hoobrik's band, are you?" he inquired off-handedly.

"Too right it's not by chance," the Tsugg said emphatically. "I went through the Ordeal, same's the other lads."

"Lucky we met," Retief said. "I'm on my way to pay a call on His Truculence. Can you lead me to him?"

The Tsugg straightened his two-hundred-and-ninety-pound bulk. "Tell yer crony to do his worst," he said with a small break in his voice. "Fim Gloob's not the Tsugg to play the treacher."

"It wasn't exactly treachery I had in mind," Retief demurred. "Just ordinary diplomacy."

"Yer threats will avail ye naught," Fim Gloob declared.

"I see what you mean," Retief said. "Still, there should be some way of working this out."

"No outsider goes to the camp of Hoobrik but as a prisoner." The Tsugg rolled his shiny black eyes at the Terran. "Ah, sir—would ye mind asking yer sidekick not to poke so hard? I fear me he'll rip me weskit, stole for me by me aged mums it were, a rare keepsake."

"Prisoner, eh, Fim? By the way, I don't have a sidekick."

"That being the way of it," Fim Gloob said carefully, after a short, thoughtful pause, "who'd be the villain holding the blade to me kipglands?"

"As far as I know," Retief said candidly, "there's nobody here but you and me."

The Tsugg turned his head cautiously, peered behind him. With a grunt of annoyance he snapped a finger at the offending bough.

"Me and me overactive imagination," he snorted. "And now—"

He turned to Retief with a scowl.

"Remember, I still have the bow," Retief said pleasantly.

"And a mort o' good it'll do ye," Fim snarled, advancing. "Only a Tsugg born and bred has the arm to draw that stave!"

"Oh?" Retief set the arrow and with an easy motion pulled until the arrowhead rested against the bow, the latter being bent into a sharp curve. Another inch—and the stout laminated wood snapped with a sharp *twang*.

"I see what you mean," Retief said. "But then the Groaci always did produce flimsy merchandise."

"You—you broke it!" Fim Gloob said in tones of deep dismay.

"Never mind—I'll steal you a new one. We have some ladies' models in the Recreation Kits that ought not to overstrain you."

"But—I'm reckoned the stoutest bowman in the band."

"Don't give it another thought, Fim. They'll love you when you bring in a live Terry, single-handed."

"Who, me?"

"Of course. After all, I'm alone and unarmed. How could I resist?"

"Aye—but still—"

"Taking me in as a prisoner would look a lot better

than having me saunter in on my own and tell Hoobrik
you showed me the route.''

''Wouldst do such a dirty trick?'' Fim gasped.

''I wouldst—unless we start immediately,'' Retief
assured the Tsugg.

Fim sighed. ''I guess I know when I'm licked. I
mean when you're licked. Let's go, prisoner. And let's
hope His Truculence is in a good mood. Otherwise he'll
clap ye on the rack and have the whole tale out of ye in a
trice!''

IV

A few dozen heavyweights lazing about the com-
munal cooking pot or sprawling in the shade under the
striped awnings stretched between the trees looked up
in mild interest as Retief appeared on struke-back, Fim
Gloob behind him astride his Vorch, glowering ferociously as he verbally prodded the lone Terran forward.

''Ho, that's far enough,'' he roared. ''Dismount,
while I seek instruction o' His Truculence whether to
h'ist ye out of hand or ha' a bit o' sport wi' ye first.''

''Ha, what be this, Gloob?'' a bulky outlaw boomed
as Retief swung down from the saddle. ''An off-
worder, I trow!''

''That he's no Oberonian, is plain,'' another offered.
''Mayhap a two-eye variety o'Five-eyes.''

Fim yelled. ''Clear the way—I've fetched this Terry
here to divert the great Hoobrik wi' his saucy sayings.''

''Here, what passes?'' a familiar baritone cut
through the clamor. A large Tsugg in a red sash pushed
through the mob, which gave way grudgingly, with

much muttering. The newcomer halted with a jerk when his eye fell on Retief.

"Methinks," he said, "I've seen you before, sir-rah."

"We've met," Retief acknowledged.

"Though all you Terries look alike to me." Dir Blash fingered his jaw gingerly. "Meseemeth 'twas in the Street of the Sweetmakers—"

"So it was."

"Aha! I've got it!" Dir Blash clapped Retief on the shoulder. "My boon companion! Ah, bullies," he addressed his fellows, "this Terry gave me a shot of something with a kick like a Vorch—though for the life of me I can't recall the precise circumstances. How wert thou yclept again, sirrah?"

"Retief; lucky you have the kind of memory you do, Dir Blash; your compatriots were just debating the best method of putting me out of my misery."

"Say you so?" Dir Blash looked around threateningly, his hand on the hilt of his cutlass. "Nobody murders my drinking buddies but me." He turned back to Retief. "Say, you wouldn't chance to have any more of the same, would you?"

"I'm saving it for a special occasion," Retief said.

"Well, what could be more special than a reprieve from being staked out on a zing-wasp hive, eh?"

"We'll celebrate later," Retief said. "Right now I'd appreciate a short interview with His Truculence."

"If I use my influence to get you in, wilt let me have another sample later?"

"If things work out as they usually do," Retief said, "I think you can be sure of it."

"Then come along, Dir Retief. I'll see what I can do."

Hoobrik the Uncouth, lounging in a hammock under a vari-colored canopy, gazed indifferently at Retief as Dir Blash made the introductions. He was an immense Tsugg, above the average height of his kind, his obesity draped in voluminous beaded robes. He selected a large green berry from a dented silver bowl at his elbow, shook exotic salts over it from a heavy gold saltshaker and popped it into his mouth.

"So?" he grunted, spitting the seeds over the side. "Why disturb my meditations with trifles? Dispose of the creature in any way that amuses you, Blash—but save the head. I'll impale it on a pike and give it to the Terry chieftain—gift-wrapped, of course."

Dir Blash nodded, scratching himself under the ribs. "Well, thus doth the tart disintegrate, Retief," he said in tones of mild regret. "Let's go—"

"I don't want to be a spoilsport, your Truculence," Retief spoke up, "but Ambassador Clawhammer only allows his staff to be decapitated at Tuesday morning staff meetings."

"Staff meetings?" Hoobrik wondered aloud. "Is that anything like a barbecue?"

"Close," Retief agreed. "Quite often a diplomat or two is flayed alive and roasted over a slow fire."

"Hmm." Hoobrik looked thoughtful. "Maybe I should introduce the custom here. My wish is to keep up with the latest trends in government."

"In that connection," Retief said, offering the stiff parchment envelope containing the invitation to the reception, "His Excellency the Terrestrial Ambassador

Extraordinary and Minister Plenipotentiary presents his compliments and requests me to hand you this.''

"Eh? What be this?" Hoobrik fingered the document gingerly.

"Ambassador Clawhammer requests the honor of your company at a ceremonial affair celebrating the election," Retief explained.

"Ceremonial affair?" Hoobrik shifted uneasily, causing the hammock to sway dangerously. "What kind of ceremony?"

"Just a small semi-formal gathering of kindred souls. It gives everyone a chance to show off their clothes and exchange veiled insults face to face."

"Waugh! What kind of contest is this? Give me a good hand-to-hand disemboweling any day!"

"That comes later," Retief said. "It's known as Dropping by the Residence for a Drink. After the Party."

"It hath an ominous sound," Hoobrik muttered. "Is it possible you Terries are more ferocious than I'd suspected?"

"Ha!" Dir Blash put in. "I myself dispatched half a dozen of the off-worlders only this morning when they sought to impede my entrance to a grog shop in the village."

"So?" Hoobrik yawned. "Too bad. For a moment, things were beginning to look interesting." He tore a corner off the gold-edged invitation and used it to poke at a bit of fruit rind wedged between his teeth. "Well, off with you, Blash—unless you want to play a featured role at my first staff meeting."

"Come, Terry," the red-sashed Tsugg growled, reaching for Retief's arm. "I just remembered the part of yesterday's carouse that had slipped my mind."

"I think," Retief said, evading the sub-chief's grab, "it's time for that jolt I promised you." He stepped in close and rammed a pair of pile-drive punches to Dir Blash's midriff, laced a hard right to the jaw as the giant doubled over and fell past him, out cold.

"Here!" Hoobrik yelled. "Is that any way to repay my hospitality?" He stared down at his fallen henchman. "Dir Blash, get up, thou malingerer, and avenge my honor!"

Dir Blash groaned. One foot twitched. He settled back with a snore.

"My apologies," Retief said, easing the Groaci pistol from inside his shirt. "Protocol has never been my strong suit. Having committed a *faux pas*, I'd best be on my way. Which route would be least likely to result in the demise of any of your alert sentries?"

"Stay, off-worlder. Wouldst spread tidings of this unflattering event abroad, to the detriment of my polling strength?"

"Word might leak out," Retief conceded. "Especially if any of your troops get in my way."

" 'Tis a shame not to be borne!" Hoobrik said hoarsely. "All Oberon knoweth that only a Tsugg can smite another Tsugg senseless." He looked thoughtful. "Still, if the molehill will not come to Meyer, Meyer must to the molehill, as the saying goeth. Since thou hast in sooth felled my liegeman, it follows you must be raised at once to Tsugghood, legitimizing the event after the fact, as it were."

"I'd be honored," Retief said amiably. "Provided, of course, that you authorize me to convey your gracious acceptance of His Excellency's invitation."

Hoobrik looked glum. "Well—we can always loot the Embassy afterward. Very well, Terry—Tsugg-to-be, that is. Done!" The chieftain heaved his bulk from the hammock, stirred Dir Blash with a booted toe, at which the latter groaned and sat up.

"Up, sluggard!" Hoobrik roared. "Summon a few varlets to robe me for a formal occasion! And my guest will require suitable robes, too." He glanced at Retief. "But don't don them yet, lest they be torn and muddied."

"The ceremony sounds rather strenuous," Retief commented.

"Not the ceremony," Hoobrik corrected. "That cometh later. First cometh the Ordeal. If you survive that I'll have my tailor fit you out as befits a sub-chief of the Tsugg."

The Ceremonial Site for Ordeal Number One—a clearing on forest slope with a breath-taking view of the valley below—was crowded with Tsugg tribesmen, good-naturedly quarreling, shouting taunts, offering and accepting wagers and challenges, passing wine-skins from hand to grimy hand.

"All right, everybody out of the Ring of the First Trial," Dir Blash shouted, implementing his suggestion with hearty buffets left and right. "Unless ye plan to share the novitiate's hazards."

The mountaineers gave ground, leaving an open space some fifty feet in diameter, to the center of which Retief was led.

"All right, the least ye can do is give the off-worlder breathing space." Dir Blash exhorted the bystanders to edge back another yard. "Now, Retief—this is a sore trial, 'tis true, but 'twill show you the mettle of the Tsugg, that we impose so arduous a criterion on oursel's!'' He broke off at a sound of crashing in the underbrush. A pair of tribesmen on the outer fringe of the audience flew into the air as if blown up by a mine, as with ferocious snorts, a wild Vorch, seven feet at the shoulder and armed with down-curving tusks, charged from the underbrush. His rush carried him through the ranks of the spectators into the inner circle, his short tail whipping, his head tossing as he sought a new target. His inflamed eye fell on Dir Blash.

"Botheration," the latter commented in mild annoyance as the beast lowered its head and charged. Leaning aside, the Tsugg raised a fist of the size and weight of a hand-axe, brought it down with a resounding *brongg!* on the carnivore's skull. The unlucky beast folded in mid-leap, skidded chin-first to fetch up against Retief's feet.

"Nice timing," he remarked. "Ye'd think the brute did it a-purpose, to plague a serious occasion," Dir Blash said disapprovingly. "Drag the silly creature away," he directed a pair of Tsugg. "He'll be broke to harness for his pains. And now," he turned to Retief, "if ye're ready—"

Retief smiled encouragingly.

"Right, then. The first trial is—take a deep breath and hold it for the count of ten." Dir Blash watched Retief's expression alertly for signs of dismay. Seeing none, he raised a finger disappointedly.

"Very well. Inhale."

Retief inhaled.

"Onetwothreefourfivesixseveneightnineten," Dir Blash said in a rush and stared curiously at the Terran, who stood relaxed before him. A few approving shouts rang out. Then came scattered hand-claps.

"Well," Dir Blash grunted. "You did pretty fair, I suppose, for an off-worlder. Hardly turned blue at all. You pass, I suppose."

"Hey," someone called from the front rank of the gallery. "He's not—"

"Not still—" someone else queried.

"Still holding his breath?" a third Tsugg then asked wonderingly.

"O' course not, lackwits!" Dir Blash bellowed. "How could he? 'E'en Grand Master Cutthroat Dir-dir Hooch held out but to the count of twelve!" He looked closely at Retief. "Thous hast indeed resumed respiration?" he murmured.

"Of course," Retief reassured the Tsugg. "I was just grandstanding."

Dir Blash grunted. "In sooth, I've a feeling ye went a good thirteen, if truth were known," he muttered confidentially. "Hast made a specialty of suffocation?"

"Staff meetings, remember?" Retief prompted.

"To be sure." Dir Blash looked disgruntled. "Well, on to the Second Trial, Terry. Ye'll find this one e'en a straiter test of Tsugghood than the last!" He led the way upslope, Retief close behind, the crowd following. The path deteriorated into a rocky gully winding up between nearly vertical walls of rock. Pebbles rattled around the party from the crumbling cliffs above as members clambered toward choice vantage points. A medium-sized boulder came bounding down from a crag to whistle overhead and crash thunderously away among the trees below. The journey ended in a small natural amphitheater, the floor of which was thickly littered with stones of all sizes. Spectators took up positions around the periphery above as pebbles continued to clatter down around the tester and testee, who stood alone at the center of the target. A head-sized rock smashed down a yard from Retief. A chunk the size of a grand piano poised directly above him gave an ominous rumble and slid downward six inches amid a shower of gravel.

"What happens if one of those scores a bull's-eye on the candidate?" Retief inquired.

"It's considered a bad omen," Dir Blash said. "Drat the pesky motes!" he added as a small fragment bounded off the back of his neck. "These annoyances detract from the solemnity of the occasion."

"On the contrary," Retief demurred politely. "I think they add a lot of interest to the situation."

"Umm. Mayhap." Dir Blash gazed absently upward, moving his head slightly to avoid being brained by a baseball-sized missile. "Now, off-worlder," he addressed Retief, "prepare for the moment of truth. Bend over—" he paused impressively—" and touch your toes!"

"Do I get to bend my knees?" Retief temporized.

"Bend whatever you like," Dir Blash said with airy contempt. "I trow this is one feat ye've not practiced at your Ordeal of the Staff Meeting!"

"True," Retief conceded. "The closest we come is lifting ourselves by our bootstraps." He assumed a serious expression, bent over and, with a smooth motion, touched his fingertips to his toes.

"He did it in one try," someone called.

"Didn't even take a bounce!" another added.

The applause was general.

"Lacking in style," Dir Blash grumbled. "But a pass, I allow. But now you face the Third Ordeal, where ye're tricks will do ye no good. Come along." They moved off. The stone piano crunched down on the spot he and Retief had just vacated.

V

The route to the Third Site led upward through a narrow cut to emerge on a bare rock slope. Fifty feet away a flat-topped rock spire loomed up from the depths, joined to the main mass of the peak by a meandering ribbon of rock some six inches in width, except where it narrowed to a knife edge, halfway across. Dir Blash sauntered out across the narrow bridge, gazing around him at the scenery.

"A splendid prospect, eh, Retief?" he called over his shoulder. "Look on it well; it may be thy last. What comes next has broken many a strong Tsugg down into a babbling Glert."

Retief tried the footing; it held. Keeping his eyes on the platform ahead, he walked quickly across.

"Now," Dir Blash said, "you may wish to take a moment to commune with your patron devils or whatever it is you off-worlders burn incense to."

"Thanks, I'm in good shape incantation-wise," Retief reassured him. "Only last night I joined in a toast to the auditors."

"In that case—" Dir Blash pointed impressively to a flat stone that lay across two square rocks, the top of which cleared the ground by a good twelve inches.

"Leap the obstacle in a single bound."

Retief studied the hurdle from several angles before taking up his position before it.

"I see you hesitate," Dir Blash taunted. "Dost doubt thy powers at last, Terry?"

"Last year an associate of mine jumped fifty names on the promotion list," Retief said. "Can I do less?" Standing flat-footed, he hopped over the barrier. Turning, he hopped back again.

There was a moment of stunned silence.

Suddenly pandemonium broke out. Dir Blash hesitated only a moment, then joined in the glad cries.

"Congratulations, Dir Tief!" he bellowed, pounding the Terran on the shoulder. "I warrant an off-worlder of thy abilities would be an embarrassment to all hands—but in sooth thou'rt now a Tsugg of the Tsuggs, and thy attainments are an adornment to our ilk!"

"Remarkable," said Hoobrik the Uncouth as he stuffed a handful of sugar-coated green olives into his mouth. "According to Blash you went through the Ordeal like a Tsugg to the pavilion born. I may keep you on as bodyguard, Dir Tief, after I get the vote out and myself in."

"Coming from your Truculence, that's praise indeed," Retief said. "Considering your willingness to offer yourself as a candidate without a whimper."

"What's to whimper?" Hoobrik demanded. "After my lads have rounded up more voters than the opposition can muster, I'll be free to fill my pockets as best I may. 'Tis a prospect I face calmly."

"True," Retief said. "But first there are a few

rituals to be gotten past. There's Whistle-stopping, Baby-kissing, Fence-sitting, and Mud-slinging, plus a considerable amount of Viewing with Alarm.''

"Hmm.'' Hoobrik rubbed his chin thoughtfully. "Are these Ordeals the equal of our Rites of Tsugg-hood, Retief?''

"Possibly even worse,'' Retief solemnly assured the chieftain. "Especially if you wear an Indian war bonnet.''

"Out upon it!'' Hoobrik pounded his tankard on the table. "A Tsugg fears neither man nor beast.''

"But did you ever face a quorum of Women Voters?'' Retief countered quickly.

"My stout lads will ride down all opposition,'' Hoobrik declared with finality. "I've already made secret arrangements with certain Five-eyed off-worlders to supply me with all the write-in ballots I need to make everything legal and proper. Once in office, I can settle down to businesslike looting in an orderly manner.''

"But remember,'' Retief cautioned, "You'll be expected to stand on your Party Platform—at least for the first few weeks.''

"W-weeks?'' Hoobrik faltered. "What is this platform, Retief?''

"It's a pretty shaky structure,'' Retief confided. "I've never known one to last past the first Legislative Rebuff.''

"What, yet another Ordeal?''

"Don't worry about it, your Truculence; it seldom goes as far as Impeachment.''

"Well? Don't keep me in suspense!'' Hoobrik roared. "What doth this rite entail?''

"This is where your rival politicians get even with you for winning, by charging you with High Crimes and Misdemeanors—"

"Stay!" Hoobrik yelled. "Is there no end to these torments?"

"Certainly," Retief reassured the aroused leader. "After you retire, you become a Statesman and are allowed out on alternate All Fools Days to be queried as to your views on any subject sufficiently trivial to grace the pages of the Sunday Supplements."

"Arrrhh!" Hoobrik growled and drained his mug. "See here, Retief," he said. "On pondering the matter, methinks 'twould be a gracious gesture on my part to take second place on the ticket and let a younger Tsugg assume party leadership; you, for example, Blash," he addressed the sub-chief.

"Who, me?" the latter blurted. "Nay, my liege—as I've said before, I am not now and do not intend to be a candidate."

"Who, then?" Hoobrik waved his arms in agitation. "We need a Tsugg who'll appeal to a broad spectrum of voters. A good scimitarman for beating down opposition inside the party, a handy club-wielder to bring in the Independents, a cool hand with a dirk, for committee infighting—" He paused, looking suddenly thoughtful.

"Well, I'll leave you gentlemen to look over the lists," Retief said, rising. "May I tell the Ambassador to expect you at the post-election victory reception?"

"We'll be there," Hoobrik said. "And I think I have a sure-fire Tsugg standard-bearer in mind to pull in the vote—"

In the varicolored glow of lights strung in the hedges ringing the former miniature golf course pressed into service as Embassy grounds, the Terran diplomats stood in conversation clumps across the fairways and greens, glasses in hand, nervously eyeing the door through which Ambassador Clawhammer's entrance was expected momentarily.

Magnan said to Retief, glancing at his watch, "The first results will be in any moment."

"I think we need have no fear of the outcome," Saddlesore stated. "Guru Hoobrik's students have been particularly active in these final hours, zealously applying posters to the polling places."

"And applying knots to the heads of reluctant converts," the Political Officer added. "What I'm wondering is—after Hoobrik's inauguration, what's to prevent his applying the same techniques to foreign diplomats?"

"Tradition, my boy," the colonel said soothingly. "We may be shot as spies or deported as undesirables—but shaped up by wardheelers, no."

A stir crossed the lawn. Ambassador Clawhammer appeared, ornate in the burgundy cutaway and puce jodpurs specified by CDT Regs for early evening ceremonial wear.

"Well? No word yet?" He stared challengingly at his underlings, accepting one of the four drinks simultaneously thrust at him by alert junior officers. "My private polls indicate an early lead for the Tsugg party, increasing to a commanding majority as the rural counties report."

"Commanding is right," Magnan muttered behind

his hand. "One of the ruffians had the audacity to order me to hold his gluepot while he affixed a poster to the front door of the Embassy."

"What cheek," the Political Officer gasped. "You didn't do it?"

"Of course not. "He held the gluepot, and I affixed the placard."

Happy shouts sounded from the direction of the gate; a party of Tsugg appeared, flamboyant in pink and yellow, handing out footlong yellow cigars. A throng of lesser Oberonians followed, all apparently in good spirits.

"A landslide victory," one called to the assembly at large. "Break out the wassail bowl!"

"Is this official, Depew?" the Ambassador demanded of his Counselor, who arrived at that moment at a trot, waving a sheaf of papers.

"I'm afraid so—that is, I'm delighted to confirm the people's choice," he panted. "It's amazing—the Tsugg candidate polled an absolute majority, even in the oppositions' strongholds. It looks like every voter on the rolls voted the straight Tsugg ticket."

"Certes, Terry," a Grimble confirmed jovially, grabbing two glasses from a passing tray. "We know a compromise candidate when we see one."

" 'Tis a clear mandate from the people," a Tsugg declaimed. "Hoobrik will be along in a trice to help with sorting out the spoils. As for myself, I'm not greedy; a minor Cabinet post will do nicely."

"Out upon thee!" a jovial voice boomed as the Tsugg chieftain swept through the gate, flanked by an honor guard of grinning scimitar-bearers. "No undignified rooting at the trough, lads—there's plenty to go around."

"Congratulations, your Truculence," Ambassador Clawhammer cried, advancing with outstretched hand. "I'm sure that at this moment you're feeling both proud and humble as you point with pride—"

"Humble?" Hoobrik roared. "That's for losers, Terry."

"To be sure." Clawhammer conceded the point. "Now, your Truculence, I don't want to delay the victory celebration—but why don't we first just sign this little Treaty of Eternal Peace and Friendship, set up to run for five years with a renewal option—"

"You'll have to speak to the new Planetary President about that, Terry," the chieftain waved the proffered document away. "As for myself, I have some important drinking to catch up on."

"But—I was informed by a usually reliable source—" Clawhammer turned to glare at the Counsellor—"that the Tsugg party had carried off all honors."

"True enough. By the way, where is he?"

"Where is who?"

"Our new Chief Executive, of course—" Hoobrik broke off, pushed past Clawhammer, rushed forward with outstretched arms, narrowly missing a small water hazard, to embrace Retief, who had just appeared on the scene.

"Stand aside, Retief," Clawhammer snapped. "I'm in the midst of a delicate negotiation—"

"Employ a more respectful tone, Terry," Hoobrik admonished the Ambassador sternly. "Consider to whom you're speaking."

"To whom I'm speak?" Clawhammer said in bewilderment. "Whom *am* I speaking to?"

"Meet Planetary President Dir Tief," Hoobrik said

proudly, waving ahand at Retief. "The winner—and new champion."

"Good lord, Retief," Magnan was the first to recover his speech. "When? How?"

"What's the meaning of this?" Clawhammer burst out. "Am I being made sport of?"

"Apparently not, Mr. Ambassador," Retief said. "It seems they put me on the ballot as a dark horse—"

"You'll be a horse of a darker color before I'm through with you—" Clawhammer went rigid as twin scimitars flashed, ended with their points pressed against his neck.

"But how can a Terran be elected as head of the Tsugg party?" the Political Officer asked.

"President Tief is no Terry," Hoobrik corrected. "He's a Tsugg after my own heart!"

"But—doesn't the president have to be a natural-born citizen?"

"Art suggesting our President is unnatural-born?" Hoobrik grated.

"Why, no—"

" 'Tis well. In that case, best you present your credentials at once and we can get down to business."

Clawhammer hesitated. A prod of the blade at his jugular assisted him in finding his tongue.

"Why, ah, Mr. President—will your Excellency kindly tell your thugs to put those horrible-looking knives away?"

"Certainly, Mr. Ambassador," Retief said easily. "Just as soon as we've cleared up a few points in the treaty. I think it would be a good idea if the new planetary government has a solemn CDT guarantee of noninterference in elections from now on—"

"Retief—you wouldn't dare—I mean, of course, my boy, whatever you say."

"Also, it would be a good idea to strike out those paragraphs dealing with CDT military advisors, technical experts and fifty-credit-a-day economists. We Oberonians would prefer to work out our own fate."

"Yes—yes—of course, Mr. President. And now—"

"And as to the matter of the one-sided trade agreement—why don't we just scrap that whole section and substitute a free commerce clause?"

"Why—if I agree to that they'll have my scalp, back in the Department!"

"That's better than having it tied to a pole outside my tent," Hoobrik pointed out succinctly.

"On the other hand," Retief said, "I think we Tsuggs can see our way clear to supply a modest security force to ensure that nothing violent happens to foreign diplomats among us as long as they stick to diplomacy and leave all ordinary crime to us Oberonians."

"Agreed," Clawhammer squawked. "Where's the pen?"

It took a quarter of an hour to delete the offending paragraphs, substitute new wording and affix signatures to the imposing document establishing formal relations between the *Corps Diplomatique Terrestrienne* and the Republic of Oberon. When the last length of red tape had been affixed and the last blob of sealing wax applied, Retief called for attention.

"Now that Terran-Oberonian relations are off on a sound footing," he said, "I feel it's only appropriate that I step down, leaving the field clear for a new election. Accordingly, gentlemen, I hereby resign the office of President in favor of my vice president, Hoobrik.''

Amid the clamor that broke out, Clawhammer made his way to confront Retief.

"You blundered at last, sir," he murmured in a voice aquiver with rage. "You should have clung to your spurious position long enough to have gotten a head start for the Galactic periphery! I'll see you thrown into a dungeon so deep that your food will have to be lowered to you in pressurized containers! I'll—''

"You'll be on hand to dedicate the statue to our first Ex-President, I ween?" President Hoobrik addressed the Terran envoy. "I think a hundred-foot monument will be appropriate to express the esteem in which we hold our Tsugg emeritus, Dir Tief, eh?"

"Why, ah—''

"We'll appreciate your accrediting him as permanent Political Advisor to Oberon," Hoobrik continued. "We'll need him handy to pose."

"To be sure," Clawhammer gulped.

"Now I think it's time we betook ourselves off to more private surroundings, Dir Tief," the President said. "We need to plot party strategy for the by-election."

"You're all invited to sample the hospitality of the *Plump Sausage*," Binkster Druzz spoke up. "Provided I have your promises there'd be no breeching of walls."

"Done!" Hoobrik cried heartily. "And by the way, Dir Druzz—What wouldst think of the idea of a coalition, eh?"

"Hmm—Twilprit sagacity linked with Tsugg bulk

might indeed present a formidable ticket,'' Binkster concurred.

"Well, Retief,'' Magnan said as the party streamed toward the gate, "yours was surely the shortest administration in the annals of representational government. Tell me confidentially—how in the world did you induce that band of thugs to accept you as their nominee?''

"I'm afraid that will have to remain a secret for now,'' Retief said. "But just wait until I write my memoirs.''

PIME DOESN'T CRAY

I

A DRIVING rain lashed the tarmac as Retief stepped from the shuttlecraft that had ferried him down to the planetary surface. From the direction of the low, mushroom-shaped reception sheds a slight figure wrapped in a voluminous black rubber poncho came splashing toward him, waving excitedly.

"You got any enemies, Mac?" the shuttle pilot asked nervously, watching the newcomer's approach.

"A reasonable number," Retief replied, drawing on his cigar, which sputtered and hissed as the rain struck the glowing tip. "However, this is just Counselor Magnan from the Embassy, here to welcome me to the scene with the local disaster status, no doubt."

"No time to waste, Retief," Magnan panted as he came up. "Ambassador Grossblunder has called a special staff meeting for five pee em—half an hour from now. If we hurry we can just make it. I've already seen to Customs and Immigration; I knew you'd want to be there, to, ah—"

"Share the blame?" Retief suggested.

"Hardly," Magnan corrected, flicking a drop of moisture from the tip of his nose. "As a matter of fact, I may well be in line for a word of praise for my handling of the Cultural Aid Project. It will be an excellent opportunity for you to get your feet wet, local scenewise," he amplified, leading the way toward the Embassy car waiting beside the sheds.

"According to the latest supplement to the Post Report," Retief said as they settled themselves against the deep-pile upholstery, "the project is scheduled for completion next week. Nothing's gone wrong with the timetable, I hope?"

Magnan leaned forward to rap at the glass partition dividing the enclosed passenger compartment from the open-air driver's seat. The chauffeur, a rather untidy-looking local who seemed to consist of a snarl of purple macaroni topped by a peaked cap with a shiny bill, angled what Retief deduced to be an ear to catch the Terran's instructions.

"Just swing past the theater on your way down, Chauncey," Magnan directed. "In answer to your question," he said complacently to Retief, "I don't mind saying the project went off flawlessly, hitchwise. In fact, it's completed a week early. As Project Director, I fancy it's something of a feather in my cap, considering the frightful weather conditions we have to contend with here on Squale."

"Did you say theater? As I recall, the original proposal called for the unusual Yankee Stadium-type sports arena."

Magnan smiles loftily. "I thought it time to vary the program."

"Congratulations, Mr. Magnan." Retief sketched a salute with his cigar. "I was afraid the *Corps Diplomatique* was going to go on forever inflicting bigger and better baseball diamonds on defenseless natives, while the Groaci countered with ever-larger and uglier Bolshoi-type ballet arenas."

"Not this time," Magnan stated with satisfaction. "I've beaten the scamps at their own game. This is Top Secret, mind you—but this time *we've* built the Bolshoi-type ballet theater!"

"A masterful gambit, Mr. Magnan. How are the Groaci taking it?"

"They've come up with a rather ingenious counterstoke, I must concede. Informed opinion has it the copycats are assembling an imitation Yankee Stadium in reprisal." Magnan peered out through the downpour. The irregularly shaped buildings lining the winding avenue loomed mistily, obscured by sheets of wind-driven precipitation. Ahead, a gap in their orderly ranks was visible. Magnan frowned as the car cruised slowly past a large erratically shaped bulk set well back from the curb.

"Here, Chauncey," he called. "I instructed you to drive to the project site."

"Thure shing, moss-ban," a voice like a clogged drain replied placatingly. "Weer we har."

"Chauncey—have you been drinking?"

"Woe, nurse luck." Chauncey braked to a stop; the windshield wipers rotated busily; the air cushion sighed heavily, driving ripples across the puddled street.

"Book, loss—we're right astreet the cross from the Libric publary, *nicht vahr?*"

"The Lublic Pibrary, you mean—I mean the pubic lilberry—"

"Yeah, mats what I thean. So—there's the piblary—so buts the weef?" Chauncey extended the cluster of macaroni that served as his hand, to wave like seaweed in a light current.

"Visibility is simply atrocious here on Squale." Magnan sniffed, rolling down the window and recoiling as a blast of rain splattered his face. "But even so—I shouldn't think I could get confused as to the whereabouts of my own project."

"It looks like a collapsed circus tent," Retief commented, studying the half-acre of canvas apparently supported by a half-dozen randomly placed props.

"An optical illusion," Magnan said firmly. "The structure is under wraps, of course; it's a secret, you know. It's just the lighting, no doubt, that makes it look so—so sort of squatty and unplanned." He was squinting ferociously into the rain, shading his eyes with a hand. "Still, why don't we just pop out and have a closer look?"

Magnan thrust the door open and stumbled out; Retief followed. They crossed a walk of colored, glazed tile, skirted a bed of footwide green blossoms. Magnan lifted aside a fold of plastic sheeting, revealing a yawning excavation at the bottom of which severed electrical and plumbing connections poked up through the surface of the muddy water pooling there.

"A treat nick," Chauncey said admiringly over his shoulder. "Do'd you how it, Master Mignan?"

"Do'd I how what?" Magnan croaked.

"Dis it makappear," Chauncey amplified. "The meaning, I build."

"Retief," Magnan whispered, blinking hard. "Tell me I'm seeing things; I mean, that I'm not seeing things."

"Correct," Retief said, "either way you phrase it."

"Retief," Magnan said in a breaking voice. "Do you realize what this means?"

Retief tossed his cigar down into the empty pit, where it hissed and went out. "Either you were kidding me about the project—"

"I assure you—"

"—or we're standing on the wrong corner—"

"Absolutely not!"

"Or someone," Retief said, "has stolen one Bolshoi-type ballet theater."

"And I was dreaming of feathers in my cap," Magnan moaned as the car braked to a halt before the imposing facade of the Terrestrial Embassy. "I'll be fortunate to salvage my cap from this fiasco—or my head, for that matter. How will I ever tell Ambassador Grossblunder I've misplaced his pet project?"

"Oh, I'm sure you'll be able to pass the incident off with your usual *savoir faire,*" Retief soothed him as they stepped out into the drizzle. The Squalese doorman, loosely packed in a regulation CDT-issue coverall, nodded a cluster of writhing violet-hued filaments at the Terrans as they came up.

"Jowdy, hents," he said as the door whooshed open. "Rice nain, eh?"

"What's so rice about it?" Magnan inquired acidly. "Harvey—has His Excellency gone in?"

"Men tinutes ago—in a masty nude. Didn't even hey sello."

Inside, Magnan groaned, put a hand to his brow. "Retief—I seem to have come down with a splitting headache. Why don't you nip along and mention this development just casually to the Ambassador. Possibly you could play it down a trifle. No need to upset him unduly, eh?"

"Good idea, Mr. Magnan," Retief said, handing his weather cape into the check room. "I'll hint that it's all a publicity trick you dreamed up to publicize the grand opening."

"Excellent notion! And if you could subtly plant the idea that you'll have it back in place in time for the festivities—" Magnan looked hopefully at Retief.

"Since I just arrived fifteen minutes ago I think that would be rather pushy of me. Then, too, he might want to know why you were lying down at such a critical moment in Terran/Squalian relations."

Magnan groaned again, resignedly.

"Let's hurry along, gentlemen," a short, black-eyebrowed man in uniform called from the open elevator door across the lobby. "We're holding the car for you."

Magnan straightened his narrow shoulders. "Coming, Colonel Otherday," he croaked. "Remember, Retief," he added in an undertone, "we'll behave as though it were the most natural thing in the world for a ten-million-credit building to vanish between breakfast and lunch."

"Did I hear someone mention lunch?" a portly diplomat inquired from the back of the car.

"You just ate, Lester," a lean commercial attaché

said. "As for you, Mr. Retief, you picked an inauspicious moment to put in an appearance; I gather the Ambassador's in a towering pet this evening."

Magnan glanced nervously at Retief. "Ah—any idea what's troubling his Excellency?"

"Who knows?" the attaché shrugged. "Last time it was a deteriorating man/bean ratio in the Embassy snack bar."

"This time it's even bigger than the bean crisis," Colonel Otherday stated flatly. "I have a feeling that this time heads will roll."

"Does it have anything to do with, ah, anything that might be—missing?"

"Ah-hah!" the lean attaché pounced. "He knows something, gentlemen."

"Come on, Magnan," the portly First Secretary urged. "Let us in on it."

"How is it you always have the word first?" the colonel inquired plaintively.

"Well, as to that—" Magnan started.

"Mr. Magnan is under oath to reveal nothing, gentlemen," Retief cut in smoothly as the car halted and the doors slid back on a wide, deep-carpeted conference room.

II

A long, polished table occupied the middle of the floor, unadorned but for long yellow pads and ballpoint pens at each place. A few seconds of unobtrusive scuffling ensued as the diplomats, all veteran campaigners, vied for choice positions, balancing the prestige of juxtaposition to the Ambassadorial chair against inconspicuousness in the event of scapegoat selection.

All hands stood as the inner door was flung wide. The stern-visaged, multi-chinned figure of Ambassador Grossblunder entered the room under full sail. He scanned the assembled bureaucrats without visible approval, seated himself in the chair the Agricultural Attaché leaped to pull out, shot a piercing glance along the table and cleared his throat.

"Lock the doors," he said. "Gentlemen, be seated. I have solemn news for you." He paused impressively. "We," he concluded solemnly, "have been robbed!"

A sigh passed along the table. All eyes swiveled to Magnan.

"Robbed," Grossblunder repeated, emphasizing the point with a blow of his fist which made the pencils, plus a number of the diplomats, jump. "I have for some time suspected that foul play was afoot; a short time ago my worst fears were confirmed. Gentlemen, there is a thief among us."

"Among us?" Magnan blurted. "But how—I mean, why—that is to say, Mr. Ambassador, how could one of *us* have purloined the—ah—loot in question?"

"You may well ask. One might also logically inquire as to why any person connected with this Mission could so far forget himself as to hide the feet that banns him. That is, bite the fan that heeds him. I mean beat the hide that fans him. Confound it, you know what I mean." Grossblunder grabbed a glass of water and gulped a swallow. "Been here too long," he muttered. "Losing my grasp of the well-rounded period."

"A thief, you say, sir?" Colonel Otherday prompted. "Well, how interesting—"

"Interesting is hardly the word for it," Grossblunder barked.

"Apalling is a cut nearer the mark. Shocking, though a trifle flaccid, carries a portion of the connotation. This is a grievous blot on the CDT copybook, gentlemen. A blow struck at the very foundations of Galactic accord."

A nameless chorus rose.

"Right, chief—"

"Well phrased, sirs—"

"You said it, Boss—"

"Now, if anyone here wishes to come forward at this juncture—" Grossblunder's ominous gaze travelled along the table, lingered on Magnan.

"You appear to be the focal point of all eyes, Magnan," the Ambassador accused. "If you've a comment, don't hesitate. Speak up."

"Why, as a matter of fact, sir—" Magnan gulped—"I just wanted to say that as for myself, I was utterly appalled—that is to say shocked—when I discovered the loss. Why, you could have knocked me over with the feather in my cap—I mean—"

Grossblunder looked ominous. "You're saying you were already aware of the pilferage, Magnan?"

"Yes, and—"

The Ambassador glowered.

"And failed to confide this intelligence to me?"

"I didn't actually know until a few minutes ago," Magnan explained hastily. "Why, sir, you are positive miles ahead of me. I'm simply able to confirm your revelation—not that any confirmation is needed, of course."

"There, gentlemen," Grossblunder said with admiration, "is my conception of an alert officer. While the rest of you went about your business, oblivious of the light fingers operating to the detriment of this Mission, my Counselor, Mr. Magnan, alone among my subordinates, sensed mischief afoot. My congratulations to you, sir."

"Why, ah, thank you, Mr. Ambassador." Magnan essayed a fragile smile. "I do try to keep abreast of developments—"

"And since you seem to have the matter in hand, you're appointed Investigative Officer to get to the bottom of the matter without delay. I'll turn my records over to you without further ado." Grossblunder shot his cuff, allotted a glance to his watch. "As it happens, my VIP copter is at this moment warming up on the roof to whisk me over to the Secretariat, where I expect to be tied up for the remainder of the evening in high-level talks with the Foreign Minister regarding slurb-fruit allocations for the coming fiscal quarter. It seems our Groaci colleagues are out to cut us out of the pattern luxury-trade-wise, a consummation hardly to be tolerated on my record." He rose. "You'll accompany me to the helipad, Magnan, for last-minute briefing. As for the rest of you—let Magnan's performance stand as an example. You, there—" he pointed at Retief—"you may carry my briefcase."

On the roof—aslosh with rainwater under the perpetually leaden sky—Grossblunder turned to Magnan.

"I expect fast action, Ben. We can't allow this sort of thing to pass unnoticed, as it were."

"I'll do my best, sir," Magnan chirped. "And I do want to say it's awfully white of you not to hold me personally responsible—not that anyone could actually blame me, of course—"

"You responsible? No, I see no way in which I could

benefit from that. Besides which," he added, "you're not an Admin man."

"Admin man, sir? What—"

"My analysis of the records indicates that a steady trickle over the past two years at the present rate could account for a total discrepancy on the order of sixty-seven gross. Think of that, Magnan."

"Sixty-seven Bolshoi-type ballet theaters?" Magnan quavered.

Grossblunder blinked, then allowed a smile to quirk a corner of his mouth.

"No need to hint, Magnan. I haven't forgotten your magnificent performance in the completion of the project six days ahead of schedule. The grand opening tomorrow is the one bright spot on my Effectiveness Report—on my horizon, that is to say. I wouldn't be surprised if there were a citation in store for the officer responsible." He winked, then frowned. "But don't allow the prospect to drive the matter of the missing paper clips into eclipse. I want action."

"Paper clips, sir?"

"A veritable torrent of them, dropped from Embassy records as expendable items. Outrageous! But no need to say more, my boy; you're as aware as I of the seriousness of the situation." Grossblunder gripped his junior's thin shoulder. "Remember, Magnan—I'm counting on you." He turned and clambered into his seat. With a rising flutter of rotors the light machine lifted into the overcast and was gone. Magnan turned shakily to Retief.

"I—I though—I thought he knew—"

"Yes," Retief said commiseratingly. "Still, you can always pick an opportune time to tell him later. While he's pinning on the medal, perhaps."

"How can you jest at such a moment? Do you realize that I have to solve not one but two crimes, before the Ambassador and the Minister finish a bottle of Port?"

"That's a thought; maybe you can get a quantity discount. Still, we'd better get started before they run the ante up any higher."

Back in his office, Magnan found awaiting him a letter bearing the Great Seal of the Groacian Autonomy.

"It's an *Aide Memoire* from that wretch, Ambassador Shinth," he told Retief. "Announcing he's moving the date for the unveiling of his Cultural Aid project up to midnight tonight." He groaned, tossed the note aside. "This is the final blow, Retief. He's ready to throw out the opening ball—and I'm without so much as a kiosk to offer in rebuttal!"

"I understood the Groaci were behind schedule."

"They are. This entire affair is impossible, Retief. No one could have stolen a complete building overnight—and if they had, where would they hide it? And even if they found a place to hide it—and we were able to turn it up—how in the world would we get it back in position in time for a ceremony scheduled less than twenty hours, local, from this moment?"

"That covers the questions," Retief said. "We may have a little more trouble with the answers."

"The building was there last night; I stopped to admire the classical neon meander adorning the architrave on my way home. A splendid effect; Shinth would have been green with envy—or whatever color Groaci diplomats turn when confronted with an esthetic coup of such proportions."

"He may be quietly turning puce with satisfaction at this moment," Retief suggested. "Rather coincidental timing, isn't it? His project ready to go and ours missing."

"How will I ever face Shinth?" Magnan was muttering. "Only last night I assayed a number of sly jests at his expense. I thought at the time he took them rather blandly—" Magnan broke off to stare at Retief. "Great heavens," he gasped. "Are you hinting those sneaky little five-eyed Meyer-come-latelies could have so far abused diplomatic practice as to be behind this outrage?"

"The thought had crossed my mind," Retief admitted. "Offhand I can't think of anyone else who might have a yen for a Bolshoi-type ballet theater."

Magnan leaped up, yanking the pale mauve lapels of his early mid-afternoon hemi-demi-informal cutaway into place.

"Of course," he cried. "Call out the Marine guard, Retief. I'll march right up to that underhanded little weasel and demand the return of the purloined edifice on the spot."

"Better be careful what spot you're on," Retief cautioned. "A Bolshoi-type ballet theater occupies a full block, remember."

"An ill-timed jape, Retief," Magnan snapped. "Well, what are you waiting for?" He paused, frowning. "Am I to deduce from your apparent lack of enthusiasm that you see some flaw in the scheme?"

"Just a small one," Retief said. "His Groacian Excellency has probably covered his tracks quite carefully. He'll laugh in your face—unless you can show some proof."

"Not even Shinth would have the cheek to deny the facts if I catch him red-handed." Magnan paused, looking troubled. "Of course, I haven't actually found any evidence yet—" He nipped at a hangnail and cast a sidelong glance at Retief.

"A ballet theater isn't the easiest thing in the world to hide," Retief said. "Suppose we try to turn it up first—then we can start on the problem of how to get it back."

"Good notion, Retief. Just what I was about to suggest." Magnan looked at the watch on his thumb. "Why don't you just pop around and have a look here and there while I whip my paperwork into shape. After dinner we can get together and agree on a story— formulate a report, that is, indicating we've done everything possible."

Leaving the Counselor's office, Retief went along to the Commercial Section. A chinless clerk looked up from among baled newspaper clippings.

"Hi, there, Mr. Retief. I see you made it."

"Freddy, I'd like to see a listing of all cargoes imported by the Groaci Embassy during the last twelve months."

The clerk poked the keys of the data bank, frowned at the list it disgorged.

"Flimsy construction they must have in mind," he said as he handed it over. "Cardboard and pick-up-sticks. Typical."

"Anything else?" Retief persisted.

"I'll check equipment imports." The clerk tapped out another code, eliciting a brief clatter and a second slip of paper.

"Heavy-duty lift units," he said. "Funny. They don't need heavy duty units to handle plywood and two-by's—"

"Four of them," Retief noted. "With wide-aperture fields and gang interlocks."

"Wow! With that, you could pick up the Squalid-Hilton."

"You could indeed," Retief agreed. "Thanks, Freddy."

Outside dusk; the car was still waiting at the curb. Retief directed Chauncey to drive back along the wet, tree-fern shaded avenues to the vacant edge-of-town site so recently occupied by the stolen building. Stepping out into the steady, warm rain, he entered the tent, circled the yawning excavation, studying the soft ground by the beam of a hand light.

"Look are you whatting for?" Chauncey inquired, ambling behind him on feet that resembled dishpan-sized wads of wet magenta yarn. "Ardon my pasking—but I taught you Therries lidn't dike feeting your get wet."

"Just getting the lie of the land, Chauncey," he said. "It appears that whoever pinched the theater lifted it out of here with grav units—probably intact, since there doesn't seem to be any evidence of disassembly."

"I goant dett you, chief," Chauncey said. "You lawk tight this roll houtine isn't trust a jick Master Magnan add off to pulvertise the And Gropening."

"Perish the thought, Chauncey; it's just my way of heightening the suspense." Retief stooped, picked up a pinkish dope-stick butt, sniffed at it. It gave off the sharp odor of ether characteristic of Groaci manufacture.

"We Squalians are no runch of boobs, you understand," Chauncey went on. "We've treen a few sicks in our time. If you howns want to clam up, that's jake;

jut bust betwoon the tea of us—how the heck dood he dee it?''

''I'm afraid that's a diplomatic secret,'' Retief said. ''Let's go take a look at the Groaci answer to our cultural challenge.''

''Mot nuch to owe seever there,'' the local said disparagingly as they squelched back to the car, idling on its air cushion above a wide puddle. ''Gothing noing on; and if were thuzz, you souldn't key it; they got this buy foard hence aplound the race and a tunch of barps everying coverthing up.''

''The Groaci are a secretive group,'' Retief said. ''But maybe we can get a peek anyway.''

''I bon't know, doss; there's a gunch of buards around there, too—with yuns, get. They don't clett lobody net goase.''

Steering through the rain-sleek streets under the celery-like trees, Chauncey hummed a sprightly little tune, sounding first like a musical comb, then a rubber-stringed harp, ending with a blatter like a bursting bagpipe.

''Bot nad, hey?'' he solicited a compliment, ''all but that cast lord; it was subeezed to poe a tourish of flumpets, but my slinger fipped.''

''Very impressive,'' Retief said. ''How are you on woodwinds?''

''So-so,'' Chauncey said. ''I'm stretter on bings. Vile this getolin effect:'' He extruded an arm, quickly arranged four thin filamets along it and drew a hastily improvised member across the latter, eliciting a shrill bleat.

''Gutty pred, hey? I can't tay any plunes yet, but I lactice a prot; I'll pet it down gat in toe nime.''

"Groaci nose-flute lover will come over to you in a body," Retief predicted. "By the way, Chauncey, how long have the Groaci been working on their ballpark?"

"Lell, wet's see: stay tharted it fast lall, bust ajout the time too Yerries foured your poundations—"

"It must be about finished, eh?"

"It hasn't changed such mince the worst feak; and a thunny fing: you sever seem to knee any jerkers around the wob; gust the jards." Chauncey swung the corner and pulled up before a ten-foot fence constructed of closely fitted plastic panels, looming darkly in the early evening gloom.

"Ear we har," he said. "Sike I lezz, you san't key a thing."

"Let's take a look around."

"Sure—but we petter beep an eye keeled; those dittle levels can squeak up awful niet."

Leaving the car parked in a pool of shadow under the spreading fronds of a giant fern, Retief, followed by the Squalian, strolled along the walk, studying the unbroken wall that completely encircled the block. At the corner he paused, looked both ways. The street lamp glowed mistily on empty sidewalks.

"Give me a chord on the cello if you see anyone coming," he directed Chauncey. He extracted a slender instrument from an inner pocket, forced it between two planks and twisted. The material yielded with a creak, opening a narrow peep-jole, affording a view of pole-mounted lights which shed a yellowish glow on a narrow belt of foot-trampled mud stacked with 2 x 4's and used plywood, a fringe of ragged grass ending at a vertical escarpment of duncolored canvas. A giant tarpaulin, held in place by a network of ropes, completely concealed the massive structure beneath it.

"Moley hoses," Chauncey's voice sounded at Retief's elbow. "Looks like they've been chaking some manages."

"What kind of changes?"

"Well—it's sard to hay, tunder that arp—shut the bape of it dooks lifferent. Wa've been thirking on it, no bout adout that."

"Suppose we cruise over and pay a call at the Groaci Embassy," Retief suggested. "There are one or two more points that need clearing up."

"Boor, shoss—but it don't woo you any good. They pard that glace like it was the legendary Nort Fox."

"I'm counting on it, Chauncey."

It was a ten-block drive through rain-soaked streets. They parked a block from the fortresslike structure, prowled closer, keeping to the shadows. A pair of Groaci in elaborate uniforms stood stiffly flanking the gate in the high masonry wall.

"No hole-poking this time," Retief said. "We'll have to climb over."

"That's bisky, ross—"

"So is loitering on a dark corner," the Terran replied. "Let's go."

Five minutes later, having scaled the wall via an overhanging slurb-fruit tree, Retief and Chauncey stood in the Embassy compound, listening.

"Don't their a hing," the Squalian muttered. "Now what?"

"How about taking a look around, Chauncey," Retief suggested.

"Okay—dut I bon't like it—" Chauncey extended an eye-tipped pseudopod, which snaked away around the corner. Two minutes ticked past. Suddenly the chauffer stiffened.

"Giggers, the Joaci!" he exclaimed. "Let's cho, gief!" The eye-stalk retracted convulsively.

"Bammit, a dacklash," Chauncey yelped. Retief turned to see the driver struggling to untangle the hastily retracted eyestalk, which had somehow become snarled around one of it's owner's feet, which was in turn unraveling, an effect resembling a rag rug unknitting itself.

"Datt thid it," Chauncey grunted. "Bam, scross, I'll never let goose in time—"

Retief took two swift steps to the corner of the building. The patter of soft-shod feet approached rapidly. An instant later a spindle-legged alien in a black hip-cloak, ornamented leather greaves, GI eye-shields and a flaring helemet shot into view, met Retief's extended arm and did a neat back-flip into the mud. Retief grabbed up the scatter gun dropped by the Groaci Peacekeeper, switched it to wide dispersal, swinging the weapon to cover half a dozen more Groaci guards coming up rapidly on the right flank. They skidded to a halt. At the same moment a yell came from behind him; he glanced back, saw Chauncey struggling in the grasp of four more of the aliens, who had appeared from a doorway.

"To throw down the gun and make no further move, Soft One," the captain in charge of the detail hissed in Groaci, "or to see your minion torn to vermicelli before your naked eyes."

III

Broodmaster Shinth, Ambassador Extraordinary and Minister Plenipotentiary of the Groacian Autonomy to the Squalian Aristarch, lolled back at ease in his power swivel chair, a pirated Groaci copy of a Terran diplomatic model. A cluster of aides hovered behind him, exchanging sibilant whispers and canting multiple eyes at Retief, who stood at ease before them, flanked by guards whose guns prodded his kidneys. Chauncey, pitiably trussed in his own versatile limbs, lay slumped in a corner of the underground office of the Groaci Chief of Mission.

"How charming to see you, Retief," Shinth whispered. "One is always delighted to entertain a colleague, of course. You'll forgive Captain Thilf's zeal in insisting so firmly on your acceptance of my hospitality—but he was quite carried away by your demonstration of interest in Groacian affairs."

"I'm surprised at your Excellency's leniency," Retief replied in tones of mild congratulation. "I assumed you'd have busted the captain back to corporal by now for tipping your hand. There's nothing like diplomat-napping to cause vague suspicions to congeal into certainties."

Shinth waved a negligent member. "Any reasonably intelligent being—I include Terry diplomats as a courtesy—could have deduced a connection between the vanished structure and myself."

"Oh-oh—I nink I thow what was tunder that arp!"

Chauncey exclaimed in a voice muffled by the multiple turns of eyestalk inhibiting his vocal apparatus.

"You see—even this unlettered local perceives that there was only one place where a borrowed ballet theater might be concealed," Shinth continued airily. "Specifically, under the canvas stretched over my dummy stadium."

"Since we agree that's obvious," Retief said, "suppose you assign a squad to untying the knots in Chauncey, while Captain Thilf and ourselves enjoy a hearty diplomatic chuckle over the joke."

"Ah, but the punchline has yet to be delivered," Shinth demurred. "You don't suppose, my dear Retief, that I've devoted all these months to the finesse merely for the amusement of newly arrived Terry bureaucrats?"

"It seems rather a flimsy motivation," Retief concurred. "But you can't hide half a million cubic feet of stolen architecture forever."

"Nor do I intend to try. Only a few hours remain before the full scope of my coup bursts upon the local diplomatic horizon." The Groaci adjusted his facial plates in an arrangement expressing bland self-satisfaction. "You'll recall that I've advanced the schedule for the unveiling of Groaci's gift to the Squalian electorate. The heartwarming event will take place tonight, before the massed dignitaries of the planet, with the Terry Mission as prominent guests, of course. Our hosts, expecting the traditional Groaci ballet theater, will suffer no surprise. That emotion will be reserved to the Terrans, to whom I've carefully leaked the erroneous impression that a ballpark was rising on the site. At a stroke, I will reveal you Terries for the Indian givers you are, while at the same moment bestowing on the local bucolics imposing evidence of Groacian generosity—at the expense of you Soft Ones! A classic gambit, indeed, as I'm sure you'll agree, eh, Retief?''

''Ambassador Grossblunder might have a few objections to the scheme,'' Retief pointed out.

''Let him object,'' Shinth whispered carelessly. ''The operation was carried off under cover of night, unseen and unheard. The lift units left the planet today via our supply shuttle. What matter substanceless accusations? Grossblunder was thoughtful enough to carry on erection under heavy security wraps; it will be his word against mine. And a ballet theater on the site is worth two in the Project Proposal folder, eh?''

''You won't wet agay with it,'' Chauncey blurted. ''I'll bill the speans.''

''Bill whatever you like, fellow,'' Shinth said loftily. ''*Ex post facto* rumor-mongering will have no effect on a *fait accompli*. And now, I really must be robing myself for the festivities.'' He snapped an eyelid at the guard captain. ''Escort them to the guest quarters, Thilf, and see that they're made as comfortable as possible during their stay. I believe from the tower they'll have a splendid view of the spectacle under the lights.''

''To defenestrate the rogues at once,'' Thilf suggested in a stage whisper. ''To eliminate the blabbermouths completely—''

''To be silent, litter-mate of drones,'' the Ambassador hissed. ''To propose no unfortunate precedents which could rise to haunt a less ingenious functionary then myself.'' He waggled three of his five oculars at Retief in a placating fashion. ''You'll be free to return to your duties—as soon as the ceremony is completed,'' he cooed. ''In the meantime—happy meditations.''

''Ithalways ought that stiguring out who loll the foote was the pard hart,'' Chauncey mourned as the door to the tower apartment slammed on them. ''We know shoo hiped it, and hair they wid it—and a lat got of food it does us.''

''Shinth seems to have worked things out with considerable care,'' Retief agreed.

''Luff tuck,'' Chauncey commiserated. ''I sate to hee those feepy little crive-eyes tut one over on you Perries.''

''Well, Chauncey, I'm glad to know you feel kindly disposed toward us.''

''It's thot nat, exactly,'' the Squalian said. ''It's bust I had a jet bown with my dookie,'' He sighed. ''Well, you can't wick a pinner every time.''

''Maybe our side hasn't lost yet,'' Retief said. ''Chauncey, how are you at poking around in dark places?''

''Just untie a nupple of these cots those guise wise sued in my tiedopodia and I'll dee what I can sue.''

Retief set to work; ten minutes later, with a groan of relief, the Squalian withdrew the last yard of himself from the final knot.

''Peether, what an exbrothience,'' he sighed. ''Wust jate until I get a lupple of coops around that nise-guy's weck—'' He writhed inside his polyon coverall, redistributing his bulk equitably among the sleeves and legs thereof. ''And I've shost my looze,'' he lamented. ''Nazzy snumbers, they were, bright with wown tingwips,'' he added.

Retief had gone to the window, was examing the sweep of wall which extended vertically to an expanse of hard-looking pavement far below, across which armed Groaci were posted at intervals. Chauncey came over to peer out past him.

"Forget it," he said. "You clan't cimb down there. And if you could, the nards would gab you. But jet's lust see if there's a lonn in here—" He prowled across to a connecting door, poked his head inside the bathroom.

"Daypirt," he exclaimed. "The gums boofed when they esterundimated a Squalian. Thawch wiss." He extruded a stalked eye, plunged it into the bowl; yard after yard of pencil-thick filament followed, paying out smoothly down the drain.

"Oh, boy," Chauncey said happily. "Will those toobs be bartled when I tit in gutch with an out on the palside. All I dot to goo is reach the plewage sant, gook around for a lie I know and—" Chauncey went rigid. "Oh-oh," he said. He planted his feet—rather loosely organized in the absence of shoes—and pulled backward. The extended cable of protoplasm stretched, but failed to yield.

"Why, the dirty, skousy lunks!" he squalled. "Way were thaiting! Gray thabbed me and nide me in another tot! I can't foe any garther and I can't bet gack!"

"Tough break," Retief said. "But can't you just slide the rest of you down the line?"

"Bat, and awondan a sellow-fufferer?" Chauncey replied indignantly. "Besides, my integnal internaments gon't woe through the pipe."

"Looks like they've outthought us again, Chauncey."

"Indeed, so it appears," an unctuous whisper issued from a grill above the door, followed by Shinth's breathy chuckle. "Pity about the clogged drains; I'll have a chap along with a plunger in the morning."

"Hey—that posy narker can weir every herd we say," the Squalian exclaimed. "A dreavesopper, yet!"

Retief went to the door and shot the heavy bolt, securing it from the inside. He caught the chauffeur's remaining eye and winked.

"Looks like Ambassador Shinth wins," he said. "He was just too smart for us, Chauncey. I suppose he knows all about the bomb we planted in his Embassy, too—"

"What's that? A bomb? In my Embassy?" Shinth's voice rasped in sudden alarm. "Where? I insist you tell me at once!"

"Don't tell him, Chauncey," Retief said quickly. "It's set to go off in eight minutes; he'll never find it in time."

There was a sibilant gasp from the intercom, followed by feeble Groaci shouts. Moments later, feet clattered in the passage beyong the door. The latch rattled. Fists pounded.

"What do you mean, locked from the inside?" Shinth's voice was audible through the panel.

"Seven minutes," Retief called. "Chins up, Chauncey. It will all be over soon."

"To flee at once!" Captain Thilf's thin tones squalled. "To leave the dastards here to die!"

"Retief—tell me where the bomb is and I'll put in a word for you with your chief!" Shinth called through the door. "I'll explain you shouldn't be judged too harshly for bungling your assignment; after all, a mere Terran, pitted against a mind like mine—''

''That's good of you, Mr. Ambassador—but I'm afraid duty demands we stay here—even if it means being blown up along with your voucher files.''

''My final offer, Retief. Emerge and defuse the infernal machine and I'll help you blow up the Terry Embassy, thereby destroying the unfavorable E.R. your shabby role in the present contretemps will doubtless earn for you.''

''That's a most undiplomatic suggestion, Mr. Ambassador.''

''Very well then, self-doomed one. To learn the meaning of Groaci wrath. To watch as I evacuate the premises, leaving you and your toady to your fates.''

Retief and Chauncey listened to the sound of retreating footsteps. They watched from the window as Shinth darted forth, crossed the courtyard at a brisk run, followed by his entire staff, the last of whom paused to lock the door behind him.

''I adfun that was a lot of mit.'' The Squalian broke the profound silence that fell after the last of the Groaci had departed. ''But in mix senutes they'll dealize they been ruped. So put's the woint?''

''The point is that I'll have six undisturbed minutes inside the Groaci Chancery,'' Retief said, unlocking the door. ''Fold the hort until I get back.''

It was ten minutes before Retief reentered the room, locking the door behind him. Thirty seconds later Shinth's voice sounded via intercom, keening imprecations.

"Thilf! To batter the door down, to take vengeance on the Soft One for making a jackass out of me in full view of my underlings—"

"Instead, to hasten to the scene of the up-coming ceremony, Exalted One," the guard captain caviled. "Otherwise, to miss the big moment."

"To myself attend the unveiling, whilst you deal with the evildoers."

"To grasp the implication that I am to take whatever action seems appropriate to deal with the interlopers?" Thilf inquired in his unctuous whisper.

"To ask no foolish questions," Shinth snapped. "The impossibility of permitting the lesser beings to survive to spread abroad reports prejudicial to the dignity of the Groacian state!"

"To see eyeball to eyeball with your Excellency," Thilf murmured.

"That's a bot of eyelalls," Chauncey commented. "Well, Mr. Retief, it was a farrel of bun lyle it wasted but I kess it's gurtains now." He twitched violently as an axe *thunked* into the door, causing it to jump in its frame. Retief was at the window, stripping off his powder-blue early-evening informal blazer.

"Chauncey, how much stretch do you have left?" he asked over the battering at the door.

"Hmmm, I gee what you've sot in mind. I'll dee what I can sue—" Chauncey unlimbered a length of tough cable from his left sleeve, sent it over the sill; his coverall hung more and more loosely as he paid out coil after coil of himself.

"There's thuch a sing as oving getter-extended," he panted; by this time his garment hung limply on a single thumb-sized strand that extended from the water closet around the door jamp, across the room and down into the darkness below.

"Can you handle my weight all right?"

"Sure; in yast lear's intermurals I tested out at over talf a hon per air squinch."

"Tell me exactly where the other end of you is trapped."

Chauncey complied. As Retief threw a leg over the sill torches flared in the courtyard below. The Groaci Ambassador appeared, clad in full ceremonials, consisting of a ribbed cloak, pink and green argyles and tricorner hat. Jeweled eye shields winked on each of his five stalked oculars. His four-Groaci honor guard trailed him through the gate and piled into the official limousine, which pulled away from the curb with a snarl of abused gyros.

"Thell, wat's wat," Chauncey said dejectedly, in a tight-stretched voice that emanated from the slight bulge that represented his vital centers. "He's on his say to the weremoney; in atither nun minutes it'll be ove aller."

"So it will," Retief agreed. "And we want to be there to see it, eh, Chauncey?"

"Why? If there's hateything I an, it's a leerful chooser."

"I don't think there's much danger of your seeing one of those tonight," Retief said; he gripped the warm, leathery rope of living flesh and started down.

Fifteen feet above the cobbles the cable ended. Retief looked down, gauging the drop. At that moment the door below him opened and two tardy guards emerged at a trot, adjusting their accouterments on the run. One happened to cock an eye upward, saw Retief, skidded

to a halt, dropping his ceremonial pike with a clatter.
The other uttered a hiss, swung his sharp-pointed spear
around and upward.

Retief dropped, sending the groaci spinning. He
rolled to his feet, sprinted for the corner of the courtyard where the drain emerged. Chauncey's mournful
blue eye gazed at him apprehensively from atop the
large bowknot into which the extended stalk had been
tied. Hastily, but with care, Retief set to work to untie
it. Weak Groaci shouts sounded from behind him.
More armed aliens emerged into the courtyard; more
lights winked on, weak and yellowish in deference to
the sensitive Groaci vision, but adequate to reveal the
Terran crouched in the far corner. Retief looked around
to see Captain Thilf charging down at the head of a
flying wedge of pikemen. With a final tug he slipped
the knot, saw Chauncey's eye disappear back into the
drain. He ducked a thrown spear, heard Thilf hiss an
order. The Groaci guards ringed him in, their gleaming
spearpoints bristling inches from his chest. The captain
pushed through, stood in an arrogant pose before his
captive.

"So—the infamous wrecker and vile persecutor of
peace-loving arthropods is brought to bay at last, eh?"
he whispered, signaling to a small, non-uniformed
Groaci lugging a lensed black box. "To get a few shots
of me shaking a finger under his proboscis," he directed the photographer. "To preserve this moment for
posterity, before we impale him."

"A little to the right, your captaincy," the civilian
suggested. "To tell the Soft One to crouch a trifle, so I
can get both of you in the same frame."

"Better still, to order it to lie on its back so the captain can put a foot on its chest," a corporal offered.

"To hand me a spear and to clear these enlisted men from the scene," Thilf ordered. "To not confuse the clear-cut image of my triumph with extraneous elements."

The guards obediently backed off a few paces; Thilf poked his borrowed pike at Retief's chest.

"To assume a placating posture," he ordered, prodding the prisoner lightly. Abruptly the captain's expression changed as a sinuous loop of tough-looking rope shot out of darkness and whipped around his slender neck. All five eyes shot erect, causing two of his semi-VIP zircon eyeshields to fall with a tiny clatter. Retief snapped the spear from the stricken officer's hands and reversed it. The encircling guards jumped forward, weapons poised; Thilf seemed to leap suddenly backward, to burst through their ranks and hurtle across the courtyard, heels dragging. Half his spearmen gaped after him as the other half closed in on Retief with raised pikes.

"Drop those stig-pickers!" Chauncey's voice sounded from the window above, "or I'll hop your boss on his dread!"

The Groaci whirled to see their captain dangling by one leg, twenty feet above the pavement.

"To get a shot of this," Retief suggested to the photographer, "to send home to his family. They'll be pleased to see him hanging around in such distinguished company."

"Help!" Thilf keened. "To do something, culling-season rejects, or to be pegged out in the pleasure pits!"

"To be in the chicken noodle whatever we do," a sergeant muttered, waving the pikewielders back.

"Mr. Retief," Chauncey called. "Shall I nop him on his drob, or bust jash his brocks out on the rain?"

"I propose a compromise, Captain," Retief called. "Instruct your lads to escort us out of here and Chauncey will leave your internal arrangements intact."

"To never yield—" Thilf started—and uttered a thin shriek as the Squalian allowed him to fall a yard, or two, caught him in mid-air and hoisted him up once more.

"But on the other hand, to what end to die in the moment of victory?" the captain inquired reasonably, if shakily. "To be nothing the meatfaced one can do now to halt the unveiling."

"To stick this Terry and take the consequences," a corporal suggested furtively to the sergeant. "To suffer the loss of the captain philosphically."

A flash-bulb winked. "To not worry," the cameraman said blandly. "To distribute a few prints here and there if His Captaincy tries to throw his weight around."

The sergeant signaled; the Groaci formed up in two ranks, spears grounded. He motioned Retief through.

"To leave by the side exit," he said. "And to not hurry back."

"Better hand me your side arm," Retief suggested. The NCO complied silently. Retief backed to the gate.

"See you outside, Chauncey," he called. "And hurry it up—we're on a tight schedule."

IV

"Shoe would have lean the sook on his face when I deft him langling from a fedge lifty feet up," Chauncey was saying exuberantly as he gunned the car along the wet night street of the Squalian capital. "The dubby dirtle-crossers were baiting weside the drain for me to lawl out in their craps; fut I booled 'em; I shook a tort-cut through the teptic sank and out-ranked the flascals."

"A neat manuver," Retief congratulated his ally as the latter wrenched the vehicle around a corner with a deafening hiss of steering jets. Just ahead, a clump of Terran officials stood under the marquee of the Terran Embassy. The car slid to a halt behind the gleaming black Embassy limousine. Magnan leaped forward as Retief stepped out.

"Disaster!" he moaned. "Ambassador Grossblunder got back half an hour ago; he was furious when I told him about the Groaci unveiling their project at midnight—so he ordered our Grand Opening moved up to 11:59 tonight! He'll be down in a moment in full formal regalia, with all media in attendance, on his way to upstage Shinth. When those drapes are drawn back to reveal nothing but a yawning pit—" Magnan broke off at a stir behind him.

The imposing figure of the Terrestrial Ambassador appeared, flanked by a covey of bureaucrats. Magnan uttered a stifled wail and scuttled to attend his chief. Retief stepped to the limousine chauffer's window.

"Drive straight to the Groaci project site, Humphrey," he ordered. "Make it snappy."

"Mate a winute," the Squalian demurred. "Master Mignan distoldly stink me to drive to the Serry tight—"

"Change in plan."

"Well—oh say if you kay so," the driver grunted. "Wish somebody'd mind up their makes."

As the limousine pulled away, Retief jumped back into the staff car.

"Follow them, Chauncey," he said. "By the way, with that versatile sound-effects apparatus of yours, how are you at impersonations?"

"Nitty prifty, Chief, if I sue day so myself. Thet giss: it's a Baffolian bog-fellow crying for his mate—"

"Later, Chauncey. Can you do Ambassador Grossblunder?"

"Just between the tee of us, me and the boys have a lillion maffs taping the old boy's owns."

"Let's hear you do Shinth."

"Lessee: *To joil in your own booses, tile Verry* . . . How's that?"

"It'll have to do, Chauncey," Retief said. "Now, here's what I want you to do . . ."

"What's this?" Ambassador Grossblunder was rumbling as Retief joined the Terran delegation alighting before the bunting-draped, flood-lit entry to the tarpaulin-covered structure looming against the dark Squalian sky. "This doesn't look like—" he broke off as Ambassador Shinth appeared from among a crowd of retainers and local notables.

"Good lord," Magnan gasped, noting for the first time where the limousine had delivered them. "Your Excellency—there's been a mistake—"

"Ah, so delighted to see you, Mr. Ambassador,"

the Groaci Chief of Mission murmurred. "Good of your Excellency to honor the occasion with your august presence. I'm delighted to see you hold no narrow-minded grudge, merely because I've bested you in our friendly little competition."

"Hah!" the bulky Terran snorted. "Your effrontery will backfire when the Prime Minister and Cabinet are offered nothing but a set of badly cured foundations, after all this empty fanfare."

"Au contraire, Mr. Ambassador," Shinth replied coolly. "The edifice is complete, even to the pennants atop the decorative minarets, a glowing tribute to Groaci ingenuity which will forever establish in the minds of our hosts an unforgettable image of the largesse-bestowing powers of the Groacian State."

"Nonsense, Shinth. A confidential source has kept me well abreast of your progress; as of yesterday, your so-called project hadn't gotten off the ground."

"I assure you the deficiency has been rectified. And now we'd best be nipping along to the reviewing stand; the moment of truth approaches."

"Magnan," Grossblunder said behind his hand. "Did he say pennants atop the minarets? I thought that was one of the unique details of our project."

"Why, what a coincidence," Magnan quavered.

"Ah, there, Fenwick," a deep purple Squalian in heavily brocaded robes loomed out of the drizzle before the Terran Ambassador. The local's already imposing bulk was enhanced by the ropes of pearls and golden chains intertwined with his somatic elements, producing an effect like an immense plate of multi-colored lasagna. "I hardly exceeded to speck you here. An inspaying displire of inter-aiming specity!"

Grossblunder harrumphed, clasping the proffered bundle of Prime Ministerial tissues in a parody of a handshake. "Yes, well, as to that—"

"You'll poin my jarty, of course?" the Squalian Chief Executive urged cordially, turning away. "Pee you on the sodium."

Grossblunder looked at the impressive timepiece strapped to his plum wrist. "Hmmph!" he muttered to Magnan. "We may as well. It's too late now for me to stage my unveiling ahead of Shinth, a grave disappointment, regarding which I'll have words with you later."

"Retief," Magnan hissed as they accompanied the group toward the brightly lit platform. "If we slip away now we may be able to sign on as oilers on that tramp freighter I saw at the port this afternoon. It looked unsavory enough for its skipper to be willing to dispense with technicalities—"

"Don't do anything hasty, Mr. Magnan," Retief advised. "Just play it be ear—and be ready to pick up any dropped cues."

On the platform, Retief took a position at Ambassador Shinth's bony elbow. The Groaci gave a startled twitch when he saw him.

"Captain Thilf didn't want me to miss anything," Retief said. "He decided to let me go after all."

"You dare to show your face here, after assaulting my—"

"Kidnappers?" Retief suggested. "I thought under the circumstances perhaps we could agree to forget the whole incident, Mr. Ambassador."

"Hmm. Perhaps it would be as well. I suppose my role might be subject to misinterpretation—" Shinth turned away as the orchestra, composed of two dozen Squalians doubling as brass and strings, struck up a rousing medley of classic Elvis Presley themes. As the music ended a spotlight speared out, highlighting the slender figure of the Groaci Ambassador.

"Mr. Prime Minister," he began, his breathy voice rasping in the PA system. "It gives me great pleasure—"

Retief made an unobtrusive signal; an inconspicuous strand of pale purple that had glided snake-like across the platform slithered up behind Shinth, and unseen by any but Retief, deftly whipped around the Groaci's spindly neck, quite invisible under the elaborate ruffs sported by the diplomat.

A soft croak issued from the speakers spaced around the plaza. Then the voice resumed.

"It grates me pleazh givver, as I was saying, to tray pibute to my escolled teamleague, Amblunder Grossbaster, by ungaling the Verran tift to the palion Squeeple." The Groaci's spindly arm, assisted by a tough length of Chauncey, reached out and yanked the tripline holding the tarps in place.

"What in the world did he say?" Grossblunder growled. "I had the distinct impression he called me something unprintable—" He interrupted himself as the canvas tumbled away from the structure to reveal the baroque pile dazzling under the lights, pennants awave from the minarets.

"Why—that's *my* Bolshoi-type ballet theater!" Grossblunder blurted.

"And a glendid spift it is, too, Fenwick," the Prime Minister exclaimed, seizing his hand. "But I'm a fit conbused—I was inder the umpression this decereful little lightemony was arranged by Amshisiter Balth—''

''Merely a bit of artful misdirection to keep your Excellency in suspense, ha-ha,'' Magnan improvised hastily.

''You mean—this strendid splucture is a sift from the GDT?'' the PM expressed confusion by writhing his features dizzyingly. ''But I had a direct stinkollection of ceding the site to the Groaci Mission—''

''Magnan,'' Grossblunder hissed ''What's going on here?''

As Magnan stuttered, Retief stepped forward, offering a bulky parchment, elaborately sealed and red-taped. Grossblunder tore it open and stared at the Gothic lettering.

''Magnan, you rascal! You staged all this mummery just to add an element of suspense to the proceedings, eh?''

''Whom—I—your Excellency?'' Magnan croaked.

''Don't be bashful, my boy.'' Grossblunder poked a meaty finger into Magnan's ribs. ''I'm delighted! About time someone enlivened the proceedings.'' His eye fell on Shinth, whose body was twitching in a curious rhythm, while his eye stalks waved in no discernible pattern. ''Even my Groaci colleague seems caught up in the spirit of the moment,'' he boomed heartily. ''Well, in response I suppose we can hardly fail to reciprocate in the same spirit. I suggest we all troupe off now to witness the presentation of the Groaci project, eh?''

''Laybe mater,'' a faint voice croaked. ''Night row I got to boe to the gathroom.'' Shinth turned stiffly and tottered away amid shouts, flashbulbs, bursting skyrockets, and a stirring rendition of the *Dead March* from Saul.

"Retief," Magnan gasped as the Ambassador and the PM moved off, chatting cordially. "What? How—"

"It was a little too late to steal the building back," Retief said. "I did the next best thing and stole the deed to the property."

"I still feel we're skating on very thin ice," Magnan said, lifting a plain ginger ale from the tray proffered by a passing waiter. He cast a worried eye across the crowded lounge toward Ambassador Grossblunder. "If he ever finds out how close we came to having to write a Report of Survey on one Ballet Theater—and that you violated the Groaci Embassy and stole official documents—and that one of our drivers laid the equivalent of hands on the person of Shinth himself—" he broke off as the slight figure of the Groaci Ambassador appeared at the entry beside them, his finery in a state of disarray, his eyes canted at an outraged angle.

"Good lord," Magnan gasped. "I wonder if it's too late to catch that freighter?"

"Thievery," Shinth hissed, catching sight of Retief. "Assault! Mayhem! Treachery!"

"I'll drink to that," a portly diplomat said blurrily, raising his glass.

"Ah, there, Shinth," Grossblunder boomed, advancing through the press like an icebreaker entering Cartwright Bay. "Delighted you decided to drop by—"

"Save your unction," the Groaci hissed. "I am here to call to your attention the actions of that one." he pointed a trembling digit at Retief. Grossblunder frowned at the latter.

"Yes—you're the fellow who carries my brief-case," he stared. "What—"

There was a sudden soft thump, merged with a metallic clatter. Grossblunder looked down. On the polished floor between his feet and those of the Groaci were spread several hundred chrome-plated paper clips.

"Oh, did you drop something, your Excellency?" Magnan chirped.

"So!" Grossblunder bellowed, his face purpling to a shade which aroused a murmur of admiring comment from the Squalian bearers gathering to observe the byplay.

"Why, however did those paper clips get into my pocket?" Shinth wondered aloud, but without conviction.

"Ha!" Grossblunder roared. "So that's what you were after, eh? I should have known—"

"Bah!" Shinth responded with a show of spirit. "What matter a few modest souvenirs in the light of the depradations of—"

"Few! You call sixty-seven gross a few?"

Shinth looked startled. "How did you—that is to say, I absolutely deny—"

"Save your denials, Shinth!" Grossblunder drowned the Groaci out. "I intend to prosecute—"

"I came here to speak of grand larceny," Shinth cut in, attempting to regain the iniative. "Breaking and entering! Assault and battery!"

"Decided to make a clean breast of it, eh?" Grossblunder boomed. "That will be in your favor at the trial."

"Sir," Magnan whispered urgently. "In view of Ambassador Shinth's magnanimous blunder—I mean gesture—earlier in the evening, don't you think it might be possible to overlook this undeniable evidence of red-handed theft? We could charge the paper clips up to representational expenses, along with the liquor."

"It was his doing!" Shinth pointed past Magnan at Retief.

"You must be confused," Grossblunder said in surprise. "That's just the fellow who carries my briefcase. Magnan is the officer in charge of the investigation. His harassment got to you, eh, Shinth? Conscience found you out at last. Well, as Magnan suggests, I suppose I could be lenient just this once. But that's one you owe me—" Grossblunder clapped the Groaci on his narrow back, urging him toward the nearest punchbowl.

"Heavens," Magnan breathed to Retief. "What a stroke of luck! But I'm astonished Shinth could have been so incautious as to bring his loot along to the reception."

"He didn't," Retief said. "I planted it on him."

"Retief—you didn't—"

"Afraid so, Mr. Magnan."

"But—in that case, the paper clip thefts are still unsolved—and his Groacian Excellency is being unjustly blamed."

"Not exactly; I found the sixty-seven gross stashed in his office, concealed under a flower box full of jelly-blossoms."

"Good lord—" Magnan took out a scented tissue and mopped at his temples. "Imagine having to lie, cheat and steal, just to do a little good in the world.

There are times when I think the diplomatic life is almost too much for me.''

''Funny thing,'' Retief said, easing a Bacchus brandy from a passing tray. ''There are times when to me it seems hardly enough.''

MORE *SCIENCE*

FICTION
ADVENTURE!

☐ 20726-X **ENSIGN FLANDRY**, Poul Anderson	$2.50
☐ 21889-X **EXPANDED UNIVERSE**, Robert A. Heinlein	$3.95
☐ 01685-5 **ALIEN ART & ARCTURUS LANDING,** Gordon R. Dickson	$2.75
☐ 73296-8 **ROCANNON'S WORLD**, Ursula K. Le Guin	$2.50
☐ 65317-0 **THE PATCHWORK GIRL**, Larry Niven	$2.75
☐ 78435-6 **THE STARS ARE OURS!**, Andre Norton	$2.50
☐ 87305-7 **THE WARLOCK IN SPITE OF HIMSELF,** Christopher Stasheff	$3.50
☐ 80698-8 **THIS IMMORTAL**, Roger Zelazny	$2.75
☐ 89853-X **THE WITCHES OF KARRES**, James Schmitz	$2.75

Prices may be slightly higher in Canada.

Available at your local bookstore or return this form to:

ACE SCIENCE FICTION
Book Mailing Service
P.O. Box 690, Rockville Centre, NY 11571

Please send me the titles checked above. I enclose _____. Include 75¢ for postage and handling if one book is ordered; 25¢ per book for two or more not to exceed $1.75. California, Illinois, New York and Tennessee residents please add sales tax.

NAME _____

ADDRESS _____

CITY _____ STATE/ZIP _____

(allow six weeks for delivery.)

SF 10

BESTSELLING
Science Fiction
and
Fantasy

☐ 47810-7	**THE LEFT HAND OF DARKNESS,** Ursula K. Le Guin	$2.95
☐ 16021-2	**DORSAI!,** Gordon R. Dickson	$2.95
☐ 80583-3	**THIEVES' WORLD,**™ Robert Lynn Asprin, editor	$2.95
☐ 11456-3	**CONAN #1,** Robert E. Howard, L. Sprague de Camp, Lin Carter	$2.75
☐ 49142-1	**LORD DARCY INVESTIGATES,** Randall Garrett	$2.75
☐ 21889-X	**EXPANDED UNIVERSE,** Robert A. Heinlein	$3.95
☐ 87330-8	**THE WARLOCK UNLOCKED,** Christopher Stasheff	$2.95
☐ 05480-3	**BERSERKER,** Fred Saberhagen	$2.75
☐ 10264-6	**CHANGELING,** Roger Zelazny	$2.95
☐ 51553-3	**THE MAGIC GOES AWAY,** Larry Niven	$2.95

Prices may be slightly higher in Canada.

Available at your local bookstore or return this form to:

ACE SCIENCE FICTION
Book Mailing Service
P.O. Box 690, Rockville Centre, NY 11571

Please send me the titles checked above. I enclose _____. Include 75¢ for postage and handling if one book is ordered; 25¢ per book for two or more not to exceed $1.75. California, Illinois, New York and Tennessee residents please add sales tax.

NAME_____

ADDRESS_____

CITY_____STATE/ZIP_____

(allow six weeks for delivery)   **SF 9**